Trying to rescue a kitten, I had bitten off more than I had bargained for...

I sank beneath the gelid water's surface, clipping my chin on a rock hard enough to bite my tongue. The tangy iron of my own blood filled my mouth. I flailed to the surface. Managing to take deep breaths, I swallowed back vomit. I held my breath before I went under once more. I tried to ignore the hard, rough rocks tearing and poking my clothes and body. I reached to free myself and felt long fingers, complete with sharp nails, curled around my ankles.

Tugging at the hands, I struggled to open them. The fingers were so long that they overlapped the thumb by at least three inches. Panicked, I forgot to hold my breath and opened my mouth to scream. I bucked and flailed. The water was up to my waist when I briefly surfaced. I spit and gulped air before being sucked in deeper.

I thrashed my legs and tore at the fingers binding me. A nail bent back and one hand released me. As the other clenched claw let go, I placed one foot precariously underneath me. A monstrous, bald head sprang from the water. It had three ridged, bumpy slits on the side of its neck like gills on a fish, but there, the resemblance ended. It was greenish blue in color and had black, pupil-less eyes. The thing gawked at me, revealing double rows of sharp teeth like a shark.

Danger lurks in the forest...
But Greg Gillie, a handsome Scot with a mysterious past, protects the Shrouded Isle and the lands beyond from the menacing fae.

A woman's arrival disturbs the wee folk...
Becca Shaw, an American widow, takes a family vacation to the island. Each day she remains, Greg struggles as more and more fae steal away from the forest hill and threaten the people.

Can the exodus be stopped?
As the danger increases, Becca strives to repair her relationship with her still-grieving girls and befriend the suspicious villagers. Resisting their blossoming feelings for one another, Greg and Becca team up to find answers. Why are the fae escaping? How can Greg and Becca stop them?

For their sake and the sake of the world, let's hope they're up to the task...
Kilts and Catnip, the first book in a new fantasy series, is filled with sweet romance, delightful humor, and exciting adventure.

KUDOS for *Kilts and Catnip*

"The settings are well-drawn, especially the author's descriptions of the tree-lined streets ("Roses twined up trellises along the walls, splashing yellows, pinks, and reds. Sun shone down on the leaves of the honeysuckle-garlanded oaks dappling the bright sidewalks with shade"). This promising new fantasy series with strong characters should appeal to fans of Charlaine Harris." ~ *Kirkus Review*

"By building a powerful atmosphere of family ties and then introducing a romantic and mysterious figure into the mix, Zoe Tasia has created an original, gripping story that draws readers in with not just evolving romance and fantasy, but strong interpersonal ties which lie at the heart of any truly compelling read. *Kilts and Catnip* is highly recommended for paranormal and romance audiences who want their writing vivid, personal, and as strong in psychological connections as it is in a sense of place and an atmosphere of danger; all set against a search for connections and home." ~ D. Donovan, Senior Reviewer, Midwest Book Review

"Well written, fast paced, and intriguing, this is a story of magic, mystery, and romance. I thoroughly enjoyed it." ~ *Taylor Jones, The Review Team of Taylor Jones & Regan Murphy*

"A delightful combination of mystery, fantasy, and romance, *Kilts and Catnip* is charming, clever, and full of surprises. It's a story that should appeal to romance and fantasy fans alike." ~ *Regan Murphy, The Review Team of Taylor Jones & Regan Murphy*

ACKNOWLEDGMENTS

My deepest thanks to:

My wonderful family, for supporting my dreams; my dear friends, especially G. and L., for reading and editing my early drafts; S.H., you're like a sister to me, and I can depend on you to always have my back.

KILTS AND CATNIP

THE SHROUDED ISLE ~ BOOK 1

ZOE TASIA

A Black Opal Books Publication

GENRE: FANTASY/PARANORMAL/SHIFTERS

This is a work of fiction. Names, places, characters and incidents are either the product of the author's imagination or are used fictitiously, and any resemblance to any actual persons, living or dead, businesses, organizations, events or locales is entirely coincidental. All trademarks, service marks, registered trademarks, and registered service marks are the property of their respective owners and are used herein for identification purposes only. The publisher does not have any control over or assume any responsibility for author or third-party websites or their contents.

KILTS AND CATNIP
Copyright © 2019 by Zoe Tasia
Cover Design by Hampton Lamoureux
All cover art copyright © 2019
All Rights Reserved
Print ISBN: 9781644370476

First Publication: FEBRUARY 2019

All rights reserved under the International and Pan-American Copyright Conventions. No part of this book may be reproduced or transmitted in any form or by any means, electronic or mechanical, including photocopying, recording, or by any information storage and retrieval system, without permission in writing from the publisher.

WARNING: The unauthorized reproduction or distribution of this copyrighted work is illegal. Criminal copyright infringement, including infringement without monetary gain, is investigated by the FBI and is punishable by up to 5 years in federal prison and a fine of $250,000. Anyone pirating our ebooks will be prosecuted to the fullest extent of the law and may be liable for each individual download resulting therefrom.

ABOUT THE PRINT VERSION: If you purchased a print version of this book without a cover, you should be aware that the book is stolen property. It was reported as "unsold and destroyed" to the publisher, and neither the author nor the publisher has received any payment for this "stripped book."

IF YOU FIND AN EBOOK OR PRINT VERSION OF THIS BOOK BEING SOLD OR SHARED ILLEGALLY, PLEASE REPORT IT TO: lpn@blackopalbooks.com

Published by Black Opal Books **http://www.blackopalbooks.com**

DEDICATION

*To Larry and Mary Lou,
my beloved, extraordinary parents,
You are missed.*

CHAPTER 1

Shrouded Isle, Scotland:

"Mom! Mom, wake up!"
I lifted my head as my eldest's finger jabbed me in the ribs three times in rapid succession. *Teen must maintain minimum touching to avoid icky mommy cooties, no doubt.* Despite lack of sleep, my inner monologue continued to function well. The dim night-light from the hall glowed bright enough to reveal Jessie standing beside the bed.

"What?" I rubbed my dry, gritty eyes and winced at the soreness. Late yesterday evening, we arrived at the summer cottage after a grueling drive and a vomit-inducing ferry trip. When the bags still weren't unpacked by eleven, I opted to go to bed and deal with it tomorrow. *Hello, tomorrow.*

"Tate's gone."

As I swung my legs over to sit up, Jessie stepped back. Her gaze alternated between me and the bedroom the girls shared next to mine. Jessie hugged her chest and fidgeted in that gawky, yet attractive way only fifteen-year-old girls can.

I shook my head. "What do you mean she's gone?" I squinted at the clock, but I had neglected to reset it to the correct time. A glance out the window revealed the star-filled sky. "Jess! It's the middle of the night! What the—" I said, barely checking myself before I blurted out a profanity. "Did you check the couch? She probably snuck out to read and fell asleep." I glanced at my pillow with longing.

Jessie's nails bit into my forearm and drove the sleep from my mind. My cool, unconcerned teen looked panicked. "I saw a boy take Tate into the woods. We gotta go now or we'll lose her!" she cried.

Fear drew an icy finger down my spine. Jessie tugged at me. Her eyes opened wide, large, like an anime character's.

"Tate? Tate, honey, where are you?" I received no answer. I shoved my feet into wellies and threw on my green, corduroy jacket I'd left on a chair. Jessie dragged me toward the door, but suspicious, I pulled free. "What *exactly* did you see? And I swear, if this is some kind of prank, you and your sister cooked up—"

"No prank."

"Then what?"

Jessie ran to the living room. "Come on!"

I followed, glanced at the girls' empty beds in the next room as I passed, then turned up the gas lamp, and blinked owlishly.

"I heard shuffling noises. I looked up and the window was open wide."

I drew close and squeezed her shoulder. "We left the window open, honey."

"Not wide open, Mom. We left it cracked this much." She held up her hands, showing a four-inch gap between them. "I went to lower it and saw a little boy dragging

Tate into the woods. Tate was moving slowly, like she was sleepwalking."

I opened the front door and switched on the porch light. The girls' room was on the right side of the small house. I rushed around the corner in time to see a bluish light illuminate two figures, one in a nightgown and the other so much into the shadows that I couldn't make out any detail. They disappeared into the foliage. I knew the ruffled, pink pajamas. They were Tate's favorite. *What was she thinking?* She had turned ten this spring and knew better than to wander off with a stranger.

Despite wanting to rush after her, I paused. *Bad idea to go into a forest, especially in the dark, Becca.* I remembered seeing a large flashlight on top of the refrigerator. Ignoring my warning, I raced back into the kitchen and rose on tiptoe to reach the light, so I could follow.

Jessie gripped my arm. "I'm coming too," she pleaded.

"Jess, if I hurry, I should be able to catch up with her before I get completely turned around. I need you to stay here and call nine-nine-nine, in case I can't find her." Jessie opened her mouth ready to protest. Before she could speak, I added, "My cell is in my purse on the table." Then I remembered the friendly local we'd met when we first arrived. "Better yet, call Mr. McNeil from the grocery. His number is in my contacts, and he's sure to know who best to call."

Jessie rushed to the table for the phone.

Yelling Tate's name, I ran into the night and dashed toward the forest, thanking God the boy hadn't taken her to the ocean side of the cottage and carried my baby away in a boat. The forest felt too quiet as I dodged around an enormous oak. I ran until my boot heel caught on a root, I stumbled on the uneven ground. Frantic, I swung the light back and forth searching for my youngest. How could they have gotten so far ahead of me?

"Tate!" I called.

Scuffing my feet and tearing at bushes, I hoped to mark my path so we could find our way back or at least *be* found. The branch on a log snagged my clothes, and I fell to my knees.

Come on, Becca. Stop panicking. I stood, flipping off the flashlight. After listening for a few seconds, I heard rustling ahead to the north. Once more, though much dimmer, the blue light flickered ahead. I was afraid to switch on my light because it dimmed the indistinct blue. The eerie glow grew fainter. I kept calling and blundered forward, crying out as the light vanished.

"Tate!" I screamed, pausing to turn on the light. I spun, lighting up the dark earth around me. *My baby's gone.* I realized my mistake after making one full circle. I'd forgotten which direction I was going and where I'd come from. My heart beat a tattoo on my ribs, and I fought the primal urge to run—to find her. Find her now! But ingrained knowledge stilled my feet. I had to stop. I'd only injure myself rushing around in the dark, and I couldn't risk it. My girls needed me. Sinking to the ground, I rested my back against a tree. My breath came in gasps. I didn't want to just sit here, but when lost in the woods, the best thing you could do was stay put—and I was very lost. I choked back a sob, hoping in the silence, I would hear them. No telling how long I would be stranded in the forest and, when the searchers arrived, they would call my name, so I turned off the flashlight, conserving the battery. My head spun and I took deep breaths, trying not to hyperventilate. I forced myself to close my eyes and stop searching the night for the bobbing blue light that had long since vanished.

I didn't know how much time passed when I heard a twig snap. If it was an animal, I doubted I was in any danger, but I turned on the light, all the same, blinking as my pupils adjusted. Could Tate have gotten away? Was she making her way back to me? I shined the light into the darkness toward the noise. A hand brushed aside a large tree limb, revealing a dark-haired man in a kilt holding my daughter. As he stepped forward, he released the limb and it sprang back into place and quivered.

"Could you not shine that in my eyes?" he called out, squinting.

I kept the torch on but pointed it toward the ground as I struggled to my feet.

Glassy-eyed, Tate yawned. "Mama?"

I held out my arms. "Sweetie."

One moment, the man stood yards away—the next, the stranger deposited my daughter into my embrace then retreated. I gasped, hugging her close. The flashlight bobbed as I juggled it and Tate. I focused the light ahead. Starlight gleamed off the shoulder-length, wavy, black hair of a man paused in motion. I panned the light down, revealing a broad back clad in a white tunic. The hem of a green and blue kilt swung against his legs. He glanced over his shoulder at me and squinted once more. A look of surprise crossed his face.

As he stared, he turned and took a step closer. "It canna be," he whispered, as his harsh, stern features softened in wonder. He regarded me for a moment then frowned and shook his head.

"What were you doing with my daughter?" I demanded.

His lip curled. "Saving her from a worse fate than having a neglectful mum."

"She was sleeping! Someone took her from her bedroom. Was it you?" I sputtered. Jessie said it was a little boy, but maybe she was mistaken.

He ignored my question. "I would thank you kindly to

leave my forest," he said, his countenance stern and his green eyes narrowing.

A thick lock of raven-colored hair hung down, almost covering his left eye. His expression warmed when he looked at Tate, but his voice remained gruff. Before he turned and disappeared, he added, "And dinna come back."

Tate mewled like a kitten, very unlike her usual bawl.

"Hey, wait! Where are you going?" I yelled. I cast my light in his direction, but only saw him for a moment before the forest swallowed him. I couldn't believe he'd left us alone. I patted Tate. "Someone will find us. Try not to worry." She nuzzled my neck and sobbed. Ahead, an orange light flickered. "What in the world—"

I recognized a blaze in the distance and used the flashlight to weave around trees and over bushes to the edge of the forest. When I stepped out, I heard a cry. Jessie ran to me, nearly bowling me over.

"Mrs. Shaw? Are you and the wee one all right?" Mr. McNeil, the grocer, called from the fire pit.

The man bore a striking resemblance to the ranger who traveled with a dwarf and an elf in that fantasy movie the girls loved. His tangled, dark hair fell an inch short of brushing his shoulders. I decided he must be one of those men who could grow a beard practically overnight because he looked as if a couple of days had passed without a razor touching his ruggedly handsome face. As he drew closer, I saw he wore unlaced hiking boots, creased jeans, and a white sleeveless undershirt which revealed tanned, toned arms.

"We're fine, Mr. McNeil. Thank you so much for coming."

Tate was getting heavy, so I put her down and led the two girls back to the house. Mr. McNeil followed us inside.

Tate's tears subsided, and she calmed enough to release my hand and sit on the couch.

My eyes brimmed with grateful tears. "Lighting the fire was a brilliant idea."

"I canna take the credit for that. By the time I arrived, your oldest had all the lights on and the pit burning."

As I looked at Jessie, I started, newly aware that she was almost my height. She ducked her head. "I saw the marshmallows on the table and remembered. I thought it could guide you home. Mr. McNeil was taking so long. I know you don't like me to light even a candle without supervision, but I had to do something."

Though she rolled her eyes at my protectiveness, I knew she wasn't as sanguine as she wanted to appear.

I tugged her close for a side hug. "It's okay, honey. I forget how mature you are."

"How did you find Tate, Mom?"

"I didn't. A man found her—maybe one of our neighbors." Though he was annoyingly abrupt, I didn't really think the stranger took Tate. Why would he bring her back to me if he had?

Jessie took Tate's hand and whispered in her ear as she draped a quilt from the back of the sofa around her.

Mr. McNeil touched my shoulder in concern. "You sure you're okay, ma'am? Was a long time to be out in the woods."

As he followed me to the foyer, I assured him I was fine. "Do you have any idea who the stranger was?" I described the man in the kilt.

"Aye. Best you avoid that one."

I asked why but he just shook his head.

The door stuck a bit as I pulled it open. "Stay inside, girls. I'm just going to walk Mr. McNeil out," I said, motioning for them to remain there.

We stepped out onto the porch. Embarrassed and now

feeling a bit like Chicken Little, I turned to him. "I'm not a survivalist, but I can manage being outdoors for twenty minutes," I said then chuckled.

Mr. McNeil ran a hand through his hair, tousling the locks, and tried to smother a yawn. I regretted inconveniencing him because, after all, we were strangers, and now I repaid his kindness by practically shoving him out the door. So relieved that Tate and I came back safe and sound, I'd forgotten my manners. "Would you like to come back inside for a glass of water or a beer?"

One side of his mouth quirked up. His eyes shone with something I might have identified as attraction, but I was too tired to be sure and was definitely not up to addressing it tonight if it was.

Before he could respond, I said, "Then again, it looks like Jess woke you up—and I'm sure you must be missing your bed and needing to rise soon."

His grin grew broader and his eyes met mine then traveled southward.

"To wake up early…to get the shop ready…" I fumbled for words, trying to balance my feelings of gratitude with this sudden unease I now felt.

"A bit too early for alcohol, but maybe tea would be nice, non-caffeinated."

His gaze focused on my bare legs. Shocked silent by the obvious interest and maybe misunderstood invitation, I tugged at my jacket, wishing it was longer. At least it covered enough so that my threadbare nightie didn't reveal what hadn't been seen by any male since my husband's death.

The sky transformed from black to a dark, steel blue. *Was I in the woods longer than I thought?* "Wow—actually, maybe another time would be better," I said, striving for graciousness. As I accompanied him to the path which led to town, I remembered what Jessie had told me about a little boy and the barely visible figure I saw. "We need to call the police. Jessie saw a little boy lead Tate into the forest."

Mr. McNeil shook his head. "Your daughter told me, but I'm sure her eyes were playing tricks on her. No one on the island would allow a child out at this time." He stopped so abruptly that I almost ran into him. "Did you see anyone?"

"I thought I did, but now I'm not sure," I answered.

"Lack of sleep can do that. Good night. You get some rest. You dinna want to send the constable on a wild goose chase." He waved as he straddled his motorcycle then revved the engine and motored away.

Inside, I found Jessie sitting beside Tate on the bed in their bedroom. Tate's eyes were at half-mast.

Jessie patted her cheek to wake her and shivered. "Brrr! Mom, she's so cold."

So happy to find her, I didn't think to worry that something may be wrong with Tate. "She might be in shock." I held the back of my hand to her forehead. She didn't feel clammy. "Are you okay, sweetie?"

Despite the warm summer weather, when I took her hand in mine, it was icy.

Tate yawned. "I'm fine, Mommy. Just tired."

I surreptitiously checked her pulse. It was strong and, if anything, slow. She didn't appear to have any of the signs of shock, except cold skin. She was pale, but only a tad more than usual. I tilted her chin and examined her face. Her pupils weren't dilated, and her breathing seemed normal.

"This night calls for some cocoa. What do you think?"

A ghost of a smile tipped the corners of Jessie's lips as she nodded, but Tate didn't answer.

After patting Tate's back, I told the girls I'd return and went to the kitchen. A few minutes of searching divulged a saucepan. Then I gathered the ingredients I had purchased and made hot chocolate. I coaxed Tate into drinking half a mug. Jessie, of course, finished hers and wanted seconds. I tried to question Tate as she sipped, but she merely yawned at my queries. When it was apparent that she would drink no more, I led her to bed and tucked her in.

"Now, no more visiting the forest alone, Tate Elizabeth," I said, my voice stern.

She nodded and sighed then curled up in a ball with one hand tucked beneath the pillow and the other fisted against her chin. After a visit to the bathroom, Jessie also turned in. She allowed me to tuck her in, which gave away how upset she was.

"Jessie, when you woke up and looked out the window—are you sure you saw a boy?"

"I thought I did, Mom, but it was pretty dark. I asked Tate about it when you walked Mr. McNeil out. She doesn't remember a little boy at all. I didn't make it up, Mom. I really did think I saw him—but I guess I didn't."

"I don't think you were lying, sweetie. I thought I saw something too. I guess we were both just over-tired." I kissed her forehead, eliciting a groan, and said good night.

Once I crawled into bed, I reflected on the event. Jessie and I must have imagined the other figure leading Tate away from the cottage. Maybe she sleep-walked off on her own. I thought again of the man in the woods. Funny how, despite his gruffness and unwelcoming way, when he placed Tate in my arms, I realized he didn't scare me.

Though terrified on Tate's account, I knew he wasn't the trigger. Despite the feminist and experienced hiker in me chafing at the way he dismissed me, I felt surprisingly at ease with him.

Settled into bed, the girls' window tightly shut, I thought back on our first day here. The people we had met on the island so far were curious, yet kind. When we rode here on the ferry, I hadn't had the correct change. The ferry operator told me not to fret. I could pay what I owed when next I needed to go to the mainland. The only way on or off the island was by boat. Mindful of the prickly plants that lined the path, we walked to the sole village there called, appropriately enough, Thistle. Our first stop upon arriving had been the grocer. The note on the window read "Be Back Soon" in a rushed scrawl. The shop door had been unlocked. We hesitantly entered and gathered our supplies. Before we finished, Mr. McNeil, the owner, returned out of breath. He apologized several times with an adorable grin. I thought him very handsome with his just-shaved look, even the small nick at the dimple in his cheek charmed me. When he turned his head, his hair swept the top of his ears. I guess sleep flattened the curls since it appeared longer when he came to help find Tate. I admired his square jaw line, heavy-brows, and wide forehead. *Strong features,* I had mused. He explained his aunt called, complaining of palpitations, but couldn't find her heart pills, so he ran up the road to find them for her.

Smiling, I remembered his comment. "I'm thinking they're naught but sugar pills. She's healthy as a horse, but to hear it from her, she has one foot in the grave and one foot on a banana peel. She's Doc's best customer, and God forbid he send her home without a concoction of some sort." His Scottish burr, melodic to my ears, had tap danced the chords on my long-forgotten libido. He had bustled about to find what we couldn't and tallied up our bill in record time. Recognizing our American accent, he had helped sack our items, though I assured him I was quite capable.

"Your trolley was chockablock with groceries for a weekend visit," he noted. I explained that we were staying at the cottage for the summer. He smiled and nodded. "Aye, you must be the Shaw family. Mrs. Grant sent word of it."

He gave me his phone number and insisted I call if I needed anything. We didn't have a car and had planned to walk, but the charming Mr. McNeil insisted that his nephew—a pimply, sullen lad with a scraggly beard—give us a ride. My acceptance was one of great appreciation. I had been tired and more than ready to arrive at the rented cottage. The landlady had informed us there were bicycles in the shed for our use, and a small bus made rounds a few times a day to pick up passengers around the island. I think she said it made about a half dozen stops, including a few places in the village, a couple around the countryside, and one at the pier. I looked forward to exploring the quaint village.

When we arrived, the cottage was cleaned and neat. All items we could possibly need were readily available. While inspecting the contents of the medicine cabinet, I had dropped a travel-size tube of toothpaste. When I crouched to pick it up, I found an old-fashioned straight razor that had dropped between the toilet and the sink. The blade was badly rusted, but the ivory handle was carved with beautiful patterns. I could just make out the initial "G" on it. I wondered how such a thing found its way into the hiding place and to whom it belonged. *Why would an elderly lady have such a thing?* She hadn't lived there in a while and, when she did, she lived alone for a long, long time. I knew a local friend of hers still cleaned and stock the place with a few necessities, like toilet paper, bread, and milk.

Thoughts danced through my head and I gave up trying to sleep. My e-reader in hand, feeling like a decadent Roman, I sprawled on the thread-bare chaise in the bedroom's alcove and sipped the dregs of my cocoa. Though the romance was written by one of my favorite authors, I remained distracted. *Who was the raven-haired man in the kilt?*

CHAPTER 2

I woke to the sound of a raucous meow. "What now?" I mumbled, skidding on the robe that puddled on the floor and stumbling to the cottage door.

Gauging from the light shining in from the window, morning had dawned hours earlier, but I still craved more sleep. Pulling the white curtain from the window at the side of the door, I peeped out. Something tapped the window. Looking down, I spotted one of the largest black cats I had ever seen. The cat stared back, meowed again, then disappeared.

Scritch, scritch. The sound of claws gouging the front door spurred me to unlock it and swing it open. The cat nudged me aside so hard that I stumbled. Turning, I watched it dart into the girls' bedroom. I shut the door and followed. The cat sat on Tate's bed, bumping its head against her chin.

Tate woke with a yawn. A grin bloomed when she saw the cat.

"You got us a kitty!" she squealed, flinging her arms around it.

"Tate, be careful, honey, we don't know anything about it. It might be sick." To my amazement, not only did the cat remain on the bed, but it purred and nestled closer to my daughter.

"Hey, what's going on? Sleeping here," Jessie complained.

The cat loudly meowed. Jessie sat up and tossed back her waist-long hair.

Shortly before we left Houston for Scotland last year, she had, without my permission, dyed the bottom six inches of her hair bright red. She swore she had wanted ombre hair for "ages."

I thought it was her way of protesting the move. Her hair was naturally straight and black like her father's had been. Tate inherited my hair, wavy and brown.

"Mom got us a kitty!" Tate gleefully answered.

With a happy yelp, Jessie jumped from her bed and rushed to her sister's. Tate relented, stopped hugging the cat, and the girls took turns petting the fawning animal. As they did, I noticed a white spot on the cat's chest on its otherwise-black body.

"I bet she's hungry," Tate said.

"Don't get attached," I warned the girls. "This cat must be someone's pet. It's too friendly to be a stray."

Jessie checked its neck. "No collar, Mom."

"I'll contact Mr. McNeil. Perhaps he knows where she belongs. If not, I can text him a photo and see if he will put up a poster with my phone number in the grocery store."

In Aberdeen, Scotland, I had no issues with unwanted male attention. I still wore my wedding band and made very clear I wasn't ready to date. I vowed to subtly cue Mr. McNeil in on this, hopefully nipping his attentions in the bud. My libido might be ready to date, but I wasn't sure I was.

"Can we keep her, if no one claims her?" Jessie asked.

"Please," both chimed in.

"We'll see. The thing is huge. Probably eat us out of house and home."

"She needs a name." Jessie stroked the cat's arched back.

It rubbed its cheek against Tate's and purred in her ear.

"Her name is Kiera," Tate said.

"That's a pretty name, Tate, but remember, we may not be able to keep her. Plus, Jessie may want to help name her."

"She told me her name's Kiera, though," Tate protested.

"It's okay, Mom. I'm good with Kiera."

I raised my eyebrows. *If the cat means no more sibling fights, it'll be worth putting out my life savings for a ton of cat food.*

The girls decided on bacon and pancakes for breakfast. They offered some to the cat who sampled a little of everything.

"She must be someone's pet. She acts like she's already been fed," I commented. I earned a frown from both the girls. Tate seemed much better this morning. While the girls explored and played with the cat, I admonished them to stay out of the forest and tried to text Mr. McNeil. After it refused to go through three times, I called using the old rotary phone. "Sorry to bother you, but a large, black cat showed up at the cottage. Do you know the owners?"

"I know several families with cats, but they keep them inside the house. Animals tend to disappear 'round here. I'll ask and see if anyone has a new black one," he said.

"Thanks. I'll send you a photo too."

We said our goodbyes. I took a photo of Tate and the cat to send later. After I tidied up, I curled up in the chair by the window so I could watch the girls and flip through the information I received from the landlady. She was an elderly lady, I had surmised from the sound of her voice on the phone, who placed an advertisement about a summer home for rent. I thought it was a mistake when I saw the price for the cottage, but called immediately, not wanting to miss out on the opportunity.

The cottage had been in Mrs. Grant's family ever since it was built. She lived in the home as a child. When she married, she moved into town. After her parents passed away, she moved back to the cottage. She was an herbalist and did her work there. Three years ago, she moved to Peterhead to be with her daughter. I drove up from Aberdeen to meet her in person. She was a dear, but a somewhat quirky woman. She insisted upon reading my tea leaves.

She had suggested visiting a nearby farm. She said if I used her name, the owner would rent out a couple of horses which we could ride. I explained that, with the exception of Jess, our riding skills were next to nonexistent, but she'd insisted that the gentleman in charge had several gentle nags to choose from—and helmets. She said he would be happy to take us out. I was reticent about calling, but Mrs. Grant promised to contact him beforehand to give him proper notice of our interest. The grocer certainly knew we were arriving, so I felt fairly sure that Mrs. Grant had indeed told everyone in advance.

I stepped outside to talk to the girls. "How would you like to go horseback riding? I thought I'd call today and set it up."

"When would we go?" Tate asked. "I don't want to leave Kiera alone."

"It depends on when is a good time for Mr. Samms. And don't worry about the cat. I'm sure it will be fine."

"Don't be a party pooper, Tate," Jessie added. "I think it will be fun. I haven't been riding since we were home in Houston."

Tate hugged the cat. She held still then smiled. "Kiera says to go."

I called the farm, and Mr. Samms's generous voice insisted we come over. His son would take us out on the trail. The farm was within walking distance. After Tate reassured the cat that we would be right back after the ride, we left.

The place, Samms Farm, had sheep, cows, and chickens, along with the horses. They planted rapeseed and rutabagas. Mr. Samms introduced me to his son, Gavin. He was sixteen with golden hair and sapphire-blue eyes. Jessie blushed when he helped her mount a horse, and I saw a summer love blossom in her eyes. Tate had begun lessons before we moved to Aberdeen and was excited to be back on a horse.

"How do you like the cottage?" Gavin asked. His horse walked toward a path, and our horses dutifully followed.

"Mom and Tate were lost in the forest last night," Jessie said to her saddle pommel, too shy to look Gavin in the eye but clearly wanting his attention.

"Best not walk around there, especially at night. Creepy stories about the forest and the cottage."

"Like what?" Jessie asked.

My horse angled close to the edge of the path, and I barely managed to duck a low-hanging branch.

"It's supposed to be haunted," he said, reining in his horse, a bay with a white star on her nose, to let us catch up.

I made eye contact with Gavin, looked at Tate, and shook my head. He caught my meaning.

"Aye, but they're just stories," he amended. The trail

led into the forest. "We'll not go too far in," he assured us. "The horses know the path well. You hardly need to hold the reins."

My horse drifted toward a tree and my leg brushed against the trunk.

Gavin noticed and clicked his tongue at the dun horse. "Honey, what are you doing?" The horse pawed at the ground and sidestepped. "I don't know what's on with her." He frowned. "These three are our most docile horses."

We rode farther into the forest and reached a fork in the trail. Gavin's horse took the left side. The other two, docile horses plodded behind. When I reached the fork, Honey neighed and yanked at her bit. I dug my heels into her sides. She shivered and shook as if a persistent horsefly bothered her.

"Giddy up, Honey," I said with more confidence than I felt.

"Is everything all right, Mrs. Shaw?" Gavin called.

The girls looked back at me.

"She doesn't want to go." I clicked my tongue and nudged her again with my heels. The horse walked backward, then, with a start, she bolted down the other fork. Losing the reins, I clung to the pommel for dear life and tightened my legs. A few yards farther, there was an opening to the left. The horse veered through it and wove between the trees. "Whoa!" I yelled.

Honey reared, and I slipped off, landing with an "oof" on the ground. The horse resumed galloping until she vanished.

Gavin quickly found me. "I'm so sorry. Honey has never acted like that." He hopped off his mount. "Are you hurt?"

"No, I don't think so. Shook up some, but not hurt."

The girls reined up near me.

"Tell you what, we'll return to the stable, and I can saddle another horse. Honey knows her way home and should make her way back soon enough. If she hasn't returned by the time we get back from our ride, I'll go back out and look for her."

"You know, Gavin, I think I'll pass on the ride." Looks of disappointment showed on the girls' faces. I continued, "If the girls want to go, can you take them out for a short trip?"

"Sure."

"We haven't ridden that far. You go on. I can walk back and wait for you at the farm."

"Are you sure, Mrs. Shaw? I don't mind taking you back."

"I'm sure. You go on and have fun." I smiled reassuringly at the girls and watched as they continued back to the fork and took the correct path. I brushed off my rear, removed my helmet, attached it to a belt loop, then ambled back, admiring the beautiful leaves of every shade of green imaginable. *Well, perhaps not neon.* I smiled at the thought of a psychedelic forest. I hadn't made the fork yet, when I heard a pained neigh. Maybe Honey stepped in a hole and hurt herself. I walked back up the correct fork and called out, "Gavin? Hey, Gavin! I think I hear Honey!"

No answer.

"Back to where you belong!" a voice shouted angrily.

I doubled back and up the other fork.

"Hello?" I yelled. "Is everything okay?"

I started when a large, male body loomed too close in front of me. He was turned away, but I recognized the dark locks and broad shoulders.

"'Tis fine now. The dunnie is back where he belongs," the man from last night said as he turned back to face me.

"Dunnie? Her name is Honey. Is the horse okay?"

"The horse isna a horse, of course. Any Scot would recognize it as a trickster dunnie," he retorted.

I shook my head. "Who are you?"

He took a step away. "That doesna concern you."

"Wait. It does." I grabbed his muscled bicep. He turned toward me again. "Who are you?" I repeated.

Once more, he ignored my question. "Something about you is stirring up the wee folk." He ran a hand through his locks then clasped my shoulders and pulled me close, staring into my eyes. "I think the better question is who are you?"

I tried to ignore the sudden zing of desire that coursed through me. "My family and I are vacationing here. We're staying in Mrs. Grant's cottage." Perhaps if I was upfront with him, he would also be so with me.

"That tells me where you are. It doesna tell me who you are."

"'Give me your name, horse-master, and I shall give you mine.'" The quote came to mind and popped out. I giggled.

He didn't even smile. "I am the Keeper of the Forest. I keep all safe."

He offered his hand to me. I hesitantly took it and shook.

Peculiar, I thought. "Nice to meet you."

His handshake was strong, but he took care not to squeeze my hand too hard. "Go home. This isna a good place for you, ma'am."

"I think it's a fine place for me, sir. We're only staying a few months. I think we can stay out of your hair if our presence bothers you so," I retorted. *How dare he tell me I have to leave?*

"I wouldna want you or yours coming to harm."

"Is that a threat?" Suddenly, I was aware of how quiet it was. Even the birds stopped twittering.

"No. The forest is dangerous. Most who live here know what precautions to take. You dinna."

"Feel free to explain what I should be doing then."

"You are a stranger and shouldna be here. I have no time to explain our ways to a Sassenach."

"I am *not* a Sasquatch!"

He looked completely baffled—almost as baffled as I felt. "You are a strange lass."

A red squirrel chattered and rustled a beech tree limb overhead. I watched it scurry toward the trunk and, in that tiny instance when I looked away, he vanished. I harrumphed and stomped back to the farm.

Mr. Samms carried a shovel with something gray balanced on the blade. As I drew closer, I recognized it as a large rat. Focused upon his steps, he didn't notice me until I neared.

He started. "I didn't expect you back so soon." He nodded at the shovel. "Cats keep the population down but leave the gruesome evidence behind at times. I hoped to dispose of it before you and your daughters returned."

"I've been brought gifts by my cats in the past, though thankfully, only small mice." The corpse was bloodless and the only damage appeared to be a bite on its abdomen—a large one. "The girls and Gavin are still out. I returned early." I quickly told him of my mishap.

"Well then—the missus is in the cottage. She'll be wanting you to join her for tea, hoping to get any updates about the American shows she watches. Just knock on the door, but go on in."

I followed his instructions.

Mrs. Samms made tea while we waited for the girls. I told her I wasn't ready for a long horse ride, allowing her to think I was tender in the seat—which I was.

"You have two bonny lasses. How old are they?" Mrs. Samms asked.

"Jessie's fifteen. Tate's ten."

"Goodness, she's a wee one. I wouldna guessed her more than seven."

"She's small for her age. She was premature."

Forty-five minutes later, the horses clomped back. Taking my lukewarm tea, I rushed out to meet them at the stables with Mrs. and Mr. Samms trailing me.

"How was the ride?" I asked, but from the matching grins the girls sported, it was obviously a big success.

"Wonderful!" Tate prattled on about the ride as Jessie helped Gavin with the horses. From his expression, I thought the attraction was mutual—something I would need to watch carefully. I was fine with a summer flirt, but a summer full-on romance was another story. As far as I knew, Jess had never dated anyone.

"Did Honey make it back, Da?" Gavin asked.

"Is Honey gone?" Mr. Samms stepped out to a fenced in paddock and whistled sharply. A raw-umber-colored horse nickered and trotted to meet him. "Honey's here, Gavin. I moved her from the stables yesterday."

"But, Da, I saddled Honey for Mrs. Shaw an hour ago."

"Not possible, son. I pried a stone from her hoof last afternoon when the Trask twins rode her and Bunny. She would be lame if you had."

"I took her from this stall." Gavin pointed to the far left-hand one. We gathered around. It was swept clean with no straw or horse droppings. "But, Da—Honey was here! There was hay and an oat bag—"

"Well, never mind that, Gavin. All is well, right?" Mr. Samms lead us back outside with haste.

"But, Da—"

Mr. Samms gave Gavin a warning look. "We will speak of the mistake later."

Mrs. Samms gave the girls cookies and Ribena, a black-currant-flavored drink. Jessie sat with us, looking at Gavin from beneath her lashes when she thought no one noticed. Tate took her large plate of biscuits outside. When she returned, I saw she had finished all twelve of them. It wasn't like her to consume so many. I hoped that it was just the results of Mrs. Samms's cooking.

The girls and I said our goodbyes, thanking the Samms's for their hospitality and walked back to the cottage. I slapped together three tuna and salad cream sandwiches, potato chips, and carrots with cukes. The cat was fed most of the remaining tuna.

A shed in back contained outdoor games. I helped Jessie set up croquet, and we played three games, each winning one. The cat cleaned itself and watched from a safe distance after one ball sailed too close.

"Where's Kiera?" Tate asked as we put up the mallets and balls.

At some point during the last game, the cat vanished.

"Kiera, here kitty-kitty," Jessie yelled.

"She probably went back home," I reassured the anxious girls.

"But what if it gets late, and she's alone in the dark?" Tate asked, her brow furrowed with worry.

"I think that cat is plenty large and savvy enough to take care of herself, sweetie. Come inside and help me decide what to fix for dinner."

When we walked around to the front of the cottage, we saw a middle-aged lady sitting on the porch. Her long, dark hair was pulled up in a ponytail. She wore faded, torn jeans and a tee shirt with *Shiny* printed on it over a spaceship.

"Hello?"

Our visitor jumped to her feet. "Hi. I'm your nearest neighbor. I'm Kay, Kay Sheey. Conall McNeil mentioned a family was renting the cottage." She stood too close to me, encroaching on my personal space, and held out her hand. I shook it. "You may want to watch out for that one." She winked at me. "I think he fancies you." She focused on my youngest and frowned. "Is everything okay? Your youngest looks a bit peaked."

I studied Tate. She did look wan. She stifled a yawn. "Well, I think so," I said. "We had a mishap last night. Oh, and the girls are fretting over a neighborhood cat. I'm Becca Shaw. These are my daughters, Jessie and Tate. Come in. Give me a few to pop some fish sticks in the oven, and I'll put the kettle on."

One thing I figured out soon was that Scots never refused a cuppa.

The girls declined tea and went to their room. Tate wanted to draw the horses and Jessie *claimed* she would begin a summer reading assignment. I was sure she would be fantasizing about the friendly, cute Gavin. "You're welcome to stay for dinner too. It's not gourmet, but we have plenty," I said, wishing I had something better to offer. I had no idea why I was so friendly. Usually, I was more reticent.

"I'd love that. Thank you. Tomorrow eve, you must come to my cottage so I can repay you with a meal. I enjoy cooking for others and rarely have an opportunity to indulge."

At dinner, Jessie scarfed her food and went back to her room. Tate dawdled. Kay and I finished eating and stepped out to enjoy the evening air. To my surprise, she pulled out a pack of cigarettes. "Do you mind?" she asked.

"Feel free." For several minutes, we sat and enjoyed the sunset. The scent of cloves wafted. I smiled. "That brings back memories."

Kay winked. "Don't tell me. Smoked them to cover up the smell of marijuana?"

I hummed a measure or two of music and said, "I won't tell," then chuckled. "Sorry, it just reminds me of a song on this show I and the girls watched," I explained.

"A musical episode in a series about vampires." Kay shook her head. "Who would have guessed it would work so well?"

Amazed she recognized it, I nodded. "Unless I'm at a convention, I don't usually run into people who have watched the show."

"Always nice to see a strong lass on the telly. Too often they're victims." She took another drag off her cigarette and turned away to exhale the smoke.

"True." I nodded. "It's nice to see good role models on television. I didn't have very many growing up, and, since my husband's gone, I've been forced out of my comfort zone many times. My girls will be much more independent and confident."

Kay nodded. "Are you liking the island so far?"

"So far it's been exciting."

"Really? Our quiet, wee village? What happened?"

"Well, Tate got lost in the woods, and then I did, too, when I went to search for her. Luckily, a man found her and brought her to me. My daughter, Jessie lit the fire pit, and I managed to find my way back to the cottage." She nodded encouragingly. *She's not bored to tears yet?* I wondered. "Then we visited Samms Farm," I continued. "My ego's bruised thanks to a horseback riding incident—or, in my case, horseback falling. I have a decent seat for a novice, usually, but the horse got away from me. I met the same man again. He has dark hair and wore a kilt." I tried to think of a way to say he was knee-weakening gorgeous without sounding like a fool.

Kay wore peculiar expression on her face. "A dark-haired man in the forest?"

"I know it sounds crazy, but it's true. Though I think I'm the only one who has had a conversation with him in quite a long time. I've been to the grocer, and he seems to know everyone well, except for this man. He cautioned me against even talking to him."

Kay flapped a hand at me. "Oh, he may seem out of sorts, but you're are safe with him as long as you steer clear of the forest"

That's the second time I've been warned off the woods. "Why's that?"

"He lost his family and still mourns," Kay answered, mistaking the question.

"That's so sad. I understand. Poor man. I'm from Houston. I moved to Scotland a year ago—after my husband died."

Kay flicked ashes from the end of her cigarette. "I'm sorry for your loss." After a pause, she asked, "What do you do?"

"I teach at the American school in Aberdeen." A cool breeze ruffled my hair, and I rubbed my arms. "How about you?"

"I make a living through my hobbies—knitting, repurposing items. If you're interested, they're sold at the Thistle Gift Shop." Kay exhaled. A heart-shaped smoke ring hovered before her, then drifted out of sight. Before I could comment, she continued.

"I'm surprised you were able to rent this cottage. You're the first person to stay in it since Mrs. Grant moved away, other than her relatives."

"She lives not far from Aberdeen. I drove up to see her, and she seemed happy to have a tenant."

"She read your tea leaves?"

"Yes, how did you know?"

My eyes met hers and she shrugged. "I would have been surprised if she hadn't. She's a hedge witch and consults with tarot cards and tea leaves before making any important decisions."

"That sounds rather…" I struggled for the right word.

"Silly? It did give you a vacation," Kay pointed out.

"True."

Kay put her cigarette out in the dirt and stood. "Well, I've overstayed my invitation. I'll come over tomorrow at seven, and we can walk to my place."

"You don't need to do that. Just give me the address." I pushed up off the step and took a step toward the door to get a pen and paper.

She chuckled. "There's no street address. I get my mail from the post office. Most find my directions difficult to follow, so I find it works much better if I collect my visitors rather than wait for them to find their way to me."

I grinned. "Okay, I look forward to it."

"So do I."

CHAPTER 3

The next morning, I had a hard time waking Tate. I felt her forehead, but she didn't have a fever. "Tate, if you aren't feeling better by noon, I'm taking you to the clinic."

"I don't wanna go," she moaned, but rolled out of bed.

Jess and I had already eaten a breakfast of Weetabix. I set a bowl, cereal, and milk in front of Tate while Jessie and I checked the back garden. It was terribly overgrown, but some herbs and plants remained.

We picked some mint, and I made a note to shop for a book to help identify the flora. I usually had good luck with gardening. Perhaps I could get this one back into shape.

Jessie ran ahead of me. I rounded the corner of the house in time to see her open the door and call out, "Tate, we found mint in the back, and—" She screamed.

I ran inside.

"What's wrong?" I asked Jessie as I looked around.

Nothing seemed out of order. Jessie, stood, her back against the wall and her hand to her mouth, staring at Tate. Tate sat at the table in front of an empty cereal bowl. The bottle of milk was half empty, and when I picked up the box of cereal, it was much lighter.

"There was this thing sitting with Tate, Mom," Jessie said.

"What sort of thing?"

Jessie was a very matter-of-fact girl and not subject to flights of fancy. Perhaps some animal found a way into the cottage when we left?

"It was small and gray and I could see through it. It sat on Tate's lap, and when Tate took a bite of cereal, the thing would lap at the spoon and eat the cereal before Tate could."

Surely, if anything had been there, I had followed close enough behind that I would have seen it. "Where did it go then, Jessie?"

"I don't know. I turned to call you and when I turned back, it had vanished." A meow came from the open doorway. The cat reappeared and padded to Tate, then jumped on the table.

"Now, now, you get down from there," I shooed it.

The cat circled the bowl. As it did, the fur rose on its back, and it hissed. I rushed forward and clapped my hands at it.

"Mom, be nice to Kiera!" Jess said.

Tate remained still and glassy-eyed.

"She hissed at your sister, Jess."

"I don't think she did. I think she smells that thing that was here earlier. Kiera doesn't like it much either."

Before I could reply, the phone rang. It rang several times before I remembered where I plugged it in the night before.

I scooped it up and said, "Hello?"

"Hello, Rebecca? Its Conall, Conall McNeil."

"Oh, hello, Mr. McNeil." I couldn't help but remember Kay's remark and was uneasy. I hoped he wasn't going to ask me on a date.

"Please, just call me Conall. This Friday there's a ceilidh celebrating my aunt's birthday at the church hall. I was wondering if you would like to go—and your two girls, of course. Sorry 'tis late notice. I rang you earlier, but you didn't answer. I'm not one for leaving messages."

I had gone to a ceilidh in Aberdeen with some of the other teachers from the school. I spent most of the night nursing a glass of wine and watching the others dance. It had been too soon after my husband's death for me to enjoy myself. "It's very nice of you to think of us, but your aunt doesn't even know me."

"Everyone in the village is invited. Please say you'll come. It will give you an opportunity to meet the rest of the people here." He was so earnest, and at least, it wasn't a date.

I sighed. It would be a good opportunity and, hopefully, the girls could meet more of the kids there. "Thank you. We would love to come. What time should we arrive?"

"Dinner will be served at six-thirty p.m. I'll pass on your RSVP to my cousin who arranged it. I would be happy to walk you over."

Conall McNeil was attractive in that rough-around-the-edges way and had been very helpful, but I didn't want to encourage him. "I'm sure I can find the church, Conall. The girls and I will be fine. Thanks again."

"Oh." He sounded crestfallen. "Well then, if I don't see you at the grocery beforehand, I'll see you at the party. Goodbye."

I found myself saying goodbye to the dial tone. "Looks like we're going to a party this Friday."

Tate perked up. "Party?"

"Oh, is it Mrs. Nivens's birthday party?" Jessie asked. "Gavin mentioned it yesterday." She busied herself with putting up the breakfast things and clearing the table.

Something she'd never do before without much prodding and reminding.

"I didn't catch the name, but I can't imagine there's another party the same night."

"Gavin asked if I was going. He said everyone was, and I should go too."

Jessie glowed. *Drats. She must really like Gavin.* I didn't want her to get too attached. We would be leaving in the fall. "We'll go. What do you think of Gavin?" I asked, fishing.

She shrugged and looked anywhere but at me. "Oh, he's nice."

"Hmmm. So, you'd be okay if we just ditched this because I'm not sure I want to go. Kinda tired."

"Mo—om!" She said it in that two-syllable you've-got-to-be-kidding-me way. "C'mon! It will be fun, and I'm so bored and—Mom, you can be such a—"

"Don't say it, Jess." I smiled, though.

"Mo—om!"

Two of them, and it's still morning. I'm surpassing myself.

Throwing up my hands, I said, "Don't blame me. If you're that obvious, anyone will figure it out."

Jessie paced the floor. "Do you think he knows?"

I shrugged. "What do you think?"

"I don't know!" she wailed.

"Jessie loves Gavin, Jessie loves Gavin," Tate chanted.

Jessie poked her sister in the arm. "Mom, make her shut up!"

"Tate, quit teasing your sister." I turned back to Jess. "We'll go to the ceilidh and find out. Sweetie, keep in mind that—"

"I know, we're leaving in the fall and this—if there is a *this*—will be over then." Jessie turned and walked to her room. She didn't slam the door, but it was obvious that she thought about it.

Ugh. Why don't kids come with an instruction pamphlet?

❧❧❧

Kay was on time. When I let her in, I glanced around. The large, black cat was nowhere to be seen. I wondered if we shared Miss Kiera Kitty with another family. She seemed to spend half of her time with us and then vanished in the evenings. I thought about bringing up the subject with the girls but decided to leave well enough alone. Tate seemed groggy and out of it. She wanted to stay home and sleep, but I didn't feel right about leaving her by herself with the way she was acting, I'd have to take her to the doctor if she got any worse or didn't get any better by Monday.

"Hope your shoes are comfy. Fables Cottage isn't too far away, but the road and path to it isn't paved and can be rocky," Kay warned.

Fables Cottage? Did I hear her right?

Tate and I wore sneakers. Jess, however was wearing her heels, the highest ones I'd let her choose. "Jess, change, please."

"But, Mom, I need to practice walking in them so I won't fall on my rear at the dance," she pleaded. "I'll walk slowly and watch where I put my feet."

Kay shook her head. "None of the other girls will be wearing such shoes. They're too high to dance in. You'd spend the dance sitting on the sidelines, bored, or needing to take them off."

I was grateful for the interjection. Teens seem to take advice better from anyone other than their own mom, and Jessie had confided to me earlier that she thought Kay had interesting taste in clothes. With Jess, interesting meant anything from nose rings—good—to puffed sleeves—bad. In this case, it was good. Jess sighed, slipped off the sandals, and went to her room to choose something more appropriate.

The walk was indeed short, about fifteen minutes, but I was very grateful I had not worn dressier shoes. In fact, I wished I had put on my hiking boots. There was little light to see by, due to the abundance of shade provided by all the trees, and the ground dipped in places. Kay's pastel pink house was quite close but hidden down a wandering path behind a copse of pines. The roof was thatched and smoke came from the chimney. When she opened the unlocked door, several cats and a litter of kittens greeted her with meows and twined between her feet. "Now, now. You be good. We have company."

The girls were quickly on their knees, cooing and petting.

In the cottage, paintings—mostly of wildlife—hung on pineapple gold walls. An easel with a canvas hinted that Kay was the artist. A leopard print throw graced a ruby red sofa with mismatched decoupage end tables bracketing it. A stained glass window tinted soft colors over the small loom that occupied one corner. "Wow your place is very—bright." *Great use of your vocabulary, Becca.* "I mean, I really like it."

Kay chuckled. "I'm a bit of a craft addict, and I love vivid colors. It's a bit much for some."

I did a quick kitty head count. "Nine cats? Goodness, you have quite the collection," I remarked as a calico butted my shin with her head.

"I found the mother cat in the village behind the butcher's, scavenging. She was obviously ready to whelp soon. She's feral but has calmed down a lot. I'll have her fixed as I have had my other two cats, Jasper and Fforde.

"Jasper and Fforde?"

"Named after one of my favorite authors." One of the kittens attempted to climb up her skirt. She bent down and picked it up. It immediately began to purr and snuggle. "I hope to give the kittens away."

Predictably, Tate cried out, "Can we have one, can we?"

"Please, please, Mom?" Jess begged at my other side. "We take good care of Kiera when she visits."

"This huge, black cat showed up on our doorstep," I told Kay. I turned back to the girls. "I allow Kiera because she just visits, but a kitten is a lot of responsibility."

"Indeed, they are," Kay pitched in. "Kiera's an older cat. She's very large and canny and can take care of herself, but the kittens can't. My cats are all indoor cats. Leaving a small animal outside is asking for trouble around here. Do it only one time, and chances are you'll awake to an injured or dead pet, if you find it at all."

Jess and Tate continued a litany of "pleases" until I hushed them. "I'll think about it," I said, including both in my gaze.

"Mom, that almost always means no." Jess crossed her arms and stood on one leg with a hip jutting out, looking put upon.

"If you cop an attitude, I won't even think about it."

"Shhh, Jessie!" Tate said, tugging on her sister's hand.

"Don't shush me," Jess said but allowed herself to be led back to the other kittens.

Kay spoke in a low voice. "If you're serious, it would be a big help. I want the kittens to go to good homes and a lot of people aren't keen on keeping cats since they have to stay inside. They hate the idea of a litter box, scratching paws, hair—oh no!" She frowned. "I've probably talked you out of it."

"No, I've had pets most of my life. My husband was allergic to animals, so I couldn't have any after we married. I'd love to have one. I just want time to think it over to make sure one will fit into our lives now."

Kay pulled out a chair and gestured for me to sit. "How long has it been since your husband passed away?" she asked.

"He died the spring before last. The kids and I were devastated. I thought we needed a change. Family, friends, everyone was supportive. I just felt like…no one knew how to treat us anymore. I was able to get a teaching position overseas, and here we are." I wondered if Kay had ever been married. The cottage held no clues.

Kay glanced at Jess and Tate. They followed the kittens to a lined box, where I imagined the animals slept, and were giggling as the little ones awkwardly climbed back inside it.

"How did the girls react?" Kay's voice was low.

"Not well," I admitted. "I was selfish. I just wasn't thinking about how much it would affect them and, when I did, I thought they'd be thrilled. They're adjusting to it slowly."

"Well, these things take time. No move is without difficulties. There's no hurry on deciding about a kitten. They aren't weaned yet, so you can think about it for a while and, like I said, I'm worried I won't have any takers. The Samms would probably take them and let them live in the barn, but I know some, if not all, would end up dead. Kittens are too curious for their own good. Mrs. Samms would try to keep them in, but cats will find a way."

"Thanks. I really will think about it."

Kay walked to the stove and, as she stirred a pot, a delicious aroma filled the air. "The venison's ready." She tossed a crocheted hot pad on the table and, with a flourish, set the pot upon it.

"I don't think the girls have ever had it. A friend of ours hunted and shared some venison sausage with us. My husband liked it, but I found it too gamey. I've seen it at the grocery store in Aberdeen but haven't been brave enough to try it."

Tate looked up at me. "What's venison?" she asked.

"Deer meat, like Bambi," Jess answered, knowing full well how Tate would react.

"Bambi!" The corners of Tate's mouth turned down.

I gave both a stern look.

"On the island, the deer have become nuisances because they have few natural enemies to cull the population. They tear up gardens and then, when they're too populous, they starve since they've eaten the entire flora. It's important to thin out the herds to keep the population healthy," Kay explained.

"Oh." Tate's forehead wrinkled up as she thought about this. "I'm still not sure that I want to eat it."

"Remember our rule," I cautioned.

Kay patted my hand and smiled then turned back to the girls. "You'll like this. It's my version of a venison Scotch broth, a kind of stew, and I've a fresh loaf of baked bread. Simple meal, but tasty."

The stew had potatoes, carrots, green beans, and leeks in a tomato broth. The venison was cut into bite-sized pieces. I sampled a spoonful. "It's delicious, Kay."

I had always insisted that the girls try everything. Not only once, but each time they came across it, because tastes changed over time and perhaps the offending food would taste good cooked differently.

They started out just nibbling at the vegetables, but Tate was too curious not to sample the venison. She fished out the smallest piece of meat she could find and took a miniscule bite then smiled and quickly ate the rest. "Yum!" She gave the dish a thumbs-up and turned to the warm, buttered bread.

Of course, since Tate tried it, the more cautious Jess had to, too.

The cats were well-behaved. They stayed off the table and out from underfoot. "I'm surprised the cats aren't begging for some meat," I mentioned.

"Oh, they've had their dinner already."

From the look of the cleaned bowls, and significantly depleted stew pot, everyone approved of the meal. Afterward, Kay brought out shortbread and fruit.

"Would you like a cuppa?" she asked.

"I'd love one," I answered gratefully.

The girls had glasses of milk with their dessert then sat on the floor and played with the cats.

"Are you going to Mrs. Nivens's birthday party?" I asked.

"Of course. You too?" Kay bustled about tidying while I started the washing up.

"Should we bring a gift?"

"Oh, no. No need for that. Mornia Nivens would be the first to tell you she already has more than she needs. She'll enjoy being fussed over and the dancing and the music. The village has a band, and they aren't half bad. They've even been asked to perform in several of the other villages on the mainland."

"Gavin's brother, Ian, is in the band," Jessie offered. He plays the violin."

"That's right. Nice lad. Bit of a disappointment to his "Da and Mum, though."

"Why's that?"

"He wasn't interested at all in the farm and left as soon as he could. Luckily, Gavin loves it."

"Since you recognize the enormous black cat, do you

by any chance know to whom she belongs? I've never seen a cat as big as that one."

"Call her Kiera, Mom," Tate interjected.

"The kids love her, but I'd feel bad if her owner is looking for her, and she's been at our cottage the whole time. I took a photo and the grocer put it up with my number, but I've heard nothing."

"Kiera is a tame stray. She doesn't have an owner."

"Is she, safe?" I whispered.

"She's sweet-natured, generally, but will claw you something fierce if vexed. Your girls seem gentle and kind, so they should be fine. I see her now and again. She's vaccinated and fixed."

"Okay. Good to know."

"Is your daughter feeling any better?"

"Tate seems off. I thought I would take her to the doctor if she doesn't improve soon."

"What's wrong?"

"She's so pale and often lethargic. She isn't acting herself. She's usually full of energy and bright and cheerful. I'm surprised she isn't chomping at the bit to explore your backyard."

"Hmmm. I'll think on it. In the meantime, I also have some herbal tea that may help."

"How kind of you."

A howl emanated from outside, startling the girls, which startled the cats. All the four-legged creatures darted for cover. The girls ran to me.

"What was that?" I asked.

"A wolf." Kay stood and went to the door. "I wonder what's brought him to this neck of the woods."

I followed her. "You aren't going out, are you? That howl sounded like it came from your front yard."

She opened the door and stepped out onto the porch. A large, gray wolf stood just visible in the porch light. It growled. Kay clapped her hands and made shooing motions. "You! Go on, then. Shoo!"

The wolf howled once more and then slinked off into the darkness.

I tugged Kay back inside and slammed and locked the door. "I don't understand it. I thought wolves were afraid of people."

Tate stayed close to my side. I absentmindedly hugged her tight. Jess stared out the window, scanning for signs of the creature.

"Odd that," Kay said as she brought out a deck of cards from the end table drawer.

She distracted the girls with card tricks, proving to be quite the prestidigitator. Soon Jessie abandoned her post at the sill, and Tate relaxed. I, however, was still on edge and fidgety.

After Kay produced cards from the girls' ears one last time, we gathered around the table and Kay and I taught the girls how to play Spades.

I happened to glance at the clock over the fireplace. "Oh, I didn't realize it was getting so late. We need to be going."

"Let me send some of this bread and the herbal tea for Tate home with you. In fact, I'll drive you home."

"You don't need to do that."

"I insist. Wild animals tend to shy away from civilization. I don't like that the Wolf came so close."

I could hear the capitalization of the word in the way she said it. I hadn't expected to be walking home in the dark. I thought we would be leaving before it got so late. I anticipated the girls not wanting to stay, but since our visit lasted so long, and with a giant wolf outside, a car ride back sounded wonderful. After the girls gave the kittens one last cuddle, Kay loaded us up in her tiny Dacia Sandero hatchback.

Later that evening, as I tucked the girls into bed, I heard another howl.

"Did the wolf follow us home?" Tate asked.

"Maybe so, but we're safe inside. Wolves can't open doors."

Tate tugged the covers up to her chin. "What about Kiera?"

"She's been here a long, long time and is still alive. I'm sure she'll be fine and knows to stay clear of a wolf or climb a tree. Sometimes she visits Kay. Maybe she went there after we left."

Before I went to bed, I looked out the window and could just make out a wolf standing in the shadows at the edge of the tree line. As I watched, a man in a kilt came out of the forest near the edge of the house. It had to be the same dark-haired Scot I'd met before. When the wolf saw him, the fur on its back raised and, stiff-legged, it approached the man. I cracked open the window to yell and warn him, but before I could, the man growled then threw back his head and howled. The wolf stopped.

Taking a menacing step forward, the man shouted, his voice deep and commanding, "Get back to where you belong!"

The wolf, to my surprise, slinked off into the night. The man turned toward me. I ducked my head, but through the sheer curtains, I saw him tip his cap at me. Then he turned and disappeared back into the forest.

The next morning, after letting Kiera in, I found the wolf's paw prints ranging around the cottage. It made me nervous. I hoped that the man had scared it off for good. I knew Kay said it wouldn't bother us, but she didn't have children. The girls both seemed unnerved by the howls, and I wanted to sit down with them and remind them about not approaching wild animals.

CHAPTER 4

Friday couldn't come soon enough for Jessie. I managed to convince her that she didn't need new clothes since everything she had was "new" to everyone here. I worried about Tate. She seemed so listless and she spent much of the day dozing. She might be depressed. Jess found someone to occupy her time and mind, but Tate hadn't found a friend. Hopefully, she would meet someone at the party. I had one daughter tugging on me and begging me to hurry up already and one who moved at the speed of a turtle missing a leg. I thought that Jess was going to hit Tate if she didn't get a move on. I finally sent Jessie to pick out some clothes for Tate. I made Tate a PBJ and talked to her while she ate.

"Your sis is really looking forward to tonight. I know you aren't as keen, but please don't make the night miserable for her because you aren't happy. You know, there will be other children there too."

The small snack seemed to revive Tate. "I know, Mom," she said as she brushed the crumbs off her mouth with a napkin. "I'll hurry. Won't take me long to get ready, especially since I don't spend an hour trying on outfits and frowning at myself in the mirror." She grinned and dodged the palm I meant to spank her butt with.

True to her word, Tate was ready in record time. Sunset in the summer here wasn't until about ten, so, the road was well lit. I wore my black espadrilles, a sleeveless, yellow blouse that I got for sale at the Galleria, and, instead of jeans, black trousers I bought the shirt right before we left Houston, whimsically choosing the color to remind me of Houston's heat. I had never worn it because the color seemed too bright and cheery for a widow, but something told me to pack it when we left for the island. Unfortunately, I didn't bring much in the way of jewelry, so my gold hoop earrings would have to do. I guess I was as self-conscious as Jess in a way, but I didn't want to show up and look like a hausfrau, especially since the village wasn't likely to have many opportunities to see me in a pseudo-dressy outfit. Despite having been told no, Conall waited at the end of the drive. He must have decided to grow a beard because the length now surpassed the five o'clock shadow he sported the other day. Even his hair seemed longer and thicker. Perhaps he just washed it. He seemed full of nervous energy and was pacing like a lion in a den. He practically danced on his toes like an excited puppy when he noticed us round the corner.

"I took a chance I might see you on your way to the ceilidh since I was on my way too."

"Kinda out of your way," I noted.

"Not really. I had to drop off some groceries to Mrs. Thomas. She's ailing and elderly."

"That was very kind and considerate of you." *And convenient.* I wondered if he really did deliver anything and if Mrs. Thomas was indeed ill. I don't know why, but something about him made me nervous. I vowed to give him a chance and not be so judgmental. "Quite a moon we have tonight." I gestured to the almost filled-in orb hovering low on the horizon.

Conall frowned as he gazed up. "I prefer the stars myself. The moon feels…moody…dangerous." He stroked his chin drawing attention to his soon-to-be-a-proper beard. I noticed it was somewhat uneven. I smothered a smile and I wondered if he was aware that there were shavers designed to give a man an even five o'clock shadow or any other length of beard.

The girls soon outpaced us. A long stretch of uncomfortable silence goaded me into making conversation. Remembering his last words, I asked, "Wished upon the first star you saw tonight?"

As soon as the church was in view, the girls capered off. "Careful," I called.

"Well, if I did, my wish came true." Conall's cheeks pinked but he maintained eye contact until I ducked my head and forced a chuckle. The man could be nervous as a thirteen-year-old altar boy and as overly familiar as a randy dog. I wasn't sure what to make of him.

Conall opened the door for me. Tate, already arm in arm with another little girl, chatting up a storm. *Now that's the Tate I know.* Kay waved at me from the punch bowl at the opposite end of the room. She tried the punch, then added soda to the bowl. I hoped I could catch her later in the night to talk. She would make me feel less like a cuckoo. Kay wore a brightly colored full skirt and a camisole topped with a bolero. Jess was alone, but I followed her gaze to Gavin, who was bringing two glasses of punch, one for him and one for Jess. Her grin was as bright as the moon.

An elderly woman dressed as a Queen Elizabeth look-a-like, possibly the birthday girl, called out and waved a lace napkin at Conall.

He nodded. "I wish I could sit with you, but we have a few tables set aside for the family, so we can be close to my aunt."

"Oh, no problem. I'm sure I can find a place to sit." When he paused, unwilling to leave, I shooed him. "Go on! Your aunt's looking for you." As soon as he reached the two tables in the front of the hall, the elderly woman practically tackled him with a tight hug. I heard her shriek of joy from the doorway where I dawdled. I hoped to sit with Kay, but she manned the punch bowl and the tables were filling quickly.

Tate and Jessie asked if they could sit with their friends, and I nodded with a small smile as I tried not to feel sorry for myself. I watched with amusement as person after person sat at the corner table by the window. Each sat down, rested arms on the table, and then jerked up when the table tilted. "Guess that's where I'll be sitting," I muttered to myself, dodging groups of happily chattering guests. The pastor stood at the front and cleared his throat. Everyone went still. He said a quick prayer and invited the guests to help themselves to the buffet. I dropped my purse on the table which, of course tipped forward. The small vase in the center wobbled.

"Here," a gruff voice said, ducking under the table as I turned. The table leveled when he placed a folded napkin under one of its legs and the very attractive, dark-haired man rose from underneath it.

"Oh! I mean, hello—I just didn't expect you here. Not that you shouldn't be here. I mean, goodness, if anyone shouldn't be here, it's me," I finished lamely.

"Is this seat taken?" he asked as he placed a hand on the back of one chair.

"No. I mean I didn't come alone, my daughters are with me, but they wanted to sit with their friends, and I don't have any friends here. Yet." I wanted to beat my head on that ill-mannered table. The more I spoke the stupider I sounded.

"You go fetch yourself something to eat. I'll make sure the table is still here when you get back."

"Thanks." *But who in the world would want the awful table that tilted by the drafty door?* There was a mishmash of dishes to choose from, and it all smelled delicious. I realized I hadn't been very good about cooking proper meals and vowed to do better as I filled my plate. When I returned, my table companion pulled the chair out for me. I gratefully sat. He joined me and sipped a beer. "Aren't you going to eat anything?" I asked.

"Nae, I had a bite before I came. Perhaps I'll have a bit of Sticky Toffee Pudding before I leave, though."

Why would he show up at a party then have nothing to eat? It had taken me a while to recognize him, out of the forest and cleaned up. His hair was combed back into a queue. He wore neatly-pressed slacks and a pin-striped, button-down shirt.

"You're the man from the forest," I said. "I almost didn't recognize you without your kilt." Heat invaded my cheeks. "I want to thank you again for helping me find my daughter."

"'Twas nothing. I was out taking care of some—wild life."

"Oh, are you a…games keeper? Do you rescue hurt animals and nurse them back to health?"

He quirked an eyebrow at me and the hint of a smile creased his face. I couldn't help but return it, struggling not to let it turn into a full-blown infatuated grin.

"Sometimes."

"You must live near the cottage where we're staying."

He grimaced. "I camp, a bit. I like to rough it during the summer when the weather is so fine."

"In the woods? Isn't that dangerous?"

"Not for me. I ken the area very well."

For a moment, we sat in silence and watched the dancers. Jess had several partners, but I saw her most often with Gavin. Tate found some other children her age. They were having their own version of a ceilidh in one corner of the large room. The music was amazing. One young man beat a drum. Another, with features so much like the drummer, that they must be related, played an accordion. Two women, one bobbing with the music, the other thoughtful and still, strummed guitars and one man a violinist—Gavin's relative, no doubt because I saw him chat with Gavin before beginning to play. As I swayed to the music, I noticed that the man from the forest tapping his foot. When there was a skip in the music, I turned to my table companion.

"I don't believe we have been properly introduced. My name is Becca Shaw." I stuck out my hand. He surprised me by placing a soft kiss on the back of it.

"Becca?"

"Short for Rebecca."

"Ah. I am Greg Gillie. Pleased to meet you. I see your little one has made friends." He motioned toward Tate. Somehow, Kiera had gotten in and was the center of attention. She must definitely be the village mascot. No one seemed upset that a huge cat was at the party. She was very well behaved and the children obviously loved her. As we watched, Kiera rubbed her cheek against Tate's and disappeared out a propped open back door.

"Yes, Tate's very friendly."

He frowned. "Warn her that not all things are as they seem."

"She's usually very cautious and well aware of strangers. We moved from Houston, Texas, and the city has a lot of crime. Even in our suburban neighborhood, our next-door neighbors were robbed, and a woman was assaulted at the supermarket the fall before—" I gulped and paused. He waited patiently. "—before my husband died."

"My sincere condolences for your loss. I admit I was curious that no man accompanied you into the woods. So, you are alone?"

"Not alone. As I said, I have my two daughters here with me," I reminded him. "My oldest is dancing with Gavin Samms, the farmer's son. I'm also sorry for your loss."

He crossed his arms in front of his chest and leaned back in the chair.

"I was told you lost your family."

"I lost my wife and child," he said and turned his chair round to watch the dancers. I struggled to think of a new topic, but words escaped me when I looked into his emerald eyes.

At this point, Conall closed in on my table and stopped just behind Greg. "Hello again, Rebecca. I needed to get my aunt settled, but if you would like, I can teach you to dance. I'm sure they'll be playing one of the easier ones soon."

"Oh, I don't know, Mr. McNeil. I'm a lousy dancer. I usually was in charge of the punch bowl back home."

"Please, call me Conall."

I sighed and resolved to try, despite worrying he would interpret the familiarity the wrong way. He reached for my hand, but I quickly put it on my lap. Then he noticed my table partner.

"What are you doing here?" he asked, his face suspicious and his tone sharp.

"Just passed by and heard the kerfuffle. Thought I would come in and see what was happening."

"I'm fairly sure you weren't invited, and you aren't welcome."

I gasped at his rudeness. "Conall!"

Greg held out his hands, placating. "Calmy doony, Mr. McNeil. Nae need to rage." Conall looked surprised for a moment, then Greg spoke again. "I was just passing through and saw the young lady. I ken she wanted something to eat and offered to save her table for her. Goodbye then. I'll be going." Greg stood, bowed to me, and turned for the door.

"Indeed, you better," Conall growled and followed the dark-haired man with his eyes as he left the building. Conall turned back to me, his face drawing with worry when he noted my expression. "I apologize. There's just bad blood between that man and my family."

"What in the world did he do?" I asked.

He shook his head. "Let's leave such a sad tale for another time. I am truly sorry for losing my temper. Allow me to make it up to you?" He reached out his hand and nodded toward the band that was starting a new number.

Deep in thought, I allowed Conall to lead me onto the dance floor. I wondered what their feud was all about, but was soon too busy paying attention to where my feet were going to think on it any further.

I danced to several more songs with various partners, and I must admit that I had a wonderful time. It crossed my mind to wonder what kind of dancer Greg was. *Get that out of your head, Becca. For all you know, he may be dangerous. Goodness knows, he's as strange as they come.*

This was probably the longest I had gone without missing my husband. I felt a little guilty but reminded myself that he had been dead just over a year, and there was nothing inappropriate about me going out. I was a bit old-fashioned in that respect, and I mourned my husband so much that I probably would have just retreated into my room and hidden under the covers for ages, but with the girls, I had to get myself out and going.

As the band packed their instruments, I realized that only the girls and I, plus the immediate family of the guest of honor, remained. Tate was having a cookie.

"Last one, Tate. I'm going to find Jess, then we're off for the cottage."

"Oh, Mom, it's a special occasion," she complained half-heartedly.

"You haven't felt well lately. I don't want you complaining of a tummy ache later tonight." I had to admit that Tate looked much more like herself. Maybe she'd had some low-grade twenty-four-hour flu and was finally getting over the hump and improving. I didn't see Jess inside and that worried me. "I'll be right back. I think Jess is outside. Don't you move," I cautioned. I found Jessie sitting on the front steps in a huddle with Gavin. Thankfully not kissing but just talking, though she did jump and looked guilty when I called her name. "Jess, time to go."

"Can't we stay a few more minutes?" She looked at me then Gavin then back at me with a pleading expression.

"The band's packing up, and soon everyone will be gone, Jess."

Gavin jumped up. "Oh, no! I was supposed to be helping. I better go." He started to leave but turned back to Jessie. "I had a great time. I'm glad you came."

"Me too," Jess said, blushing.

Ah, young love, save me from it. I sighed, and Jess and I followed Gavin in to get Tate. We made our way to the guest of honor, Mrs. Nivens, to wish her happy birthday once more. We thanked her and Conall's cousin, Marie—who planned the party—for inviting us. I didn't see Conall and was glad. He was so brusque with Greg and almost possessive of me. He had no cause to think that. We weren't dating, and Greg only saved a rickety table for me and introduced himself. I thought I might now know why a handsome man and business owner my age would still be single. When we stepped outside, the village lights made it easy to see Kay finishing a cigarette.

"I saw you when I first came in, but then you vanished. Sorry I missed you," I said.

"I helped some with the serving. Spent some time outside smoking—" She gestured with the one she had almost finished. "—and chatting with the neighbors. Did you have a good time?"

"Yes, I did. I'm glad I came. Glad you're still here and haven't left already. I wasn't looking forward to walking home with just me and the girls."

The first part of the walk was fine. The main part of the village was paved and well lit, but as we left the buildings and street lamps, it darkened. Thankfully, the full moon, Kay's flashlight, and Jess's cell phone light helped us pick out the rocks and dips in our path. We were joined by other villagers who lived our way, but we were the farthest from the town square—or at least the farthest of those who attended the party. Soon enough, it was only the four of us. We were just rounding the corner of the road leading to the path of the cottage, when we heard a howl. Both girls grabbed my hands. Kay had been in the middle of relaying a recipe to me but stopped and looked around.

"Wolf," she said. She didn't seem to be afraid and that bolstered my confidence. "It shouldn't bother us, but let's move a little faster. No running," she cautioned as Tate bent her arms and doubled up her fists in preparation to tear off. "Just quicken the pace."

We remained silent. The only noise we could hear was the wind blowing through the leaves. It felt unnatural to be outside in all this flora and fauna and hear nothing. Not the occasional baa of a sheep or moo of a cow or the bark of a dog. We turned onto the lane that led to our cottage when we heard a low growl right behind us.

"Just keep walking," Kay said. "Don't look." The hairs on the back of my neck straightened and goose bumps covered my arms.

"Our paths diverge here. You go on. The beast will be undecided."

"But what if the wolf is a decisive sort?" I asked.

Kay patted my arm. "We'll all be fine. Trust me." She shooed me and the girls down our path and continued toward her home.

CHAPTER 5

Kay disappeared, and I hoped she made it home safely. The wolf howled again—close. It sounded near enough to nip at our heels, but no one turned to check, we just picked up our pace. The night was eerily silent without Tate's usual chattering. She wasn't a quiet sort of child, but she had her mouth set. Our gaits were beginning to resemble the speed walkers from the Olympics. I let the girls pull out ahead of me. If this thing did attack, it would hopefully go for me first and then maybe the girls could run to the house while I fought it off.

"Girls, if anything happens, run. I'll take care of it," I said in a low voice.

Jess shook her head. "Mom, I'm not leaving you. Tate can run ahead and call the police."

"No. I won't!" Tate protested.

"Shhh! You will *both* run to the cottage and call the police."

I risked a glance behind. The black wolf's shoulder came to my waist. It didn't look starved. Its body was well-muscled, and its fur gleamed in the moonlight. As its eyes caught mine, it whined and ducked its head. Perhaps it really was afraid of people. We neared the forest's edge defining the beginning of the property. I tripped over a rock and tumbled to the ground. The wolf yelped and, as I sat up, it rushed toward me. The girls screamed.

"Run!" I cried out.

Before they could, the black stray rushed from the underbrush and pounced on the wolf. The wolf cried out when her sharp claws found its delicate snout. Though the wolf shook and rolled, the cat clung to its back and neck.

"Kiera!" Tate cried out, running toward the snarling beasts.

"No, Tate!" I snatched at her, but missed her hand.

She'd almost reached the animals when a bulky, dark figure burst from the forest, caught her around her waist, and lifted her. "Not a good idea, young lady." Greg held her. "You go to your mum." He pushed her my way and turned to the animals. The wolf managed to dislodge the cat, and it flew through the air. As Kiera hit a tree trunk, the beast turned toward the man.

"You dinna want to do that, Sir Wulver," Greg said. The wolf hesitated. "You need a run," he continued. "Into the woods with you. Find a wee coineanach to chase."

The wolf's lip rose in a snarl and, with stiff legs, it backed into the woods and out of sight. Tate and Jessie ran toward Kiera. By the time they reached her, she was up, walking.

"I think she's just shook up," Greg said. "Lady Sith is a hardy one."

"What did you call her?" Tate asked.

"Why, Lady Sith is the Queen of Cats."

Kiera purred, licked each girl's hand, then leapt to a low tree limb, and vanished.

Tate beamed with joy. "Wow, Mom, our kitty is the queen of all kitties."

"Rest assured that she is no one's cat but her own. You are blessed and lucky if she deigns to visit you. Remember, though—always treat her with respect and honor her desires."

"We will," Tate answered solemnly.

When he addressed me, his soft and gentle tone became gruff. "I'll walk you the rest of the way to your cottage."

"There's no need," I protested.

"No, perhaps not, but I would rest more easily if I knew you and your family made it home."

He proffered his arm, and I hesitantly took it, gingerly resting my fingertips on his hard bicep. When we could see the cottage, the girls rushed ahead. We followed at a more dignified pace.

"Thank you, again," I said when we reached the door.

"It seems that you are often in need of help. Perhaps you should find a husband? You're comely enough."

I bristled. "I don't need a husband," I said, my teeth clenched.

"A woman needs a helpmate as does a man," he stated.

"So, why aren't you looking for a helpmate?"

"That is no concern of yours," he said shortly. "Goodnight." And, with a whirl, he disappeared into the darkness.

I locked the doors and made sure all the windows were shut, even though it would be stuffy. The wolf scared me. Heck, the cat and the man were beginning to make me feel seriously uneasy.

The girls went to bed without a fuss. Jessie had a dreamy expression on her face as she tucked herself in bed. I kissed both the girls and sat at the kitchen table with a cup of tea. I couldn't sleep. I kept thinking about the feeling of his arm, the heat he radiated, and the way his blue-black hair gleamed.

"Geez, Becca. You aren't sixteen. Stop mooning!" I admonished myself. Besides, he thought I should find myself a man, and clearly, said man wasn't him.

As I put the empty teacup in the sink, I heard a howl. Though tempted, I refused to look out the window and went straight to bed.

CHAPTER 6

The next morning, we all slept in. When we did wake up, the sun was well overhead. I decided to work some more in the garden. It was overgrown, but with attention, it could be lovely. I knew it was silly since we would be gone in a few months. The hands of time would render it back to its current condition, but I hated seeing it the way it was, and I needed something to take my mind off recent events. Gavin invited Jessie back to Samms Farm to help with the horses, and I gave permission. She spent an hour getting ready and then took off like a dart since she was running late, no doubt undoing all her efforts. I shook my head and smiled. As I finished making breakfast, we heard the telltale meow. Tate opened the door, and Kiera entered regally, up on her toes and her tail erect. Though she shared half her breakfast with the cat, Tate seemed to be eating and looked better. Perhaps we could skip the trip to the doctor.

I didn't have any plans for the day other than gardening. Tate joined me, and once I pointed out the difference, helped with weeding for an hour—fifty minutes longer than I thought—then went in to finish her book. I peeked in later, and she was curled up with Kiera, making comments on what was happening. I swear, it looked as if the cat understood every word she said and when Tate paused before turning the page, the cat batted her hand in encouragement.

"That's the craziest thing," I said to myself.

I hadn't bought much the first day on the island, so I needed to replenish the pantry. Tate grudgingly stopped reading, and we walked to the bus stop. I intended to get plenty and didn't want to have to carry it home on foot. The bus came every half hour on Saturday, so we didn't wait long. I thought we would look around town at the various shops, have a tea, or in Tate's case a hot cocoa, do grocery shopping, then take the bus home.

One shop sold and rented kilts and stocked tartan. I was amazed at how expensive they were. The kilts costs more than I paid for my last dress. "That's why many men rent them for formal events and weddings," the shop keeper confided. "Men rarely wear them daily. Only a few older gents."

"I saw a younger man, around my age, wearing one."

"Well, perhaps he was off to a party."

"No, I don't think so. He was in the forest."

"We have some eccentric characters in the village as most small villages do. No doubt you've run across one."

"I suppose. He seemed gruff—maybe rustic, but sane and kind."

"Well, if he acted crazy, he would be put away, now wouldn't he?" the shop keeper opined.

"I guess so." I bought four yards of tartan to send home to my mother in-law. She loved to sew and the material was the only thing she asked of me. Even though I had been in Aberdeen since last summer, I hadn't managed to make it to a shop before to buy the gift. I'd hoped to find something local to send her from the island.

We found a sweet tea shop, Marnie's Tearoom, tucked in an alley or perhaps an old street only wide enough for pedestrian travel now. There were many such places in Scotland. The shop was well attended, always a sign of a good establishment.

I smiled at the display of miniature Sticky Toffee Puddings and couldn't help but think of Greg. While he was easy on the eyes and mostly polite, he could say the most annoying things at times. The proprietor, Marnie Wallace, introduced herself and took our order. We got tea and scones as a treat. I held back a sigh as Conall saw me through the plate glass and doubled back to enter the shop.

"How are you today?" he asked when he reached the table.

I nodded. "Well enough."

He seemed agitated and swiped a shaky hand through his hair. "I had a rough night," he admitted.

"Well, some people do. A full moon can have a strange effect." My words were whimsical as I struggled to keep the mood light.

"That's the talk of old women. The full moon has nae effect on me—or anyone else, for that matter." There was an awkward pause as we both regrouped. "I didn't mean you were an old woman—" he said, as I said at the same time, "I'm sorry, I—"

We laughed nervously.

"No harm done, I hope. As I said, I didn't sleep well. You made it home all right, then?" he asked.

"Yes, we had a bit of a fright. A wild wolf was on the lane. I think from now on, I'll carry a large stick. Kay said that they're more afraid of us than we are of them, but this one seemed quite bold."

He swallowed. "Well, we tend to leave well enough alone here. Creatures, all, have a right to live."

"As long as they cause no harm," I commented.

"Aye, that. Well, I'll leave you to your tea. G'day."

He bustled away before I could say anything. *How peculiar.*

The shop teemed with customers, and I recognized some American accents. As I gazed out the window gathering wool, a familiar voice greeted me.

"I see you survived the walk home, Becca."

"Miss Sheey! Tate exclaimed. "How are the kittens?"

"Curious as can be and constantly finding something to get into. They'll be ready to be weaned in a month."

I gestured to the chair. "Please, sit down and join us."

She pulled it out and sat. "I can only stay a bit. I often help out Marnie on the weekends during the summer when things get busy. I do have time to have a cuppa with you while I wait for the bread to finish baking."

"How many of the kittens have homes?" Tate asked

"The ginger tom and the gray and white one are already spoken for."

"Jody told me. I met her at the party last night." Tate frowned for a moment in thought. "At least she hasn't chosen my favorite."

"And which might that be?'

Tate lit up. "The black one with the long hair. She reminds me of Kiera. She's so tiny, but brave. She doesn't let the bigger ones to push her around. Even though she's tough and brave, she's gentle. Some of the others scratch accidentally." She showed her arm which had light crosshatches where the kittens had caught at her.

"You're a good judge of kittens, Tate. She will make someone a wonderful pet. Sadly, it's hard to find homes for black cats."

"Why?" Tate asked.

"People believe black cats are bad luck. Many shelters don't allow black cats to be adopted in October, because there have been cases of abuse during All Hallows' Eve.

Shelters put a moratorium on black cat adoption or step up screening at that time of the year."

"That's horrible!" I loved animals and cringed at the idea of anyone abusing the kittens.

"I'll go fetch some tea. The scones are fresh out of the oven. Would you like a couple?"

Tate gave me a pleading look, complete with hands clasped in front of her chest.

"Better make that six. One for Jess when she gets home and the others for breakfast tomorrow."

Kay glided between the crowded tables and chairs and returned with a tray.

"This is one thing I will seriously miss when we return to the States," I said as I piled my scone high with clotted cream and raspberry jam.

"They don't make scones?" Kay asked, pouring us each a cup of tea.

"What Americans call scones are different from the ones here. They're more like giant triangular biscuits. Good, just not the same."

"I've never been overseas."

"You should go sometime. There's a lot to see and do. We have family in Houston who we plan to visit next summer. If you travel then and are anywhere near us, I would be happy to take you around." *Why did I say that?* I disliked driving in the busy city and was happier letting guests make their own arrangements for sightseeing. I changed the topic. "I can't believe how crowded the shop is. It reminds me of one of the beach resorts in Texas."

"The lake island community is a novelty and many who are already in the vicinity for other reasons make a point to ferry over to hike or just to walk around the town. No cars save those already here are allowed on the island. We want to keep this a nice place and the quiet appeals to us."

"How long have you lived here?"

"I lived here with my family until I turned sixteen and we moved to Aberfeldy. We remained there for over thirty years. When my parents retired and moved to a residential care home, I visited the island. Several years later, and I'm still here."

I had to reassess my guess about Kay's age. I thought she was around my age, but from what she just said, she must be closer to fifty than forty. She did have one of those ageless faces. Carnival people would lose money guessing her age and would probably continue to do so when she was ninety. We finished our tea and scones and Kay stacked the empty cups and dishes on the tray and wiped the table.

"Are you going home soon? I thought, if it was okay, maybe I could come over and help with the kittens."

Tate studiously avoided looking at me. I was sure "help" was Tate code for "play."

"Tate Elizabeth, we do not invite ourselves over to someone's house," I admonished.

Tate opened her mouth to apologize, but Kay interrupted. "I have a few more hours of work to do here, but if it's okay with your mother, it would be a big help to me if you could check on them and see if their mama needs any water or food." Kay looked to me for the answer.

"We'd be happy to do that, but are you sure? After all, we've just met."

"I'm a good judge of character. I trust you. Besides even if you were a thief, I've got nothing anyone would want to steal—unless you're a cat burglar," she added mischievously as she squinched up her nose at Tate. Tate and I obliged her with giggles. "Well, I best get these back to the kitchen and start cleaning." Kay smiled and waved, swirling her skirt as she made her way toward the swinging doors.

"But what about the key?" I asked.

"The door is unlocked. Just make sure you pull it to and it's latched before you leave. Otherwise, I'll have six kitties to chase after. The cat food is in the pantry above the bowl."

We said our goodbyes and, after an overdue stop at the grocery, we staggered under the weight of bagged goods to the bus stop bench.

"We need to get one of the little carts other ladies use to put our shopping in, Mom," Tate commented pushing a sweaty lock behind her ear.

"There may be one at the cottage. I haven't checked, but we are definitely bringing it next time if there is one." I repositioned a bag so a box corner wasn't digging into my ribs. When, after a short wait, the bus came, it held few passengers. Most did their shopping during the weekdays when the businesses weren't crowded with tourists. "Let's go home first, Tate. We can drop off the groceries and—" I checked my watch. "Jess may be home by now and want to go with us or eat her scone as a snack."

Tate agreed quickly, making me feel bad about saddling her with two bags. They were the smallest, and I couldn't carry anymore, but guilt washed over me, and I regretted purchasing so much, since Tate had felt off the past few days. When we reached the door, she tried to mask a yawn.

"Are you feeling okay?" I asked.

"A little tired. It was a long walk with the groceries, but Mrs. Sheehy's isn't very far and we *have* to go, Mom. I've got to water and feed her cats."

I thought the cats would be fine until Kay got back, but I knew my little girl had her heart set on going. We had half the groceries unpacked when Jess rushed in, her face flushed with excitement.

"Gavin let me jump the horse!" she reported, grinning ear to ear.

"Jessie, I don't know about that—it's been a while since you've had horseback lessons."

When we lived in Houston, both the girls had English style horse riding lessons, albeit Tate had barely started when we moved. Jessie had graduated to jumping the horses, but she'd hardly ridden since our move to Aberdeen. I had asked her, but I thought she was punishing me for moving her away from her friends. She continually reminded me, "It won't be the same without Courtney and Trina."

"Mo—om, Mr. Samms was there and the fences were very low. He also gives lessons. Do you think I could take some while we're here?"

I took pleasure in seeing her excited and happy about something. The lessons gave her much joy when her dad was alive. She attended after his death, but lacked enthusiasm. He was the one who had encouraged her. I had some experience with cowboy riding, but not English.

"We'll see, honey." I put off the decision for later. "Tate and I brought back scones. There are three for breakfast tomorrow, but we got an extra one for you if you're hungry."

"Thanks!" Jessie sifted through what we had bought and quickly found the scone. She broke off a corner and stuffed it into her mouth. "Yum, thanks, Mom," she said around the bite.

"We saw Kay Sheey in town, and she asked if we could stop by and check on the cats this afternoon. Do you want to come or would you rather stay here?"

"Sure, I'll come. Let me wash off a bit. I smell like horse." She raced to the bathroom and returned with wet hair in a sloppy braid and her face scrubbed pink. She munched on the scone as we walked over. True to Kay's word, we needed no key and, when we entered, the cats immediately mewed and twined around our legs, demanding attention. The girls each picked up two kittens. After I found the food, I handed it down to Tate so she could feed the cats. She washed out the water bowls and refilled then with fresh water, nearly bursting with pride.

The girls settled down for some serious petting time while I perused Kay's bookshelves. Some appeared to be in Gaelic. The latest Booker and Orange winners were annotated and marked. Either Kay taught, was in, or ran a book club. I leaned toward believing she ran one since the books had folded articles, study questions, and reviews tucked behind the covers. The books were too recently published to be introduced into a school yet. Several books on fables and local mythology that I would have loved to have spent more time skimming lined the bottom shelf, but I wanted to be gone before Kay made her way back so she wouldn't feel like she had to feed and entertain us. I imagined she would be tired after waiting on all those customers.

"Girls, I'm going to run to the bathroom before we leave. Put the kittens back in with their mommy. They're probably hungry and have had enough attention for now."

Tate groaned but I reminded her that they were just babies and too much stimulation would be bad for them.

"I'm going to look for a big stick," Jessie said.

I doubted that the wolf would come out this early, but I didn't think it a bad idea either. When I turned to the bathroom, I heard Tate say, "As we walked up, I saw this stick almost as tall as I am."

After I made use of the bathroom, I saw that the front door was open, just a bit, but enough for a kitten to escape. Alarmed, I called for the girls and we searched for the kittens, finding all except the little black one.

Beside herself with worry, Tate said, "Oh, no! I told you she was brave."

Near tears, Jessie apologized. "I'm so sorry, Mom. I thought I shut the door."

"It's okay, honey. We'll find the kitten." *I hope.*

CHAPTER 7

After shutting the door, *properly* this time, we searched the yard, circling out farther and farther from the house. The girls called for the kitty. I thought the little one was too young to come when called, but perhaps noise would motivate her to move and reveal her presence. We reached the edge of Kay's property and still hadn't found the kitten.

"She's so tiny and the door was only open while I visited the bathroom. How in the world did she wander so far away? Jess, you go up the path to the road and see if she made it that far. I wouldn't think so, but maybe something caught her eye, and she ran."

Jessie raced toward the path and the road. From the drive onward, stone walls flanked the road. Low, but certainly too high for a kitten to manage. "Tate, we'll walk around the house again, only pay close attention to the edge of the property. Maybe we can see an obvious break in the foliage where she slipped through."

Kay had planted blackthorn sloe, raspberry bushes, and several varieties of roses, including the butter-yellow Emily Gray and the pink and white Ballerina near the edge. I assumed they were to discourage the animals from trespassing. "Tate, do *not* go into the forest. If you see something, call me." Thankfully, in the summer, the days were long. During the winter, at least in Aberdeen, by four you had to turn on the car headlights to see. Before we finished checking the perimeter, Jess returned.

"No sign, Mom."

I explained what we were doing and Jess helped. Finally, we caught a break. At the forest edge, nearest to the doorway, I found a small path worn clear of grass and shrubs. I wondered if it was a rabbit trail. *I can't believe I didn't think to search there first, but we were at the back of the house when I thought to look more closely at the forest's edge.* Kay had planted many flowers and predictably, catnip, in her small garden along with some herbs. To my surprise, Kay didn't have a vegetable garden, but I supposed with Samms Farm close, she hadn't seen the need.

I checked my watch. It was nearing five o'clock. I didn't see a small tea shop staying opened much later than that. I expected that, like most small towns, once the clock struck six, the town pulled in its welcome mats and said good night—at least to any shopping. "Jess, Tate, Miss Sheey should be back soon. I'm going to follow this trail and see if I can catch the kitten. I won't be gone long."

"Okay, Mom, I hope you find her," Jess said.

She took Tate's hand and led her into the cottage with a promise to share the third of scone she had planned to save for dinner. I watched them go inside then walked back to the trail. At first, I had to walk duck-style as the branches caught on my clothes. An old forest, once I passed the barrier of plants and bushes Kay had planted, the ground was relatively bare. With the shade of the enormous trees, it was dark and foreboding. I stumbled over rocks and knotted roots, trying to keep an eye on the time. I didn't want the girls worried, and I didn't want

Kay to think I set her up to baby-sit without asking. *Not that they're babies anymore.* I traveled almost as far as I deemed prudent and was about to turn back when I heard water splashing.

The path twisted around to expose a small pond with a waterfall. Clear water revealed a rocky bed several yards out, but then the surface darkened, indicating much deeper water. Just over the splashing of the water fall, I could hear a meow. Below the roots of a giant tree, I saw a hollowed-out space and a tiny black paw, claws out, scratched at the slimy edge. The kitten must have tumbled in and gotten stuck.

"Now, now. I'm coming to get you," I reassured the kitten.

I worried how close the hollowed tree was to the edge of the pond, and that the rocks would be slippery. As I drew nearer, I could hear something else, a wailing, morose crooning in a minor key. It reminded me of a funeral hymn, perhaps one of the older songs sung a-cappella, though I couldn't make out the words. It was odd and hypnotic, like a Gregorian chant. A mist crept over the surface of the water obscuring the farthest shoreline, but I could make out a female figure in a white gown. She was so close to the waterfall that the spray and increasing haze made her hard to see. The fog muffled her voice. As I watched, she fell to her knees and bent toward the water.

"Are you okay?" I called.

What was she doing out in the forest dressed in a gown? She either did not hear me or chose to ignore me. She sat slumped at the water's edge and moved to and fro in a rhythmic manner. I winced when I stepped closer and the cold water abruptly soaked my walking shoes through to my socks.

Cupping my hands around my mouth, I called again,

louder. "Hello! Do you need help?" I must have traveled out farther than I intended because suddenly I plunged into thigh deep water. I shrieked, as I fell to my knees. The water was abnormally cold. It felt like the temperature that teeters on the very edge of water turning into ice. "Okay, enough of this," I muttered.

I was going to be no help to anyone if I collapsed from hypothermia. I turned toward the ledge I had stepped off to search for something to grab so I could pull myself up. Reaching into the water, I grasped the base of a large rock, digging my nails into the sand underneath it to gain purchase. As I tugged, landing on the ledge, something wrapped around my calf, and before I could take a breath, I lost my balance. I flailed my arms as I fell back, soaking myself more than I would have if I had just collapsed gracefully.

The water felt heavy, almost like quicksand. It seemed to cling to me like taffy. I fought to get to my knees. Whatever encased my calf vanished. *Perhaps algae?* I dashed wet bangs from my eyes and looked for the woman. Gone.

"Well, I won't have to rouse the town to look for her, I suppose."

I began to think I had imagined it or maybe she was some sort of white bird like a large heron or swan that I mistook for a woman. I rose from the water and stepped back as I appraised the shoreline once more. My foot slid on the slippery, sloped rock, and I went down again, hard, banging my head. I coughed and sputtered, getting a nose and mouthful of freezing water—liquid so cold, that it caught my breath and yanked it away. I rolled to my hands and knees, and vertigo unsteadied me. All I could do was sway, as my wet hair dripped into the water with a loud plop-plop as each drop entered the freezing pond. I jerked my head up when I felt tendrils wrap round each ankle. My head spun, and my stomach churned at the horrific surprise. I thought I would have thrown up except, before I could, something jerked and my knees fell from under me.

I sank beneath the gelid water's surface, clipping my chin on a rock hard enough to bite my tongue. The tangy iron of my own blood filled my mouth. I flailed to the surface. Managing to take deep breaths, I swallowed back vomit. I held my breath before I went under once more. I tried to ignore the hard, rough rocks tearing and poking my clothes and body. I reached to free myself and felt long fingers, complete with sharp nails, curled around my ankles.

Tugging at the hands, I struggled to open them. The fingers were so long that they overlapped the thumb by at least three inches. Panicked, I forgot to hold my breath and opened my mouth to scream. I bucked and flailed. The water was up to my waist when I briefly surfaced. I spit and gulped air before being sucked in deeper.

I thrashed my legs and tore at the fingers binding me. A nail bent back and one hand released me. As the other clenched claw let go, I placed one foot precariously underneath me. A monstrous, bald head sprang from the water. It had three ridged, bumpy slits on the side of its neck like gills on a fish, but there, the resemblance ended. It was greenish blue in color and had black, pupil-less eyes. The thing gawked at me, revealing double rows of sharp teeth like a shark. I couldn't decide if it had tiny scales or roughened skin. I watched it bite off the nail and spit it into the water. An odd, oily-gray blood oozed from the wound.

More hands clutched my ankles and knees and tugged me underwater again. I opened my eyes this time. Six creatures clung to me and fluttered their webbed feet as they attempted to drag me farther down. I twisted and turned until I had no idea which way was up or down. My head throbbed and, exhausted, I relaxed. My breath was giving out. I thought of my children, alone. I wondered if my husband awaited me wherever I ended up after death. The water wasn't deep. Probably not even chest deep, but if my face was underwater, it wouldn't matter.

I closed my eyes.

CHAPTER 8

I felt hands, human hands, grasp me under my armpits and wrestle me upright. The other hands burned as they were torn from my body, but I didn't care. I was free. I wondered who had come to my rescue. When I tried to stand, my legs collapsed. Thankfully, whoever held me—and, from the feel of the hard chest my head rested against, it definitely was not Kay—kept me from falling.

"Steady there. You're bleeding." He lifted me, one arm across my back and the other beneath my knees, but even though he was gentle as he waded out of the pool, I felt my gorge rise.

"I'm gonna be sick," I warned.

He sat down with me on his lap and held my hair, as I leaned sideways and threw up onto the mossy shore. My long, wet bangs hampered my vision, and my head pounded like a Vulcan was using it as an anvil. I combed back the errant locks with a shaking hand and saw my savior. "Greg?"

"You remembered. 'Tis surprising since we've barely spoken." He examined my head, and I winced when his fingers encountered a cut and what would no doubt be a huge goose egg.

"Ouch!" I ducked out of reach then swayed with vertigo.

"Sorry. We need to see to that and get you warm." He chafed my hands which I could barely feel.

"I came from Kay's cottage and—oh! The kitten!"

"You're lucky. I heard the wee one crying and came looking. Usually, grindylows, while mischievous, dinna attack. What were you doing in the pool?"

"I heard a lady crying and got too close." I shivered ad bit my lip to stifle a moan. "I got my feet wet and since I was already wet, I thought I'd wade in a bit and see if she needed help."

"You were going to go wading?"

"No farther than my ankles." My teeth chattered and I felt like I'd never be warm again. "W—water's too cold for my Texan blood. Anyway, the lady wouldn't answer and then disappeared."

"What did she look like?"

"She was wearing white, like a long dress with fluttery sleeves. Her hair was down. She held something she moved in the water."

"Doing her washing?"

I coughed, sounding like a barking seal. "Maybe. But why? She sang a—" I coughed again, less deeply this time. "—sad tune. Didn't get the words." I felt uneasy sitting on a strange man's lap, but when I tried to rise, I quickly fell back.

"Just sit still."

I could hear the kitten's more insistent meows. Greg parted my hair to look at my wound again and tsked like an old maid coming upon a girl and her beau kissing. He pulled a kerchief from a pouch he wore round his waist—I thought it was called a sporran—and pressed it against the gash.

I hissed in pain. "Yow!"

"Sorry. Will you be all right if I fetch the wee kitten?" he asked.

I began to nod, but reconsidered it since my head throbbed when I barely tilted it. "Yes."

He gently shifted me from his lap to the rock he had been sitting on and stood. When he reached the trunk, he squatted and slowly lowered a finger into the hole.

"Well, she's a friendly one. A lad or a lassie?" he remarked as he picked her up.

"Kay told me it's a girl," I answered. When he unbuttoned his cream-colored shirt, I noticed a cut on his neck just under his chin. "You're hurt too. Did you get cut when you fetched me from the pond?" I asked.

He rubbed his neck. "Nae, I nicked myself shaving. I used to have a fine ivory-handled blade but lost it. I've made do with my blade." He tucked the cat inside his shirt then rebuttoned it.

As he stood, I marveled how he did so in a kilt. I, on the other hand, would have probably exposed myself. The kilt was a bit longer than I'd seen on old Benny Hill reruns but neatly pleated and held up by a thick belt on which the sporran hung. He had a knife tucked into his calf-high sock. "Home for you two." The kitten mewed, and he reached inside his shirt to pet it. Muffled purrs soon replaced the meows.

"I need to get back to Kay's house. My girls are there, waiting for me, and I've been gone longer than I thought I would, thanks to that—what did you say those things were?"

"Grindylows."

I had heard of grindylows because the girls and I loved that series of books and movies which mentioned them, but these things did not resemble those portrayed in the film. "Grindylows are real?"

"Aye, and not generally dangerous. The weeping lady—she portends misfortune." He returned and offered me his hand. I gripped it, and he slowly lifted me to a standing position. My head spun, and I clung to him, feeling my cheeks heat as I did so but having no other choice unless I wanted to fall on my rear.

"Let me see how your heid looks," he said.

I rolled my head and, when I didn't feel like it was going to tumble off my shoulders, considered it a good sign then gingerly lifted the cloth for him to examine the wound.

"'Tis clotting. I dinna think it needs stitched. Heid wounds bleed so that the damage seems much worse than it is. Needs ice though as soon as you get back."

"I don't know if I can make it back on my own," I admitted.

"No need. I'll help you."

As we walked, I asked, "What brought you out to the woods? Are you still camping or do you live near?"

"I am neither too near nor too far."

Cryptic, much? "I haven't been here long enough to do much exploring, but I know there isn't another path between my cottage and Kay's." I waited, expecting him to give me a general location to his home, but he added no further information.

"Aye, true."

We walked for several minutes in silence and made much better time than I would have without his help.

"What do you do?" I asked.

He raised one eyebrow as he stopped for a second and met my eyes.

"I mean—for a living. Where do you work?"

"Around."

Definitely in avoidance mode. I looked at my watch but was dismayed to discover that, at some point in the water, I'd lost it. "I wonder what time it is."

He looked up. I did too, but the forest was so thick it was hard to see a bit of sky. "Near to tea time, I expect."

I walked faster and tripped over a rock.

"Careful now," he warned, grabbing my elbow and jarring the kitten. The kitten mewed in protest. He frowned at me. "You'll be adding more bumps to your noggin."

I sighed and resigned myself to a more leisurely pace. "I didn't thank you. I'm afraid I was too out of it at the time, but I appreciate you jumping in the pond to save me."

"'Tis nothing. Chances are, you would have been able to beat them back and scare them away."

"I don't know about that. By the time you arrived, most of the fight had gone out of me. I'm not one for swimming."

"You dinna know how to swim?"

"I took lessons as a child, but mostly I just dog paddle."

"You must remedy that. An island is surrounded by water."

I focused on not tripping and trying to make it as easy as possible for him to support me. The kitten continued to meow. Greg periodically paused to pat it and softly tell it, "Now, now, you will be back with your mum soon."

When we neared Kay's home, he had me lean against a tree and hacked enough foliage with his knife so we could get through without crawling. We emerged and a minute later, the girls burst out of Kay's cottage, followed by Kay herself.

"Mom!" they shouted as they ran toward me.

Jessie reached me first. "Why are you all wet?" she said, fingering my blouse.

"I had an unintended dip in a pond," I answered, not sure if I wanted to tell her about the grindylows, just in case, despite what Mr. Gillie said, I imagined them. *Lack of oxygen can cause hallucinations*, I thought. *He doesn't strike me as a jokester, but perhaps he was having me on.*

Kay reached us. "Mr. Gillie."

"Miss Sheey."

They greeted each other so formally I wondered how well they knew one another.

"Greg, I mean, Mr. Gillie, these are my girls."

"Aye, Jessica and Tate."

"He saw you two at the ceildh," I explained to them. I didn't think Tate remembered him from her outing in the woods. The kitten mewed. Greg took her from his shirt and gave her to Tate. The girls cooed over her.

Kay noticed the bloody kerchief in my hand and frowned. "You're hurt," she stated. "Get yourself into the cottage and let me see to you."

Greg swept me up in his arms and carried me across the grass.

"Oh, no! You don't have to do this," I protested.

"'Tis nae trouble and will be faster." No doubt he wanted to get away from me and my bothersome family as soon as possible.

Once we reached the cottage, he lowered me on the couch then brandished his tam toward us. "I need to make my way back. I am sorry you were hurt," he said to me. "The Granite Falls is a beautiful place to sit and be lost in your thoughts. Just have a care on the rocks and avoid the water."

"I'll take that advice to heart."

"Rebecca, girls, Miss Sheey."

Kay stiffly nodded her head. "Mr. Gillie." And he left.

Kay insisted on driving us home and spending the night. "With that head wound, you need to be woken every two hours," she said when I objected.

I was dead beat and my head was killing me. She set a soup before me, which I barely sipped, then made sandwiches for the girls. As they ate, Kay helped me get ready for bed. After I took a couple of pain killers, I slept like a log.

※ ※ ※

The next morning, I rolled over and cried out when the back of my head hit the mattress. The events of the evening before came to me. I could hear whispers coming from the other room. I slowly sat up and swung my legs over the side of the bed. Kay left a glass of water on the night stand with the painkillers, and I swallowed two. Gingerly, I crept to the rocker where my robe lay, slipped it on, and clung to the furniture as I made my way through the bedroom and down the hallway to the kitchen.

"Morning, Mom!" Tate piped up.

I winced.

"Remember girls, soft voices until you mum is feeling better."

"Sorry," Tate said in an exaggerated whisper.

"How are you feeling, Becca?" Kay set a tea cup and a plate with two pieces of toast at my place on the table. I gratefully collapsed into my chair.

"Better. And thank you again for taking us home and staying over." My head wasn't throbbing quite as much and, as long as I moved slowly, I wasn't nauseated.

"What happened?" Jessie asked.

I told the story, describing the grindylows encounter as a combination of getting caught in seaweed and some sort of wild life preventing me from getting up. I had a feeling Kay knew I wasn't telling the whole of it, but she said nothing. However, she gave me a look that told me that, at some point, she had some questions.

"Did you have any special plans for the day?" Kay asked.

"Not really." I warned the girls not to go to the pond by themselves using the slippery rocks as an excuse. Kay reinforced my words. Somehow, the kitten ended up coming home with us. Too exhausted and hurting, I didn't protest when the girls told me that the kitten was so stressed that she shouldn't be left alone either. The little thing weaved back and forth around the chair legs, purring, then found a stuffed catnip mouse that Kay apparently had packed and batted it around the room.

"She's been so good, Mom," Tate said.

"She nursed a bit at the cottage, but she seems ready to wean," Kay said.

"I guess we'll keep the kitten, if it's all right with you," I said with a laugh. Kay nodded. I gestured to the little ball of fur. "We kinda bonded on our trip in the woods."

෴

It took me longer than I thought it would to feel one hundred percent. Kay wanted to call the doctor over, but since I hadn't lost consciousness, I saw no need. Living out of the village proper and being very independent, Kay had her first aid qualifications kept up, so she reluctantly agreed. I was so out of it the first night that I didn't even remember her waking me every two hours, though she did. Kay made a point to come over a couple of times during the day, to bring food and check on me and the girls. She spent the first three nights with us. When Tate wanted to play with two girls she met at the party, Kay walked her to the village. Tate informed me afterward that since Jody was getting a kitten, we should invite the girl and her cat over so all four could play together. In the mornings, Jessie helped Gavin with the horses. In the afternoons, the girls usually took our still-unnamed kitten to play with her siblings or accompany Kay to the village. Conall came once, bearing flowers. Thankfully, Kay told him I was sleeping. As my wounds healed, I noticed Tate looked listless again.

By Wednesday, I felt much better. Tuesday had been the first day Kay deemed me well enough to need only one visit a day. Kiera, the cat hadn't been over since my accident, and I wondered if Kay had seen her.

CHAPTER 9

There was a tap, tappity, tap, that I now recognized as Kay's knock. She had gotten where she would rap then poke her head in. *I guess people on the island don't worry about catching the homeowner in a compromising position.*

"You're already up and dressed?" Kay exclaimed when she saw me clad and nursing my second cup of tea of the morning.

While the rest was good and needed, I had been recuperating for days. Fidgety, I was eager to do something other than read and sleep. "Yes, I think I'm ready for the world."

Kay checked my bandages. I found additional cuts and bruises from being dragged into deeper water. My head wound was well scabbed over and the worst of the ugly bruises had faded to a sickly yellow and green.

"I thought you might be ready to get up and out soon," Kay remarked.

When I asked about Kiera, Kay reassured us that the cat was probably visiting the other neighbors. "She likes to roam," she said when the girls questioned her.

I'd been trying to think of something to do or get for Kay and Greg. I smiled remembering how my name fell from his lips. *Cut it out, Becca!* They both pooh-poohed their actions, but I didn't know what I would have done without them.

"I'd like to do something special for Greg, to thank him for his help at the pond. Do you have any idea what sort of things he would appreciate and like?"

"Best you leave him be, Becca."

"Why?"

"He can be an abrasive man. He isn't unkind. It isn't that. He's just preoccupied and gruff. He likes his privacy to the point that he rarely comes to town."

"How is that possible? Surely he doesn't make his own clothes and what about bread" Does he grow wheat and grind it for flour?"

"I know he hunts and forages because once in a while he'll bring extra meat to sell to the butcher."

"I don't think I've met him?"

"Everyone goes to him, and you will too. The meat is much better than what you can get at Conall's."

"Just one of those things the villagers knows and the strangers have to find out?" I decided to go local when it came to meat as soon as possible. "I know Greg's a loner, but maybe he's just lonely."

"Oh, Becca. You see how handsome and strong he is. Don't you know the local girls have tried to flirt with him the rare times he's seen in town? He roundly rejects their attention to the point that they avoid him."

"Well, I still would like to do something for him."

Kay smiled. "Yes, I can see your mind is set on it. I noticed you'd worked on the garden."

"Yes, I have been."

"One thing he might appreciate is herbs and vegetables, since I don't think he has a garden of his own. With the money from the deer, he usually picks up potatoes or other cultivated produce he wouldn't be able to forage from the forest."

⋐⋑⋐⋑

One of my first post-accident outings had to be grocery shopping. The girls reluctantly agreed to accompany me. It would be a rushed trip because they had plans later that morning. We bussed into town. When we got off the bus, I noticed three dead squirrels lying under a nearby tree. I shielded the view from the girls and wondered if they were diseased or had rabies. They had perished almost on top of one another. As we passed, I saw the animals had puncture wounds like the rat at the farm. There was no blood.

In the grocery store, Jessie drifted away from us exploring the aisles. Tate, oddly, tagged along with me. There was scant selection as usual, but I had expected that. One long row contained shelves of favorite regional items that I looked forward to sampling.

"Can I help you?" I heard someone stutter out. I looked up, but the blotch-faced boy was speaking to Jess. I recognized him as the young man who gave us a ride to the cottage the day we arrived.

"No Lundy, I'm good. Just looking." She barely gave him a glance as she picked up a box from the shelf. I cringed. It was very obvious that he was trying to engage her. I tried to will Jess to be less cold.

"Well, now that—" He took the carton of biscuits from Jessie's hands. "These are a favorite of people round here—for tea. With tea—for the adults. The little ones usually have Ribena and…well, a biscuit. To tide you over, you know? A snack?"

"Uh—yeah." Jess gave him her back and joined me. The boy thrust the box back on the shelf so hard that two other boxes spilled off and hit the floor. Blood rushed to his face, making the blemishes there stand out even more.

"Jessie, to be nice," I whispered, watching him bend and retrieve the items.

She frowned at me. "What?"

"That boy was trying to talk to you."

"I know. I answered him. What's the big deal?"

"I think he was flirting," I said as I added two jars of Nutella to the basket.

"Seriously, Mom? If so, he sucks at it," Jessie exclaimed.

"Jessica! I raised you to be more sensitive than that." I looked for the boy, but thankfully he was several aisles over.

She lowered her voice to a fierce whisper. "Well, I don't like him like that, and I don't want to encourage him. He drove me nuts at the ceilidh."

"You should have said something." I knew Gavin wasn't the only boy she danced with that night, but I hadn't noticed any friction.

"I didn't want to make a big deal out of it. I hoped he would find someone else to annoy."

"Well, it isn't like he has a huge selection. This is a small village. A beautiful new girl is going to get a lot of attention."

Jessie rolled her eyes. "Mom, I'm not beautiful."

"You are to me—and him and Gavin."

"I tried to be nice—I did. And then when Gavin finished getting drinks for his brother and the band members during a break and wanted to dance with me, Lundy told him I was with him."

"Oh, no."

"Oh yes. Can we talk about this later?"

"Okay, sweetie. Sorry."

"Me too. I don't want to be mean, but he just doesn't take a hint."

☙❧

When we unpacked the groceries, we found a Cadbury bar in the bottom of the bag with a Post-it note. *I remembered it is your favorite.* It was signed with the initial *L*.

"See, Mom?' Jess waved the bar at me, vindicated. "L, as in Lundy."

"I see what you mean." I didn't want to see the boy hurt, but Jess didn't have a duty to spend time with him if she didn't want to—and she didn't. She liked Gavin, and he seemed to like her. While I didn't want to encourage any major relationship, I certainly wasn't going to ask her to spend time with someone she didn't like.

"And, one of the girls does like him, Mom. I got her to ask him to dance, and he flat-out turned her down. It was embarrassing for her, and I don't know if he even noticed. If he did, he certainly didn't care."

A lot like his uncle, I thought. *Conall doesn't understand that I'm not romantically interested in him either, and he's almost as persistent as Lundy. No wonder the one doesn't have a girlfriend and the other is unmarried.*

I'd asked Kay about it earlier and she had said that Conall's mother died shortly after he was born. Conall, the youngest of twelve, was raised by his elderly father. Twelve kids—the poor mother must have died of exhaustion. When his sister-in-law, Lundy's mom, died, he started helping his brother care for his nephew, so both Conall and Lundy had been raised without a woman in their lives. And they didn't seem to know how to act around one.

The rest of his siblings had moved off the island and were doing well, except for his brother who died when he was in his teens. They did come back for the occasional visit. Their only female relative on the island was the octogenarian aunt who was described as a bit fanciful. Oh, well.

I felt for them but I was with Jess on this. The more we tried to be nice, the more it encouraged them to have the wrong ideas. *I may need to be more careful about planning my shopping so I don't need to visit the grocer very often and try to make sure that Jess never goes there alone.*

༺✶༻

I heard a tap on the door. "Hi, Kay. Come on in and I'll make some tea," I called and bustled her inside.

Both girls were at the farm. The Samms' sheepdog had just given birth to five puppies. *Hopefully, one of those won't join our kitten.*

When they left, Jess wore her riding pants, which we had thankfully remembered to pack, and a tee shirt. Tate had on jeans and a sweater.

"You're going to be burning up in that, hon," I commented. I usually kept my mouth shut about the girls' dress fashions, as long as it wasn't too crazy. I learned quickly that, with children, you had to pick your battles, and I had better things to do than argue that the pink polka dot blouse clashed with the blue tartan skirt—a pairing deemed by my daughter as proper school wear.

Tate hugged herself and shivered. "Cold, Mom."

"Come here, honey."

Slumping, Tate plodded over as if her shoes were lined with lead.

I took her hand. "Brr! Your hand is so cold." I felt her forehead for a fever, but she didn't have one. "Are you feeling okay?"

"I feel fine. I'm just tired."

"Are you sure you're up to going with Jess?"

Jess, anxious to be along, called out at the door, "She'll be fine, Mom." She turned to Tate. "Come on, Tate, let's go."

"I'm fine, Mom." Tate pulled away from me and followed her sister out, carefully closing the door behind her.

Once tea was poured and we were munching on bickies, I asked Kay, "Did you noticed anything funny about Tate when you were with her during my recovery?"

Kay set her tea down and balanced the half a cookie on the saucer. "What do you mean?"

"She's been overly tired, in spite of getting a full night's sleep. Pale. Her hands were like ice this morning, and I swear she looked bluish around the mouth yesterday afternoon, but she said she had accidenty put a blue marker in her mouth when she was coloring." *Maybe that will break her of chewing on her pencils.* "She seems to have a decent appetite," I added. "I tried to get her to drink the herbal tea you gave me, but she doesn't care for it."

"You mentioned earlier that she seemed sickly." Kay steeped her fingers together and sat back in thought. "Well, she did like to take her meals outside or to her room. I figured she was out of sorts with you being sick and didn't insist she sit at the table. She always brought a clean plate back, though."

A thought came to me. "You don't think she's anorexic, do you?" Like all girls, I had had issues with my body image, but I worked so hard not to speak negatively about myself in front of the girls—or at least I thought I had.

"She doesn't seem the type, but if I were you, I would speak to her about it."

"I hope she isn't gorging and throwing up or not eating her food and hiding it."

"You may want to visit the doctor, regardless. Just to introduce yourself. Goddess willing, you won't need medical care while you're here, but if you do—I don't know about you, but I'd rather at least have a nodding acquaintance with my physician, rather than suddenly finding myself naked with a stranger." Kay winked and waggled her eyebrows, and I had to chuckle.

"There is something else I wanted to talk to you about."

Kay tilted her head, silently encouraging me to continue.

"I would like to have you and Greg over Friday night as a thank you. A thank you to Greg for rescuing me and taking me back to your house." *Not because he's gorgeous and the first man I've been remotely attracted to since my husband died.* "And to you, for all the help you lavished on us the past few days."

"Well, I would love to come over. I can't speak for Mr. Gillie, though."

"Do you know where he lives? I imagine it has to be near the two of us, somewhere in the forest, but I can't, for the life of me, find a path or lane off the main road that would be close enough."

"I don't think he has a path."

"How do people find him to visit? How are things delivered? What happens if he needs, say, a plumber?"

"I am thinking his accommodations are very rustic. He's a simple man and not needing heaps of things from places like Amazon."

"Somebody has to know where he lives. This island isn't that big. I can probably find him online. Search engine ought to show something."

"Good luck. The internet service is sporadic and often out. We tend to hold to the old ways, leaving the web to the mainlanders. Besides, I doubt Greg Gillie would show up. He is, what you Americans say, 'living off the grid.' You could try the post office or the library."

"I can't believe everyone knows him, but no one knows where he lives."

"Well, it isn't as though anyone is close to him."

"I feel sorry for him."

"He has had more contact with you than anyone, at least since I've lived here."

"How old is he?"

Kay patted my hand. "Why don't you just let it go?"

"Perhaps I should," I said. *Fat chance.*

CHAPTER 10

Kay was due at the tea shop to help with inventory. Apparently, they needed to be well stocked because many of the goods came via ferry, so it wasn't as if you could just pop over to Sam's and find items needed in bulk.

"I think I'll walk into town with you," I told Kay then called Jess and told her where I would be.

The girls were invited over for lunch at the Samms, so Jess didn't think they would be back until one thirty at the earliest, leaving me with plenty of time to investigate. My husband used to tease me that I just couldn't stand a mystery. He said it must be part and parcel of being a university professor.

I met David when I was at a faculty dinner. He didn't work for the university but was at the same restaurant. We bumped into each other. Me, on my way out of the bathroom—I had retired there to avoid a particularly fierce debate. He had just hung up the telephone. His date had cancelled. He impulsively asked me if I would like a drink. Since my meeting had, for all practical purposes, ended, I agreed. The rest, as they say, is history. Originally, I had intended to go back to work. In fact, David insisted that I keep my maiden name since I already had numerous articles published in professional journals and magazines. Once I had Jessica, though, I couldn't bear the thought of leaving her with someone else all day. So, I stopped teaching and became a stay-at-home mother. I'd never know why they called it stay at home. I spent most of the time running to and fro, shopping, and taking the girls to dance and horseback riding lessons, carpooling to games, and so on. When the girls got old enough to stay at home alone, I found myself with too much time on my hands, so I procured a teaching certificate and began substitute teaching. I thought it would help me choose what grades I would prefer to teach. I'd finished my first year at Roosevelt Elementary when David had his fatal car accident.

ಲಾಲಾ

Once Kay and I parted ways, I searched for the red post office sign and, finally, found one—so faded it was barely legible—at the grocery. I entered, uneasy that I might be trying to question a man with a crush on me about finding a man he already disliked. Conall was nowhere to be seen, but his nephew was carefully stacking baked beans in a pyramid at the end of an aisle.

"Very nicely done," I commented, startling the boy. He wheeled around, knocking the four rows off the top. Cans rolled across the wood floor. Unable to hide it quickly enough, a look of anger and disgust flashed across his face. He turned his back to me to chase cans and when he turned back, his expression was forced pleasantry.

I had rounded up the cans that rolled my way and tried to hand them to him, then realized he had his hands too full to take them. "I'm so sorry."

"Just leave 'em on the floor. I'll fix it." He began to rebuild his monument to beans. I stood there perplexed. In the States, I would be asked if I needed help. Surly clerks were not the norm—and if that was the said clerk's norm, they wouldn't be a clerk much longer.

I cleared my throat. "I was wondering where the post office is."

"You're looking at it."

"I mean...well, who do I speak to about a postal issue?"

"My uncle, I suppose, but really people just come here to pick up post, drop it off, and buy stamps and such. Most of the real post office business is done on the mainland."

"I'd like to talk to him just the same."

The nephew heaved a great, put-upon sigh and stood.

"He's in the back. I'll go fetch 'im." The nephew sauntered toward the counter.

Thanks, I said to myself and mentally rolled my eyes.

As I waited, I began to restack and reclaim the cans that had gone higgledy-piggledy all over. As I gathered ones that rolled increasingly farther from the display, I reached the counter. The last one was behind it. The counter was old style. The nephew left the part of the countertop, which swung up to admit the clerk, open. I admired the old timey cash register that a museum would probably love to have, misjudging the distance and kicking the can. The can rolled through an open door at the back corner, continuing to bounce down a flight of stairs. It came to a stop, but the door at the end wasn't shut completely and the can bumped it ajar. I walked down the stairs and couldn't resist peeking inside. I looked behind me, but there was neither sight nor sound of either of the McNeils, so I pushed the door open.

A few more stairs continued down, and overhead, beams were exposed in the unfinished basement. I pressed the light switch near the entrance, illuminating the area, and ventured down to the landing. When I turned, I saw a barred area in the back corner. *Jeez, is this the local jail too?* Pieces of silverware were lined up in the slots between the bars and what appeared to be silver necklaces were wrapped around the door frame and lock. *Okay—this is weird.* Worried that I shouldn't be down here, I quickly retraced my steps, turned off the light, and closed the door. When I reached to pick up the errant can, I heard Conall call my name. I ran up the rest of the stairs in time to see him step out from behind the nearest shelves. I stood and smiled awkwardly.

"What are you doing behind the counter?" he asked as he rounded the corner, took my elbow, and pulled me out to the opposite side. I didn't resist but, honestly—it wasn't like my hand was in the till.

"I damaged your bean pyramid and one of the cans rolled back here." I brandished the offending one.

"Oh, well, if anything like that ever happens again, leave it, and I'll deal with it. No one is allowed past the counter, except me and those who help out on the rare occasion—which are always family members."

"I apologize. I was just trying to help." Anxious to change the topic, I asked, "How would I go about finding someone's address? The net seems to be up one moment and down the next. I thought you, being the postmaster so to speak, could tell me and might even know the address."

"Could be. Whose address are you looking for?"

I really didn't want to tell him about asking Greg over. He had been very helpful too, even though he didn't save my life and he might feel hurt if I didn't invite him. I cast my mind about trying to think of a good reason. *Aha!* "I accidently ended up with Greg Gillie's kerchief and wanted to drop it by."

"Him?" Conall said flatly. "He lives out in the forest. He never gets mail."

"Okay, he *has* to get some mail...like stuff from the government or...well, he doesn't own the forest, does he? How is it that he's even allowed to live there?"

"I don't know all of the details, but he's allowed. Tender-hearted islanders, no doubt, turning a blind eye to the unfortunate homeless man camping in the woods. We don't fash ourselves about such as that. Now, is there anything else I can do for you?"

I knew a brush off when I heard it. "No. Thanks for your help. In what direction is the newspaper?"

"The courthouse and the newspaper are two of the first buildings that were built. Most of the tourists get their pictures taken in front of them."

"Oh, you mean the impressive buildings at the very end of the block?" I had not managed to go all the way down to the edge of the village, but I couldn't help but admire their grandeur.

"Aye. Now, if you'll excuse me, I still have some work to do."

I wonder why he's so upset anytime Greg is mentioned. Did they have some sort of major falling out?

The romantic in me speculated briefly about both loving the same girl until I reminded myself that Greg was a grieving widower who, from what Kay said, never ever recovered from the loss of his wife and child. Speaking of which—I wonder exactly how they died. Perhaps I could find something in the newspaper archive. I really hoped if they didn't have it all on a computer, which I seriously doubted, they would at least have it on microfilm or microfiche. "Sorry to have bothered you, Mr. McNeil. Have a nice day."

He muttered, "And you," as he turned and went through another door that I imagined led to the office. The sullen nephew came out and, without a word to me, picked up a broom and swept as if I brought in all kinds of dirt.

Okay—fine.

As I walked down the cobbled streets, I admired the other buildings. Most appeared to be constructed of granite, but a warmer color of gray than what was used in Aberdeen. Roses twined up trellises along the walls, splashing yellows, pinks, and reds. Sun shone down on the leaves of the honeysuckle-garlanded oaks dappling the bright sidewalks with shade. Despite the penchant for the locals to use brightly colored paints on the trim and doors, the buildings really were beautiful, without being gaudy, and well kept. Not a bit of modernization had occurred, as far as I could see, and I felt as if I had been plucked up and put back to an earlier time. I walked up the stairs to the front of the building Conall had spoken of. Double doors were in the middle and then two other doors were on each side. I opened the double doors. The sign on the front indicated that this was also the library. Here, I saw my first sign of changes made to an older building. What must have once been a large room was now divided into smaller open rooms with shelves of books. A young lady sat at a gray granite counter reading, but looked up at the sound of the door opening. A bright smile crested her face as a look of recognition set in.

"Hello! You're the new boarder at Mrs. Grant's cottage. I don't know if you remember me, but we met at the party." The girl looked to be about eighteen. She came around the counter to my side and warmly shook my hand. Her wavy black hair was braided with the tail hanging down over one shoulder. She wore a collared, polo-like shirt and a short jeans skirt.

"I'm sorry, I don't remember you. I have an awful memory for names and faces and..."

"And, though we are a small village, meeting everyone all at once is enough to discomfort anyone. My name is Fiona Campbell. I'm distantly related to Kay."

"Oh, I didn't know that. She told me she had only lived here for five years."

"'Tis true, that. Her side of the family moved to the mainland, and we rarely saw them. Then Kay came over for a visit...let's see...I think I was eleven, so about eight years ago. She must have enjoyed herself because the summer next, she started looking for a house to stay in and, as luck would have it, her own family's cottage was standing empty. Wonderful coincidence, don't you think?"

"Yes, it is."

Once Fiona told me, I could see the resemblance. Their eyes were shaped the same, tilted, and a unique shade of hazel. Both were slender without being skinny and small boned without looking like a young boy.

"What can I do for you? Or are you just over to look around? Many tourists come in to take photos and have a gander. I can take you round for a tour, if you want. We aren't busy. It's too early for the first of the visitors."

"Thank you, maybe later. There are a couple of things I wanted to ask about." She looked at me expectantly. I cleared my throat. "I'm trying to find out where someone lives. The man was at the party too, briefly." I remembered how unpleasant Conall was and how quickly Greg left.

"Do you know his name?"

"Yes, yes, I do. His name is Greg Gillie."

"Oooh, he's a right looker for an older man."

Older man? Guess that makes me an older woman. I smothered a sigh.

"My mum calls him Gorgeous Gillie." She hoisted herself up on the counter top and patted it. I hopped up too, but nowhere near as gracefully. "I don't rightly know his address," she continued. "He lives in the forest. I think maybe he's one of those doomsday people that's preparing for the end of the world. He wears old-timey clothes and uses snares to catch conies. He's rarely in town."

I'd had such high hopes. *Darn!*

Noticing my crestfallen look, she said, "Let me go back to the newspaper archive. I might be able to find some mention of him. I think he's something of a local hero. The older folk go on about him saving some children. I tend to shut it out. It happened ages ago."

"Fiona Campbell, 'you're my only hope,'" I said.

Thankfully, she recognized the quote and grinned.

"Do you suppose I could go down with you and do some research?" I asked.

Fiona lowered her eyes and shook her head. "You would need to sign some papers and show ID. I'm officially only supposed to check books in and out, but I've helped my mum with the paper a bit. I know she wouldn't mind me looking around, as long as I was very careful to put everything back where it belonged. She might not be as happy having a stranger there unsupervised, though."

"That's too bad. I really wanted to find out more about the village while I was here," I improvised. "I was a literature major in school and thought I could look at the old newspapers. Maybe find out about how the village was founded and by whom, if there were any legends associated with this place. That sort of thing."

"Well, Mum's on the mainland right now, but if you

stop by tomorrow, she should be here. If you give me a few minutes, I'll hop down for a quick look and see if I can find out anything about his address. I can't stay away from the counter too long in case others come in, but maybe I'll get lucky."

She lifted her legs, spun around facing the back, and leapt off the counter top. I levered myself off and wandered over to the stacks.

The books were well kept. The front few rows contained the newer fiction and a carousel display rack that held the latest paperbacks stood in one corner. Those books showed quite a bit of wear. The romance section was twice as large as any of the other paperback sections. I trusted that Fiona would find me when she came back and if not, I would see her on my way out. I ventured to the very back of the stacks where I found the nonfiction. Some of the books were so old that I never would expect to see them outside a museum or rare books shop. A dark blue one on the bottom shelf caught my eye.

I sat Indian style on the floor and plucked it out. The gold embossed title on the spine was too worn to read. I opened the book to the title page. *Local Herbs and Their Uses* by Helga Grant. I wondered if she was related to the owner of our cottage. "Perhaps I'll give her a ring and ask her about it," I mused, flipping through the pages, and started to read.

ల/ఎ/ల

My back ached and I realized I had been sitting there a long time. I glanced at my phone *Eeep!* It was almost two o'clock. I needed to get back to the cottage. I started to put the book back but changed my mind and carried it to the front.

"Found something?" Fiona asked as she put down the

university catalogue she had been perusing.

"Yes, I did. How did you fare with the address?"

"Sorry to say, I struck out. When my mum gets back, I'll ask her about it. If you come tomorrow, perhaps she'll at least have a good idea where to start looking if she doesn't find it right away. She knows this place like the back of her hand." She reached out for the book. "Ooh, this is an old one." She opened a drawer and pulled out a paper and pen. "You'll need to fill this out to get a library card, but it won't take long." Shaking her finger at me and scowling, she said, "Don't be late or we'll hunt you down and demand the book returned plus late fees."

She grinned to let me know she was jesting, but I remembered some pretty strict librarians back in my home town. They looked like they sucked lemons and they could sniff out a fine on you as soon as you opened the library doors. I took the clipboard with the form to a table. It asked for the usual stuff—name, address, et cetera. I put the cottage address, since that's where they would find me, then in smaller letters, I wrote in my Aberdeen address.

It was unlikely that I would forget to return a book and end up taking it home, but there was a possibility that one of the girls might. Plus, maybe they needed that info too and better to just fill in something a little extra than be sent back to add something I thought was unnecessary. I returned the form and Fiona gave me a temporary library card until a proper one was made. I glanced to check the information and immediately gave it back to her with the book.

She flipped to the back. "Wow, this hasn't been checked out in ages. I don't ever even remember seeing it, and I spend a lot of time here. I thought I could at least recognize all the books even if I hadn't already even read them. Where did you find this?"

"In the very last row on the bottom shelf. It was pushed in a bit, so maybe you didn't see it."

"No, Mum is very picky about the library looking nice. She has me go down and make sure the books are lined up evenly as possible and the title and author is clearly visible. This book—I can't even read the spine. Mum would have made a jacket for it, if she saw it. Maybe a new batch of books arrived. We don't have much money to buy them, so we don't get a lot of new books. Sometimes one of the villagers will clean out the house and decide they would rather the books clutter up our shelves instead of theirs. I'll have to ask her."

I smiled and accepted the book. "Your mom is going to get a lot of questions when she returns."

"She'll think it's cool. Things can be so sleepy and dull here. She loves a good mystery novel too. If you're interested, we have more than you would expect a library of this size to have. Mum says it's a librarian perk."

I tucked the book under my arm. "I've gotta run. My daughters are waiting for me. The girls are old enough to be home alone, but my youngest is a bit under the weather. Thanks again. I'm sure I will be back."

"I'm sure you will too if only to return that book and avoid the wrath of the librarian. Hey, Wrath of the Librarian would be a cool name for a band." I thought she was kidding, but she found a scratch piece of paper and made note of it.

CHAPTER 11

Since the tea shop was on my way, I thought I would stop by and see if Kay was there. If so, maybe she'd be ready to go home and could give me a ride back.

Business seemed good but not crazy busy as it was on the weekend. Marnie waved me in as she replenished a platter and placed it back on the shelf behind the glass display. When I reached the counter, I inhaled the yummy aroma of fresh-baked scones. Just then, Kay popped out from the kitchen carrying another cookie sheet.

"Hi, Marnie—Kay," I said.

"Would you like a scone?" Marnie gestured with the spatula. "This one broke so we won't be selling it."

"I'd love one, but I need to rush home. I'm late and the girls are no doubt wondering where I am. I tried to call, but couldn't get through."

"That happens. For some reason, any complicated, new invention tends to be finicky about working regular like," Marnie commented as she emptied the cookie sheet onto another plate. "You know, Kay, I think I have things under control if you want to leave early."

"Oh, thanks, Marnie. I have a feeling that Becca's angling for a lift."

I chuckled. "That obvious, huh?"

"It's okay. I was going to ask Marnie if I could pop out and take you, but this works even better. You're lucky I brought my car in today. A package I've been waiting for came in yesterday. I didn't want to pack it home on the bus, so I waited and brought the car in today to pick it up."

"So, you need to go to the post office, before we leave?" I really didn't want to see Conall again, not after knocking over the display and agitating his good humor.

"No, I picked it up when I arrived. It's sitting in the car, so I'm ready whenever you are. Just let me hang up my apron and get my purse."

"Well, this changes things." I quickly pointed out some goodies to buy and Marnie had just handed me my change when Kay came back.

"Couldn't resist, huh?" she said with a grin.

"It's a wonder you're so slender. If I worked here, within a month, my pants would be too tight."

"Funny, you get used to it always being around," Marnie said. "Since it's readily available, you tend to crave other things that you can't get here."

After we said goodbye, I followed Kay to her car.

The girls were indeed already home, and Jessie ran out to meet me.

"Where have you been?" she asked.

"I'm sorry, hon, I was at the library and got distracted."

Jess tugged on my hand. She didn't even greet Kay which was so not like her.

"Is everything all right, Jess?"

"Hello, Jess," Kay said. "Has something happened?"

"Hello, Miss Sheey. I don't mean to be rude, but I need to speak to my mom."

"Not at all. I need to be on my way anyway."

I reached out to touch Kay's arm. "Are you sure? I'd planned to put the kettle—" I began.

Kay shook her head and backed toward her car. "Another time, certainly. I'm off tomorrow, so I might pop by, if that's okay with you?"

"Anytime, Kay. I think the only thing I have planned is another trip to the library."

"Cheerio. Be seeing you," Kay said.

Instead of going in the cottage, Jess sat on the bench beside the door. There didn't seem to be an emergency. If it was, she would have told me right away, but *something* was wrong.

"Mom, Tate is acting weird."

I joined Jess on the bench. "Weird?"

She scooted closer. "Yes, I think something's wrong with her."

"Why do you think that?"

Jessie lowered her voice and leaned toward me. "She seems bored with everything. She loves horses and riding as much as I do and cried when we moved. After her lessons ended, while she was waiting, she'd be at the fence struggling not to pet the ponies when students rode by. Today, she watched me jump a couple of times and then wandered off. Gavin told me it was fine as long as she didn't do anything silly like play with the farm equipment. I told him she wouldn't, so we rode more."

"Maybe she's just outgrown her fascination with horses. Did anything else happen?"

"Later, Mrs. Samms called us in for lunch. When she saw Tate wasn't with us, she was surprised. She said that Tate had been in earlier and Mrs. Samms had loaded her up with a plateful of snacks for all of us. It took us ages to find her. I was scared and ready to call you. Finally, we found her just outside the forest sitting on the wall. I could have sworn someone was with her, but Mrs. Samms and Gavin didn't see anyone."

"Are you sure you didn't imagine it, Jess?" I asked.

"Tate's the one who likes to pretend, not me," she said, her tone weighed with exasperation. The usual sigh and eye-rolling that *didn't* accompany the remark unnerved me more than anything she had said. She paused a moment, and continued. "The plate of cookies Mrs. Samms gave Tate was supposed to be enough to share with me and Gavin. It was empty! Then she was so tired walking back to the house, that Mrs. Samms thought she had gotten into the pesticides, but Tate said she hadn't. We sat down for lunch and, Mom, she ate *again*. You don't let her have a lot of snacks in the afternoon because she's always too full to eat her dinner later."

"Where is she now?"

"She's inside napping—which is something else she never does."

Tate lay so still on the bed. *Prone, like a corpse.* The second the thought entered my head, I banished it. I woke her for dinner. She ate and looked better for the rest, but Jess was right. This wasn't at all like my Tater Tot. Tomorrow, we would find the doctor and see what he said.

൞

The next morning, we caught the bus into town and easily found the clinic, possibly the most recent addition to the village. The cordial receptionist said the doctor was out checking on Conall's aunt, but should be back within an hour. I said I would be back then. The girls and I walked to the library where they were issued their own cards and soon were seated at a table, Tate with a stack of books and Jess with a teen magazine.

Fiona introduced me to her mother, a woman with stylishly coiffed, short hair and a gorgeous taupe pant suit of such a quality that it must be designer. She was unlike any other librarian I had ever seen. Her makeup was expertly applied and her cupid bow lips, a flattering scarlet. Once I settled the girls, I came back to the front desk.

"I told Mum what you were interested in," Fiona said.

Mrs. Campbell, or Courtney, as she insisted I call her, said she would be fine with me digging through some old records and would take me to the basement and get me started whenever I was ready. I explained that Tate wasn't well and I'd have to put my search on hold until I could take her to the doctor and get to the bottom of whatever ailed her. Though the librarian could have modeled or been on one of those British soap operas, she didn't put on airs. Courtney said this morning she had tried the usual venues for finding someone, but found no record of a Greg Gillie.

"Perhaps he has changed his name. My mother didn't name me Courtney, but I certainly wasn't going through life as Agatha." She shuddered and I have to say, I would have changed my name too if my mom saddled me with that.

We left and beat the doctor back, but, as I predicted, there were new patient sheets to fill out. After a short wait, the receptionist, who was also the nurse, escorted us to a small room in the back and took Tate's vitals. The doctor, a surprisingly gregarious man, came in and introduced himself. Dr. Murphy's hair was a shaggy brown and he had that pudge around the middle that men often get after ten years of marriage. I explained my concerns and, after he examined Tate, he asked me some questions.

"Well Mrs. Shaw, your daughter's underweight, but

not excessively so. Other than that, everything else seems to be normal. Is she eating?"

"She eats well. In fact, she's eating more than she usually does."

"I want to take some blood and get a urine sample to send off to the mainland. Has she had a recent growth spurt in height? Allergic reactions? Has something new or different entered her life?"

I shook my head no to each question. The doctor stepped out and soon the nurse rejoined us. Tate didn't complain about the needle, which was atypical. She sat and shivered on the table. When we came out, Jess wanted to know what happened. I told her what the doc said, and we decided to eat an early lunch then go back to the library. Fiona ran a teen program at one-thirty. I hoped to do some research while the girls attended the program.

҂҂҂

Courtney was happy to take me downstairs to the morgue, the place where back issues of the newspaper are kept. As she led me down there, she told me something about the newspaper. "The first newspaper here was printed—and I do mean printed, because originally there wasn't a press—in the late eighteenth century. We're lucky enough to have many copies of the original issues. At first, it was one page of information about town occurrences, births, deaths, and such. Information from the mainland was incorporated as well. My ancestor, Phineas Campbell and his family handwrote the issues, one per family. It was unusual that this small an island had a newspaper. From what I can tell, reading Phineas's journals, he tried to get one started, but no one wanted to take it on, so in the end, he did it himself. Just prior to the move to the island, he had retired from the world of publishing and had a large family who was willing to humor him and help with what was basically an expensive hobby for him. He seemed to be pretty fair-handed with the news, though he did put considerable items about his family and articles about parties they held. Eventually, a press was purchased and the paper was named *The Shrouded Isle Chronicle*, usually shortened to *The Chronicle*.

"Phineas was a bit of a character and some of his editorials are pretty funny. The newspaper has stayed in the family all these years. I don't know how much longer that will be. Fiona isn't interested in running it, and she's my only child. I have two brothers, but they rarely come to the island. I'm hoping maybe one of their children will be interested. I've been planning on inviting them all over for one of the hols but, so far, all my plans have fallen through. Since the paper, even now, isn't very big, we've been able to transfer all of it on microfiche, and I have some of it loaded up on the computer, not that many islanders read it from there. You've probably discovered that tech doesn't always work that well here."

I nodded. Jessie had given up on playing games on her phone. It'd been kinda nice not having her glued to it.

"The films are stored by date in here." She slid open one of the seven shallow drawers of a gray cabinet and plucked out one film. "The power switch for the microfiche reader is on the right side. If you want to copy anything, the power switch for the printer is on the left side of it." Courtney demonstrated how to use it. "Once you get the magnification and clarity adjusted, it's pretty simplistic. It's much like putting a slide under a microscope. Well, I'll leave you to it."

I started by looking for recent mentions using the name Greg Gillie. That proved completely futile. Then I tried local hero. I had more luck with that. Over the last thirty years, twelve children had been lost in the woods and several of the accounts, including the oldest, spoke of a dark-haired man who led them out. The children weren't the only ones who saw him. Some of the adults did too. One account with a quote read, *I met the man at the edge of the forest. My Jamie's wee face was tear-stained, but he seemed fine, other than being as dirty as a lad can get. The dark-haired man didn't say a word. He just set Jamie on his feet and pushed him toward me then whirled around and vanished. I think he was a guardian angel.*

I went through some more issues and then decided to leave off until another day. I rubbed my tired eyes. Mrs. Campbell rejoined me as I was putting things up.

"Any luck?"

"Of a kind. I couldn't find the name, but I did find a stranger in the forest who helped lost children mentioned."

"Oh that, I think the children fabricated it. It is a bit of a legend here. The gist of it is that a good man, who lost his child, haunts the woods. I don't put much stock in such things."

"Hmmm—at some point I'd like to read some of the earliest papers. I can't believe you've managed to save them all."

"Oh—not all. Some were lost, but we do have many. Fiona's finishing up with the discussion."

"Thank you."

"You're welcome to look again another day. Though it rarely happens, I do like to be here when someone is in the crypt. The papers aren't valuable—at least not to anyone but me. I want to keep them safe."

"I understand that." I had made a note of the more recent sightings and decided I would try to find a family member who was around then, maybe even one of the missing children, and talk to them about it. *In the meantime, I think a visit to the forest is in order.*

On the way out, I picked up a leaflet listing various library activities. Later in the month, a summer movie night was scheduled. As we walked back home, the girls spoke of the teen event. They seemed to have enjoyed it, though Tate was quiet. I had hoped Tate had planned to get together with some of the girls from the library, but she hadn't. Jess said that when she mentioned that she had been at Samms Farm helping Gavin, she got some envious glances.

"Don't let it go to your head, young lady," I said.

"I won't. Gavin's sister is coming for a visit this weekend. He asked if Tate and I would like to meet her—maybe even hang out. She's his only sister, and he said she always complains about not having anyone to do girly stuff with. Is it okay if we go?"

"Get the details and I want to talk to his mother first, but it shouldn't be a problem."

"Cool."

Tate pleaded being tired and left to curl up in a chair in the bedroom to read. Though I wanted to check her temperature, I resisted, reminding myself that the doctor said she was fine.

After my oldest fired off a text, I asked, "Jess, how was Tate at the meeting?"

"Quiet. Some of the girls she met at the party were there, and they tried to talk to her, but she didn't say much. She didn't answer any of the questions about the book, and it was one she liked. It's just weird, Mom. Tate loves to be the center of attention."

"I know, Jess. We should get back the blood work and results sometime next week. Hopefully that will tell us something."

※※※

Kay called and said something came up so she wouldn't be by today, so I spent the afternoon doing some light housekeeping. I didn't want things to get out of control. The girls helped by dusting the bedrooms and sweeping the floors. I bundled up the sheets and did what laundry we had then worked on the bathrooms and the kitchen. *There's something so satisfying to sit back at the end of the day in a tidy, clean house*, I thought, as I sipped my cup of tea.

The girls decided to investigate the shed to see what other games and such were there. They found a couple of bikes, but the tires were flat and probably needed replacing. I vowed to ask around in the village for where I could get them repaired so the girls and I could ride. The tires were the wide, fat type and the bikes old but sturdy, as they would need to be, considering the condition of the roads.

Kiera came over for a couple of hours which was unusual. We generally saw her in the mornings, but it had been a while, and the kids were so happy that she was okay that they lavished her with attention. She allowed the kitten to pounce on her tail and bat her ears. I still couldn't get over how large she was. When she was ready to go, she went to the door and meowed loudly.

I asked the girls what they wanted for dinner, and we decided on something simple—soup and grilled cheese sandwiches. I paid special attention to Tate. She ate all her food, but I had to jostle her twice when she started to doze off. I found some board games, and we played.

"How about we have a game night party and invite a few of the girls you've met over?" I asked.

Tate and Jess were enthusiastic about the idea, and it would give them an opportunity to talk to the villagers on the girls' own turf. My phone rang, and I stepped outside to talk since the girls were singing. Seeing that Tate had perked up a bit, I didn't want to hush them. I checked caller ID. It was the lady who owned the cottage.

"Hello, Mrs. Grant."

"Hello, dear, I wanted to call and see how you were getting along."

"The cottage is wonderful. We met Kay early on and she's been taking good care of us. There was also a ceilidh, so we met many of the villagers." A thought occurred to me. "Mrs. Grant, do you know someone named Greg Gillie? He lives in the forest behind your cottage."

"Gillie, now that name rings a bell."

"So, you know him?"

"I don't know him personally, dear, but the man who built the cottage was a Gillie. Unfortunately, his family perished without an heir. The closest relative was the wife's sister. This sister is one of my ancestors and through whom the house continued to be passed down. If you look at the fireplace, the name is carved on the mantel."

I remembered seeing the swirls and thought it was just a decoration. "Oh, so he must be some relative of yours."

"Perhaps a distant one by marriage. I inherited the cottage because my da was an only son, and he had all girls. I'm the last still alive."

"Would you mind if I looked at your family tree? What of it you have?"

"Of course not, I'll send it to you. Our tree is very detailed. I wouldn't be surprised if it doesn't at least mention the names of the parents of the man who built the cottage. How did you meet this Mr. Gillie?"

"I've seen him a couple of times now. A few times in the forest, and he came to Conall's aunt's party. I didn't get to talk to him long then. For some reason, although everyone else in the village was invited, he wasn't."

"Who was the party for?"

"It was for Conall McNeil's aunt."

"Conall—goodness. Has he married yet? If I remember, he was quite attractive, but it's been a couple of years since I have seen him."

"No. He's single."

"Well, he and his family were always an odd sort. Conall's family has been plagued with accidents."

"What kind of accidents?"

"Well, Conall's grandda was found just inside the forest with his neck broken. It was ruled an accidental death, but there were a lot of questions, like why he was in the woods in the first place. Then Conall's brother was found in the woods, too, shot by his own gun. That one was ruled a suicide, but Conall was furious and swore it wasn't. Many violent deaths, mainly of the males in the family. Perhaps if this man was in the woods, Conall thinks he was involved in his brother's death."

"Something to think on for sure, but you don't know Greg—Greg Gillie?"

"I'm an old woman. Perhaps I do and have forgotten. You have naught to worry about a Gillie. We Scots may be of stern stock, but we are honorable."

"Oh, I wasn't inferring otherwise—"

"Aye, I know, lassie." She chuckled. "You're a worrier, aren't you?"

"Being a single mom, I have to be," I said in a stilted voice.

"Enjoy the cottage, and I'll email you my family tree. If you can find out how your gentleman friend is related, I would appreciate it."

I tried to explain that he wasn't exactly a friend but she followed her statement with a goodbye and hung up before I had a chance.

CHAPTER 12

The next morning, the girls began planning the much-anticipated party. I limited the guest number to four, each girl could invite two friends and I hoped, for their sake, that the invitees would show up but comforted myself that they probably would out of boredom and sheer curiosity. The television was equipped with a DVD player and we had brought many of our favorite UK DVDs, since US DVDs wouldn't work with a UK DVD player.

I let the girls decide what they would play and, from there, we would decide what to serve. I loved themed parties and had thrown many for the girls and friends in the past. Luckily, I had a husband who enjoyed such things too. *I did have one.*

I blinked to keep the tears at bay and wished for a more stalwart personality. Surprisingly enough, the girls decided on an older movie. They wanted to show *Princess Bride*. I tried to convince them of something more recent that perhaps not all the kids had seen, but they were adamant. We set about making head bands with the name of characters upon them so the kids could play a game guessing as to which character they had on their band based on the answers to questions they asked one another—a game we often included at parties.

"Can we go to town, Mom?" Jess asked.

"I suppose. Why?"

"We want to look around and see if anything in the village would work as party favors or games."

"Okay, but you only have two hours. Are you sure you're both okay with taking the bus down on your own?"

They both scoffed at me. Tate sternly regarded me. "Mom—I'm ten years old, and Jess is older. We've been riding buses back and forth to school for *ages*. I think we can manage this teeny bus."

I hid a smile as Tate sternly regarded me.

"Okay." I gave them money and walked down the path with them to the bus stop. I thought to go to the library, but was sick of looking at microfiche and wanted a break. Luxuriating in the clawed tub sounded perfect. I'd found some bath salts in the cupboard and looked forward to a soak with a book in one hand and a glass of wine in the other. But first, I'd do some exploring in the woods.

I doubted that I'd be long, but I wrote a note for Jessie and Tate and called Kay. She didn't answer so I left a message, asking her to check on the girls if I was late and invited her to lunch. In preparation for the hike, I filled a thermos and tossed it and a handful of granola bars in a small backpack. The island was unlikely to shelter any vicious animals in the woods, and it was daytime, but I brought my walking stick and packed the ivory-handled straight blade. If Mrs. Grant had a stockpile of arms, I hadn't run across it yet and, while I did want some sort of weapon, I wasn't keen to lose her cutlery. I also cut red ribbons to tie on tree limbs to make my way back. My sense of direction was good enough that I should be able to make it to Kay's through the forest instead of via the road and wanted to test my assumption. Perhaps, since I'd encountered Greg near both cottages, if I traveled from my cottage through the woods to Kay's, I might catch sight of his home. No doubt, I could also reach the farm, but I didn't want to try to go that far, especially since I wasn't sure about the conditions.

Once ready, I set off. After I passed the earliest growth nearest to the cottage, the going was fairly easy. The tall, old trees shaded the ground and there wasn't much undergrowth to worry about. A few rocks jutted from the ground like broken teeth, but not too many and my hiking boots were more than adequate to keep me from slipping. By my reckoning, depending on how deep into the forest I went, I should intercept the pond and waterfall. I planned to stay well away from it when and if I did. I traveled twenty minutes straight into the woods and then turned toward Kay's. The tied ribbons would guide me home if necessary. I made sure I could still see the ribbon I just tied before tying a new one. After another forty minutes of walking, I still saw nothing of another cottage, nor did I see the pond and waterfall. Perhaps I'd walked far enough to circle around it? At any rate, I needed to return to the cottage. The girls would be home by noon, so I had just enough time to get back.

I turned and walked to the nearest red ribbon. When I reached it, I looked for the next which I should have easily seen, but couldn't. *Okay, this isn't good.* I decided to leave the ribbon and travel out to search for the next one, but always keep the last one I found in view so I could return to it. I walked toward what I was sure was the way to our cottage, every few minutes turning to check the ribbon and then, the last time I turned, it was gone. I froze. *This can't be happening.* I carefully moved from side to side. No ribbon. "Well, crud. Where the heck did that ribbon go?" I wondered out loud. I heard a gruff guffaw. "Who's there?" I asked.

I turned toward the sound. I stared but could see nothing. As I turned back, I saw a ribbon tied to a branch, but not in the direction I thought I should be going. *I must be totally turned around.* I sighed, glad to find the trail, but a bit discomforted that I got lost in the first place. Anytime we went anywhere, I was always in charge of the map. And mostly, I didn't need one. When I reached the ribbon, I could see the next, so I untied that one and stuck it in my knapsack and took off for the next. By the twelfth ribbon, I began to worry. I most definitely did not tie this many ribbons. Someone was leading me somewhere.

"Whoever you are—this isn't funny. Show yourself!" I called out.

There was no response but another laugh. I drew out the straight blade and opened it, feeling like a murderous barber.

The next ribbon led me to the pond and waterfall that I'd been studiously trying to avoid. "Well, darn."

I stayed at the edge of the clearing, not wanting to get anywhere near the water. As I circled the pond, I spotted what was definitely a cleared path. Finally, I thought. This must lead somewhere. Probably to Greg's home. I followed the path—and hoped he was home and could lead me back to my cottage.

After I traveled around a curve in the path, I saw a divergence. At the V was an enormous, black hound. Its lips curled, revealing sharp teeth as it growled. *I am so over canines. The girls can have cats.*

I tried to remember what I was supposed to do if around a strange dog. "Good boy. Who's a good boy?" I murmured, drawing nearer.

The dog paced in front of the two paths. As I tried to

decide which one to take, there was that chuckle again. The dog barked and tore off toward the left fork and the sound. "Okay...follow the dog and the laughing guy or not." I thought I saw a glint of light down the other path and heard a scuffling. *The devil you know or the devil you don't, Becca.*

Pocketing the blade, I walked toward the scuffling fork, away from the dog and chuckling one, and hoped I made the right decision. It was getting increasingly late, and I was lost. Yes, on a path—but a path to where? And the path kept narrowing and winding. I had no idea where I was.

I cried out when I tripped over a root and stumbled into a raspberry bush, scratching my arms on the thorns. The path closed in until my shoulders brushed the bushes at each side, then I rounded a bend, and the trail opened up. I found myself in a clearing. In the center, I saw a slight rise, which couldn't even be called a hill, with a circle of the largest mushrooms I had ever seen surrounding it. I walked around the ring.

On the first pass, I thought I could see something in the center—all blurry movement that I couldn't track. As I continued to walk around the hill, the vision seemed to be less hazy. The second pass, I saw more clearly—creatures that I should be afraid of, I knew at some level, but I found fascinating and entrancing. I wanted to see more. The third pass, I heard whispers—enticing me, encouraging me to keep walking, promising me untold treasures. I tingled. I longed to continue, but trepidation filled me. I retrieved the blade and held it ready. Before I could finish this circle, someone jerked me from the path into the woods.

CHAPTER 13

"What were you thinking, lass?"

My body was so lax that my head snapped back and forth as I was shaken to and fro, and I dropped the blade.

"Huh...nuh?" I asked fuzzily. I reached out and clung to the muscled arms which held me. A man's worried face peered down at me.

"Greg?"

"Aye," he said and stopped rattling my poor brain.

"I was looking for you." I heard the murmurs from the hill and, like a siren call, they tugged, urging me to continue my walk around the clearing.

Greg held me firm, preventing me. "Let us get shed of this place and talk." He gathered me close to his side and led me away from the clearing pausing to pick up the blade.

The farther away we went, the clearer my thoughts became. I stopped and trembled. "What was that?"

"An entrance to a place you shouldna go."

As I rubbed my aching head, I said, "I don't know what you're talking about. Why can't you answer me straight? Why does everything have to be in riddles?"

"I'm sorry."

His eyes met mine, and I could see such weariness in his. Years and years of loneliness—what I had to look forward to. I bowed my head, saddened at the thought.

"You willna have my life."

"What?"

"You need nae worry about being like me. You're too sweet—too innocent—you wouldna even know how to offend them." There was a pause, and he asked," Why did you seek me?"

"This will sound silly, but you and Kay have done so much for me, I wanted to invite you over for dinner this Friday—the two of you."

"Dinner...at the cottage?" He said it as if it were a foreign concept.

"Yes—if you can and want to. It won't be anything fancy. The girls will be the first to tell you that I'm not much of a cook, but in my defense, they tend to have simple tastes and turn their noses up at anything new." I realized I was prattling on and stopped.

"Can I...think about it?" he said carefully.

"Yes, I suppose so. Could you call me before Wednesday to let me know?"

"Call you? You mean on the telephone?" he carefully enunciated. I nodded. He chuckled. "I don't have need of one of those contraptions."

"Oh," I said lamely.

He stood still, in thought then said, "I could send you a message."

"Oh, that would be fine. I thought seven o'clock would be a good time for everyone. Would that work for you?"

"Aye, if I come, it shouldna be any trouble to be there at that time." There was an awkward pause. "Thank you for thinking of me."

"Well, I wanted to do something. You've gone way beyond neighborly kindness."

"If you wouldna go traipsing off into the woods, you wouldna need the help."

"I've been hiking my whole life. It isn't like it's late, and there aren't any dangerous animals in the Scottish woods."

"Perhaps not in other woods in Scotland, but this one is different."

"How?"

"It just is. That is enough for you to know."

Grrr, this man can be so frustrating. "It would help if I knew what I was dealing with—what these dangers are. Then I could prepare for them."

"There isna all that much that you can do to guard against them. Some know ways—wise women and the such."

Wise women? Changing the topic. "Is your home nearby? I need to rush back, but if it's close, I'd love a glass of water."

"I can cut the time. I know of many shortcuts through the woods." He took my arm and led me off the path but paused. "You dropped this," he said handing the blade to me. "I can hone the edge if you like, but I would know how you came by it?"

"I found it at the cottage in the bathroom, between the toilet and the sink."

"Aye," he said, rubbing his chin. "An excellent one, to be sure. A close shave could be had, no doubt."

"Thankfully, we now have razors. I'd be afraid to use that."

"'Tis easy once you get accustomed. I should be getting you back." His hand wrapped around my bicep, and he tugged me forward. Within five minutes, I was completely turned around. In another five, the trees thinned to reveal a path and a red-ribboned oak on the opposite side. I went to the tree, carefully untied the ribbon, then folded it into my pocket.

"You shouldna have trouble getting home from here. Just follow the trail that way." He indicated with his hand which way to go, and I turned to look. When I turned back, he was gone.

I arrived home, footsore and exasperated. After I filled the bath with water and poured in the scented salts, I opened a bottle of white wine. I didn't drink before dinner, usually, but I felt I deserved it today. As I luxuriated in the tub, I thought about what to serve to Kay and, hopefully, Greg.

"Heck, I don't even know what I'm serving for lunch today," I said ruefully. I read for about twenty minutes until I heard the girls come in, chatting gaily. It sounded like the shopping went well. "I'm in the bath," I called out.

Both girls, laden with bags, crowded in.

"They don't have all that much, but Mr. McNeil said if we waited and had our party next weekend, he was going to the mainland and would pick up some stuff for us. He also gave us this. It's for you." Jessie pulled a box of Quality Street Candy from a bag and waved it at me.

"That was nice of him." I wondered if he felt bad about our last interaction.

"We stopped by the café, and Mrs. Wallace suggested serving tarts. We said we had to ask you before ordering anything. We bought one inexpensive decoration to show you before buying a lot."

"Good idea."

Tate had been fairly quiet and let Jess do the talking.

"What about you, Tate? Did you see anything you liked?"

"I think I'll make something from my craft book."

Tate was the artsy one. Jess was my outdoorsy sports girl.

"Sounds like a marvelous idea, but will you have time? We haven't set a date yet, but I still think it will have to be a simple project."

Tate had been known to begin a small painting that, in her enthusiasm for the pastime, turned into a large mural. While the girls filled me in, I rose from the bath, wrapped a towel around my body, and let the water out.

"You girls scoot so I can dry off and dress. I invited Kay over for lunch, and I have no idea what I'm going to serve. I really need to plan meals better."

"Mom, you always say that."

Shushing them, I herded them out of the bathroom and shut the door. I had just finished dressing when I heard Kay's tap, tappity, tap.

"Hellooo?" She popped her head in and then smiled when she saw all of us. "I took the liberty of picking up some things from the café. If you don't already have something ready, I thought we could eat them for lunch."

"Kay, you're my hero!" I proclaimed. "I was out longer than I had intended and haven't started anything yet."

Kay opened the bag and pulled out irregular pastries and such that the owner didn't want to go to waste but didn't think were good enough to be sold. Kay arranged several meat and vegetable pies and at least a dozen cookies on the table. I made a small salad and cut up some fruit, so we ate quite well. When we finished and the girls left to talk more about the party, Kay helped me tidy up. "So, I heard your message. Hiking, huh? Did you go alone? It's safer to always have another with you."

"I hadn't intended to go far. I was going to just enter the forest and travel toward your cottage to see if I could find where Greg lived."

"No, luck, I take it."

"No, I didn't find his cottage, but I did find him." I relayed what had happened to me. "You don't think he was the one who stole the ribbons and caused me to get lost, do you? And what about that dog?"

"He wouldn't do that, I think. The dog—well, the dog must have been a neighbor's, maybe the Samms'."

"No, when we visited the farm, all the dogs came to greet us, except one, and Gavin introduced us to each."

"Maybe the dog you saw on the trail was the missing one."

"No, the missing one was a sheepdog. I don't know what breed the dog on the trail was, but it was definitely not a sheepdog. It was huge. If Kiera was a dog, she would have been this size. And the dog was black, too."

"So, after you saw the dog, you ran into Mr. Gillie?"

"Yes, and I asked him about coming for dinner."

"I'm sorry he said no, I told you he's a bit of a recluse."

"He didn't say no."

"He didn't?"

"Well, he didn't say yes either."

"What did he say?"

"He said he would think on it and get back with me by Wednesday."

"Seems you've had some influence on Mr. Gillie—a positive one if it gets him out of his woods and around others."

"Well, for his welfare, I hope he does come over. I feel so sorry for the poor man. I know losing a spouse is devastating enough. I don't know what I would do if I lost one—or, God forbid, both—of the girls."

"So, he told you a bit of it?"

"Not much, he's very private, but a little."

"I imagine the fact that he's a handsome man had nothing to do with you being pleased he didn't say no." Kay winked and smiled when I blushed.

"It hasn't been like that at all," I protested.

"Let's see, he rescues your daughter from some stranger leading her into the woods. He rescues you from drowning. He sits with you and chats at the party."

"That was barely a chat, and he only sat to keep the table for me so I could go get some food."

"Right. And now he's run into you in the forest and may join you for dinner. I never would have dreamed that Greg Gillie would go on a date."

"It isn't a date! You'll be there!"

"About that, would it be okay if I brought a friend of mine?"

"Sure, that would be fine."

"Amberlee is coming in for the weekend from the mainland. We met years ago, but lost track of each other. I'm a little nervous about seeing her, so it would be a big favor to me if I could bring her here. Things would be less likely to get awkward with more people around talking."

"Well, I don't know how much talking Greg will be doing, but I'll do my best."

"I knew Amberlee when my family lived here. We were pen pals for a long time after I moved, but I moved again and somehow, along the way, we lost touch with each other. When I was on the mainland today, I saw her and we exchanged information. I ran into the girls too. So, you're having two parties? One for the girls and an adult one?"

"Yes, a party for the girls but no, on the adult one. Goodness, Kay! I'm having you, your friend, and Greg over for a simple dinner—not a fancy party." Then I realized that Kay had managed to make it an evening for four instead of the odd number of three. "Are you up to something?" I asked.

"Me? Of course not! The girls said you've been spending time at the library."

Way to change the topic, Kay. Yeah, you are definitely up to something. "I've been down to the newspaper archives reading some very interesting articles. I'd love to investigate further. Do you think it would be okay if I interviewed some of the older residents?"

"I'm sure they'd love to talk. Everyone here has heard their stories, and they would love a new audience. I think the older ladies get together at the church on a regular basis, but I'm not sure of the time or day. I'm not a church goer myself. I can ask the parson if you like, or if you are planning to attend services, you may want to meet him yourself."

"I don't know. I haven't been to church since we moved to Scotland. I feel bad about it. Things were just so busy when we first moved and I didn't have time to check out the local parishes. Give me a few days to mull it over. I've found that it's better to not even talk with the clergy if you are seriously not interested in their church. Once they have a grip, they don't want to let go. I really don't want some pastor knocking on my door every Saturday inviting me to church the next day and sending…I don't know…whatever is the name of the local women's organization over to invite me to fundraisers and such."

"I know exactly how you feel. Pastor Doyles knows my family never attended, so he wouldn't try to talk me into it. Just let me know. I don't mind popping in. He has a small place beside the church. One thing I would suggest doing some day is going by the graveyard. There are some amusing, interesting tombs there. A lot of the tourists go and take rubbings to bring home as souvenirs."

"I haven't been to a cemetery since my husband died."

Kay patted my hand. "I'm sorry, Becca. I wasn't thinking."

"No, it's okay. It's been over a year. It still hurts, but it's easier now. I didn't think I would ever be able to do the simplest of things for a long while. When I was in the States, I lived near David's family. Every time I saw a relative, I got upset, and I just couldn't take all the memories that were constantly in my face. That's why I decided to make a big move. I needed some time away. Some time and somewhere where no one could pop in and check on me or tell me a remember-when story about David."

The phone rang. It was Mrs. Samms calling about having the girls over while her daughter, Heather, visited. I had second and third doubts about it until she confessed that her only daughter was coming for the weekend from school and had always wanted little sisters. She was excited to see the girls and had all sorts of plans, like fingernail painting and such.

"Glad she's enthused now," I said. "Wait until she actually *has* a daughter and see how fun it is when little Suzie demands French braids for school then complains and whines when it's halfway done and acts like you're torturing her when you insist on finishing said braid."

Yes, Jess. In all fairness, she never asked for it again.

CHAPTER 14

Friday afternoon, as I stood surveying the contents of the wardrobe, I agonized over what to wear for that night. Earlier, Greg had left a note under a rock on the cottage porch saying he would be there for dinner.

I had decided to serve roasted chicken with vegetables and spent the morning chopping and marinating. I lamented that I hadn't really brought any fancy clothing but then chastised myself for even thinking of wearing something dressy to a simple dinner party. *Crud! Now Kay has me thinking party, too.* "Jeans, I'm wearing jeans. I'm being silly," I told myself firmly.

Jess peeked around the corner into my bedroom. "What did you say, Mom?"

I hadn't realized I'd said it so loudly. "Never mind. Just talking to myself."

"So, who did you say was coming over tonight?"

I actually had tried *not* to say. Earlier, I just mentioned Kay and a couple of her friends. *Hey, she does know Greg.* "Kay and a couple of other grownups. Probably be a boring night, but I wanted to do something to thank her for being so helpful after I fell in the pond."

"Oh, it's a thank you. Then are you inviting that guy

in the skirt?" The telltale signs of a pout emerged as Jess wrinkled her forehead and her lips thinned.

"Ha, ha, Jess. You know it's called a kilt. Yes, I asked him to come too."

"Is he?"

"Is he what?"

"Coming."

My cheeks warmed. "Well, yes. He did say he could make it. Kay's bringing an old girlfriend."

"Wait a minute—is this a double date?" Jess folded her arms in front of her chest and narrowed her eyes. "Is that why you wanted us out of the house?"

"I didn't say I wanted you out."

"Yeah, but you were really fast to agree to let us spend the night at the Samms', and you're usually so weird about letting us even go over to someone's house when you don't know them well. You've never even met the daughter."

"But I've met the Samms and allowed you and your sister to go there often. Look, Jess, do you want to stay home? If you do, you can march yourself over and explain why you've changed your mind. I don't have a problem with it. I'll probably tell Tate she needs to stay home too."

"That's blackmail."

"It's not. It's fact. I feel better about both of you being together. You've been alone there more than Tate, helping out with the horses and riding, plus you're older."

Jess huffed a sigh. "Fine, you get your way. I'll go—but he better not be here when I get home." She twirled around and trounced to her bedroom.

"Jessica Elise Shaw!" I debated about following her but decided not to. I was pretty sure I knew what this was all about. Jess had told me about a friend of hers in the States whose parents divorced. The mother started dating again, which was fine, but she also had her gentlemen spend the night. Jess and her friend woke up one Saturday morning to find a man in sweats making breakfast. After that, I kept the sleepovers to my house. I knew it upset Jessie's friend because one night, when she stayed over, she burst into tears and sobbed as she told me how much she missed her father and disliked her mother's new boyfriend.

After I checked on the chicken and vegetables that were roasting in the oven, I dressed. Lazy, I had purchased dessert from the tea shop. Unsure what everyone would drink, I stocked up on wine and beer. Scots weren't known for being teetotalers.

I hadn't planned on walking the girls over but decided at the last minute to do so, hoping I wouldn't come back to a smoldering cottage. I rushed them during the walk over but took time to meet the Samms' daughter, Heather, and say a proper goodbye. She seemed very nice and was majoring in psychology, with the plan to go into counseling young adults. One more reason she wanted to be around the girls, I supposed.

છ્ચઝ

I arrived back at six. Plenty of time to get ready. I spent more time than I liked to admit fussing with my hair. So I could finish the last moment preparations of dinner without having hair droop in my face, I clipped the sides back, but left the rest down. The last time I had my haired trimmed was in Houston just before we left for the UK. It had gotten longer than it had been since before kids. I cut it off shoulder length when Jess was two and had kept it there for years. I added just a tint of color to my cheeks and a clear gloss to my lips.

"That's it, Rebecca Shaw," I told myself with resolve.

After my primping, I went to the kitchens to marinate the chicken with the drippings. While the chicken rested, I'd roast the vegetables a bit longer. I debated about appetizers and finally decided to put something out. The cottage held no fancy serving dishes that I could find, so I opened a can of mixed nuts and dumped them in a small cereal bowl. *Drat.* I thought I'd gotten nuts with no peanuts but must have grabbed the wrong can. I'd have to remember to pitch them afterward or send them home with Kay. Jessie was allergic. I'd feel awful if she accidentally ate any. I had an EpiPen but I would rather not have to use it.

I thought about asking Kay to come early, but I didn't know her friend, so I decided not to. When her friend arrived on the ferry, Kay planned to pick her up then go to the cottage to drop off luggage. Then both would walk over.

I also put out chips for a quick appetizer. "I am so overthinking this," I moaned.

Tossing the crisps back in the pantry, I exchanged them for dip, crackers, and veggies. "There, that's enough."

In the bathroom, I studied my reflection in the mirror. Deciding I looked wan, I added more blush then wiped it off because, geez, who puts makeup on for a simple meal with friends? I checked the poultry and, when I noticed a dry leaf in the entry way, stopped to sweep. I put the dip back in the fridge because it was too early. The chicken was ready.

"Ugh!" I gasped with worry, debating whether I should leave it in the oven and have it too dry or take it out and have it cold when they arrived. I turned the oven down.

Kay's signature knock struck the door. When I rushed to the entryway, I was almost smacked in the head as

Kay opened the door. "Oops, sorry," she said when I bounced back to avoid it. "I thought you'd be busy cooking, and I didn't want to interrupt you to get the door."

"Oh, no—everything's ready."

"Are we late?"

"No, I think I'm a bit early."

When Kay entered the cottage, a slight woman with huge brown eyes, wearing oddly patterned green and yellow tights, followed her. Her hair was parted in the middle with a zigzag pattern. She met my eyes then ducked her head.

"This is my friend, Amberlee."

"It's so nice to meet you," I said, thrusting my hand out like a politician after a vote. Her eyes widened, but she gingerly took my hand and shook it. Kay looked at me like I had turned into a turnip. To cover the awkward silence, I said, "Hi, I'm Becca, Becca Shaw. I've heard so much about you."

Amberlee's forehead crinkled. "You have?"

Kay's mouth hung open then she mouthed, *What?* at me.

"I mean, any friend of Kay's is a friend of mine." *Oh, God, kill me.* "Come in, come in. I have some dippy crackers and nuts here."

Amberlee hesitantly followed.

As Kay passed me, she leaned in. "Are you okay?"

As I nodded. I pushed the door shut, but before I could close the door, something stopped its progress.

I eeped. Thoughts of the large wolf and weird creatures filled my head. I pushed harder to close it.

"Becca, I think you're trying to shut out your other guest," Kay said.

I turned to face her and pressed my back into the door. "Huh?"

"Mr. Gillie was coming up the road when we knocked. It's probably him."

I yanked open the door. Greg had turned to walk away. Before he got too far, I reached out and grasped, catching the hem of his kilt. He spun and grabbed my hand.

"Oh," we both said.

I dropped the material and opened the door wider. "Please come in."

"These are for you," he said as he shoved a bouquet of wild flowers into my hands. In a whirl of tartan, he shouldered past me then froze in the middle of the room. "This—it has changed much."

"Oh, well, I imagine Mrs. Grant took much of her stuff with her when she moved in with her son. Did you know her well? Incidentally, the person who built this house was also named Gillie. Any relation to you?" *Babbling again, Becca.*

"The island is small and many of the villagers are related, if not through blood, then through marriage," he replied.

"Mrs. Grant is sending me her family tree. I'll let you know the first name of the Gillie she's related to through marriage."

"Ta," he said.

I busied myself with finding a vase for the flowers. "Please, sit down and have some appetizers." *Appetizers. Sounds like some fancy, posh party.*

Kay introduced Greg to Amberlee as Mr. Gillie. A look of surprised crossed Kay's face when he asked them to call him Greg. Kay kept a running commentary on the food and the flowers, thankfully filling the air with noise while I wanted to crawl under the table. I stole glances at Greg. He wore a patched, but clean shirt, the color that white material got when it was old. His kilt hitched up a bit revealing one scabbed knee. My glance traveled down to his muscled calves. I wondered if he owned more than one kilt. I was no expert on survivalists, but the ones I saw on the news were rough-looking and in camo. Greg never looked scruffy and, while not a metrosexual, he seemed to take pride in his appearance. When I finally arranged the flowers in a large jar, having failed to find any other viable container, I put them in the center of the table.

"Amberlee also brought you this from the mainland." Kay handed me a bag. Inside was a bottle of single malt whisky, a brand I recognized.

"Oh, thank you so much! We can have some after dessert."

I came around the table to Amberlee and bent to hug her but straightened when she failed to react, just as she tried to hug me. We settled on patting each other awkwardly. I could smell the chicken, so I feared it was getting overcooked.

"Kay, could you get drinks for everyone?" I gestured to the red wine on the table. "There's white wine and beer in the fridge."

After I removed the chicken from the oven, I transferred it to a platter. Then I scattered the veggies on the pan, put them back in, and turned up the temp.

"What's this?" Greg asked, holding up a small piece from the nuts bowl.

I thought he was just trying to make conversation. "Looks like half of a peanut," I answered.

He popped in his mouth and chewed.

"What do you think?" I asked.

He took a drink of water that Kay had poured for everyone. "Is it supposed to make my lips tingle?" he asked.

To my horror, bumps rose on his face and his lips began to swell.

"Oh no!" I grabbed the offending bowl and tossed it in the trash. "Rinse your mouth out and wash your hands!"

I practically dragged Greg off his chair. Though he insisted he was okay, his face was swollen, and he had a blotchy, red rash. I eyed the bathroom and debated about getting the EpiPen, but Kay said she thought he would be fine as long as he didn't have breathing problems or eat more peanuts.

Poison one guest, check.

By then the veggies were done and the chicken had rested. I put out the food and invited everyone to sit. Not knowing if I should say a prayer, in the end I decided to bow my head and hold my hands together as a compromise. Greg surprised me by making the sign of the cross. Thankfully, he offered to carve the chicken. My attempts in the past looked like a caveman had at it. I passed the bread and veggies around as he wielded the knife. When he finished, we passed the meat which was divided into light and dark.

"Thank you." I smiled gratefully at him. He smiled back. I cleared my throat and raised my glass of wine. "I would like to propose a toast to Greg and Kay for their help in making my stay on the island happy and safe."

We clicked glasses and sipped our wine.

"This is a beautiful island," Amberlee commented. "I've never been here before."

"Really?" I commented.

"Amberlee and I met when we were children while I was on a field trip," Kay said. "Our friendship wasn't approved of. We wrote to each other, and I tried to get to the mainland when I could but was unable to invite her to my house to visit. My parents were…intransigent."

"That's so unfortunate. Why did they object?" I asked.

"Many people here on the island have a…legacy. Some choose to ignore it and hope it goes away. My parents felt that way. They were very conservative in their outlooks."

I was so totally lost. "Is that why you left?"

"Partly. I never knew about it until later. Thankfully, someone—" She looked at Greg. "—pointed me in the right direction."

Greg studied his plate.

"I'll always be grateful for that."

Amberlee looked about as confused as I felt. Kay squeezed her hand. Everyone seemed to enjoy the food. In the States, I often served baked chicken and always received compliments. Most everyone would eat chicken and with a medley of vegetables—there should be at least one in the dish that everyone liked.

"I havena had chicken in some time," Greg commented.

"Really? What do you generally eat?"

"I hunt—so, rabbits, the occasional deer, and such."

"You're welcome to take some home with you if you would like."

"That's not necessary. I can provide for myself."

Great, I guess he thought it sounded like I thought he was beggared and needed charity. I debated about trying to explain but figured to leave well enough alone. Once dinner was over, I placed the cake I bought at the tea shop on the table. Kay removed the dirty dishes while Amberlee passed around the deserts plates and I cut the cake.

"I hope everyone likes chocolate." I had tea and coffee. Of course, they all wanted tea. I thought I would offer the whisky when we finished. My phone chirped. "Excuse me a moment, it's my daughter."

Jess texted that they were having a wonderful time and sent a couple of photos of the three of them. Heather had French braided Jessie's hair and curled Tate's in ringlets. The girls combined efforts on their poor hostess, and she sported three braids that then had been braided together and numerous ribbons. I quickly texted back to say I was glad they were having fun and to be good and I loved them.

"They're fine and having fun." I explained where they were at and Greg asked me what color Heather's hair was. "Brown, I think."

"Ah, not blonde then?"

"Nooo."

"So, she isn't attached to the land as her kin."

I wasn't sure how to respond to that. "No, I guess not. She's visiting, but it sounds like she has her own life on the mainland. I think she's planning to move to London if she can afford it. Her mother said she had visited and loved it there."

"The one boy, at least, he will stay," Greg said decisively.

"Well, yes, their son, Gavin, does seem to be attached to the farm, but there's always a possibility that he may decide to venture out too."

"Nae, glaistig blood runs through him, as his da."

"Glas...what?" I asked.

"Pay no mind. I have a fanciful nature at times." He stood. "Where is your water closet?"

Kay whispered, "WC."

I motioned toward the hallway. "The first door on the left."

I wanted to ask Kay about the comments she and Greg made that I didn't understand, but I wasn't sure if I should. It was as if she and Greg were in some secret club, and Amberlee and I were in the dark. I didn't like that feeling.

After a few minutes, Greg peeked around the corner. "I think your pull cord is broken."

"Oh, let's see." When I reached the bathroom, he halted me just in the doorway and tugged the light, which came on then off.

"I think it works fine."

"Well, it turns the lights on and off, but it doesna..." He gestured at the toilet.

The toilet was newer and had a small handle that went two ways, one way for number two and one way for number one. I guessed he hadn't seen such.

"It was a surprise to me, too. Kay had to enlighten me." I explained and left him to it. No way was I going to ask him if the result was number one or two.

When he returned, I offered the whisky. Everyone wanted a glass, which in the States was fairly unusual. Kay and Greg preferred it neat, but Amberlee and I had a cube of ice in ours. I savored the scent and sipped. "This is such a treat, Amberlee. Thank you."

Her cheeks dimpled, and she sipped her glass.

A wolf's long howl pierced the air. Amberlee splashed her whisky on her hand. Kay tsked and brought a towel from the counter for Amberlee to dry herself. Thank goodness the girls weren't home. This creature was starting to make me very uneasy.

"Sorry, Amberlee. Apparently, there's a wild wolf in the area, and he or she—"

"He," Greg interrupted.

Okay, this guy can sex a wolf? "He seems to be fixated with this cottage. At least this area. We've seen him over by Kay's too."

"I think he may be more fixated with you," Greg said.

"Why would you say that?"

"Wolves can be like that. Something about you attracts it."

"Well—any ideas on how to distract it?"

The wolf howled again louder. It sounded like it was just outside the door. Amberlee edged her chair closer to Kay. Greg stood and walked to the door.

"What are you doing?"

"Going to check."

"Do you think that's safe?"

"I'll be fine. Stay inside." He opened the door and slipped out. I paced. The howls escalated to snarls.

"Do you think he's okay?" I asked Kay.

Amberlee rubbed her palms on her legs.

I peered out the curtain, but could see nothing in the pool of the porch light. "I'm going out."

"Becca, Greg said to stay." Kay pushed her chair back and stood, but before she could say more, I opened the door and stepped out, closing it behind me. I could just make out Greg and the wolf—no, *two* wolves standing near the edge of the forest.

"Greg!" I called out. He turned to look at me and when he did, one of the wolves darted in and nipped at him.

CHAPTER 15

I looked for a weapon. Seeing a hoe, I grabbed it and ran toward him. While Greg dodged the first wolf, the second darted in and snapped at him. *Wild animals are supposed to be afraid of people!* I ran, screaming, toward them, waving the hoe in what I hoped was menacing way. I raised the hoe to slam the sharp end on the smaller of the wolves when Greg blocked me.

"No, don't hurt them."

"They're trying to bite you." I sidestepped Greg, determine to swing the hoe at the creatures, but Greg gripped the shaft, preventing me. Though the wolves backed off, their hair still bristled on their backs.

"They dinna mean to. They dinna understand and react emotionally."

"Well, I'm about to go all emotional on their heads with this," I said, trying to shake it loose from Greg.

He pointed to the wolves. "Look—"

The larger one nipped at the smaller one's heels. The smaller one barked once but allowed itself to be herded back into the forest. When the smaller one disappeared, the other turned and howled at us, then it followed.

When we returned inside, Kay was speaking earnestly with Amberlee but stopped when we entered. The women finished up their whiskies and thanked me for the invitation. I worried about them walking home alone, but they seemed fine about it, especially when Greg reassured them that the wolves had moved on.

When I turned back from the door, I saw that Greg had begun clearing the table. "You don't need to do that," I said as I took the whisky glasses from him.

"Nae bother. 'Tis the least I can do to repay your hospitality. Long has it been since I've been invited into someone's home."

"Well, I'm glad you could make it. I'm still not completely clear on exactly what you do in the forest. Who owns the wooded area?" Why he would live there by himself? I knew he was a mourning widower, but I still thought it was unusual. Perhaps if it was also a part of his job, it would make more sense.

"No one owns the forest—or all do," he said enigmatically. He smiled at my furrowed brow. "That dinna really answer the question, did it?"

"No, not really."

"I guess you could say the National Trust owns it. They are responsible for the treasures of our land."

One of the first things I had done when I arrived in Scotland was to become a member. We took advantage of it often, especially since we lived in the Grampian region which was awash with castles, standing stones, and the like.

"So, you take care of the land?"

"In a manner of speaking."

"Does that pay well?"

"'Tis rewarding."

I searched my mind for other topics as I filled the sink. When I reached for the wash cloth at the same time as he did, our hands met. A thrilling zing ran up my hand and arm. I didn't want him to move his palm which covered the top of my hand. We froze like that, then he cleared his throat and pulled away. "Would you rather I dry?" he asked, finding the towel.

"You really don't need to do this," I protested.

"I'd like to. Perhaps with the girls gone, you would enjoy my company a little longer?"

I hadn't been looking forward to the night without them. The girls rarely had spent a night away from me since their dad died. I suppose I had been overprotective. Even now, though I trusted the Samms family, I had misgivings about my decision. It was nice to have Greg here. If left alone, I would probably worry myself into a frenzy. Having him here was…distracting, in a good way.

"Unless you had other plans for this evening?"

"No, I thought I might read a bit, but that was it. Tell you what, why don't we leave the dishes for later and sit and have another glass of whisky and talk—unless you would prefer tea?"

"Whisky would be grand."

I couldn't remember which glass was whose, so I removed two clean glasses from the pantry and poured another glass for each of us. Good that he chose whisky. Tea combined with worrying over the girls would probably assure me of little, if any, sleep. Hopefully, the whisky would have the opposite effect.

We moved to the sofa and sat at either end. As I nursed the drink, I asked, "How long has your family lived here?"

"In the 1800s, my kin moved to the island. The family has been here ever since."

"I've been doing some research about this place—at the library and in the newspaper archives. There are photos. It doesn't appear that much has changed here over time."

"True, we like to keep things the same."

I wondered if it would be all right to ask him more about his family or if it would be too personal. Americans tended to come off as brash to many Europeans. I didn't want to ask any awkward questions—or any *more* awkward questions. I took another sip of the delicious whisky when my phone rang.

"Excuse me." After the girls texted, I'd plugged the phone in to recharge. I really didn't expect anyone one else to call. I checked the phone and recognized the Samms' number. I hoped everyone was okay. "Hello?"

"Mrs. Shaw, I don't mean to alarm you, but Jessie's in hysterics. I can't get the whole story out of her, but she said she saw a small creature sitting beside her sister. I swear I couldn't find anything of the sort. She said it was grayish, and we are a farm, so the occasional mouse isn't unheard of, but she said it was larger than that." Voices talked in the background, but I couldn't understand what they were saying. Then Jess came on the phone.

"Mom—that thing I saw around Tate was back! It's creepy, and I think it's the reason Tate gets sick. When Mrs. Samms came in, the thing disappeared, but now Tate's so pale, and she won't answer me!" Jessie's voice grew shrill with panic.

Mrs. Samms came back on the line. "Tate does seem unwell. I can't get her to answer my questions either."

"I'm on my way. Thanks for calling me."

"Wait, Mrs. Shaw. We'll bring the girls over. I know you don't have a car."

I reluctantly agreed. I ended the call and turned to Greg.

"Trouble?" he asked.

"Something's wrong with Tate. The Samms are going to drive the girls' home." I paced in front of the window and mentally hurrying them.

"Is she ailing?"

"I don't know what's wrong. Sometimes she seems fine, and then she gets all wan, tired, and lethargic. I've taken her to the doctor, and we're waiting on test results. Jess swears she sees some creature around Tate when she has these spells."

"Creature?"

"Something small and grayish. I'm sorry, that isn't much help, but that's the best description I've gotten from Jess. She says it's like smoke, hard to see."

"Hmmm." He grew quiet.

I was beyond making conversation and, though we kept drinking the whisky, I paused often to look out the window. I'm sure it didn't take long at all, but it seemed to take ages before I finally saw the truck headlights. Mrs. Samms climbed out, carrying Tate in her arms. Gavin had driven and helped a shaky Jess toward the door. Too impatient, I didn't wait and ran outside to meet them. I took Tate from Mrs. Samms.

"Tate, sweetie?"

Tate looked up at me groggily. "Mama?" She closed her eyes and went limp in my arms. Her head fell back on my chest.

"Tate!" I rushed inside the cottage.

Mrs. Samms followed. "I have no idea what happened. You have to believe me. They were fine one moment and then the next, Jessie was screaming and Tate was like this."

Greg held the door open and nodded greetings at Mrs. Samms and her son. I sat on the couch and tried to get Tate to stir. Gavin held Jessie's hand and patted it helplessly.

"I know it sounds crazy, Mom, but something's somehow zapping the strength from Tate. I don't know how, but every time it appears, she gets weak."

Greg gestured to the couch. "May I?"

I nodded and he sat beside me.

"Come on, baby," I said. "Wake up."

Tate blinked at me. "I'm sleepy."

"How do you feel?"

She yawned. "Sleepy—told you..."

I sighed. "Mrs. Samms, Gavin, thank you for bringing them home."

"It was no trouble. I just feel horrible that she fell ill. I didn't know she was so delicate."

"She isn't, usually. We've been to the doctor, and he's mystified, too."

"Well, we'll be going then. Let us know if there is anything we can do."

The boy murmured to Jess and the family said goodbye.

Tate seemed—faded. When I pressed on her arm, a dent remained, as if she were dehydrated.

"Jess honey, could you make some tea with sugar and milk for Tate?"

Showing how worried she was, Jess didn't complain but immediately started the kettle. Tate slid off my lap and curled up on the couch, tucking her hand beneath the pillow. I brought the tea, encouraged her to sit up, and left her with her hands around the mug to go get a blanket to wrap around her shivering body. I used a stepstool to reach the blankets at the top of the linen closet when I heard Jess gasp.

Then I heard Greg say, "Aye, I see it too, Jessica." Then he muttered something in Gaelic.

I rushed back to the room in time to see a hazy outline of something gray, small, and humanoid—the size and shape of a child only with more adult proportions. The hands were overly large and the head too small but with an elongated, gaping mouth. It was pressed tightly against Tate. My stomach clenched at the sight of it.

"What is that?" I gasped.

"Something that has no business here. Away, you wicked creature! Back to where you belong!" Greg slashed his hand where the creature and Tate's bodies met and, like a knife cutting through bread, the gray thing fell from Tate's side and lost its shape as it wafted toward the door. Greg leapt up and opened the door. By the time it crossed the threshold, it resembled nothing so much as smoke. It vanished into the night. "She should be fine now. She must have picked it up in the forest that night. I apologize. I should have seen the marks, but didn't think she had been in the forest long enough to arouse the attentions of the darker fae."

"What's fae?"

"Creatures of power."

I wasn't sure exactly what he meant by that but let it slide. "Jessie said someone led Tate into the forest that night."

"Yes, but that which did, while mischievous, isna evil." He scratched his chin.

"Taking a little girl out of her bed in the middle of the night and into a dangerous forest is pretty darn evil in my books," I snapped.

In the short time since that the thing had left, Tate already gained color. She took interest in the tea and relished it, when before she could barely hold onto the cup and only gingerly sipped it. "Good tea, thanks, Jessie." She smiled at her sister and her sister, her expression relieved, smiled back.

Turning to Greg, Jessie asked, "How did you make it go away? Can you teach me?"

Greg slowly shook his head, but I didn't think it was in answer to Jessie's question. "I dinna understand why such as it was so near the edge of the forest. This is worrisome." He paced. "I thank you for your hospitality, but

I must take my leave. Something is amiss, and I need to discover the truth of it." He caught each girl's eyes as he said, "Goodnight, lassies." He then surprised me by taking my hand and holding it as he said, "I hope that I may call on you again, soon—if it pleases?"

"Um...of course...I would like that. Thank you for...well, for..." I didn't know exactly what to call what he did.

"'Tis nothing and only my duty as keeper. I'm sorry that I didna realize earlier. Young Tate should be fine now." He turned to leave but then turned back. "You and Jessica—you both saw it?"

Jessie tilted her head. "The gray thing leeching on Tate? Yes."

"Unusual. I would also like to talk to you about that, but another day. Rest easy, Tate will quickly improve and become her old self soon. No lasting harm has been done to her. Best if everyone stays away from the forest, at least until I can look into this."

I nodded.

After he left, Jessie, who had been frowning, asked, "What was up with him holding your hand?"

I blushed. "I think he's old-fashioned."

"Humph."

I hoped Jessie's attitude toward Greg would change, but maybe she was right to feel the way she did. David had been so reliable and normal. Greg was reliable, too, after a fashion, but was far from normal. Before he died, David began the preparations for Jessie's college education. I doubted Greg would have a clue about how to proceed. I was jumping the gun, but I was a mother with two children. I had to think of these things.

"Why don't you get ready for bed, Jess?"

"Mom, could we all sleep in your room tonight?"

"Yes, I guess it has been an eventful night." I wasn't sure I trusted that Greg had indeed rid us of the creature, and no mention was made about how many more crept about in the woods. When we were snug in bed, I reached over to turn out the light then paused. "Jess, are you supposed to go over to the Samms and help Gavin with the horses tomorrow?"

"After the fit I threw, I doubt if he wants me anywhere near him." Before I could object, she continued. "Plus, his sis will be there, too, and she was looking forward to spending time with the horses. She rarely gets to ride when she's at school."

"You may want to text and make sure, Jess." I hoped she was wrong about the boy, but teens could be cruel at times. It probably was best that I hadn't said anything about the boy surely understanding her outburst.

Jessie's thumbs speedily texted a message on her ever-present phone. She frowned at the screen for a few minutes, and then muttered, "Finally, it actually sent it," then put it on the table beside the bed.

CHAPTER 16

The next morning, Jess asked if she could go to the library. She even offered to take her sister. I hoped my surprise didn't show because Jess wasn't always keen to include Tate. When in a particularly snarky mood, she once told me if I wanted a babysitter, then I needed to pay for one instead of asking her to watch her sister. Also, Jess rarely darkened the steps of a library. She didn't read unless it was for an assignment, despite the hours I spent reading aloud to her when she was young, hoping to encourage a mutual love of books. Tate was my little Miss Imagination Girl. She constantly read and her reading level was very high. I had to closely monitor her book selections. I didn't like to ban any novel, but some topics needed a mother's weighing in. Stifling my surprise, I told Jessie she could go.

After a hearty breakfast of pancakes, I walked the girls to the bus stop and waited with them until the bus arrived. I said I would meet them for lunch. Jess wasn't sure if she would be done with whatever she had planned at the library and I didn't know if Tate, despite her love of books, would want to spend that many hours there, nor did I really want to be separated from her that long. Maybe I was being overly protective, but it was tough not to feel that way. Because Tate didn't seem to understand what happened, I didn't want to scare her by bringing up the subject. Though Jess had calmed down once Greg got rid of the gray creature, I didn't want her agitated about something she had no control over. Plus I felt bad about doubting her. And as well I should. She wasn't one to tell stories or imagine monsters under her bed—it was just so Alice in Wonderland that it was hard to believe.

Today, I had my own plans. Greg elicited mixed feeling in me. He was gruff, but kind, and goodness knows he was utterly gorgeous in that broody kind of way, but something was going on with him, and it was driving me insane. And Kay. She and he, they shared knowledge about…the forest? The island? I didn't know and frankly didn't care, but when it involved my children—not to mention my own experiences with the horse and the pond—I wanted to get to the bottom of it and wouldn't feel safe until I did. I guessed I could just leave. Call Mrs. Grant and explain that it wasn't working out and hope that she might consider a partial reimbursement, as unlikely as that was, but something made me stubborn. I ran away once from Houston. I wasn't going to run away from this.

Kiera had shown up to eat a few rashers of bacon with the kitten, but left when the girls did. I remembered that Kay's friend intended to catch the ferry early this morning. Why not stay the whole weekend? It was as if Kay had something to hide or—she wasn't sure what her friend would make of the island and wanted to introduce her in small increments.

Scotland never got very hot, but today the cold air nipped at my nose and the gray sky drizzled—more like a fall day than a summer one. The sun had been slow to rise, reluctant, and seemed…dimmed. I waved to the girls as the bus pulled away. The grass rustled and swept from side to side, despite that I only felt a breeze from behind me. When I got home, I eyed the leftover dessert and decided use it as an excuse to visit Kay. As I finished packing, the sound of thunder drew me to the window. A lightning bolt tore a white slash across the angry clouds. I felt silly, it rarely rained hard, just drizzled, but crammed my feet into an old pair of wellies and donned an ancient mackintosh that smelled of mothballs. As I turned to shut the door, I reconsidered leaving it unlocked. I went back inside and checked all the windows and the back door, then locked up, and pocketed the key usually hidden above the sill. "I don't know what's going on, but I'm tired of it," I muttered as I stomped toward Kay's cottage.

The wind picked up as I drew closer to her house. I wished I had braided or tied my hair back. The broken tie string snapped my cheek as I held the hood tightly closed with one hand, but wisps of my hair still escaped to fly into my eyes and my mouth.

"Vanity—drat it," I muttered.

Since my hair had turned out so well last night, I'd decided to leave it down today. Now I paid for that. I was almost at Kay's when the sky opened up. Not a smattering of rain, but a downpour like I hadn't experienced since Houston. I struggled to the door and had raised my hand to knock when Kay opened it before my fist could land. After I got inside, we fought against the wind to shut the door. When she did open her mouth to speak, I motioned her to wait. I handed her the dessert then dredged my cell from my pocket and called Jess.

"Mom?" she answered.

"Did you make it to the library okay? This weather's crazy. If it doesn't get better, just stay there, and I'll meet you at the library for lunch. Don't try to make it to the shop."

"We...and Tate is reading...I can barely hear you." Her voice faded in and out.

"Jess? Are you okay?" I tried not to panic.

"...fine, Mom. We're fine. See...at lunch."

I thought she said goodbye but, regardless, the phone cut out.

Without a word, Kay helped me out of my coat and waited while I wedged my feet from the tight wellies. Kay's cats played with a ball of yarn, and a half-finished striped scarf she must have been working on lay on the arm of the chair. She asked if I'd like a cup of tea, but I was too wound up to drink anything.

I hadn't really thought about how I would start this conversation. I just knew she had information that she wasn't sharing with me—an outsider. "After you left last night, I got a call about the girls." I told her what happened at the farm house and later with Greg. "Kay, what's going on? Do you know anything about all this?" She sighed and went back to her knitting. I suppressed the urge to yank it from her and toss it out the door. "Kay? We *are* friends—aren't we?"

"Of course, we are." She paused to turn her work. "I think—you've stirred things up. Put something into action, something old."

I slapped my hands on the coffee table. "What?" I demanded.

"Don't be angry with me, Becca, but it isn't my tale to tell."

"Kay, confound it! I think I *need* to know. Me? I don't give a hoot about what happens to me, but my kids—this thing was eating my baby, Kay. I have never seen anything like it or felt so helpless."

"I know how you feel—"

I stopped her. "No, you don't. People without children say that, but you don't. You don't know."

Kay tossed the knitting down and paced round and round the room. I'd never seen her like this. She was *never* agitated. The Queen of Calm and Collected. I tried to be patient, but on the fifth round, I broke.

"Kay!" I pleaded.

She took her shoes off and strode to the door. "Come on, then."

While I stood there confused, she peered out the glass set in the door and frowned. "Could you have chosen a more dreich day?"

She opened the door. The wind tore it from her hand and flung it so hard against the wall that I expected to see a hole. As Kay walked out, hair, tugged from her braids, floated like a nimbus around her head. As the downpour fell, her drenched plaid tunic clung to her body.

I rushed to the doorway. "Kay?"

She stepped off the porch and onto the grass. She turned to face me and smiled, then closed her eyes and raised her face to the heavens as she scrunched her toes into the earth. Then it was as if I looked through a window clouded with moisture that continued to fog. Kay blurred and shrank, and all the colors of her swirled and darkened. I didn't know how long it took, but when my vision cleared, the enormous, black cat, Kiera, stood before me. The cat shook herself hard, hissed, and ran inside.

I dodged, shut the door, then turned to the cat. "Kay?"

The cat jumped into the seat of the armchair and from there, to its wide, green velvet-covered back. The kittens mewed and tried to claw their way up. Kiera gave a plaintive meow.

"Kay?" I asked again.

Kiera tilted her head and nodded once. "Yerrrow."

I felt stupid talking to a cat. *Wait, Kay's a cat?*

I wouldn't have believed it, if I hadn't seen it with my

own eyes. The cat hissed as if she sensed my incredulity.

I shook my head in dazed wonder as Kiera gnawed on a claw and spit out a sheaf. "We'll have to clean that up, yes?" I asked.

The cat...chuffed?

I'd never seen a cat laugh before, but this one did. Kiera/Kay leapt off the chair. The kittens surrounded her. She gave each a lick, went to the door, and turned to look at me.

"Uh...okay."

I opened the door and Kiera padded out to the grass. The same fogginess occurred.

Instead of shrinking, the cat grew and the colors of Kay's skin and her clothing threaded in, obscuring the black until Kay stood before me.

She rushed back into the cottage, rubbing her arms. "Brrr!" She slipped her shoes back on. When I raised my eyebrows, she said, "I could have changed with them on. They would have just vanished and reappeared as my clothes did. It's just a bit easier and faster to shift if my body has some contact with the earth." She returned to her chair but set the knitting aside and scooped kittens into her lap until she had all of them. "Yes, they are mine. All cats are. No, they are not all like me."

"Okay." I backed until my legs met the cushions, and I collapsed onto the couch. "Kay...how, why?"

"I guess it's hereditary. Like being left handed? My family—we have this in our blood. My parents thought if they ignored it and refuted it, it would go away. I should have been raised to expect this, but I wasn't. Do you have any idea what it's like to turn into a cat and have no idea what's going on? Sorry, of course, you wouldn't. Just like I have no idea what it's like to have children."

I ducked my head and blushed.

"I tried to make a go of it on the mainland, but there

were too many questions," Kay said. "I do have control of my change, but if I go too long without changing, the change will assert itself. It is the way of the fae."

"So...what? Are you fae? And what is a fae?"

"Fae are magical beings. Don't ask me why, but at some point, a fae or fae with human blood thought it would be brilliant to turn into a cat and didn't think through to the consequences. It's genetic manipulation, I guess. And with fae blood, one can do this easily. Now undoing it—another story. Imagine this. It's easy to push a glass full of water over and watch it pour out, maybe direct the flow in a certain manner, but to take that glass, upright it, and put the water back? Now that is not easy."

"So...you're a cat...well, a part time cat?"

Kay stood tall and regal. "I'm no mere cat hybrid. I am of Cat Sith. We are fae royalty. When we choose to grant the courts our attendance, we are heralded and sit upon a throne."

"Wow—royal. We?"

"Actually, yes, it is."

"So, the night of the ceilidh, you didn't urge us to continue to the cottage because there was no danger, but so you could change into your cat form and attack the wolf."

"Yes. I'd hoped to dissuade it. As Kiera, we have crossed paths before with little or no incident. It's strange that the wolf was so determined and aggressive."

"That was very brave."

Kay shrugged. "Something about you and your daughters called to me. It entreated me to reach out to you. I hope my senses were not mistaken."

"I don't know anything about senses, okay, but I thought you were my friend because you liked me."

"We are friends. I do like you. But when we first met, it was curiosity that drew me."

"Curious as a cat?" I asked wryly. "Is that why you

decided to check me out as a kitty before meeting me as Kay?"

"If you continue to make cat jokes…" Kay warned.

"I'm just a little freaked out. I'm sorry."

"You can tell a lot about a person by seeing how they treat animals. I did, the times I came to you as Kiera. I saw you were a good person and wanted to get to know you better. We grew to become friends, just like any other women do. I've told you some of Greg's background. There's quite a bit more, and I believe you are wrapped up in it. I think he knows this, too, and expect he will share his secret with you soon."

"Do you know the secret? Wait, is he a fae too?"

"Greg isn't fae, and I know part of his secret, but not all of it. To be honest, I don't even know if he is allowed to talk about it."

"Allowed? What do you mean allowed?"

"There are…rules, I guess is the best way to explain it…for the fae. You don't break them. It isn't like running a stop sign at an empty street corner. Fae won't slap you on the wrist and fine you. Breaking fae rules comes with a greater cost."

"Wait a minute." I remembered something that Greg had said about Mr. Samms and his son. "The Samms—they have fae blood too. Were my girls in any danger there?"

"No, Becca. They are good people."

"No, they're fairies."

"The Good People *are* fairies—or fae, as we prefer."

"So, somehow my coming to the island changed things here. Well, there's a simple answer. The girls and I can pack up and leave. We should easily be able to catch the last ferry back to the mainland."

"I don't know if that would help. Indeed, it may make things worse."

"What do you suggest then? The weather is crazy—weird things are coming from the forest. There has got to be something I can do."

"I believe it will take the efforts of you and Greg to set things rights."

"Well, it will be hard for me to help if he won't tell me anything about what's going on."

"He can't tell you until he recognizes and accepts what is happening."

"Now, you're going all weird on me again. Not like you haven't been since I've arrived, but it's getting old—the not getting any useful answers."

"I'm sorry, Becca, I am. Know that I am your friend, and I will help you in any way I can." Kay tapped her chin. "There may be someone I can talk to and find out more. I don't like to visit her, though."

"Why, is she one of those bad things?"

"Not exactly. I think she's so unlike humans, even half humans, that she can't quite relate and speaking to her may not give us the results we want."

"Would it help if I came with you?"

"No, I fear that would make it worse. At least I know what to expect and how to act."

I looked at my phone and was unsurprised to find a blank screen. The battery life seemed shorter on the island than the mainland. "What time is it?"

Kay gestured to an old analog clock on the mantle. It seemed to be keeping time, at least. It was drawing close to the time I needed to get to the bus stop to meet the girls. "I need to go. The girls will be waiting on me. I hope the weather is better at the village than here."

"Let me give you a ride so you don't have to stand in the rain."

I gratefully accepted. Kay's car was old and very reluctant to start, but the engine finally turned over. The windshield wipers did more smearing than clearing off the water. She had to turn the lights on and drove very slowly on the muddy lane. Mentally, I urged her to drive faster, even though I knew it was safer to be cautious. I didn't want to be late.

※※※

The girls beat us to the tea shop. I guess Jess hadn't heard me when I told her to wait at the library. Good thing I saw them through the window. Thankfully, Fiona had an extra umbrella and let them borrow it and oversized raincoats from the lost and found. Their feet, however, were soaked. They both seemed to be in good moods. Marnie had served them hot chocolate and scones.

I really wanted them to eat a proper lunch *then* have scones. I would have complained but this was turning out to be a weird day. Tate appeared so much better since Greg had rid her of that thing, and I hoped Jessie and my relationship would improve since she was vindicated when we saw the creature.

Tate waved at me. "Hey, Mom!" Her hair was damp and drying into ringlets. Jess had braided her own back in the morning.

"I hope you didn't drive the librarian nuts." It just occurred to me that perhaps Courtney would prefer that parents accompany their children when visiting. Even after a year, I wasn't always sure how I should behave. About the time I thought I had Scottish customs down, I would do something abysmally stupid or unthinking. The Scots would be understanding, but tsk to each other and, I knew, later speak of "that American."

A grin lit up my baby girl's face. "There wasn't anybody there, Mom. Mrs. Campbell let me help her unbox some brand-new books that just came in and guess what?"

"What, Tate?"

She gestured to her sister who opened the back pack she brought and handed her sister a stack of novels. "I'm the first person to *ever* check these books out!"

"Good for you, Tate!"

She chattered and waved the books at me, until I finally took them and returned them to Jess, admonishing Tate that she would end up with clotted cream on them if she didn't stop.

"What were you up to in the meantime, Jess?"

"I've been doing some research. I want to go back and read some more after we eat."

"I don't know about that, honey. What are you researching?"

"Just curious about some folklore I read a bit about."

I wanted to ask more, but was afraid my curiosity would, rather than encourage her, make her decide to forgo the library completely, so I let it go for now. "The weather's atrocious. Kay has offered to take us back home. If this downpour continues, I don't want you stuck waiting at the bus stop and walking home." Then the sky made lie of my words by the rain abruptly stopping and the sun burning the clouds away in a matter of moments.

"Odd weather we've been having today," Marnie said bringing a pot of tea and without asking. "What else will you be having?"

I ordered one of all the sandwich types available. There wasn't that big a choice, and I thought it might be nice to share. I vowed to treat Kay to the meal. Sure enough, the girls had spoiled their appetites with the scones and barely touched the sandwiches, so we could take them back and finish them off for dinner. I wondered about stopping by the grocer to get some chips to go with but dreaded seeing Conall and didn't want Kay to have to wait on me. This dilemma was solved when Kay asked if it was okay if we stopped by there before she took us back. She had some items she wanted to pick up. Certain favorites ran out fast, and she knew Conall was expecting some stock on today's morning ferry.

CHAPTER 17

Funny what Scots thought were "specialty" items. Often some staples that we took for granted in the States were unusual and exotic here, especially in small towns and villages. No doubt getting Jif or marshmallow crème was much easier in London. We hadn't spent much time there, and it was on my list of things to do before going back home. I had rented my house out and had a friend keeping an eye on it. When I left, I wasn't sure where I would end up, but I wanted to keep my options open. The rent had helped with the more expensive clothes and such sold here. I was okay with the clothing situation, but Tate had gone through two growth spurts and even Jess, I suspected, had a bit more growing to do. Her body had yet to fill out in more womanly curves. She had been slow to menstruate and was still blossoming. And, yes, if I shared that with anyone, she would kill me—or pout for a year.

When our items were packaged up, we stepped outside to find it almost dry. We shed our coats and left them in the car, hoping the rain wouldn't return. The forecast hadn't predicted the weather correctly thus far. An older American couple came in shortly after us, soaking wet and grumbling about being stuck on this teeny island with nothing to do and no way to get back to the mainland for hours. They had holed up in the church during the rain and made their way here when the sky cleared up. Hopefully, they would have a more pleasant time in the next couple of hours before the ferry arrived. I knew the island needed the tourism. When we reached the grocery, it was quiet and dark. I tried the door. It was unlocked. "Do you think they blew a fuse?" I asked.

Kay shook her head and gripped the doorway as she peered into the unlit store. "Maybe I'll just come back another day," she said. "I don't see anyone here to help us anyway."

Just then, we heard a crash from the back of the building and a scratching sound.

"Mr. McNeil?" I called out. "Is everything okay?"

The girls had preceded us in and Tate rushed down the candy aisle, collecting several different chocolates which she would, no doubt, insist she *had* to have.

Suddenly the light blinked on and off then stayed on. "They must be working on the fuses. They should be in pretty soon," I said hopefully. I didn't like it, though. "With his nephew helping out, you would think someone would be here while the other worked on the fuse."

"Mom, can I try this?" Tate waved a new candy at me.

"I guess, Tate. Please don't go overboard, though. Too much rich food after an illness will make you sick."

She hadn't exactly had an illness, but I didn't know what to call what happened. Tate skipped back to the counter and unloaded her arms. She was very spontaneous. Jess was taking more time with her selections. Kay wasted no time in finding the foreign foods aisle where the American foods resided and loaded up a basket she found at the door. I picked up a few more things, since we were here, and I was trying not to make as many trips. I heard another crash. It seemed to be coming from the basement. I remembered what was there. The silver and the cage. *Uh oh.* Surely Conall wasn't in the middle of some weird sexcapade when the storm messed things up. "Surely not," I muttered.

"What?" Kay asked.

"Oh, nothing. Or I'll tell you about it later."

Jess looked up and rolled her eyes at me, recognizing my code for "not in front of the children." Tate, blissfully unaware, decided in which order she would eat her sweets. Thuds came from the basement as if several someones were coming up the stairs. The door was shut, but as I watched, the handle bobbed up and down erratically.

"Mr. McNeil, are you okay?" I asked.

We froze when we heard a low growl. The door shook as something rammed into it hard.

Staring at the door, Jess backed up toward me. "Oh, shit!"

I had never heard her say anything stronger than shards. "Jess!"

"Sorry, Mom."

The door reverberated with another hard bump, and the lever jiggled again, almost turning far enough to open but not quite.

Tate arranged her candies at the counter. Only a few feet stood between her and the door.

"Tate, just leave it. I think we should go."

"But, Mom! I want to try this new bar!" The candy slid from her fingers and plopped onto the counter top.

Kay rushed forward and swept the goods into her basket. "Come on, let's go *now*!"

"But what about paying?" Tate gaped at Kay but followed, needing to jog to keep up with Kay's long strides.

"We can pay later," Kay assured her.

As I held my basket, undecided, I searched for Jess. "Jess!" I called.

When she crept beside me and brushed my arm, I flinched.

Jessie's hand trembled on my shoulder. "Mom?"

The door flew open with a bang. Two wolves burst from the basement, tumbling over each other in their haste to get out. The smallest jumped on top of the counter. The larger one slinked out from behind it. That wolf, all black except its gray legs and muzzle, bared its teeth. The wolves were huge. Even the small brindled one looked like it outweighed me. I glanced back. Kay and Tate had reached the exit and waited for us. I froze, inanely torn between leaving money on the counter, maybe a note, or just leaving.

"Becca, Jessie. Come now!"

The panic in Kay's voice and Jess's tug on my arm decided me. The hackles raised on both animals, making them appear even larger. The smaller one sniffed the air then howled. He leapt to the floor, putting him mere feet away from Jess and me. Jessie gasped as I pushed her behind me.

"Back out slowly," I whispered as I tried to remember what you were supposed to do around a wild dog.

My mind went blank. I wanted to run, but I didn't want my back exposed to them. My eyes darted back and forth at the shelves, hoping to find a broom or something. As I crept back, my hand brushed the items on the shelves.

"Here, doggie, come here!" Jessie called.

I turned. Jessie had snuck to the next aisle and torn open a package of tuna. She waved it to get the wolf's attention.

"Jessica! Get to the door!" I squeaked, managing not to yell. *No freaking out the wolves, Becca.*

I couldn't see the large one, but said a quick prayer that it found the meat department. The smaller wolf sniffed and weaved around to the aisle where Jess stood. I backed more quickly and sidestepped to reach her just as the wolf did. Jess placed the package in the center of the aisle and backed away.

"Good doggie—you're a good doggie. Tuna is way better than icky people," Jessie crooned.

The wolf sniffed the fish and then lapped up some. Something bumped my hip. I wheeled around. The other wolf had flanked us. This time I couldn't contain myself and shrieked. The wolves shied, their claws chattered on the tile as they scrambled back. I swallowed an eep.

"Go!" I shoved Jessie toward the door where Tate and Kay waited, Tate's hands gesturing for us to come. I raced after Jess.

"We tried to get your attention, but we didn't want to startle the wolf," Kay said as she threw open the door.

The girls ran out. Kay and I fled seconds later. Just as I was pulling the door closed, the larger wolf leapt up, hitting it, and slammed it shut. The wolf rested its front paws on the wood and stared through the glass at us with intelligence showing in the dark eyes. Raising its head, it let out a spine-chilling howl.

"What in the world are wolves doing in the grocery? Do you think Mr. McNeil and Lundy are okay?" I asked.

Kay's eyes didn't meet mine as she played with the strap of her purse. "They're fine, I think," she postulated.

Suspicious, I said, "Those look like the same ones we saw earlier. Kay, what do you know about this?"

Kay shrugged. "I know that wolves shouldn't be in the village. And these wolves weren't acting wolfish."

I fished out my phone, but it still had no bars. "Is there any way that they can get out?"

"I don't think so. There's a back door, but surely the

grocer keeps it locked. Anyway, wolves can't open doors."

After poking buttons on the phone with no results, I tossed it back into my purse with a grunt. "We can't just leave. What if someone comes to buy something? They would walk right in on those animals. We need to contact the police or animal control or somebody so they can be captured and taken back to the forest." Kay and Jess checked their phones with the same results that I had. "Kay, why don't you walk to the station? We can stay and make sure no one enters."

"No, I'll stay. You take the girls to the station. They look pretty shook up."

I studied at the girls. Tate didn't seem to understand the danger we had been in and was excitedly watching the wolves eat the tuna. Jess was proud that she had done something to distract them enough for us to leave. Neither seemed upset. I had the feeling that Kay wanted us away, but I wasn't going to argue with her.

"Okay, we'll be back as soon as we can."

"Can't we stay, Mom?" Tate pleaded.

"No, honey. I think Kay's right that it would be better for you two to come with me. Watching them may unnerve them, and I don't know how strong those wolves are. There's a possibility that they could break the glass and get out if antagonized."

Tate pouted for a few moments but quickly forgot the issue when I let her try one of the new candies she had chosen. Their appetites were ruined so much that she might not even want dinner, considering the sweets she had eaten. With all that sugar, I wasn't surprised that she skipped ahead of us, bursting with energy. While Jessie retold the details of what happened, I kept my responses to noncommittal "Uh, huhs," my mind busy wrestling with why Kay would want us gone. We reached the station and, in short order, were escorted back to the store by Constable Ian Gow, a ginger who didn't look old enough to shave. Kay wasn't in front. And the door was open. "Oh, no!" I was torn between running to check for Kay and staying back in case the wolves were close.

"Stay here," the constable said and cautiously moved to the door. He looked in then turned back and smiled at us. "It's safe!" he called out.

When we reached the store, we saw Kay with Conall and his nephew cleaning up the tuna and the few items that had been knocked to the floor when the animals ran down the aisles.

When I reached Kay, I asked, "What happened to the animals?"

She busied herself with digging in her purse to pay for her items. "Conall and Lundy returned. They had run out to check on Aunt Mornia. I told them about the wolves but, when we investigated, they had vanished. Conall checked and he said the back door was open. He said he must have forgotten about it in his haste to see to his aunt, and the wolves must have left that way."

"But how did they get inside in the first place?"

"Probably the same way."

Maybe, but how did they get shut up in the basement?

Kay went to the counter, paid, and packed up her purchases along with mine.

"Wait, Kay! You don't have to pay for ours."

"It's no trouble at all. I don't know about you, but with all this excitement, I'm anxious to just get home, put my feet up, and have a cuppa."

The police talked to Conall while Lundy gave Kay her change.

Lundy reached for a rag and polished the counter. "Hi, Jessica. I hope you weren't so scared that you won't want to come back to the store to shop," he said.

"I don't scare that easily," Jess said airily. "They may have just been very large dogs. They seemed awfully tame to me. Now you—are you going to be too afraid to come to work because of the scary doggies?"

I frowned. Jess was being a real pill, and she needed to stop it. She didn't have to be rude to discourage him.

Conall's nephew was rightfully indignant. "They were two wolves and the biggest wolves in the forest, I warrant!" he protested.

"How would you know? You weren't even here. Why did both you and your uncle have to go, anyway?" Jess retorted.

Lundy said nothing and rubbed harder at the spotless countertop.

I intervened. "They were wolves, Jessica." I agreed with Jessie, they were acting suspicious, but poking at Lundy wouldn't get us any answers. I gave her a meaningful look and frowned.

She rolled her eyes at me. "Fine, I guess they were wolves. It was weird that they would come into a grocer. I could see them trying to get into the butcher shop, but why a grocer?"

"I guess we'll never know," Kay said.

The constable and Conall finished up and said goodbye to each other.

When Conall came to the counter, I asked, "How's your aunt?"

He scratched his head. "What?"

Kay cleared her throat. "She's fine. It was a false alarm." She tilted her head at Conall. "Right, Conall?"

His eyebrows raised as some unspoken communique occurred. "Oh, right." Turning to me, he said, "My mind's in a muddle. We've never had wolves in the store before."

My eyes narrowed as I studied the two of them. "Hopefully, they won't return."

"Ready?" Kay asked, bright as a Barbie doll.

We said goodbye and Kay drove us back to the cottage.

CHAPTER 18

The kitten greeted us at the door, and Tate cuddled her up as soon as she could.

I wanted to see if I could tease more information from Kay. "Would you like to join us for some tea?" I asked when she sorted the groceries, leaving my items on the table.

Kay bundled up her goods and slipped the bag over her wrist. "No thanks. I have a few things I want to get done before I have that cuppa."

The lame excuse tasked me. A Scot never turned away tea. "Okay…well, thank you for the ride." I walked her to the car. "Those wolves—Conall and Lundy, are they like you?" I waited, but Kay didn't answer. She didn't even look at me as she busied herself carefully putting her items on the passenger seat. I grabbed her shoulder. When she turned, I asked, "You can shift into a cat. You said you are Cat Sith. Are they Wolf Sith?"

"Don't be silly, Becca. There's no such thing as Wolf Sith." She absentmindedly said goodbye. I watched her back out.

When I got back inside, Jess said, "Mom, I think Lundy and Mr. McNeil were lying. What do you think is really going on with those wolves?"

I patted Jessie's hand. "I'm not sure. I've asked Kay about it but haven't gotten much in the way of answers. Can you help me with the groceries?"

Tate wanted to read her book, so I told her she could as long as she helped get dinner ready.

As we put up the groceries, I tried to broach the subject of Conall's nephew again. "Jess, you really need to stop baiting the boy. It isn't nice." *And I'm still not convinced he isn't some sort of shapeshifter, despite what Kay said. But, surely, if they were dangerous, she'd tell me.*

A can thumped when Jessie slammed it in the pantry. "Well, he isn't very nice. When we were over at the Samms', Nessa came over to ride. Her horse is boarded there. She was still upset about the dance, Mom. Lundy really hurt her feelings. Gavin felt bad for her, too."

When she came back to the table, I nudged her with my elbow to get her full attention. "Sometimes teenagers are so busy focused on themselves that they say things without thinking. Also, when you live in a small town and you're around the same people all the time, it can be hard for someone to see another person as a prospective date. That girl and that boy have probably been raised together, almost like siblings."

Jessie sighed. "I'm sorry. I guess I should have been nicer. I just talked to Nessa yesterday and it made me so sad, and mad, to see her practically cry over the dummy."

"Well, you insulting him and being a snot isn't going to make him like her."

"I suppose not."

"He'll eventually see the young woman she now is and decide to ask her out—or not. Boys tend to mature slower than girls."

A gust of air escaped Jessie's lips as she sat at the table. "If I were her, I would say no, even if he *did* ask me out, but I bet she would say yes. She just kept saying there must be something wrong with her and asking me what she should do to make him like her. If a boy treated me like that, I wouldn't be wondering what was wrong with me. There would be something wrong with him, and then I wouldn't want to go out with him anyway."

I sat across from her. "You know, everyone makes mistakes, Jess. As you get older and start dating, I'm sure you'll mess up along the way."

Jess stubbornly shook her head, and I let the conversation go.

"What were you researching at the library?" I asked as a topic change.

"Oh, I was thinking about what Mr. Gillie said about the thing that I saw…well, the things, the one that led Tate into the woods and the one that he sent away. I wanted to see if I could find any books to read up on it. I thought there might be something about how to get rid of them."

"What did you find out?"

"Well, I found several books, and the librarian helped me find some others. Most of them are pretty old and some bits are boring. I kinda skipped around with the reading. I haven't found anything that sounds like either of the things, so I guess I need to just begin at the beginning and read them all. I'll probably need to check them out again. There's no way I'll get through all of them before they need to be returned."

"If you want, I can help you." I knew that, while Jess was quite a capable reader, she really wasn't fond of it and found reading a chore.

"Really? I thought you might think it was silly. You know, reading stupid fairy tales."

"Learning something new is never silly or stupid. When I was young, I loved fairy tales."

"The librarian gave me some adult books and some very old fairy tales. I started with the fairy tales. I thought they would be easy to read since they were written for children, but, Mom, these fairy tales aren't like the Disney movies. Some of them read more like a horror shows."

I rubbed my bottom lip as a mélange of childhood memories shuffled through my mind. "She must have pulled out some of the original *Brothers Grimm*. The tales those films are based on are often very violent."

"You've read them?"

"Not all, of course, but some."

"Also, some of the books are about Scottish tales and creatures."

"Tell you what, we can sit down and pour through it. I'm thinking maybe the library is a good place to study, with internet access going on and off." I waited and Jess nodded. I knew she would be checking up on it much more frequently than I would. "At least there, we have other references we can use. I'm kind of old school with research. Just about anyone can put something up on the internet that isn't true."

Jess rolled her eyes. "Tell me about it. You still read books."

Someone knocked on the door. And it wasn't Kay's usually tap, tappity, tap, but an almost tentative rap. We looked at each other, and I shrugged, not having a clue who would be visiting. I rose and opened the door. To my surprise, Greg stood shifting from one foot to the other.

"Good afternoon, Rebecca. I hope I'm not interrupting anything."

"No. Jess and I were just putting up some groceries. Come in." I moved to the right at the same time he moved to the right to walk inside and then, we exchanged grins and both of us moved to the left, doing an odd dance. Jess snorted. I felt my face redden.

"Mom, I'm going to my room to read some more. Will you be in soon to help?" Her voice raised meaningfully on the word *help*.

"In a few, honey."

Jessie flounced off to her room. I also apparently needed to speak to Jess about trying to restrict my social life. *Social life?* The poor man had never asked me out. I didn't know why I was being so silly. He was handsome but hadn't shown any more interest in me than anyone else. Not really.

Greg slipped round me and shut the door. "I am interrupting something. Sorry."

"No, no you aren't. Have a cup of tea." I busied myself at the sink. "I'm glad you're here. I have a question."

"I willna take much of your time. I wanted to see how you were. I expect where you come from, you rarely have *power outages*." He said the last two words slowly, as if he wasn't accustomed to the term. I supposed if he lived in the rough in the woods, he wouldn't have much experience with it.

Greg looked at me expectantly.

I realized I had missed the last thing he said. "Sorry, I was gathering wool. Could you repeat that?"

"You said you had a question. What's on your mind?"

"It's nothing really." *Perhaps I can get him to talk about this.* "Actually, it involves you, in a way."

"What do you mean?"

"Yesterday, when you got rid of that thing that was hurting Tate, it made Jess curious. So, she went to the library to try and find more information about it. I told her I would help her with her research. In fact, I should thank you. She never reads unless she has to for a school assignment. It's nice to see her reaching for books without being coerced into it."

"'Tis odd. These are not creatures that appear many places or very often. Places less populated, as this island, tend to draw the fae. Even here—"

"Even here what?"

"There are constraints in place to prevent men from seeing or having contact with them." I wanted to ask him more about that, but he quickly continued. "The storm and the odd weather we had earlier—I came to check and see if you and the lasses were all right."

"We're fine, but thank you for checking on us." I brought the sugar, cream, cups, saucers, and spoons to the table. "The tea shouldn't take long."

"You really didna need to trouble yourself, but thank you."

"It's okay. I've lived in Scotland long enough for the practice to grab hold." Unable to stop myself from asking, I said, "I'm curious about your home. It is unusual for someone to live alone like you do—off the grid."

"Off the grid?"

"I mean, without the usual conveniences of electricity, plumbing, and the like. Kay mentioned your living circumstances."

"Aye, I suppose so, especially to someone from the New World like you."

"Do you think..." *In for a penny, in for a pound.* "...do you think I might be able to visit some time?" His face went blank, and I was afraid I had insulted him or been too much of a brash American. I continued. "I mean, I know you like your privacy. I wouldn't dream of imposing. I just thought—I used to camp quite a bit." *Great, Becca, way to sound like a blonde.*

The tea was ready, so I prepared the pot and strew some biscuits on a plate to give him time to compose himself.

"Well, I supposed I could take you to my place."

I noted he did not say his home.

"I havena had many visitors. I'm not sure what you would think of it. 'Tis quite rustic and simple."

I want to see if you're a crazy survivalist. "Oh, I was curious to see how much your home differed from...say...the cabin we stayed in during our last camping trip. What kind of permanent arrangements have you made? How do you minimize the ecological footprint?"

"That term is unfamiliar to me."

"How you take care not to harm the earth or the animals around you."

"Oh."

There was an awkward pause. I poured the tea, put the kettle back on the stove, and picked up the biscuits. "Cookies," I said over-brightly. I spun back to the table too fast and several of the shortbreads flew off the plate. Almost faster than I could see, Greg's hand snatched all three from the air.

"I'm sorry," I said, flustered.

"No harm done." He placed the cookies in a circle around the edge of his saucer and sipped his tea.

"You're a leftie," I noted. "So is Tate."

"Aye, cack-handed. Though my mother tried to train it out of me, I just couldna write as well with the other. Finally, me mum just let me be about it."

"Well, it can be difficult in a world set up for righties. Perhaps your mother thought it would make life easier for you if you were like everyone else."

Greg sipped his tea. "How has your visit been?"

I chuckled. "You mean outside the weird weather, the energy leech, a come and go horse, a ghostly lady by a pool, and large wolves in the grocery?" I was not going to mention the creatures in the pool that tried to drown me. I wasn't sure I didn't imagine that myself, and Greg had been pulling my leg with the grindylows explanation.

He added a teaspoon of sugar to his tea. "Aye. I guess this has been a visit full of surprises. Did you see the wolves again, only in the village?"

"Kay, the girls, and I went to the grocery to pick some things up. Two huge wolves came up from the basement. Maybe they were just scared and looking for a way out, but they came at us, growling. Before, they've always shown up near the forest. You seem to have some sort of power over them."

"Not power, exactly. They just have a healthy respect for me. How did you get away?"

I stirred my tea to cool it. "We were close to the door, and Jess distracted them with some tuna."

Greg rubbed his chin. "An odd time to see wulvers, that."

"What did you call them?"

"Wolves."

I let it go, but that wasn't what he said. I shook my head. "We think they escaped out the back door because when Conall and Lundy came back from checking on their aunt, the wolves were gone. I'm not sure I believe that."

"I'll look into it. Though we are not on the best of terms, I may check on the grocer and his nephew."

"Do you think Conall and his nephew are—"

Before I could finish the question, Greg interrupted. "I said I would look into it. Dinna fash yourself."

So much for getting anything out of him about it.

"What happened between you and Conall, if you don't mind me asking?"

"Ancient history. I married the lass that a McNeil wanted."

"He was interested in your wife? A Mr. McNeil?"

"He was and was quite mad about losing out, even though the lass never gave him reason to think the attraction was mutual. Scots have long memories and Conall continues to begrudge me."

"Seems to run in the family," I muttered. He tilted his head. I shrugged. "I mean the pursuit of a woman who doesn't return the man's affection."

"Oh? How so?"

"Conall's nephew seems to be hot for Jess, and she isn't interested. He won't take the hint. I wonder if some men never get over not getting the woman of their dreams, and it makes them socially awkward, or maybe they are socially awkward and that's why they didn't get the woman of their dreams," I mused.

"Perhaps," Greg agreed.

Jess poked her head around the corner. "Mom, are you coming?"

Tate appeared beside her. "Yes, Mom. I need help with…" She looked at Jess.

"You need help with that word you don't know the meaning of and I don't either," Jess filled in as she nudged Tate. I could tell that Tate had been put up to it.

Greg ate the last bite of his last cookie and finished his tea. "I thank you, Rebecca. I'll think about your request. I value the sanctity of my home."

"I hope I didn't offend…"

"Not at all."

I opened the door for him.

He took my hand again, and I think he was going to kiss it, but caught sight of my no-doubt-glaring oldest and just squeezed it. "Ta."

"Goodbye." As soon as I shut the door, I turned to Jess. "Okay, what do you have against Greg? You were just talking about how he helped us earlier with the soul leech thing."

"I don't have anything against him. I just think it's a little too early for you to be—"

"Be what?" Tate asked, oblivious to what Jess was about.

"Greg's a friend and, though I'll admit he's a bit strange, he's done nothing to warrant your distrust and hostility."

"Well, sometimes he seems a little too friendly."

I realized that I hadn't had another male in my home other than the relatives after David had died. I guess Jess was protective and seemed resentful of my replacing her father. I would have to address that. I wasn't sure how I felt about Greg, but I did like him, despite his strange ways. A summer flirtation may be just what the doctor ordered. It wasn't as if I could have anything more. We would leave in time for school to start. But for the first time in a long time, I felt attractive and desired. It was time for me to shed the metaphorical widow weeds.

೭ೂಲ

I pored over tracts from the tourist agency. I read about a park opened to the public, which had guided cave tours. Over dinner, I discussed it with the girls, and we planned to visit it the next morning if the weather was nice. When I told Jess I could help her with her research, she shoved the books into her backpack and told me she would continue it another day—probably to punish me. I had hoped to peruse the books in the evening after she slept, but Tate wanted to play a game. One game turned into several and, by the time the girls were in bed, I was more than ready myself.

I slipped into my short sleeved, V-necked nightgown, the bottom of which had small slits on each side and the skirt floated down to just above my knees. On the front was a large book case with the words "I'd rather be reading." I sighed as I looked in the mirror. I could barely read the tee's faded letters and the hem sagged on one side. I used to have some beautiful gowns and teddies, but when David died, I couldn't stand wearing them. The girls bought me this nightie for Mother's Day a few years back. It was my summer nightie. I had flannel pants and shirt pajamas for winter that were so generic that a boy could wear them and be totally secure with his masculinity. Maybe I'd do a little shopping on the mainland later in the week. The girls could go to Mickey D's and we could see a movie. We tried to watch movies online, but with the internet problems, it proved to be too much trouble. I would ask the girls about it or maybe I would just tell them we were going. Ever since I made the executive decision to move to Aberdeen without consulting them first, I'd been trying to make it up to them. I thought my time of atonement was over.

CHAPTER 19

The next morning, true to her word, Jessie was up and out the door in time to catch the bus, aiming to be on the library steps waiting for Courtney and Fiona Campbell to open. Hopefully, not a long wait. I assumed they kept regular hours, but from my visits to the grocery store and the doctor's, I quickly discovered that popping out for a bit and leaving a sign was quite acceptable. If Jess had to cool her jets and wait, maybe she could aim her annoyance to that inconvenience, instead of keeping me in her crosshairs. For some reason, Jessie's phone failed to charge, so she left it plugged in at the cottage. I didn't like her being out of touch. The land lines continued to work, so I called Kay. Kay said she would be at the tea shop working if Jessie needed anything and that Jess was welcome to join her for lunch there. Then I called the library. After Fiona assured me that Jess could use the phone there, if necessary, she put my daughter, Jessie the Grouch, on the line so I could relay the news.

When I finished, Jess grunted and mumbled, "Sure."

Jess had left with a granola bar and a bottle of Coke—Breakfast of Champions. Though I'd planned a leisurely meal of French toast and milk, Tate bounced on her chair and barely finished one piece. She'd never been in a cave before. We'd take the bus to the cave formation which was locate near the shore on the other side of the island. The bus dropped tourists off near enough to walk to a small museum which contained artifacts from the cave.

The cave tours, which started at ten a.m. with the last one at two p.m., were scheduled every two hours. The tour had two sections, one accessible to people with less mobility and another section that went farther into the cavern that was more rigorous. I warned Tate that we may not be able to go as far into the cave as all the other tourists, but she was excited just to get to go in one at all. I sighed. I loved both my girls very much, but I related more with Tate. I knew that a part of it was age. Teenagers tended to test their limits. Jessie lost her dad, who she adored, during this stage of her life and was stuck with me as a single parent. I fully admitted that I stank at it. Focused on my own grief and taking on all that David had done, perhaps I hadn't addressed her loss as well as I should have. One of the reasons I chose to travel to the island cottage was to mend this breach.

The full bus disgorged many riders as we trundled through the cobblestone streets of the village, but we also picked up a few tourists bound for the cave. Two students from Spain, several older German couples, and an American family, who latched onto us as soon as they heard our accents, joined us. The American mother, like me, was of Scottish descent and the family was traveling throughout Scotland during the summer. The mother's professionally bleached hair hung just below her shoulders, and she wore a gray Patagonia hoodie. When her husband handed a brochure to her, I noticed his manicured nails. Prior to the birth of their children, the couple had visited to the UK but never ventured as far north as Scotland. Though the children, two boys, were younger than Tate, they seemed well behaved, thank goodness. Tate immediately regaled them with her stories of getting lost in the forest and being attacked by the energy-sucking creature. The parents spoke to me, but I could tell that they were listening to Tate too.

"My, your daughter certainly has an imagination. What a story!" the mother, whose name I had already forgotten, said.

Tate overheard her and paused. "Oh, it isn't a story. It really happened. Didn't it, Mom?"

I wasn't sure about how to address this and since I had been on the island with all the eccentric people, it hadn't dawned on me that people outside the island would think her accounts were made up. I wished I'd thought to talk to her about it beforehand.

One of the boys...Timmy, I think...asked, "Will the monster get us too?"

Tate had, unfortunately, told her tale as effectively as a certain individual on his one hundred and eleventh birthday and, like the children there, the boys were convinced of what she said. The mother played with the clasp on her purse, flipping it open and shut, open and shut, with her eyes on me.

I chuckled. "She's very imaginative. She is correct, though. She was very ill and had to see a doctor."

"Oh, but she didn't have some creepy creature attached to her that a Scottish gentleman banished, now did she?" asked the husband, whose name was Matt or Mark...something that began with the letter M, I thought. The two boys sat on the edge of their seats, goggle-eyed.

"She was very sick and bacteria can be considered a monster banished by our Scots doctor," I whispered to the parents then more loudly said, "Tate, honey, why don't you talk about something else? I think you're frightening the boys."

"Okay, Mom." She turned to the two boys. "You don't need to worry. You won't go near the woods, because it isn't safe, and there's something special about me and my family that attracts strange stuff." Then she told them about one of her field trips in Aberdeen, thankfully. I guess she realized that she needed to change topics. *Goodness, my little girl is growing up.*

The couple didn't press it and seemed to accept what I said. After the bus pulled to our stop, the door wheezed open. The bus driver informed us the time he would be back to pick up everyone and advised us not to be late. "I won't wait, and I won't be held responsible for anyone who neglects getting here on time," he cautioned.

We thanked him and, once the last passenger stepped out of the bus, he drove off.

"Rather dour, wasn't he?" the husband said.

His wife shrugged and smiled. "Well, he is Scottish."

The walk was as advertised—short, but rocky, and overgrown with wild flowers and nettles. I warned everyone to stay far away from them, but one German lady toddled into a thistle. She shrieked, and her arm soon turned bright red. I hoped the museum had a small medical kit. She complained the rest of the way there, sounding like a snarling Schnauzer. Her husband pulled a linty toffee from his pocket and gave it to her. The caramel stuck her teeth together, and the husband slyly turned to wink at the rest of us.

Our timing was perfect. I assumed that the various tourist sites consulted with the bus service to make sure they could keep to their schedule. A short woman with fair skin and wispy hair, who introduced herself as Greer Ogg, greeted us. She ushered us inside the building and took her place behind a desk labeled *Admissions*. I paid our entry fees, and we sat on a bench as we waited. Once everyone had paid, Mrs. Ogg announced that a tour guide would be with us shortly. We hadn't waited long when a young lady opened a door marked *No Admittance*. Her hair was white and, when she closed the door, tendrils curled and uncurled like fog about her shoulders. I would have thought she was an albino, so fair and pale, except her eyes were a blue-gray, so dark as to be almost black. She seemed flustered and spoke to Mrs. Ogg for such a time that I worried that there was something wrong at the museum. Mrs. Ogg seemed to be reassuring her. Eventually, the young lady stood in front of the desk to address us.

"Hello, my name is Davina Ogg please call me Davina." She gestured to her name tag. "And yes, this is a family-run establishment. You've already met my mother. The displays are under glass, but I ask that you look only. I'm almost out of Windex."

We dutifully laughed at the comment.

"After a brief tour of thirty minutes, you will be taken through the caves. Depending on what group you're in, you should return here in anywhere between thirty minutes and an hour. The first half of the tour is very easy. The decline is slight and there are rails to hold onto along the way. The second part of the tour is more rigorous. My brother, Fingal, may take some of you farther, depending on your interest and ability."

"I want to see the entire cave!" one of the Spanish girls called out. "I do have some experience in spelunking." Her accent would have been enchanting had she not taken a snooty tone.

"I'll let my brother know, but he decides who continues and who returns. Of course, if you don't want to go, you won't be required to."

The young lady looked as if she was about to protest,

but her companion spoke to her in Spanish. They giggled at whatever she said as Davina led us into a large room with several display cases. One contained a map showing the known tunnels that ran through the cave.

"These are the tunnels which we have mapped out. This cave system is quite extensive and parts are dangerous. There's much that we haven't been able to access." She waited a moment for us to look at it and then moved onto the next exhibit. "These are some of the artifacts we found in the cave. The skulls, we believe, are from people who were sacrificed. Ritual objects were discovered with them and bone chipping indicated they were murdered. It's said that deep down in the cave, there lives a goblin. As long as she is happy and people stay out of her home, she will remain where she is, and the island will prosper. If her domain is violated, there will be death."

"Have there been any deaths in the cave more recent than these?" the snooty girl with spelunking experience asked.

"Yes, there have been a few. Three teens on vacation snuck into the cave ten years ago, and they were never found."

"Oh, come now, you are just trying to make the caves interesting and scare us so your brother won't have to take us all the way through," one of the Spanish girls said and rolled her eyes at the other.

"You did ask," Davina pointed out and spoke about more of the relics found.

One glass display case held tools and bits of clothing made from animal hides. There were also items that were thought to be gifts to the goblin. Plates, that Davina said may have held food, and empty sacks.

"I'll bet someone just snuck in after the sacrifices and stole whatever was left, making everyone think there was some goblin," one Spanish girl commented in English, loud enough to be heard.

"Perhaps so," Davina said, completely unruffled. "We shall probably never know for sure."

As Davina led us through the building, she told us more about the original settlers and what their lives were like, given what had been found and by extrapolating. The last ten minutes, Davina allowed us to explore the whole of the museum and focus on what exhibits we were most interested in as she looked on. A young man, sharing Davina's white hair and dark eyes, entered and motioned to the tour guide. They spoke for a few moments, then he left.

"If you're all ready and want to see the caves, now is the time to go. If you choose not to come and don't want to remain here, you may wait at the café where we'll meet up afterward."

The German lady with the plant rash had been given some anti-itch ointment that must have worked because the only time she scratched was when she noticed someone was looking at her. I felt sorry for her poor husband, but he was a good-natured sort and patted her, making reassuring murmurs when she told him she would rather not go. Another German lady also declined attending the cave tour and said she would accompany the wife to the café. Before he joined us, the husband kissed his wife goodbye. I heard the American couple discussing the venture. She was fine with the boys going, but he was resistant. When they realized everyone was waiting on them, the wife asked Davina, "Do you think the boys can manage the trip? I don't think I'm strong enough to carry them and my husband has back issues."

"They should be fine. The first part of the trip is only fifteen minutes in and fifteen minutes out and, as I mentioned, it is very gently sloped. We'll be stopping several times for me to point out some features, and there are places to sit at some of the stops. We haven't ever lost anyone yet."

The German wife looked at the husband and took a step toward him.

He waved her back. "See, I'll be fine, dear," he said.

As the boys chattered and teased each other, Tate practically danced in anticipation. Seeing her so enthusiastic, brought home how unlike herself she'd been acting while that energy-sucking thing leeched from her. Smiling, I gave her a hug. She returned both.

We stepped outside. Davina admonished us not to walk ahead of the lead guide. If anyone did so, they would be escorted back to the top and the second part of the tour would be canceled since they would be one guide short. *Nothing like peer pressure to get people to behave.* I thought.

Once we stepped outside, Davina introduced her brother, Fingal. The young Spanish girls quickly latched onto him. While his coloring was almost as pale as his sister's, I had to admit he was attractive in a striking way.

The senoritas crowded directly behind Fingal, then the American family and Tate and I fell in line, followed by the elderly crew. A switchback trail zigzagged down. Thanks to the rain, it was a bit slick, but manageable. The Spanish girls chattered at Fingal whose answers were monosyllables. The young man forced the girls to wait for the rest of us at each turn. Davina and her brother shared glances and frowned as the young girls chattered obnoxiously. As the senoritas wove down the path, they turned back and forth to take in their surroundings and narrowly missed hitting Tate with their backpacks twice.

When a backpack hit one of the little boys hard enough to send him into his father, the man gripped the backpack's strap as he said, "Hey!"

The girl whirled around, one corner of her mouth raised in a snarl.

Not an attractive look, I thought.

"You need to be careful with that thing," the father said with his hand on his son's shoulder. "You almost knocked that little girl down twice already, and you just hit my son with it."

One of the girls poked her friend and snickered. "Well, just walk a bit farther back."

Before the father could respond with what I was sure were going to be some harsh words, Davina said, "The backpacks will need to be left outside the cave."

"But they have our passports and money!" one girl protested.

"They're too large and will get in the way. If you intend to go farther into the cavern with them, you wouldn't be able to get through some of the tight spots. Size is one of the factors that Fingal considers when deciding who to take farther and who to send back. Plus, the gentleman is correct, wearing them and not being ever-aware when moving is perilous. You wouldn't want to knock someone down into a sinkhole, would you?"

The girls looked ready to complain again, but Davina had one last thing to add to close the conversation. "There's a locker where we have spelunking equipment. We can lock your backpacks in there where they'll be perfectly safe."

The path ended at the mouth of the cave. The girls reluctantly gave over their bags, which Fingal locked into a chest. Small lights hung from the top of the tunnel. Davina and her brother carried flashlights. Fingal led us into the cave, which turned sharply to the left and narrowed quite a bit, but not claustrophobically so, at least not to me. After walking for a few minutes, the Spanish girls complained about not seeing anything and wanted to know how much longer they would have to walk down the tunnel.

I admitted to being a bit disappointed but kept it to myself. Tate passed the time by chattering with the two boys. She told them about the Samms and the horseback riding.

The boys' mother turned to me. "Did you think it was worthwhile to go riding? Was it safe?"

"I believe so. My oldest daughter enjoyed it so much that she's going there to help out some while we're here."

"So, you actually live on the island?"

"Yes, we rented a cottage."

"We're only here for the day, but if you have the information, I'd like to call and set it up."

"No need to call. We were told to just go over. The boys can meet and feed the horses and other farmyard animals like ducks, chickens, and cows, if you decide you would rather not have them ride. Tate and her sister both took riding lessons in the States. I should look into riding lessons for them in Aberdeen when we get back there."

We talked about Scotland and the differences between here and the US. The small lights illuminated, but not enough to give a view very far down the tunnel. We heard a gasp before we saw anything. Then the tunnel opened up into a chamber. As we walked closer, I realized that we stood on a manmade balcony, projecting us out into an open cavern. Stalactites and stalagmites festooned the chamber, some several stories high and meeting to form one long rock strand. I listened as the guide gave some basic information about caves to the group. The Germans took advantage of the available benches in short order while they paid attention. The rest of us ranged back and forth in front of the opening, looking up, down, and around in awe. Majestic rock pillars, with shining white curves, stood wider than a person.

"We'll stay here a few minutes so you can enjoy the view," Fingal said.

Very few people tarried at the edge farthest from the way we entered. That area lacked as interesting rock formations and some of the lights had gone out. I sat and turned so my back rested on the rock. I shivered at the coolness and rubbed my goose-pimpled arms. I hadn't been in a cave in ages and forgot how much colder it could be. I saw some movement out of the corner of my eye, turned, and gazed into the darkness. Tate, noticing my attentiveness, joined me.

"What do you see, Mom?" she asked.

"I don't know. I thought I saw something moving...maybe a bat?"

Davina overheard me and joined us. "Unlikely in this part of the cave unless it is a rabid one. We do have bats living farther back in the cave. There's another entrance. We don't take people back there because we don't like to disturb the bats. They're one of the rarer breeds in Scotland. The whiskered bat is quite small and has long hair. I plan to add an exhibit to the museum about it, but don't have the funds." She rushed to the opposite end where the girls were standing on their seats. One hung onto the other one's jeans waistband as she leaned over the abyss snapping photos.

Geez, to be young and stupid.

Again, I saw something move.

"Did you see that, Mom?" Tate asked.

CHAPTER 20

"I saw something." I squinted at the darkness. "What did you see?"

"I saw a woman. I think she—" Tate grabbed my arm and pointed. "There! Look!"

I followed the line of her finger to a figure smaller than I, under five foot tall, for sure, but lithe—almost, but not quite, emaciated. The pale skin glowed. Light appeared to be attracted to it, and the figure seemed to absorb weak brightness. I could see the undeniable curves of a small bosom. She wore a form-fitting bodysuit that shimmered gray, but changed colors as she moved—like an oil slick. I swallowed hard as my stomach roiled when I looked at it too long. Her long, pointed ears flicked and moved independently then angled toward me. She moved faster than my eyes could follow. One minute she crouched at the bottom of the cavern, and the next, she clung to a stalagmite, half way up. Her bare toes and finger tips adhered to the rock surface like one of the anoles that lived in our garden in Houston. No one else seemed to notice. Fingal and Davina argued with the girls who, in frustration, regressed to speaking Spanish which the Oggs obviously didn't understand. The Germans had grown weary of the sights and were, in equal parts, conversing or resting. The American family sat angled away from our guides. The mother surreptitiously fed the boys Cheerios, despite the sign at the entrance which said eating in the cave was not permitted.

"Mom—" Tate whispered.

While I'd checked the locations of the guides and other members of the tour, the creature had traveled all the way up the column and, as I watched, leapt to the next one and continued to hopscotch until she was at the one nearest to us. She turned and grinned. I swallowed. Her teeth were sharp and long. She swung and propelled herself off the rock to land out of my sight. Then I could hear a sound. Not quite a hissing, but almost like a barely audible exhalation.

"Mom—" Tate whispered again.

"I know, honey."

I stood and pulled Tate away from the bench. As I did so, the creature peeped around, only half her face visible. The one eyebrow rose. Time froze.

At the sounds of two loud claps, the creature's head jerked up then vanished.

I turned to see what had made the sound. Davina stared at me with her hands clasped together and eyes so wide open that I could see the whites around the irises. Her brother, with a hand on the arm of each of the Spanish girls, wore an expression of wonder.

"The tour is over," Fingal said as he propelled the protesting girls in front of him. No one else objected. The American mother encouraged the boys to stuff the remaining oat treats into their mouths and move. The Germans wearily stood and followed. Soon, Tate and I were the only ones left, along with Davina. She came and stood next to us.

"Who are you?" she asked.

I shook my head. "I don't know what you mean."

She gripped my elbow and turned me toward her. I was so startled, I didn't resist. She stared into my eyes. "You have the Sight," she said.

Before I could speak, she bent toward Tate and peered into her eyes too. "As do you." Her shoulders slumped as she gazed at the stone ground. "How is this possible?" she murmured.

I tugged Tate's arm. Mesmerized, my daughter stared into the darkness where something glinted and moved.

"Tate, don't look." I pulled her toward the exit—toward the others. I was relieved when Davina didn't move. Instead, she turned and looked out over the chasm, searching for…I didn't wait to know for what.

Tate protested as I hurried us closer to the others. "I think she wanted to speak to us," she ventured.

"Honey, I don't know that I want to speak to her."

"Mom," she admonished. "You've always said not to judge others by their appearance. Besides, she really was beautiful—" She paused. "—until she opened her mouth."

I couldn't argue with her about that. The lights overhead flickered. Tate and I sped up until we were jogging. We almost ran into one of the Germans lagging behind. She paused with her hand over her heart.

I stopped. "Are you okay?"

"Yes," she said in perfect English. "I don't know what the hurry is, though."

"I think those girls broke the rules."

"Well, no surprise is it?" She took a deep breath. "I think I am ready now. Where is the other one?"

"Oh, you mean the other guide, Davina?"

"Yes."

"She was behind us." I looked back and saw a shimmering figure definitely not Davina.

"Let's go." Grabbing Tate's hand and the German lady's arm, I rushed us forward. We burst through the opening, startling the group.

"Where is Davina?" Fingal asked.

"I don't know, but the lights started going out." I knew it sounded silly, I mean, after all, even a person with an awful sense of direction could get back here in the dark. It wasn't like there was any other way to go once you were turned in the correct direction, which we had been.

Fingal rounded us up. "Come along," he said, turning toward the stairs.

"What about your sister?" the American mother asked.

"I will return after I accompany you all back to the café."

"I think we can make it back on our own," one of the Spanish girls said.

"Most of you could," Fingal said pointedly.

As he led the group back up to the café, I listened as the Spanish girls demanded their money back because they felt shorted. They expressed that they were not told not to stand on the seats. Fingal argued that there was indeed a sign and even the children in attendance had not done something so immature, not to mention unsafe. "You're too juvenile to go on the extended tour, at any rate. You would have been sent back with the rest. Of the group, I think I saw maybe five that I would take farther, from the point we were, and we weren't even done with the first leg that *everyone* can handle." They huffed, and as soon as they entered the café, pushed up to the front to order. Before we could go inside, Fingal stopped us. "I'm going back to check on my sister. I would appreciate it if you would wait for us to return."

I mutely nodded.

"What do you think the creepy lady wanted?" Tate asked.

"I'm not sure, honey."

She reminded me of a cuter version of a lizard, though both could be pretty creepy. I ordered a pot of tea and Tate asked for a Ribena. After collecting our drinks and a plate of biscuits, we sat. When everyone from the tour had an opportunity to finish their light snacks, the museum was showing a short movie which you could choose to watch or remain in the café. I noticed that the person behind the counter in the café also resembled the guides, and I assumed she was some relation.

A little while later, Fingal returned along with his sister. She took those who were interested in to watch the film. Fingal came to sit at our table. Most of the group decided to watch the movie, even, surprisingly, the Spanish girls.

"My sister will start the movie and return," he said then rose, helped himself to some tea, and chatted with the lady behind the counter. Ten minutes later, Davina returned and sat with us. Fingal brought a cup of tea over to the table and gave it to her. They stared at Tate and me.

About the time that I started to feel uncomfortable, Tate piped up. "Do you know the lizard-toed lady?"

The siblings looked at one another. "They both could see her, and she rarely shows herself. I think we should tell them," Davina said.

Fingal rubbed his chin. "I don't know, Davina. They aren't family or even islanders."

"They did not see merely the briefest of glimpses. She *showed* herself to them. Besides, look closely—they have the Sight. They would fit in on the island."

I wasn't sure what she meant by that comment.

Her brother stared first into my eyes then Tate's, nodded then cleared his throat. "You remember the legend Davina told you in the museum?"

"Yes, a goblin lives in the cave and likes presents but doesn't like people coming over uninvited," Tate answered around a mouthful of biscuit.

"Tate, swallow what's in your mouth, then speak," I gently admonished.

Fingal continued. "Pretty much. It isn't just a story, it is true. However, there is more to the story than just that."

"The creature, we saw? Was she the goblin?" I asked, wanting to get to the crux of the matter before the bus arrived. I had no intentions of missing it and needing to wait for the next one.

"Yes. Her name is...well, it's difficult to pronounce even for me. We call her Blanca."

"Does she like living in the cave?" Tate asked.

"Tate, honey? Why don't we just listen for a bit? I bet if we're patient, all our questions will be answered." I *hoped* anyway.

"Blanca used to live somewhere else, but she did something that caused her to be expelled from her home to this cave system," he said. Tate opened her mouth but closed it at a look from me. Fingal sighed. "I'm...well, Davina and I are related to Blanca. She's our grandmother."

"She certainly has aged well."

"Goblins have longer life spans than humans. Blanca took a human lover and married him. This is anathema to the goblin people. They cast her out and shunned her. In the beginning, she lived in the cottage above. At first, it was enough for her to be with her beloved husband, but she missed the caves and spent more and more time there. Then, one day, she didn't return. Our grandfather raised the children she left behind. We are told that our grandfather went to the caves and camped for days at a time, but he couldn't stay there any more than she could remain above. He brought their children to visit her. She was never very motherly, but she was kind when she saw them and told stories about her home. After her husband died, the children, now adults, found her and told her. Mad with grief, she cried out and ran deep, deep down into the tunnels. For years, there was no sign of her. Her children eventually believed her dead and thought she would never be seen again.

"Davina and I often see something when we entered the caves, the shape of a woman in the dimness. My da thinks that Blanca stopped showing herself to him and his siblings because they reminded her too much of the husband she gave up everything for and lost. It's customary to always leave things for her. To let her know she is remembered."

"When did this happen?"

"My grandparents married in the eighteenth century," Fingal answered.

If anyone would have told me this before I had been to the island, that I would have laughed in their faces and accused them of having me on, but after all I had seen and heard here, I was inclined to believe.

He nodded at me then Tate. "Then you came, and you saw her. Not just a glimpse, but you clearly saw her. This is unusual for several reasons, but the most important one is that the only ones who have ever seen her were relatives. Others on the island rarely saw her. They thought it was odd, but our grandfather told them she had a disabling skin condition and couldn't abide light. Considering how light-skinned our family is, the islanders believed it.

"My grandmother would, in the earlier days, go to the village and walk amongst them camouflaged. She wore a large bonnet and long sleeves, only venturing out in winter months. This is the first time she has shown herself to an outsider. Sometimes she has teased folks with little glimpses, so brief that all the viewer could say was that he or she saw something but knew not what. She has never shown herself so plainly as she did to you. She revealed herself to you clearer than she has ever even appeared to us."

"Why do you think that is?"

"I don't know, but it concerns me. I don't know if it is a good thing or a bad thing. She's fae and has unorthodox views, not always in keeping with human sensibilities."

"Well, this island has been full of surprises for us." I debated about telling them about all that had occurred but decided first I wanted to talk to Kay and see what she knew about the family.

Fingal glanced at his sister. She nodded and he cleared his throat. "We would like you and your daughter to return when we are not guiding the tours and go into the caves with us."

I paused. "If I do come back, I'll come alone."

"But she showed herself to me first, Mom!" Tate protested.

"I know, honey, but her family isn't even sure she is...well, safe."

"She wouldn't hurt a child," Davina protested.

"Once, a little boy squeezed between railings and fell," Fingal said. "He hit his head and was unconscious. She carried him to a safe place where he could be found."

"What about those most recent deaths?" I asked.

"I don't know. I don't want to think she did anything, but I am not sure."

"Well, I won't put my daughter at risk. I want to have some time to think this over. Can I reach you at the number for the tours?"

"Here." Davina produced a business card and pen and wrote on the back. "This is my cell number, too. Call me anytime. If I'm working, I'll get back with you as soon as possible. Please think about it. It would mean so much to us."

The doors to the film room opened. I glanced at my phone for the time and realized the bus would be coming soon.

"Thank you for the tour," I said.

"Thanks!" Tate parroted.

Our group seemed oddly taciturn, even the Spanish girls, as we traipsed to the bus stop to wait. The bus was prompt and, in no time, we found ourselves back at our stop. I was so involved in my thoughts that time flew by.

Since the little boys fell asleep, Tate read pamphlets we'd collected. We walked back in silence to the cottage. My mind sprinted in various directions. The kitty meowed, and Tate refilled its water dish and gave it a little food. I tried to watch how much she fed the little one. With the excitement of the day and still a bit weak from the strength-sapper, Tate curled up on the bed and fell asleep with the kitten.

CHAPTER 21

With dinner in mind, I dug through the cabinets for ingredients I could cobble together into a main dish. Afterward, I checked my phone. No one had called or texted. Although I hadn't asked Jess to, I'd hoped she'd thawed enough to let me know her plans. I texted Kay to ask if Jess had joined her for lunch. Kay texted back that Jessie had indeed and also wanted to stay in the village longer and catch a ride back home with Kay. I said that would be fine, resisting the urge to ask Kay to hand Jess phone. I'd talk to Kay about the cave family when she dropped off Jess. In fact—I fired off another text, asking Kay if she would like to eat dinner with us tonight.

She texted back, ~ *YES!*

Since I had a little time before I needed to start dinner, I changed into jeans and an elderly tee to work in the garden. It was coming along nicely.

I was at the door, when I paused. I hadn't checked emails in ages. "Crud," I murmured to myself.

I sat down and pulled them up on my phone. Mrs. Grant sent her family tree. That, I'd look at later. Conall also emailed. *Ugh. Definitely checking that later.* Conall, and, for that matter, his nephew, too, behaved so perplexingly that I'd just about reached the point where I just wanted to avoid the whole family. *Great, now I sound like Jess.* I stuffed the phone into my back pocket. Next, I went to the little shed to find gardening tools, gloves, and a pad I could kneel on. As I pulled the door open, something rustled. Was it a mouse or some other kind of rodent? Scotland didn't harbor as many snakes Houston did.

It doesn't hurt to be cautious. I picked up the closest implement, the hoe, and poked at the shelves. My shoulders scrunched up toward my ears, and I squeezed the handle so hard that my knuckles whitened. If something was going to rush out at me, I wanted to be ready to either bash it or run, depending on what it was. Hopefully, neither would be needed and some sweet little field mouse would run out, more scared of me than me of it. Wouldn't be too surprising, I guessed. Maybe one was frightened by the wolves, hid in here, and got shut in. I leaned forward and poked the very back of the shed.

"Oof!" someone called out.

"Who's in here?" Items teetered on the back-most shelf and a jar of marbles tipped and rolled off the warped wood. A small hand darted out, caught it in mid-air, and replaced it.

A child? "It's no use hiding. Stand up and show yourself."

"I *am* standing," the low, pleasant voice sang and I swayed as if I were listening to a favorite music. "However, elevation may indeed aid me," he continued.

Two hands appeared on the top shelf. It teetered dangerously as a boy hoisted his body atop it and sat, dangling his legs. He grinned at me, displaying bright white teeth.

"What are you doing hiding in my shed? You shouldn't be here. It's dangerous."

He laughed and swung his legs. "I assure you that I am the most dangerous thing in this shed at the moment."

"Mom, that's the boy who led me to the woods the night we arrived." Tate had awakened from her nap and stood behind me.

"Hello, Tate!" he said as he rose to his feet and bounded over objects like a mountain goat on steroids.

I stepped aside so he could get out.

He looked like a young boy except around the eyes. To look into his eyes was to look at someone much, much wiser...older.

"What's your name?" I asked.

"That isn't important. I decided to pop over and see how you were. You've met Greg, I know. What do you think of the lad?" He walked away and, after looking at each other, Tate and I followed him to the bench where he sat. He patted beside himself, but I shook my head. If this was another fae, we'd keep our distance.

"So..." He paused expectantly.

"So?"

"Greg. What do you think of him?"

One thing was for sure, he certainly didn't talk like any child that I knew of either.

'He's...nice. How do you know him?"

"You might say we're neighbors."

I wasn't sure exactly what to do or think. He was obviously not ordinary, though he did look like a child, and I wasn't one to send a young boy off alone.

"I think you should be getting home. Why don't you let me walk you there?"

"Oh, not that I wouldn't like the company, but the cost would be more than I'd be willing to pay. I can make my way alone." He hopped off the bench and sped toward the forest.

I shook my head, amazed at how fast he moved. "Hey!

Those woods aren't safe! There are wild wolves. Come back!"

"Those wolves are more afraid of me than I am of them, and rightly so," he called back. "Say, when next you see young Greg, give him a kiss for me." Then he bounded off into the woods.

I turned to my daughter. "Tate, you always said you couldn't remember what happened that night."

"It was all fuzzy until I saw the boy and remembered."

"Why in the world would you wander off with a stranger, even another child?"

Tate frowned. "I don't know. He just made it sound like it was a good idea to go with him."

After I retrieved the gardening tools, I hoed at the stubborn weeds and made a note to see about the fertilizer in the shed.

༺◦༻

I hadn't realized how much time had passed until I heard Kay's car. Tate had remained outside to help me, so I asked her to run to the front and tell them I'd be inside in just a minute, while I put up the tools we had been using. The garden looked much better. When I went in the back door, I could hear Jess talking excitedly. Thank goodness, she seemed to be in better spirits—at least around others. I washed my hands and steeled myself to expect any one of her mercurial moods.

"Hi, Mom!" she said, beaming as if she hadn't been ticked at me for over a day.

"Hi, Jess. How did the library research go?"

"The library didn't have all that much more than what I already had checked out, but Kay gave me a cool book. I found recipes in it. Spells, I guess. Kay's looked at them, and she says they're safe." She waved an old book, so worn that I couldn't read the title. I looked at Kay, and she waved her hand slightly at me and smiled to assure me that it was indeed okay, but I still wasn't sure I liked the idea of my daughter doing spells.

"Jessie's gonna be a witch! Can I be one too?" Tate asked, Jessie's excitement catching.

"We'll see."

"Look, there's one for protection. If we had it the first night, that fairy creature never would have taken Tate. And there are ones you can carry around with you to ward off evil spirits."

Of my two daughters, I never thought Jess would be the one interested in fairies. The girls went to their room to make a list of the spells they wanted to try and what they would need for them.

Noticing my discomfort, Kay patted my hand. "Don't worry about it, Becca."

"Normally, I wouldn't. But things aren't normal here. Those spells probably work. And I'm sure there are some that I would *not* want her using."

"There's nothing evil in that spell book. It belonged to a white witch. Jessie will find no black magic inside."

I wasn't happy at all, but I had some other questions, so I'd put that issue on the back burner.

"Tate and I had a strange experience at the cavern." I told her about what happened.

Kay's forehead wrinkled. "That is odd. I do know the story, everyone does, but I don't know anyone who's ever seen her, except for the fleetest glimpses."

I also told her about the boy. "Was he even a boy?"

"Yes, but he shouldn't be out and about."

"So, you know this boy? Is there something...wrong with him?"

"I know him—not well, but I do know him. He lives in the forest."

I couldn't stay still and leapt to my feet and paced. Spinning around to face Kay, I asked, "Wait, I thought the forest was dangerous? Why would a boy live there? Why is Greg living there? Are you sure he isn't fae or part fae too?"

"No, Becca. Greg is a man."

"How many people live in that forest, anyway? Is it some kind of survivalist camp? Is that what Greg is? Is he one of those weirdoes who thinks an apocalypse is about to happen and is readying himself for Armageddon?"

"It is...well, an island peculiarity."

"You know, Kay, for being friends, you keep a lot of secrets. Dangerous secrets! This boy led Tate off, and she came back with that...that life-leeching thing. If it hadn't been for Greg—" I gulped. "We've dealt with wolves, a crazy goblin chick, and a weepy ghost at a pond—at least she didn't do anything other than weep. This—this is a lot, Kay, and you're hiding something!" It wasn't in my nature to be accusing. I was shocked by my own shaking finger. "At this point, I'm thinking seriously about packing it up and going home to Texas."

Kay clasped my hand in hers. "Oh, don't go, Becca. Please stay. You know the Scots are reserved and slow to confide."

"This is more than just being Scots. Why don't you trust me enough to tell me what's going on?"

"I trusted you enough with my own secret." Kay closed her eyes for a moment then opened them. "Maybe I should just go home. Maybe you don't trust me." She wrung her hands and glanced at the door.

"Kay, wait, I'm sorry. You've been wonderful. I'm just so confused, and I worry about the girls."

There was a knock at the door. Kay looked at me. I shrugged. "I'm not expecting anyone other than you."

I opened the door and Greg filled the doorway. "Hello," I said, surprised and frankly, happy for the interruption.

"Hello. Sorry for my timing. I hope I'm not interrupting your dinner."

"I haven't started it yet, come in."

Greg entered, and he and Kay exchanged greetings. Then Kay excused herself to wash up.

Greg turned to me. "I was wondering, have you been bothered by a boy about yea-high." He motioned with his hand at a height about his waist.

"I did find a boy in the shed. He ran off into the woods. Is he a relative?"

"No, but I am responsible for him. Has he caused you any grief?"

"No, no grief this time, but he was the boy who led Tate into the woods. Did you know this?"

"I suspected it might be so. He's a mischievous imp."

I got right in his face…well, his chest, and glared up at him. "Why didn't you do anything?"

His hands landed on my shoulders and slid down to my arms. I fought to hold onto my anger.

"I did, Rebecca. I brought your daughter back to you," he said softly.

"But if he's leading children into the forest, shouldn't he be in juvie?"

Greg shook his head. "Juvie?"

"A jail for youths."

He gave my arms a gentle squeeze. "You must ken he's no mere child?"

Overcome with the stress of the day and the feelings Greg unknowingly coaxed from me, I merely nodded. "He did ask me what I thought of you."

"Aye? And what did you say?"

"I said you were nice."

"Nice," he said flatly.

"He also had a message that I was to give to you."

"And what was that?"

I had intended to give him a quick kiss on the cheek, but when I moved closer, I couldn't look away from his eyes. Our lips met briefly and parted. It was an innocent kiss, except for the passion which filled me. I gasped when we tenuously separated. He composed himself more quickly than I, but I knew that the kiss had meant something to him too.

"Well, now. That isna a message I ever expected to get from the lad."

"Sorry, I—" Before I could explain, not that I had any idea how I was going to, the girls came in followed by Kay. I rested my hand on his muscled bicep. "I'm making dinner. You're welcome to stay if you want."

And just like that, Jess went from cheerful and smiling to pouting and frowning. "Is it okay if I read in my room until dinner?" she asked.

Not wanting to subject anyone to her mood, I nodded. Kay helped me with dinner while Tate cheerfully regaled Greg with our trip to the cave, leaving nothing out. As she spoke, Greg's brow furrowed. We jumped when lightning flashed and thunder abruptly roared with no warning. The sky seemed to open, and rain poured down. We went to the windows to look.

"Okay, is the weather always so weird here? Because in Aberdeen we haven't had downpours like this. This is more like the weather we saw in Houston."

"No, 'tis not typical," Greg said thoughtfully.

Someone knocked at the door—though more heavy-handed than Greg.

"Who would be out in this weather?" I received blank stares as an answer.

Shrugging my shoulders, I opened the door. Conall

and his nephew, Lundy, stood shivering on the porch.

Conall cleared his throat. "I wanted to apologize for not being in the store the other day and for the attack."

The storm roared so loudly, I could barely hear him.

"It wasn't your fault." A strong gust sprayed a freezing mist of water in my face. Thunder rumbled and a bolt of lightning slashed a tree on the edge of the property. We watched it burn red for a second before the rain doused it. "Goodness, come in."

After they entered the cottage, I pushed the door shut.

Conall shook his head. "It was. We need to be more diligent about the door being shut and locked. I've been after my nephew to remember."

A look of surprise flashed across Lundy's face, then he grudgingly nodded. He shot dagger eyes at his uncle that I recognized from having been on the receiving end of them from Jess.

Lundy and Conall, their clothes, dark with water, dripped on the entry rug.

I hadn't heard a car. "Did you walk here?"

"We didn't expect the weather to be bad, and…well, I thought the lad could use the exercise."

Lundy sent laser eyes this time. I was surprised Conall didn't turn into a pile of ashes.

I couldn't send them back out into that maelstrom. "Let me grab some towels so you can at least get dried off. Hopefully, the weather will let up." This evening, I'd originally planned to pick Kay's brains about the goings-ons. I hadn't expected to host an impromptu dinner party. The food was ready and there was plenty, so…

"Would you two like to stay for dinner?"

With a sullen expression on his face, Conall eyed Greg. "That's quite generous of you. If you're sure it is okay?" Conall asked

I nodded.

"We accept," Conall said, triumphantly gloating at Greg, who ignored him.

This seemed to bother Conall even more. The timer dinged. The casserole was ready, but I took a detour to get Jess and pick up some towels. They'd have to stay in wet clothes, but at least they wouldn't be dripping.

I tapped on the girls' door once then entered. Tate was trying to teach the kitten to fetch, while Jess studied the spell book. "Jess, we have extra guests. Could you set three more plates?"

Jessie marked the place in her book and sat it on the bed. "Three?"

"Yes, three."

When I returned, I passed out towels I got from the linen closet and the two men removed their shoes and dried off as best they could. I turned back to the kitchen. After donning oven mitts, I opened the oven, removed the dish, and placed it on a trivet. I turned just in time to see Jessie's reaction to discovering Lundy. Pretty priceless. She, of course, glared at me like it was my fault.

"They came to apologize and were caught in the downpour, Jess."

"Great," she muttered as she slid three more plates from the shelf.

Greg addressed Conall. "I dinna ken if you should be out so far from home at this time. I heard about the…mishap at your store."

"We have it under control, and if we didn't, it would be your fault and your responsibility to answer for it. Wouldn't it, Keeper?"

"Are you talking about the wolves?" I didn't see how Greg could possibly be blamed for that.

Dinner was delayed when I realized I'd need to add a leaf to the table. Both Greg and Conall tried to help which made it take even longer then it would have if I'd just done it alone. In the end, I had them both fetch the other chairs and Kay helped me.

Then it came time to be seated. I sat at my usual place at the head of the table and was immediately flanked by Conall and Greg who glared at each other from across the table. Kay sat at the opposite end, mainly, I think, to avoid the musical chairs game that Jess and Lundy were participating in. Conall's nephew jockeyed to sit by Jess, who moved three times before grudgingly snagging a place between Greg and Tate. She wasn't pleased with sitting by him, but her other two choices were by Conall and no doubt become sandwiched between him and his nephew or by Kay which would put her between Kay and Lundy. Apparently staying away from the nephew at all costs was more crucial than avoiding Greg.

"Why are you sitting on this side?" Tate asked Jess.

"I just did, hush," Jess grumbled.

Lundy settled for sitting across from Jess. I bowed my head. We weren't a particularly religious family, but I was raised Catholic and remembered Greg apparently was too. So, I made the sign of the cross with him. The girls, used to seeing me do it, folded their hands and bowed their heads too. I said a quick, heart-felt prayer of thanks.

"Amen," Tate whispered.

Lundy picked up his fork then grunted in pain and dropped it when, I suspect, his uncle kicked him under the table. I had originally planned on putting the casserole in the middle of the table and letting everyone serve themselves, but now the table was too big to do that and the dish too hot to easily hand around. So instead, I placed it in front of me.

"Since this is so hot, if everyone could pass your plates, I can serve. We can pass around the other dishes." Conall held up his plate.

"Jess, Tate—could you two get everyone a glass of water?"

The girls worked together with Jess putting ice and water in cups and Tate bringing them to the guests.

I took Conall's plate and served him.

He shook out his napkin and put it on his lap. "It looks delicious."

"Thank you," I said. "It's a Mexican casserole. My mother used to make it. It has some ingredients not usually found here." Before we came to the island, I bought some American ingredients that I thought I might have trouble getting. I congratulated myself for having the foresight after seeing the limited choices at the grocery here. The dish was supposed to last the three of us at least a couple of meals. Looking on the bright side, at least I had enough to feed my unexpected guests. I served everyone and then myself. "Oh, I almost forgot." I pushed away from the table and stood. "I have a couple of bottles of red wine, if anyone wants some. I'm having a glass." The wine glasses were washed and sitting out on the counter.

"I'd love a glass," Kay said and stood to help me.

"I'll have one too," Conall said.

I looked at Greg and he nodded at me.

"Me too," Lundy said.

Conall frowned at him.

"I suppose that it's okay, I guess it's legal here," I commented.

"Does that mean I can have some too?" Jess asked. The last time she had tasted wine she hated it, but I decided not to mention it.

"I suppose so." I measured out a small portion for Jess because I doubted she would even finish it and the same amount for the nephew, because I didn't want her complaining that he received more. *Teens*. Then I passed the salad, refried beans, salsa, and chips around. Since Greg was left-handed and Jessie was right-handed, they kept bumping elbows.

With some urging from Conall, Lundy tried to engage Jess in conversation. "You really danced well at the ceilidh for someone who didn't know the steps until then. Did you take lessons like, uh, ballet?"

"No." Jessie crunched on a chip.

Though clearly flustered, Lundy soldiered on. "What do you like to do?"

Keeping her eyes on her plate and shrugging, she answered, "Ride."

"Oh, like horses?"

"No, like camels." Jessie's sarcasm reared its ugly head. Unfortunately, Lundy took her seriously.

"Camels? I've never ridden a camel before."

I caught Jessie's eye and frowned. She abandoned the eye roll she had started and sighed. "I was kidding. Yes, I ride horses."

Lundy frowned. "I don't ride anymore. I used to."

"Why not, "Tate asked.

"The horses, they get nervous around me now."

"Why, did you accidentally hurt one?"

"Probably his cologne," Jess muttered just loud enough to be audible.

Lundy blushed. Greg bit his lip in an attempt not to smile. *I'm glad someone is getting a kick out of it.*

When Greg and Jessie's elbows bumped yet again, Jess lost a forkful of food. She scooted her chair farther from Greg and jarred Tate's.

"Hey!" Tate protested.

With a sigh, Jess moved her chair back then turned toward Greg and opened her mouth. I hoped to apologize and not to complain. Her elbow connected hard with Greg's as he reached for his glass. The goblet tipped over. The merlot sloshed across the table onto Conall and his nephew. Lundy, in his rush to stand, knocked his knees under the table and jostled his own glass. More wine splashed on his pants. I rushed for the towels as Greg and, to my delight, Jess, apologized.

"I'm so sorry. This will probably stain," I said as Conall and Lundy blotted themselves, and I hurried to keep the wine from running off the table and onto anyone else.

"It's okay," Conall said. "It isn't your fault." He glared at Greg.

"Let me get everyone some more wine." Kay stood and fetched the wine bottle. Once the table was cleaned as best it could be, we finished our meal. Everyone seemed to enjoy the food despite the mishap. Only two servings of casserole remained in the pan. Kay left the wine bottle on the table, and Conall poured the last of it in his own glass.

"I'll open another," he said.

Thankfully, I bought more than one. The rain was still coming down hard when I finished clearing the dirty plates. "I have coffee, tea, and whisky," I announced as I moved the casserole to the counter to cool.

"Whisky sounds grand," Conall said a little too loudly.

He'd drunk the lion's share of the wine and was flushed. Lundy, noting that Jess barely finished her half glass, didn't have any more. The rest of us stuck with just one glass. I would have loved to have more, but between Jess and Lundy and Conall and Greg, I wanted to have my wits about me.

However, I was going to have some of the whisky and, as soon as I poured a glass for those who wanted it, the bottle was going back up to keep Conall's intake down to one. I kept glancing out the window, hoping that the weather would clear up, but if anything, it looked worse. The kitten meowed. Tate had accidentally shut it up in her room. She went to get it. All the adults said yes to whisky. I put out a box of cookies.

"Sorry, they're store-bought," I said as I passed around the assortment. "If I had known I would have so many guests, I could have made a trifle or something."

"We should apologize. You didna expect so many guests," Greg said.

Tate returned holding the kitten. When it caught sight of Conall, it hissed and clawed. Tate cried out and dropped the kitten that ran under the couch.

"Tate, are you okay?" Dots of blood beaded on her forearm.

"I dropped the kitty!" As she held her arm, she rushed to the couch and knelt to look underneath.

"The kitten's fine, I'm sure, but let me check while your mother looks at your arm."

I smiled at Kay gratefully. Tate's arm wasn't bad, but I put antibiotic and a bandage on it. Kay coaxed the kitten out, and it seemed to be no worse for wear.

When Kay approached them, Conall and Lundy pushed away from the table. "Keep it away from us," Conall said. "We're allergic to cats. I didn't know you had one."

Shrugging, I said, "We didn't when we arrived. Kay's cat had kittens, and we decided to adopt one."

"Dogs are much better pets," Lundy said.

"They are not!" Tate burst out, loyal to her kitten.

Lundy snorted. "You can train a dog. You can't train a cat to do anything."

"I bet we can train our cat," Jess added.

"No, won't work. They just aren't smart enough."

Honestly, no wonder the boy isn't getting dates. Why would you talk down something the girl you like is fond of?

"Cats are actually quite bright," Kay said.

The kitten hopped from Kay's arms to Greg's lap.

Conall scowled. "Seems like we're outnumbered."

"Pretty wee thing," Greg said as he ran a thumb over its head. The kitten purred.

Wishing to smooth things over, I took the cat from Greg and backed away from the table. "Why don't we move her food and water into the girls' room so she won't bother Conall and Lundy?"

Jess picked up the water dish and Tate took the food dish.

On her way out, Jess snagged some cookies and smiled. "I'll stay in the room with the kitty so she won't be afraid."

"Me too," Tate called out.

As I followed the girls to their room, I made sure I had a secure hold on the kitten.

In hopes of removing stray cat hair, I ran my hands down the front of my shirt as I returned. "Sorry about that. I had no idea you were allergic, or I would have made sure to keep her away."

I did notice that neither of them seemed to be sneezing or acting like the encounter had bothered them. I had friends who were allergic and sneezed as soon as they walked into a house with a cat. They didn't need to touch it or be near it.

Conall and his nephew hadn't reacted adversely upon arriving.

We sat at the table to finish our whisky and cookies. The evening was a disaster, and I didn't see how it could get much worse. I decided to pursue the topic I began with Kay. Maybe I would get some answers from the men too. "We went to the cave for a tour today," I began. "We saw something unusual."

Greg tilted his head as he regarded me. "Oh?"

"Yes. There was a…well, it couldn't be called a woman, because it wasn't human, but it was female." I described the goblin.

"That is odd. I will have to go visit the caverns," Greg said.

Conall's eyes narrowed. "What do you plan on doing?" he asked.

Greg toyed with his napkin. "Well, I am interested in such occurrences."

"What will you do if you see her?" I asked. The conversation's direction was making Greg uncomfortable, and I had no idea why, but I was going to try to find out. "Anytime something weird or odd happens, you seem to be involved or know about it. You weren't at all surprised when I described the woman. Why is that?"

"Well, of course we know the story. Everyone on the island does," Conall explained.

"Yes, but the story doesn't describe the woman. It just mentions that she's a goblin. Jess brought books from the library. I haven't looked at them all, but I did see some pictures of supposed goblins. They looked nothing like the creature we saw."

Greg folded his napkin and placed it on the table. "I havena seen her, but I ken others who have and described her. She causes no harm. The stories are just to keep nosy people away."

"My understanding was that nobody has actually seen her in decades. How is it you spoke to someone who described what she looked like?"

"The family, the Oggs, they ken, but they prefer to keep it to themselves."

"You aren't family and you know." As soon as I realized I was pointing at Greg, I drew back and put my hands behind my back. Lundy was as twitchy as a rabbit's nose, and Conall didn't bother to hide his glee at Greg's discomfort, so I turned to him. "And you, what is it with these wolves? I know you two know something about them. Kay and Greg do too. Are they an endangered species you're trying to protect?" I tried to think of some reason for the secrecy, but just couldn't come up with anything. "Kay says they kill pets. For a lot of people, at least in the States, that alone would be reason enough for destroying them or at least relocating them, but you people—" I stood and paced around.

My guests stared at me as if I was about to roll my eyes up in my head and puke pea soup.

Greg reached out and took my hand when I passed him. "Please, please, sit."

"Tell me what's going on!" I demanded.

"I'll tell you what I'm able," Greg said.

Conall gasped and stood.

Lundy cried out, "You can't tell her!"

"Sit down," Kay said.

The two bristled at her.

"We hold to the white way. We've earned trust, respect, and protection." Conall loomed over Greg who remained sitting, I think, to try and diffuse the situation.

Greg shook his head. "The wolves shouldna have been in the store."

"That's your fault, not ours."

"It isn't Greg's fault," Kay said. "It is the way of it, that's all. Perhaps you two should stay close to home."

"Are we now prisoners? Besides, it hit so fast today, we had not the time," Conall protested.

"Ahem—I'm still here and apparently the only one who has absolutely no idea what you all are talking about. It's like you're speaking a different language in front of the only person who can't understand. It's rude."

Greg nodded. "Rebecca's right."

"She brought it up," Lundy said with a begrudging edge to his voice.

Jessie peeked around the corner, but when she realized I had seen her, she came in like that had been her intent in the first place rather than trying to listen in. "I just came to get some more cookies," she said, with all eyes on her. "Does anyone else want some?"

"We're good, Jessie, but thanks. Take one to Tate in case she wants it, but that's it for the night."

Jess blushed as Lundy snickered. "Mom, I'm old enough to decide what I can eat." She tromped out, but somehow flounced with grace.

Kay spoke quietly. "I told Becca about myself—me being Sith. I think it would be okay to tell her...other things."

She looked meaningfully at Conall and Lundy, but neither would meet her eyes. Lundy slouched as Conall crossed his arms in front of his chest.

"If you ken about Kay and Blanca, then you ken that some of the legends and tales are true, but the books dinna always get it right," Greg said.

I nodded. I had a chance to look through some of the books that Jess checked out from the library. "There's one legend that described something a lot like the woman by the pond, the one washing. How much of it is true?"

"You saw a bean nighe," Kay said.

"Oh, I wasn't sure how to pronounce it." I turned to Greg. "I was out of it after I fell in the pond and didn't get a chance to ask you about it. You said something about being worried?"

Kay sipped her whisky. "She's supposed to be a harbinger of death."

My mouth went dry and I swallowed. "So, she's evil?" I stared at Greg.

He sipped his whisky.

"No, she's just the messenger." Kay again answered my question even though I addressed Greg. "She doesn't cause the misfortune to happen. However, some tales say, she did do evil in life, and The Morrigan has her do this as penance."

"Depending on the country, people have different names for these beings. I don't always use the ones which originated here. I'll use ones that more people are familiar with," she continued.

When I tried to catch Greg's eye, he looked down at his hands.

"And in the water? Those weren't ferns or grasses. I really was grabbed by some things."

"Grindylows, though they aren't usually aggressive."

I frowned at Kay then looked at Greg, trying to get across to her that I wanted to hear what he had to say. She blithefully ignored me.

"When Rebecca was hurt, I think they were being mischievous and didna realize their prank had gone wrong," Greg reasoned.

I threw my hands up in the air. "So now you're going to talk?" I was so confused.

Conall cleared his throat. "I think the rain's cleared up."

I'd been so intent on the conversation that I had not even noticed the lack of sound.

"Aye, 'tis late."

The three men rose. Neither seemed to want to be the first to leave, but finally, when it was obvious that Conall and his nephew weren't moving,

Greg said goodbye. He surprised me with a soft kiss on my forehead. Lundy kept looking back toward the bedrooms.

"If you want to say goodbye to Jess, the girls share the first room to the left in the hallway, just be sure to knock."

Conall shuffled his feet. "It seems that I always end up appearing to be the bad guy," he said once his nephew left the room.

"Why would you say that?"

"Well, me not wanting to talk about the legends and such. It's just very...personal for me. I hope you take no offense."

I smiled and he looked relieved. If he always acted like this, I might be tempted to go out with him—no, not even.

Jess came into the room followed by Lundy who was speaking to her earnestly.

"It won't just be me," Lundy insisted. "There will be other girls and guys. It will be fun. The ceilidh was the only time you really had to meet everyone, and the music was so loud. We all didn't get to talk. The movie is supposed to be very good. I'll make sure you get back on the ferry in time."

I saw the volcano that was my daughter, Jessica Shaw, bubbling and simmering and about to blow.

"I said no. I said no several times. I am not going to change my mind. Why don't you ask Nessa? I bet she would love to go."

"Oh, no. Besides, she's already going."

"I bet she would love it if you did, all the same."

Lundy shook his head.

"Why not?"

"She isn't my type."

"Well what is your type?"

"You."

They both stopped talking when they realized we were all listening to them. Jess looked at me. I subtly shook my head. She gritted her teeth.

"I don't want to go out with you. I will never want to go out with you. If you ask me again, I am going to make sure you couldn't ride a horse, even if the horse was still enough to let you mount it."

Lundy took a minute to puzzle that out and when he realized to what she was referring, his hands went in front of his jewels.

Jess scowled. Lundy turned bright red, mumbled something to us, and left the cottage, slamming the door so hard that it bounced back open. Conall caught it before it hit the wall.

I turned to Conall. "I'm sorry. She's just—"

"Well, I'm not sorry! And I mean it. I want him to leave me alone!" Jessie practically ran back to her room.

Tate had followed the two of them out and was almost run over by Jessie. Tate carefully shielded the kitten she cradled.

"He really wouldn't stop asking, Mom," Tate said, taking up for her sister. "It upset Jessie."

"I know, honey. I'll be in later and we can talk about it."

"Okay. Are you mad at Jessie?"

"No, just a little upset."

"Maybe the kitty will cheer her up." She went back to the room with the kitten snug in her arms.

"I'm sorry. He gets a little over eager, I guess. I was the same at his age, stuck on a girl who didn't want me." Conall frowned. "Well then, I'll be off and catch up with my nephew. Thank you for the dinner."

Once he left, I shut the door and leaned back against it. "Whew." I turned to Kay who was getting her coat. "Kay, why wouldn't Greg talk to me about the stuff that's happened?"

Kay thought for a moment. "Perhaps, living in the woods, he's too close to all of it. If he deals with things like that every day, maybe he doesn't want to deal with it at other times."

"He doesn't have to live in the woods."

"I suspect he does—or at least he feels he must. Hopefully, someday that will change."

"I think the girls and I are going to the mainland tomorrow. I think we all need some time away."

"That may be for the best." She reached for the door, but turned back to me. "We do have our secrets, but let me ask you this, Becca—if you could turn into a huge cat, how many people would you tell? Who would believe you if you told them about a goblin lady with sharp teeth crawling like a spider in a cave? Who would have believed you if you said you were almost drowned by grindylows?"

"I know that, Kay, but—this island has tourists. Surely they see things."

"Actually, no, they don't. If they see something, it's easily explained away, usually by the tourist who saw it. Their minds try to make it be something they can deal with—something they're familiar with. Also, no one I have ever heard of outside the islanders has had so many, and so close, interactions with the fae as you and the girls have. It's unusual. It's unusual even for islanders to have so many close encounters."

"At the cave—it was a bit frightening, but I may go back and see if I can talk to her," I said.

"I would have one of her family there too. She's been wild and alone for a long time."

"Are there any stories about other strangers that see the fae on the island?"

"Not that I'm aware of—not like your experiences. Perhaps you have the Sight."

"What's the Sight? Davina mentioned it. I thought that was seeing into the future like Cassandra."

"The Sight is a gift that few humans have. It grants you the ability to see fae. The fae are curious about those who can see them. That's how Thomas the Rhyme ended up in a fairy hill. The fae keep to themselves, usually. It's safer for all that way. Can you imagine what would happen if everyone knew of them? And they freely wandered the Earth with no camouflage?"

"Do they?"

"Do they what?"

"Roam?"

"Rarely, and rarely does anything bad happen, but sometimes some of the disasters attributed to nature or man—fae were involved. It was more common a long time ago."

"Why do the fae hide?"

"Do you know the tales about the leprechaun?'

"Yes, if you catch him, he'll give you three wishes, and he has a pot of gold hidden somewhere."

"Humans are jealous of the fae's powers and beauty. Mankind harassed them. Their numbers dwindled to the point that the fae thought they would be no more than stories. They live in a different place, and they closed the door between, so none could get out and none can get in. Some fae want to be seen. They want to be a part of Man's world. Most of them want to rule over humans, have slaves. Some find human babies a…um…culinary delicacy."

I shivered. "Well. If you wanted to scare me, you succeeded. Eep."

"You should be fine. Don't take risks—like walking off into the woods alone."

"In any other woods, I would've been perfectly fine. I never was that far from civilization—at least I shouldn't have been."

"Distance and time aren't always the same in the fae's home and the land near it. Guess I should be leaving, unless you want some help cleaning up?"

"Thanks, but no. It isn't like it was a six-course meal." I touched Kay's shoulder. "Will you be okay walking home alone?"

"I think I'll be careful too." She took her shoes off and placed them in a bag then stepped out on the ground. Seconds later, a huge black cat stood curling its back up then stretching and kneading the lawn with its very large claws.

"Well, I'm glad you're friendly. Those claws could cause some damage. And I know you can't answer me now, but where do your clothes and purse go when you change and how do they come back?"

"Mrrr-ow," the cat said and then padded off into the dark.

"Wow." Tate stood at the doorway. "Miss Sheey is Kiera?"

Great. There are all these secrets and, of course, my girls manage to see these things too. "Yes, she can turn into a cat. And don't ask me how, I don't know."

"Jess is crying and won't stop."

I sighed. "I'll go talk to her. Could you stay out here? I'd like to have a moment to ourselves."

"Okay, Mom."

I should have known better with my background, but I spoiled the girls. I was the helicopter mom. Always at school, always volunteering. I didn't like confrontation, so I'd talk to David about any problems, and if he felt an issue had come up that we needed to deal with, he'd go with me to talk to the teacher. Show a united front, he said. I think he thought I couldn't deal with it. He did everything for me. He even put gas in the car. We both tended to talk to the girls like adults. When the girls were little, they would say Mommy and Daddy were their best friends, but they outgrew it. I started to realize that I didn't do them any favors by being so easy going.

I went to the bedroom. Jessie's face was mashed into the pillow to muffle the sound, but I could see her shoulders heaving and heard a low moan. "They're gone, Jess."

She immediately sat up and glared at me. "I want to go home," she gritted out through clenched teeth. "If you want to stay here, fine. I know Grandma or Aunt Jan will let me stay with them. I texted them."

She texted them? "When did you do that?"

"When school ended and you said we weren't going back to Houston for the summer but coming to this dumb island."

I couldn't believe that my sister-in-law and mother-in-law never said a word to me. We had traded texts and emails several times. I didn't call all that much because of the time difference. My husband was the one religious about keeping in touch regularly about everything.

"First of all, moving out of your home is not an option, so take that off the board right now."

"That's just it! We aren't home. We aren't even home when we're in Aberdeen. This is *not* home. Houston is home—or it used to be, before you rented the house and put most of our stuff into storage."

"I think both of you girls need to hear this." I called out, "Tate, come here for a moment."

Tate appeared so fast that it was a sure thing that she had been listening at the door.

"Come here and sit by me."

Tate sat Indian style on the bed with Jess. We formed a triangle—I hoped—and not my side and their side. "Losing your father was hard for all of us." Jess started to speak, but I held my hand up. They were going to hear me out without interruption. "Your dad did a lot. He paid the bills and the taxes. He put gas in the car. He programmed the DVR. I shouldn't have become so dependent on him, but I did. When he died, I was overwhelmed." I took a deep breath. "But I managed. I figured it all out. I made some mistakes, sure, but I found out that I was capable of doing things. I love your father's family, but they hovered too close. They constantly reminded me of your dad, and I was always upset. I think they did so because your dad took care of everyone. He took care of his siblings, his parents—and I think they were having a harder time dealing with him being gone than we were."

"Grandma cried every time we saw her," Tate pointed out.

"Shhh," Jess said.

"I told them that, while the insurance money would last for a while—your dad was good that way—it wouldn't last forever. I needed to continue teaching. There was a major dip in income since your father made quite a bit, but we're just fine financially. However, I told your father's relatives that I couldn't fund their ventures as your dad had. I told them that I adjusted, and they needed to as well." I looked at each of them. "When they saw that I was handling everything that your dad had with only a few problems, they started asking for my help. Uncle John was the last straw."

"What did he do?" Jess asked.

"The restaurant lost a load of money in the two months after your dad died. I don't know how your uncle managed to botch things so badly. Quarterly taxes were due, and he didn't have it. I had already given him a few loans from the money your dad left for us, but that was slowly dwindling."

"Didn't they get something when dad died?" Jess had apparently heard some of the will talk.

"Yes, they did. It wasn't as much as what we inherited, but it was a tidy sum. They spent it instead of investing it or paying off credit cards." One of the things David did was talk to the girls about finances. He didn't want them to turn out like his mother—or me, I guessed. When I was single, I had my own place, a career, a bank account, and managed just fine. But after I married, David wasn't happy with the way I budgeted, balanced the checkbook, filled out the tax forms. Slowly, he took over these tasks and others. I guess he didn't think that I could do it, or do it well enough. *Ouch.*

"We know to save money for a rainy day and don't buy something you don't have enough cash for," Tate said.

"Yes, you do. Some people never learn those valuable lessons. I was getting calls all the time and visits. I finally decided that I would go far enough away that they wouldn't be able to try to get me to help them, and I wouldn't be badgered and guilt tripped. I guess I didn't think it through as to how you two would react. When I was little, I would have given anything to go on a trip to Scotland, but I was a bit of a loner." I handed Jessie a tissue and she blew her nose. "We're here now. I would like to stay until you, Jess, graduate from high school."

"Mom, that's three years!" Jess wailed.

"I've already spoken to the school. I asked them if I could think about it. I have and we're going to stay."

Tate clapped.

Jess tossed her tissue at Tate. "Oh, shut up, Tate."

"Ewww! Mom!"

"Stop it now!" I called out over their voices, then I grasped each of them by the forearm. Their eyes widened. "I need your support. What I don't need is you two fighting with each other."

Jess wrapped her arms around her knees. "I hate this place, Mom. Can we at least go back to Aberdeen? I don't like it there, but at least I don't have a dork following me around town."

"I'll consider your request, but for now we're staying. You two will be helping me around the cottage."

"With what?" Jess asked suspiciously.

"The garden, for one. If you're interested in those spells, Jess, Kay told me a lot of them need herbs. A lot of herbs grow in the garden, and we can plant more."

"Why?" Jessie asked.

That was a good question. When I originally started tidying the garden, it was because David always hired a gardener, and I was rarely able to get my hands dirty between car-pools and PTA meetings. I did work in the garden as a youngster and missed it.

"I think it would be a nice gift to Mrs. Grant. The price to rent this place was ridiculously low and whoever she rents the cottage to in the future can enjoy it."

"I guess we can help out," Jessie said with a resigned sigh. "It isn't like there is anything else to do on this stupid island."

Tate petted the cat as we spoke, but I knew she had listened carefully to the exchange.

"What about you?" I asked her.

"I can help. I already do by taking care of the kitten," she answered.

"While we're here, I want both of you to be very careful. Tate, no going anywhere without an adult or your sister. Jess, I want to know exactly where you are at all times and that doesn't mean calling me and telling me when you're already somewhere. It means letting me know beforehand."

Jess groaned. "I'm not a baby!"

"No, you aren't. You're a young woman in a new place where large wolves roam. We've seen them out during the day around people. I think that's highly unusual. Despite that, I've found being here restful. Well, it would be more so if I knew what was going on—but still much better than the hustle and bustle of adjusting to a new school, new grade, new class, new country—new everything. I thought we could get off the island tomorrow and go to town. See what movies are on. Do some shopping."

Jess threw her arms around me. "That sounds wonderful!"

Jessica, your name should have been Quicksilver.

"I picked up some more brochures from the visitor's center while we were waiting for the ferry. We can look at those, and you two can decide what you would like to do and then we can see what we have time for. It's kinda late, but you can stay up for another hour. We won't catch the first ferry out." I winked. "The brochures should all be in a pile by the phone, Tate. You go and start looking. We will be there in a moment."

Jess studied her fingernails. The sparkle polish was starting to peel off, and she picked at it.

"Jess, you're old enough to know how to act. Your outburst was that of a much younger, ill-behaved brat. I didn't raise you to act like that. I've cut both of you a lot of slack this last year. Especially you. I hadn't realized how hard it would be leaving your friends and your school, but you've had time to adjust. I'm not going to punish you. I am, however, going to expect from you behavior that's appropriate for a well-mannered young lady."

Jess snickered. "Going to send us to charm school?"

"Don't tempt me. It would probably do both of you some good. So, are we clear?"

"Yes, Mom." She stood and trotted to the door, her shoulders rounded, and her feet dragging.

I caught up with her and hugged her tight. "I love you, Jessie Jellybean."

Jess snorted. "I love you too, Mom."

ぐっぐっ

I let the girls pore over the brochures. The town wasn't that large, and I didn't think they could pick anything that would be so far away that we couldn't manage to get there or that was too expensive. I checked my phone and to my surprise, had internet, so I went to my email and opened the one from Mrs. Grant—the family tree. *I wish I had a printer.* The print was small and faded. She, or I am guessing a younger relative, scanned the pages and sent them. I was surprised to see that many of the women kept their maiden names. Mrs. Grant, however, had taken her husband's last name. One of the last names looked familiar. It tugged at me. "Puldreach—I know I've seen that before, but where?" I paid more attention to the men's names. I wanted to find Greg's, but the print was so tiny, and I was so tired that I decided to look through it again tomorrow. Maybe I could find some of those magnifying glasses. *Oh no! I'm going to be wearing glasses around my neck like a little old librarian if I'm not careful.*

I told the girls it was time for bed. They didn't argue with me, thank goodness. I didn't know if it was because they took what I said to heart, or they were tired from the events of the day. I should have talked a bit to Jess about Greg, but one step at a time. I didn't know why it mattered. It wasn't like I was dating, and even if I was, we would be leaving soon.

CHAPTER 22

"Hurry up, girls, or we'll miss the ferry," I yelled, rushing into their room and tripping over my untied laces.

Jessie stood in front of the bureau mirror. She yanked a brush through her hair, sending the scarlet ends flying. "It's not my fault. I set my phone alarm. It didn't go off."

After I shoved the comforter and pillows to the center of an unmade bed, I sat and tied my shoes in double knots. "Where's Tate?"

"She's in the bathroom."

"Tate, we've got to go now." I didn't stomp my feet, but I wanted to.

Tate poked her head around the doorway. "I need to brush my teeth. Jessie hogged the sink."

"Forget the teeth. You can chew a piece of gum." I herded the girls to the door and outside.

"Mom, I want to get back in time to go to the library," Jessie said as she walked backwards.

"Let's see how the day goes. Now turn around before you fall on your rear."

Thanks to our late start, we decided to explore the town and eat an early lunch since we skipped breakfast to make the ferry. Afterward, the girls opted to see a movie, the latest comedy from the States. We hadn't wandered the cobbled streets for long before Jess spied Quaich Shopping Centre, and we had to go in for a brief look-see. The center housed a McD's and it was nothing doing that we had to eat there. After our McMeals, we had ample time to find the Cine Theatre and purchase tickets and sweeties.

I would have liked touring the ruins and seeing the circle, but Jess and Tate thought the aquarium would be cool, so we spent the rest of the afternoon staring at fish. Jess wanted to go on the ghost tour, but I vetoed it, for today, at least. I didn't want to return to the island after dark. The trip to the mainland turned out to be a good break. We all needed some time away from the strangeness. When we got back to Thistle, Jess and Tate wanted to visit the library. Tate had finished two books and wanted to check out more, and Jess wanted to chat with Fiona about school and driving. While she and Tate went there, I popped into the grocer for dinner supplies.

༄༅༄

The next day, I visited Mrs. Nivens, the oldest living person in the town. I didn't want to show up empty-handed. Conall insisted that she wouldn't mind me dropping in, but I was glad that he promised to tell her about it on his way home. I remembered visiting David's grandmother when she was in the nursing home. The trips always went better in the morning, so I would stop by around ten o'clock. I shopped at the tea shop for scones and biscuits. On a whim, I also purchased a vase of flowers.

As I approached Mrs. Niven's home, I admired the oak double entry door that featured beautiful stained glass at the sides and above. Seeing no doorbell, I lifted the knocker which looked like the head of a snarling wolf with a ring gripped between its teeth. I let it drop and waited. Soon the door opened, revealing an older woman with graying hair styled in a bouffant that went out in the sixties.

"Hello, you must be Mrs. Shaw."

"Yes, but please call me Becca."

"Come in, come in." She ushered me in an entry way which held a coat rack and an umbrella stand with two lonely black umbrellas in one corner. On the opposite wall stood a full-length mirror beside a shelf filled with dusty figurines and vases. The spotted glass reflected a mottled image of us. I could have sworn I saw someone peeping from behind my shoulder. I wheeled around, but no one was directly behind me. Shaking my head, I turned my attention again to the woman.

"My name is Dorcas Anderson," she said. "I come over in the mornings and evenings to help Mrs. Nivens."

"Nice to meet you, Mrs. Anderson."

"Please—Dorcas." She led me through another set of double doors into to a large foyer. A beautiful staircase, marred only by a chair lift, curved upward. I followed Dorcas down a hall and into what must be the parlor. A fireplace easily big enough to cook a boar was centered on the back wall. Two groupings of chairs, sofas, and tables were arranged around it. A thread-bare Aubusson rug with a still-vibrant red floral pattern lay on the wood floor.

"Please have a seat." She gestured to two chairs and a sofa with matching faded gold upholstery grouped around a recently cleared-off table, judging from the spots clear of a light layer of dust. Dorcas shook her head, tugged a rag from her apron pocket, and wiped it down. "Housekeeping never ends, especially in a house of this size."

As I waited for Dorcas to tell Mrs. Nivens I'd arrived, I admired the wood carving along the upper left wall. Animals cavorted in a forest. The setting was so detailed that it was difficult to pick out the animals. The wolf family featured in the center of the carving were the only animals that I didn't have to do a Where's Waldo to find. I heard a shuffling and an elderly lady entered with Dorcas anxiously mother-henning her. I stood.

"I told you, Dorcas. I am quite capable of walking to the parlor. Stop hovering like a hummingbird."

Dorcas reached for the lady's elbow but drew back at her scowl. "I know you can normally, but these shoes you've chosen to wear are higher than your usual ones. I don't want you to fall."

"Especially on your watch. Be missing that paycheck." It took her a while to traverse the floor, so I met her halfway. "Hello, dear, you must be Rebecca. I am Mornia Nivens."

Though I felt the urge to curtsey, instead, I took her hand and gently shook. "It's a pleasure to meet you."

She gestured at the small vase. "Oh my! Are those for me?"

"Yes, I also stopped by the tea shop and bought some scones and biscuits."

"Delightful. Thank you so much." She turned to Dorcas. "Please add some of these to the platters and then bring the tea. The flowers will look lovely on that side table, the one with the Limoges boxes."

Dorcas bustled about to do her bidding.

Mrs. Nivens gestured. "Sit down, sit down."

I took a seat on the couch while Mrs. Nivens sat on a large, upholstered chair. A pair of glasses and a pitcher of water sat on the side table beside a Tiffany lamp and a paperback book with a place marker in it.

When the tea came, Mrs. Nivens asked me to be

mother. I poured for each of us. We chose a cookie and scone to nosh. Dorcas remained and Mrs. Nivens encouraged her to get something. Dorcas sat on one of the chairs at the other grouping. Close enough to help if needed, but far enough to at least suggest privacy.

"Conall tells me you are interested in the history of the island," Mrs. Nivens said.

"Yes, yes, I am." Originally, I had intended to ask about Greg, but with everything else that had happened, I had more questions and wasn't sure where to start. I decided to start with her family. Most people love to talk about themselves. "I noticed your unusual door knocker and the carvings. The wolves are quite realistic looking."

"This home has been in my family since the McNeils first moved to the island. My maiden name is McNeil. I suppose when I die, it shall go to Conall. He's the only one left. The others have moved away or died."

"Is there a reason for the wolves—aside from them being attractive?"

"There's a tale. There were several reasons the first McNeil family moved here. One was the privacy. Another was the animals. There used to be more wildlife diversity before my family moved here, but my ancestor was an avid hunter. I shall take you into the trophy room when we finish our tea. The story is that he was out hunting one day and saw a beautiful, rare, white wolf. He was determined to have it. He finally cornered it in a cave and discovered the wolf had pups almost ready to be weaned. Hunters leave nursing mothers alone most of the time, so there will be more animals to hunt later, but my ancestor didn't care. He wanted the pelt at any cost. The cornered wolf attacked the man so that the young pups could escape. He was able to get his gun up and shot the wolf several times, eventually killing it, but he didn't come out of it unscathed.

"Though the man had been wearing several layers of clothing and a thick coat, the wolf bit his forearm hard enough to pierce the skin. The man bragged of his prowess and decided to stuff the wolf, which we still have. The wound became infected, but eventually healed. I'm told that he was cursed to turn into a wolf at the full moon. I don't know about that. I do know that his wife had one more child with him and then moved out. A nanny was hired to care for the children. The man remarried. Years later, he was found in the woods, dead from a gunshot wound. Some believe that he transformed into a wolf when he was in the forest and someone shot him.

"I think its rubbish, of course. Conall and his nephew, Lundy are the first adult males in the family for a long time—at least the first to have remained on the island. The McNeil family has had mostly daughters and the few sons that were born died early, to the despair of most of the kin.

"The wolf touches were added by the eldest McNeil son. He built onto this part of the house and incorporated many wolves in the décor—I am thinking more to scare the peasants than anything else. By all accounts, he was a grim man who eschewed company."

"Well, that's some story. Did your ancestors keep any records or journals?"

"Not really. As an exercise, one of the tutors had the children use a journal to write an entry a day about what they did. I believe they're still in the nursery upstairs. You're welcome to look for them. Dull things, for the most part. Childish and devoid of much detail."

"Incidentally, thank you for inviting us to the ceilidh. We got to meet most of the islanders there."

"Nae trouble. I had no idea anyone had moved in for the summer. The cottage has stood empty for many years, since Mrs. Grant moved out. Conall told me. The entire village was invited and since you now live here, the invitation was extended to you and your family too."

"A man chatted with me for a bit at your party, a Mr. Gillie. Do you know Greg Gillie? I had the impression that he and Conall weren't on good terms."

"A handsome man, that one. I was surprised to see him there. He keeps to himself. Seems like there has always been a Greg Gillie in the forest, though of course, it must be a family name passed down to the sons. There's some story about the Gillie family dying in a fire, but of course that must be a falsehood since a Gillie is still here. I've never been to the man's home. I don't know if anyone has. Like a hermit that man is. Wouldn't surprise me if he has a wife and kids hidden there."

Now that's a sobering thought. "How in the world would he even meet anyone if he never leaves?"

"Goodness, you don't imagine that the ferry is the only way on and off the island? Several people here have boats and make the trip when the urge comes. And there are people on the mainland who have boats and can boat over here if they have the urge. We don't live on the moon, dearie." Mrs. Nivens laughed then started coughing. Dorcas rushed over to pour her a glass of water. When she stopped coughing, I decided to move to another topic.

"What do you know about the people who live near the cave and do tours?"

"Oh my, you're interested in the people more than the island. They arrived here sometime after my family did. I believe the Gillie family did too, but I'm not sure. The Oggs are a creepy family, all pale and quiet. I think they're albinos or have some sort of hereditary skin disorder. They have their groceries delivered and don't tend to venture into town at all. They were invited to my party, but they sent their regrets. No reason was given, just that they couldna come. The few others who couldna make it gave me a reason, but not them. Tight-lipped, they are. As bad as that Gillie, I'd say, though there are more of them, so slightly more likely to see them than Mr. Gillie. Could you pour me another cup of tea, dear?"

I poured her and myself more. "Dorcas, would you like more?"

Dorcas came and proffered her cup. "Just a half cup, please."

I asked about the hero-in-the-woods story, but Mrs. Nivens pooh-poohed it. "Children have been rescued from the forest many times over the years. There are always tales of that sort."

I chatted for another fifteen minutes but noticed that Mrs. Nivens's head began to droop.

Dorcas quietly went to her side and took the tea cup from her before it spilled down the front of her dress. "Mrs. Nivens? Why don't you lie down for a bit?"

She snorted. "Huh, what? Oh, no, Dorcas. I am not tired in the least.' She looked up at me. "Well, hello, dear. Now what were we talking about?"

"Thank you for your time, Mrs. Nivens, but I do need to get going. Before I do, would it be okay if I looked in the nursery?"

"Why ever would you want to go there? It is perfectly fine with me if you want to. Just be warned, it's a dusty mess. No one has been in there in ages. Dorcas?"

"Yes, ma'am."

"I think I will read a bit on the chaise."

"Of course. I'll get you situated and bring you your book."

"Now, Dorcas. What have I told you? I'm not an invalid." Mrs. Nivens slapped Dorcas's hand away and heaved herself off the chair. She wobbled a bit but found her balance and tottered off. "Good bye, dear. Thank you for visiting," she said as she left.

"I'll be right back," Dorcas said as she snatched the book from the end table and hurried after Mrs. Nivens.

I finished a biscuit and a short time later, Dorcas returned.

"She's already asleep. She doesn't like to admit she needs more rest, and she was so excited that you were coming that she wore herself out."

"I noticed she was beginning to fish there."

"Aye. Now you wanted to go to the nursery?"

"If you don't mind, yes."

"I haven't been in it, but I imagine it shouldn't be too hard to find." I followed her out the room and to the stairs. I admired the wood banister as I bypassed the chair lift and walked upstairs. We went down a long hallway lined with doors. She opened the one farthest from the stairs. "I think they put the children as far away from the rest of the family as possible. In those days, it seems like other people raised the gentry—nannies and tutors and such. I think they only saw the children once to say good morning and once to say good night and on the occasional special holidays or events. Sad that."

"Yes, it is."

We stepped into the room. Dingy sheets covered much of the furniture. There were so many boxes and trunks that there was hardly any room to move about.

"Goodness. It looks like the nursery has been enlisted to double as a storage room." She peeked under a few sheets. "Aha, a bassinet. We must have the right place. Well then, I'll leave you to it. I'll clean up and then be in the parlor reading. Just get me when you're ready to go."

"Thank you."

Dorcas turned to leave.

Well, Becca. What have you gotten yourself into? I

peeked under sheets to see what the larger items were. I saw the usual furniture you would find in a nursery, plus some pieces from other parts of the house that needed repair. Nothing resembling journals lie there. I left one of the chairs uncovered to sit on while I tackled a box.

I hoped that I would recognize immediately which box should have such items because if I had to open and examine every single one, it was going to take ages. I found old moth-eaten clothes, books, toys, linen for the crib, and a layette. Finally, one trunk held what looked to be exercise books. *Promising.* I carefully looked through and found items dating back to the late eighteenth century. Finally, underneath an art project made of old buttons, I found five journals in childish scrawl. They were faded and difficult to read. I gathered them up and went down stairs. Dorcas was exactly where she said she would be.

"So, you found it?"

"I believe I did. Do you think that it would be okay if I took them home to look at?"

"I think that would be fine. Mrs. Nivens's youngest sister should be over soon to take over. The family tries to have someone with her at all times during the day. So far, she's been sleeping during the night, thank goodness. So many older people become nocturnal and up at all hours into mischief."

"Halloo?" An elderly woman peeked around the corner. "There you are, Dorcas. How is she today?"

"Happy as can be. She had a visitor. This is Rebecca Shaw. She's staying in Mrs. Grant's cottage over the summer."

"Hello, nice to meet you and thank you for visiting. Sissy can't get out on her own very well."

"I'll try to come by again. Talking to her was quite fascinating. But now I need to be getting back home. So nice to meet you."

She walked Dorcas and me to the door. I didn't really think any light would be shed on the happenings on the island by the children's writing, but I had to check into it just in case.

⁂

The girls Skyped with their aunt. I wanted to talk to her too, but when the girls weren't around. It still rankled me that she said nothing about her conversation with Jessie and promised to let her stay with her without mentioning any of it to me. As I opened the door, I called out. "Tate, Jess? How did your chat go?"

They were on the floor playing Chinese Checkers. "Okay, I guess," Jess said.

"She was mad," Tate added.

I sat on the couch. "She was? What about?"

"Uncle John's gonna lose the restaurant and his house. She said it was because you wouldn't help him out."

That biddy!

"Jessie stuck up for you. She said that it was his fault not yours, and that he needed to be better with his money if he didn't want to lose his home. Then Aunt Jan blew up at Jess."

"Oh, Jess. I'm sorry, hon. You should've just let it go. I plan on talking to your aunt and grandma later on."

"You're our mom. She had no business blaming you because Uncle John's an idiot."

"Jess, let's not call people idiots."

"Well, he is."

I had to smile. "Yes, he is, but we don't call people names. Thanks for taking up for me. Did you two have lunch?" I wasn't hungry since I ate all those cookies and drank all that tea.

"We made grilled cheese sandwiches."

"Good. Let's get started on some gardening."

The girls groaned, but stood and put on their shoes. We spent much of the afternoon weeding. We also tried to identify all the plants. Jess told me what all she had learned from Fiona. She was excited about the younger drinking age, but nervous about the driver's test. I reassured her that it would be easier for her because we had an automatic, and I would take her out a lot to get practice. When I decided we had done enough, Tate scampered ahead while Jessie and I took a more leisurely pace.

"When I was at the library, Fiona tucked her hair behind her ear. Do you know her ear is pointed?" Jessie said.

"Really?"

"Yes, I asked her about it and she seemed embarrassed. Should I have not said anything?"

"Well, sounds like she's sensitive about it, so I would probably not bring it up again."

"I thought it was kind of cool, but I guess being different can bother people just because they *are* different. Even if the difference is better or just...well, different."

"True."

Jessie followed me to the bathroom, and we scrubbed our begrimed hands at the sink. "Mom, do you like that Greg guy?" she asked, picking at the soil under her nails.

"Yes, I do."

She slid the soap in the dish and looked at me. "Don't you miss Dad?"

"Yes, every day. But I've been lonely."

"You have us—and Kay."

"I do. But I think I can care about more than one person, don't you?"

"Yes—I just sometimes wish you wouldn't."

"I kinda got that." I finished washing my hands and tugged the towel off the rack. "Maybe you could help me with something. Mrs. Grant sent me her family tree and I'm having a hard time reading it. Could you see if you can write it down on a sheet of paper for me to read?"

"Sure."

We finished cleaning our hands and joined Tate in the living room. During our foray at the library, I printed off the email. I wanted to be able to look at it even if the power went out—which seemed to be a regular occurrence. I handed it to Jess and she sat at the table to work. Tate helped me with dinner.

I was about to interrupt Jessie so I could set the table when she said, "Well, I think I've deciphered it." She handed me several pages.

I scanned the notes toward the end that were the most faded. I had thought one name said Williams, but Jessie read it as Ghillie, Grieg Ghillie. "Looks like this Ghillie married the sister of one of Mrs. Grant's ancestors. Hmmm—Mrs. Grant may be related to Mr. Gillie. I think that's an alternative spelling. Thanks, honey, for doing this." Unfortunately, I had no way to contact Greg, because I would love to hear what he had to say.

"What's that?" Tate asked.

"It's Mrs. Grant's family tree. It looks like she may be related to Mr. Gillie."

Tate bent over to look over my shoulder. "Do we have a family tree?"

"I don't have one of your dad's, but I'm sure your aunt and grandmother can give you some information. I do have some information about my side of the family. I saved it as a doc at some point. Would you like to see it?"

"Is it just a bunch of names? "

"Names and dates."

"I'd like to see it," Jess said.

"I'll pull it up, if I can." I smiled. "Let's do it after dinner."

We ate dinner and cleaned up the dishes. I pulled up my documents and found the family tree hidden amongst my other information. I gave my phone to Jess to look at. After a few moments, she said, "Hey, Mom. Here's the name Puldreach. She came from Scotland."

I remembered seeing the last name on Mrs. Grant's family tree. "Maybe it's a common Scottish name." I studied the tree. "Tomorrow, we'll go by the library and get my tree copied down so we can compare them side by side. It would be kind of funny if we were related to Mrs. Grant."

"Then we would be related to Mr. Gillie too?"

"By marriage, maybe."

CHAPTER 23

The next day, I woke up early. The girls were sound asleep, and I didn't want to rouse them, so I went out to the garden. All the seeds we had planted from the shed were already growing and some of the other bushes, that I thought were dead, had buds on the branches. Small apples hung from a tree, and it wasn't the season for it.

"How in the world…"

Kay was walking down the lane when I went back to the house. I waved and she came over. "How was your outing?" she asked.

"Okay. We visited the aquarium, did some shopping, and went to the library when we got back. Do plants typically grow well here?"

Kay shrugged. "As well as any other place, I guess. Why?"

I gestured. "Come back here to the garden. The girls and I planted seeds just a few days ago, and they've already sprouted."

Kay followed me and I pointed out the new plants and apples.

"I guess you have a green thumb."

"I do, but this is crazy. Normal plants don't grow that fast. Do you think it's the seeds? Is this stuff even safe to eat?"

"I would think so, but why don't you ask Mrs. Grant if you're worried about it."

"I guess I will. We do have enough plants that Jess can try one of the spells in the book. A simple one that doesn't involve eating."

"So, you'll let her keep the book?"

"I'm still nervous about it. But, surely, it's harmless, right? It isn't evil? Mrs. Grant isn't a devil worshipper, is she?" I was sure I sounded daft, but I had to ask.

Kay laughed. "You really think she is? She's a little old woman with grand kiddies."

"Hey, I bet there are little old grannies who worship the devil!"

Kay chuckled. "Let's go in. I'll let you make me a cup of tea."

∞∞∞

We were just sitting down to tea when the girls woke. Kay had brought some scones from the tea shop and the girls made short work of them.

I told the girls we could try a spell and pored over the book to see our options. We decided to make something that would keep away wolves. It seemed useful, and we had the ingredients. We had to gather the herbs and grind them with a mortar and pestle.

"It would be a lot easier to use a food processor," Jess commented.

Kay hid a smile behind her hand. "Yes, but a part of what makes the spell work is the effort you put in making it. Using a food processor would take less effort. I'm betting the spell wouldn't even work then."

"How will we know for sure if it does?" Jessie asked as she blew at a strand of hair hanging in front of her face and wiped her forearm over her brow.

"Well, those wolves should stop coming around." Kay advised Jess what to do, but let her do all the spelling.

Tate watched for a while, but when the "herb smushing," as she called it, began, she retired to the bedroom.

"I wonder if we could put the stuff in a sachet and wear it?" Jess asked.

I was gratified to see her clearing the counters of utensils and wiping them down without being reminded.

I glanced at Kay, wondering what her answer would be.

"I haven't heard anyone doing that, and I would be curious to see if it worked," Kay said.

"Do you know many witches?" I asked.

"Not many. But I'm renewing a friendship with one."

"Is that the lady you brought on Friday?"

"Yes, she is."

"I would love to talk to her and find out what she knows."

"I'll let her know. I'm sure she would be happy to talk to you if you really want to learn more, as long as you weren't trying to make fun of her. Sometimes it's hard to openly be a witch. People can get nasty. I'm trying to talk her into moving here. She has a very good job on the mainland, and hates to lose the income, even though she doesn't particularly like the work."

The finished potion required one last step which was to let sit in a muslin cloth overnight to drain off the liquid. "The resulting powder is the potion," Kay said.

There was a knock at the door. To my surprise, it was Greg.

He held burlap bundles with green peeking from the tops and shifted for foot to foot. "I saw you were working on the garden. Some rare plants grow in the forest and I dug a few up for you to plant here."

"Thank you! So far, we've weeded and prepared the soil. We planted some old seeds I found in the shed, but that's all. I was going to go to the village and see what they sold."

"Well then, I'm off," Kay said as she dried off her hands.

After Kay left, Greg told me the names of the plants he brought and helped me plant them. Once Jess noted the plant names, she went to the bedroom to read the spell book and see what other spells she could do with the additions.

Tate was trying to teach the kitten to walk on a leash—with very little success. I finally told her to take the poor thing inside to get something to eat and drink and pointed out that cats, typically, didn't walk on leashes well.

Greg patted dirt around a plant and sat back on his heels. I still marveled at how he managed the kilt better than I did a skirt. I would have asked him for pointers but was pretty sure it would fluster him.

We worked in silence for a while. I wanted to ask him a question but was afraid of being gauche. After a few moments of wavering, I finally decided I would brave inquiries. "Greg, have you helped other lost children? Are you the forest hero I read about in the newspaper? Why do you continue to live out there?" I blurted out in a rush.

"Aye, I've helped lost bairns like yours before. As for living in the woods, I like it, for one. And I have much to do."

"What *do* you do all day?"

"Take care of the forest."

"Won't the forests take care of itself?"

"Not this one. Would you like to come someday and see my home?"

The change of topic was abrupt, but I'd take it. My heart did a little jig and I tried not to sound too eager. "Yes, I'd love that."

"Tomorrow, then? I can come and escort you to my place in the afternoon around two, if that time is convenient for you."

"Let me talk to the girls about it."

"They are, of course, welcome to come." Considering the happenings in the forest, I was reluctant for the girls to spend any time in there, though I did trust Greg. Also, I wanted to spend time alone with him.

A thought occurred to me. "How will I be able to let you know?"

"I can stop back by here in the evening."

"Would you like to eat dinner with us?" I couldn't believe I asked him to dinner again. It would be the third such invitation in just a few short days.

"I would love to, if it's nae trouble."

"None at all. We have to eat dinner and making enough for one more is no problem." I was yammering. How embarrassing.

We washed our hands under the outside faucet. As he washed his, I noticed a red, angry-looking spot. "What happened there?"

"Oh, it's a splinter. It will work its way out eventually."

"Can you see the tip?"

"Aye, 'tis too small and deep to grasp."

"If you can come inside for a few, I can try something that might work."

"Aye."

One of the items that the girls bought when out and about was glue. I took his hand, it was warm and large. I thought how my hand fit in his and hurried to examined the splinter.

"That's a pretty big piece." The splinter broke off flush with the skin but the end I saw was as big as the head of a pin.

"It tapers," he explained.

I found the glue and squeezed s blob out on his finger. "Now, we wait." I enjoyed his perplexed expression. "Would you like some tea?" Though I already had some with Kay, I was fine having another. Cups of tea had taken the place of the tons of diet cokes and coffee I used to drink in the States.

"Aye, that would be nice."

I started the pot and gathered the sugar and cream. Something else I never bought until I lived in Scotland.

"I'm glad to have met you, Rebecca," Greg said when I brought the tea.

"I'm glad to have met you too." Then there was one of those awkward moments when you don't know what to talk about. The tea was ready. I poured a cup for each of us. "I'm going back to the caves, but I don't want the girls to come. I don't really want to go alone either. Would you come with me?" *Good way to fill dead air, Becca.* I willed myself not to redden.

"Me?"

I wished I could stick my head in a bucket of ice water as I felt my cheeks stain pink. "If it's any trouble, I can ask Kay—"

"Nae trouble, I was just surprised. When were you thinking to go?"

"Well, if we go tomorrow morning, I can give you the answer about the afternoon visiting your house."

"Yes, it sounds like a date." He flushed after he said the word date. It was unexpected on his broad form, but becoming. It lent an innocence to his masculine presence that endeared me even more.

Jess came and started when she saw Greg.

"I'm trying to get a splinter out of his finger to repay him for bringing the plants over."

"Mom? I changed my mind about that movie. Is it okay if I go? It got a U certificate. I can take Tate." Jessie had been pretty adamant about not wanting to be anywhere near Lundy, and since Gavin wouldn't be at this outing, she firmly declined. Now, all of a sudden, she wanted to go? I knew something was going on, but I had no idea what.

"I guess it's okay. What time is the movie?"

"It isn't 'til six, but some of the girls are getting together earlier at Nessa's. Tate knows Nessa's little sister."

"What time would that be?"

"In the morning, around nine."

"And you're sure this is okay with the family? That seems awfully early to show up for an evening movie."

"Mo-om! We just want to hang out. Play some games. Have fun." Jess heaved a put-upon sigh. "Here's the number if you want to call. I warned her you'd probably want to. Nessa's dad is Dr. Murphy."

Jess dialed the number, and I spoke to Mrs. Murphy, Nessa and Jody's mother. I remembered her from the party vaguely. Her husband was the village doctor. She had been very happy to see her daughter playing with Tate. Her daughter was very shy and didn't make friends easily. Mrs. Murphy reassured me again and again that it would be her pleasure, and she planned on going to the movie theater to keep an eye out on the kids.

'Sounds perfect." *Too perfect.* I added in my head.

"Then we can go?"

"I guess so."

Tate and Jess danced out of the room squealing.

Greg sipped his tea. "You're a good mother, Rebecca."

"Thank you."

He sighed. "I miss having a bairn about."

"I am so sorry."

"So am I."

The glue was dry so I carefully peeled it up and, sure enough, the splinter came up enough for me to grasp it with tweezers and pull it out. It had to have hurt, but he didn't make a sound. When I was done, I swabbed antibiotic gel on the wound then covered it with a band aid. I only had kid ones so it was neon green.

"Thank you. That was kind."

"No prob. Splinters are horribly uncomfortable and, frankly, if that one had stayed in any longer, I think you would have had been going to a doctor with an infection."

"Well, thank you for saving me the trip. So, tomorrow?"

"Let me give the Oggs a ring and see if the day is good for them." I searched through my purse, embarrassed by the amount of junk I had to shift out, but eventually found the card. I phoned and spoke to Davina, and, after quickly consulting her family, she said tomorrow would be fine. "We'll catch the bus out to the cave and you can go with me when I talk to this relative of the Oggs. If you're sure you want to."

"Aye, I am."

"Mom, come here and look," Tate called from the bedroom. "Hurry up!"

What now? I rushed to the room with Greg following me closely. The girls were gazing out the window pointing at figures near the edge of the forest. They looked like little men. Standing next to me, they'd come up to about to my knee. Their heads were red. I peered closer. The red wasn't hair and it dripped down their backs and shoulders like paint.

"Red Caps," Greg said. "I must deal with this." He turned to me. "I willna be able to stay for dinner."

"It's okay. I'll see you for—"

But Greg had already rushed out the room.

I followed him and was out in time to see him throw open the door and speed outside. "Well, goodbye then," I said to the closed door.

"They ran into the woods when they saw Mr. Gillie. He's following them," Jess yelled.

I turned to go back to the room, but before I could, the girls joined me.

"They're all gone. What was wrong with their heads?" Tate asked.

"I'm not sure, but now that they' gone, let's see to dinner." I locked the door and felt both disappointed and relieved that my guest had been called away.

CHAPTER 24

That night, I made sure to set my alarm. The last thing I wanted was for Greg to show up with me still in pajamas. In the morning, I walked the girls to the bus stop and waited with them. They were admonished to call me when they arrived and again when they reached the movie theater. I wished I had just waited to get ready after the girls left. Now, I was so nervous about it that I found myself completely ready and with plenty of time on my hands. I would have loved going out to work in the garden, but I didn't want to get dirty. Instead, I flipped through the pages of the spell book. It was not the original. This was a copy. I wondered where the first one was.

One of the recipes had notes in the margins. There was a change suggested and initials of the person who made the comment. I searched for more notes, in hopes of detecting who wrote the book. Based on the entries, you could tell it was written by multiple authors. The earlier entries were typed, beginning with an old manual typewriter and the last ones shifting to a newer one or perhaps even a computer because of the lack of corrections.

There was a tap at the door.

"Come on in," I said as I placed a receipt as a place marker and closed the book.

Greg cracked open the door and peeked around. He noticed the book. "What are you reading?"

"A book Kay gave Jessie. It's a book of potions."

"Oh? My wife had one." His face fell and I wished I hadn't had the book out when he arrived.

"Your wife? She was…"

"Aye, she was a witch."

I heard meowing. "The girls must have shut the kitten in their bedroom. I'll be right back." As soon as I opened the door, the kitten darted out. When I returned, the cat sat on Greg's lap as he petted it.

He gave the kitten one last stroke before dropping her to the floor. "I see you already have a potential familiar," Greg said.

"What?"

Greg gestured toward the kitten.

I shook my head. "Oh, the cat belongs to the girls."

"You all have the ability to be excellent witches with a little practice."

"Thank you, I think."

"The water bowl is running low, I see. Let me refill it."

While Greg took care of that, I thought about where my search for Greg's story had taken me. So far, I'd had no luck with finding anything on a Greg Gillie in the newer papers. I thought his family would be found in the obituaries, but my search in the library came up empty. I would check the cemetery when I had the time. There was a small plot located behind the church. The tourists enjoyed visiting the site. I also made a mental note to check the paper for information about fires and accidents.

Greg helped me into a jacket. I needed one since the cave was cooler inside than outside. While we waited for the bus, we spoke of mundane things like the weather at first. He was very interested in hearing about my life in Houston.

"I havena been to the New World. I rarely travel."

"You should see it someday. Houston has a lot to offer."

"Perhaps—someday." Although the bus was packed with tourists, Greg and I were able to sit together. The majority of our fellow riders seemed to be Canadians on an alumnae trip and a handful of other nationalities. When we reached our destination, Mrs. Ogg manned the front as she had when I visited. After she greeted the tourists, she came over.

"Thank you for coming. It means a lot to the children," Mrs. Ogg said. "After this tour, there's a break. If you can wait until then, that would be grand."

"Do you know Greg? I hope you don't mind that I brought him."

"Not at all."

Davina entered and began the museum tour. When she reached the point where the group was free to roam, she joined us. The day had been gray and chilly, even for a spring day in Scotland, let alone a summer one. The sky grew darker. "I hope it isn't going to storm again," I commented.

"Aye," Davina said distracted. "I ken of you, Mr. Gillie. How is it you are out of the forest?"

"There might be something I need to tend to here. I live in and see to the forest, but in my duty to keep the island safe, I am allowed to roam."

Now that sounded very odd. Almost like he was a prisoner. I started to ask him but decided to wait and talk about it on the way home.

"If you have any thoughts of hurting my nana—" Davina said.

"Nae, but she may be needing my help."

When it became evident that the group was ready to move on, Davina said, "I think it's best if you both stay here and not go on the tour—especially considering what happened last time."

"We will go after the tourists leave," Greg said.

"Because you'll miss the bus, we're happy to drive you back home, so you don't have to wait for the next one."

"I guess part of that will depend on how long we're in the cave." I hoped Blanca would show herself, and we wouldn't need search for her.

"True." Davina rounded up the group and announced that they would be entering the cave in a few moments.

Soon enough, Fingal joined his sister and they set off. Mrs. Ogg led us to the tea room which was redolent with the smell of fresh baked goods. Since I had been too nervous to eat earlier, my stomach emitted a loud borborygmus. "Excuse me," I murmured, hand on the errant tummy.

"Dinnae fash yourself. I'll bring tea and scones to tide you over," Mrs. Ogg said.

True to her word, she fetched two scones and a pot of tea. Greg refused his. Though I broke off small pieces and nibbled to make mine last, I eyed his with longing. To distract myself, I glanced out the window. The sky darkened and storm clouds roiled in the distance.

"Will we meet Mr. Ogg?" I asked, hoping I hadn't offended and wanting to take the attention of me and my wayward appetite.

"Aye, but he's wary of strangers. He actually takes a lot from his mother. Davina and Fingal told us about what happened during your tour of the cave. We were very reluctant to share our personal lives with you." She was silent for a moment then cleared her throat. "We're private folk, but she deemed to show herself to you, so we've decided to be candid. We've long worried about her." She took a deep breath. "You would nae guess from his looks that my husband is half goblin. You've seen Fingal. He looks much like his da. I think in his heart, Fingal's da is more so goblin, though. He seems cold to some—the few who meet him. But to me he's like a cool stream, calm and steady." Her eyes sparkled and a soft smile graced her face.

"You love him very much."

"That I do. If there's anyone he would be likely to meet, it would be the two of you. You, Mrs. Shaw, because of your abilities, and Greg—well, because of who you are."

Yep, another strange thing to say. I mean, who is Greg really? As far as I knew, he was a strange man who lived in the forest like a forest ranger. Last time I checked, it didn't have a certain stigma, like Conall and his nephew acted, nor the distinction Mrs. Ogg gave to him. I resisted the lonely scone, and Mrs. Ogg cleared it and the other dishes away to the counter. After she glanced at the utilitarian metal clock on the wall, she said, "When the children return, and the tourists leave, we can have something more substantial before you go to the cave to investigate."

I brushed the crumbs of the table into the palm of my hand and dusted them in the brown plastic bin in the corner. "Oh, I don't want to trouble you."

"It's the least I can do. You would be resting my husband's heart. He worries about his mother. The rest of his siblings, decided to go and live with the goblins. When they left, they tried to find their mum to take her with them, but she wouldna show herself."

Mrs. Ogg returned with a cloth to wipe down the table. "I wish that there was some way for my husband to visit his brothers and sisters. He misses them, but never had any desire to move to the hill."

"The hill?" I wondered if it was the same one I encountered.

"Yes, where the goblins live and the other fae."

"Where is it?" I asked. Lightning flashed and the lights flickered, but stayed on.

Mrs. Ogg organized the sugar and sugar substitute packages. "The hill's in the forest."

Curious. "Seems like a lot of people live there. Are they all fae or part fae?"

Greg answered the question. "Aye, most are. It really isna a suitable place for humans to spend much time."

I remembered the odd effect the hill had on me. "Why not?"

"Well, time moves differently there." He turned to Mrs. Ogg. "I am thinking it would be better if your husband's relatives visit him here instead of him going there. I believe I can arrange that—if his siblings are willing to come."

Dropping the last sugar package in the ceramic dish, Mrs. Ogg clasped her hands together. "Thank you. I didn't know if you made exceptions."

"I think I'm free to in this particular case. I will find out."

"How will you find out?" I asked.

"If it canna be done, I'll know it isna allowed."

The man was full of weird comments. We passed the time listening to Mrs. Ogg regaling us about artifacts they had in storage until displays could be made. The rest of the tourists drifted in, and Mrs. Ogg rose serve them. I offered to help but she shushed me and sent me back to the table.

The small scone wasn't enough and with lunch time approaching, my stomach gurgled to let me know. As

Greg tried to smother a laugh, I shrugged. "Sorry, a dainty girl, I'm not."

"I like to see a woman with an appetite. Dinna worry. Unlike you, I did eat breakfast."

Guess he wasn't as nervous about seeing me as I was about seeing him. That was kind of deflating.

Finally, the tourists filed out the door. The occasional splat of a raindrop fell while the last climbed on the bus, and we told the driver we would be staying. While we were at the bus stop, Mrs. Ogg had busied herself in the kitchen. When we returned, she brought out a plate of sandwiches and bags of chips. Davina and Fingal joined us and handed out bottled water.

"Yum. Salt and vinegar," I said, snagging a package.

"Eat up. There's plenty. I ate some as I made them, so in a few, I'll find Uisdean."

The siblings were quiet. I think they were nervous about the prospect of meeting their long-distant grandmother. We'd finished up the meal and were clearing the table, and Mrs. Ogg still had not returned.

When she had swallowed the last of her water and tossed the bottle in the bin, Davina said, "I'm going to check on Mum. I'll be right back." Only a few moments passed before, I heard raised voices. Davina, Mrs. Ogg, and a gentleman who I assume was Mr. Ogg were arguing.

"I'll not come and risk her not showing herself," Mrs. Ogg said as they entered the room.

"But you're a part of my life," the gentleman insisted. He did indeed look like an older version of Fingal.

"That I am, but not of hers."

"Let it go, Da. She's right, you know," Davina said.

"I suppose, but I don't have to like it."

Mrs. Ogg tenderly kissed her husband. "You don't have to, love. Now go on, the lot of you. I'm going to check and see what state these have left my kitchen. Probably nothing's put in the right place." Mrs. Ogg bustled off to the back.

"Greg, Becca. I'd like to introduce you to my father, Uisdean Ogg," Davina said.

"A pleasure to meet you." I didn't offer my hand.

He seemed a bit shy now that his wife stepped away. He nodded in my direction.

"Good day, sir," Greg said, also getting a nod.

"Well then, let's go," Davina said.

When thunder shook the house and lightening flashed so bright in the windows that it momentarily blinded me.

"I guess we should get the rain gear," Fingal said, eyeing the sky.

We wore sensible hiking boots. Though my windbreaker was waterproof and Greg wore a light poncho, neither Greg nor I had expected the downpour that seemed imminent.

Mrs. Ogg called from the back, "I'll fetch something for our guests and meet you at the door."

I accepted a mac and a hard hat with a headlamp, but Greg took the hat and nothing more. Davina and Fingal were in rain gear similar to mine. Mr. Ogg added nothing to his attire. Mrs. Ogg also gave a bag to Fingal.

"I packed water and food. You can never be too careful in a cave. Besides, I'm sure Blanca would appreciate it." We walked down the steps in pairs except for Mr. Ogg, who led. The wet, slippery stone steps slowed me down. Greg took my elbow and I smiled gratefully at him. We barely got inside the cave when the sky opened up. Fingal and Davina pulled backpacks from a storage unit at the cave's entrance and split the food and water between them. The light bulbs inside flickered.

"How do we want to do this?" I asked. "We can't just wander around for ages, hoping she'll notice."

Fingal shouldered a backpack. "I don't think that will be necessary. She notices everything. We'll go on the longer tour, the one that we had to skip thanks to those silly girls. If she hasn't made herself known by the end, then she doesn't want to communicate with us."

We made it to the observation point without seeing her. "I'm not surprised. She doesn't like the lights," Mr. Ogg said. "I can't say that I care for them much either."

We paused briefly for a drink then continued past it. The cave floor sloped downward and the walls of the cave narrowed until we could only go single file. Then the ceiling lowered until the stalagmites reduced the headroom enough that we needed to dodge them. Too busy watching our steps and heads, we didn't speak. Caught up in admiring a stalactite and I bumped my noggin. My helmet spared me from a nasty bump. The light bulbs vanished at some point, but I could still see. A lone bulb gave off a sickly, yellow light at the end of the tunnel. At the dead-end, I saw a rough-edged hole flush against the back wall, so dark, I couldn't see the bottom. "Fingal will go first and help you in," Mr. Ogg told me. "It isn't too far drop." *Drop?* I gulped.

Fingal, effortlessly, in one, seamless motion, sat and hung his feet over the edge then, with a push of his hands, disappeared from sight.

"Show off," Davina called out. She turned to us. "The ledges are difficult to see, but they're there. Fingal will help you with your footing. Just sit on the ledge then turn on your stomach to face me. Fingal will direct your feet to the first ledge and help you down. Come, Becca, you're next."

I took a deep breath. "How do we get back up?"

"It's much easier to climb up because you can see where your feet go. It looks scary and people get a kick about having to kind of crawl through. This is one of the photo opportunities."

I sat on the edge facing the wall. Glancing back, I asked, "Uh, why doesn't Fingal turn on some lights?"

"Now Becca. We'd be cheating you out of the full, cave tour experience then." The Oggs exchanged grins and I would have questioned my decision to come, except Greg nodded and a hint of a smile crossed his face.

"I'm going to touch your legs to help you find your footing," Fingal called out.

Even warned, I narrowly avoided kicking out when I felt hands on my calves. Davina crouched before me. "Do you need help turning?" I shook my head. If everyone else could do it, I could.

The lip of the opening sloped down from the wear of constant use. I carefully let myself slide and, as I did so, turned. Fingal guided my foot to the first ledge, but in my eagerness to get down, I missed the second and slipped. Jarring to a halt, I glanced down. Mortified, I realized I was practically sitting on Fingal's shoulder.

"Sorry."

"It happens all the time," he reassured me, with a cheeky grin.

Once my feet hit the ground again, I turned around and looked. The top of the cavern opened to the sky. I imagined that it was quite beautiful when the sun shone in, but with the bad weather, rain poured down and obscured the sky.

"Are we in any danger of flooding?" I asked as Greg came down next with little help from Fingal.

"We never have before and our family has been living here for decades."

One of my fears was of drowning. I didn't like getting in the water. My husband used to tease me that I wasn't in the shower long enough to get clean. I hoped Blanca appeared and whatever conversation her relatives wanted to have with her, quickly concluded. Once Davina and her dad joined us, we hugged the rim of the overhead opening to avoid the downpour. Where people from numerous tours had trod, the narrow, smooth path was smooth, but beyond, the way was rocky, so I watched my footing with care.

"This is where the tour ends. Then we have everyone go back up," Davina said. "We're going to continue." At the far side of the open cave, we came upon a large rock. Between the rock and the wall, there was just enough room to slide in behind it. The shadows hid the entrance and, because of an odd shimmer, I thought Blanca must have magic that also shrouded it. Davina started to go through, but her dad stopped her.

"I'll go first. You follow only when I call for you. You ken?"

"Oh, Da, we've been this way before and nothing ever happens."

"Well, it's different now. I don't want my mother startled. A frightened creature will attack."

"Da, you speak about her like she isn't even a person."

"Love, she isn't." And with that, Mr. Ogg disappeared.

We waited. A couple of minutes passed.

"Should I go?" Fingal asked.

"No, Da said not to," Davina answered.

About the time that we were all nervously fidgeting, Mr. Ogg's voice called out, "Come through one at a time, slow like. Fingal, you first, then Davina, then Mrs. Shaw and lastly Greg. Family first then the least intimidating to the most."

"I'm coming in."

Fingal vanished and, after waiting a tick or two. Davina turned to me. "We don't normally do things like this. Usually, we always bracket our tourists. I don't like leaving you, but—"

"But you're going to do what your father says. It's all good. We will be fine."

Davina followed her brother. I waited while I took five slow breaths and went through. It was going to be a very tight squeeze for Greg, I thought, as I slithered between the wall and the rock. The siblings had their lights off. Only Mr. Ogg's was lit.

"Please, douse your light, Mrs. Shaw," Mr. Ogg directed.

When I did, I couldn't see past the Oggs.

"Ouch," Greg muttered under his breath. He practically popped out of the opening like a cork. "I thought for a minute that I wasna going to make it."

"Shhh," Mr. Ogg admonished. "I saw a flit and I'm sure it was her. We'll travel down. There will be water, but very shallow. At that point, it shouldn't even go over the tops of your shoes. The cave opens up to a water fall and small pond. It's one of my favorite places to come when I'm feeling—not right."

We walked one by one. When I came out, I couldn't help but gasp. To the left and slightly behind me a waterfall splashed. I could feel droplets on my face. The low waterfall gurgled quietly, so we could still hear each other, despite the proximity. Mr. Ogg motioned us to the right. The ground sloped ever so slightly up, and very soon we were on a dry surface again. The rocks, tan with white streaks in places, seemed to shimmer and reflect the light back to us. The pond was about the size of a swimming pool, with water a beautiful shade of jade. I could see some small, eel-like fish darting about. Davina opened her mouth, but her father stared at her, frowning. Then across the pond, where I could have sworn there were only rock formations and stalactites, the creature we saw at the observation point slowly emerged from behind a towering stalactite.

"Uisdean? You came and brought one of the two that saw and the Gillie," she said, and while her voice was strange, it wasn't unattractive. The lisped words seemed to glide about me.

She defied gravity as she sinuously crawled to us. I watched her and, though her movements seemed slow, in seconds she was—not near enough to touch, but close enough to see clearly. One tufted ear swiveled in our direction. She crept to a particularly thick stalagmite then clamored up about five feet, spitting a stream of green, glowing liquid. An amazingly straight, horizontal line appeared on the rock. She waited a moment then shoved the top. Sheared off, it fell and crashed to the ground. She crawled atop the now-flat surface and looked down at us.

"Something happens," Blanca said. "The fae are restless. I have seen those who should not be here. So far, only little creatures have slipped through the net. I have sent them back where they belong, but others will follow. I feel it too. A stirring. The air smells strange. You can taste it in the water."

She stared at the waterfall. Her ears twitched and rotated toward Greg, her head and eyes followed. "You are ever stalwart, Gillie. But one of my kin sent a message that the geas weakens and, with it, your ties and powers over the fae doth too. What can you tell me?" The goblin tilted her head with interest.

Greg stepped closer. "Those with fae blood, the blood exerts itself. There are wolves when there should be none. Weather that has never been. You, who have been out of sight for so long, appear. Puck ventured out of the forest."

"Ah, Puck. That trickster!" Her laughter harmonized with the falls. "On what errands was he? What mischief did he wreak, Greg Gillie?"

I cleared my throat. "Actually, he visited me—twice. At least the cottage I'm staying in."

Her attention turned to me. "Tell me of it."

"Well, the first time, he came and took my daughter to the forest at night. Thankfully, Greg brought her back to me."

"How was it you found the child, Gillie?" Blanca asked.

Greg's forehead wrinkled as he thought. "Something woke me. I went to investigate. It was odd, now that I think harder on it. Puck led the girl by the hand. Then he called out, 'Make haste, Greg Gillie—I have found something for you.' He danced away and I went to the girl. She sat beneath a tree. When Puck left her side, she had swooned. I heard Rebecca calling. I picked the child up and took her to her mother."

"The second time?"

"Well, I found him inside the gardening shed." My eyes focused on the goblin, and I shuffled, unwilling to share the conversation, but continued anyway. "He asked me if I liked Greg. He said some other strange things. Wait a minute! Could he be the one who left the seeds I planted?"

"Ah." She looked from me to Greg. "So, the time has come."

"Okay, I'm confused as usual. What time has come?" I wanted to stomp my feet like a child. *Why can't these islanders speak plainly?* When she looked at Greg, I did too. "It has something to do with you," I continued. "The whole of the island is strange and hiding secrets."

"A moment, child," she said to me. The goblin skittered down the stalactites. She went to four others, that were almost in a circle between her and us, and touched them. As soon as her hands left each, the rocks began to glow green. "You've seen the magic and you think it is separate from you. You are wrong, child," she said.

"My name is Rebecca Shaw. You can call me Becca."

"Rebecca, you have magic, and we have need for it. You have need for us."

"No offense, but no, I don't need—" I tried to rethink a way to phrase what I wanted to say without sounding rude. "I'm fine on my own. I don't need any help—thank you," I added lamely.

"Well, there lies part of it. A problem cannot be solved if one cannot accept the problem exists in the first place. Puck has set things in motion, and now washes his hands of it. You two will need to work together." She turned and leapt to the wall of the cave.

"Wait! Work together to do what?" I called up.

"Be selfless, and you shall be rewarded. It is time. I sense I am needed."

"Aye, Mother, take care."

"And you, my son."

The light from the rocks began to fade as soon as she left. We quickly turned on the helmet lights, and Mr. Ogg led us to the slit. This time, when Greg eased between the rock and wall, his poncho snagged on the rough surface and ripped. "When we get back, remind me, and I'll stitch it up for you," I told Greg as he fingered the hole.

When we reached the opening, I discovered the Oggs were correct. It was much easier to climb up then it had been to slide down. I'd had my fill of caves and longed to be outside. We said nothing, each of us deep in thought. As we exited, I realized I hadn't heard my phone beep. The girls should have called or messaged. When I pulled out my phone, I saw why. I didn't have a signal. "Oh, no!"

"What is wrong?" Greg asked.

"My phone's out of commission—again."

"It happens often, but won't last too long," Davina said to comfort me. "Soon enough you'll have it beeping away as you get all your messages and texts."

When we reached the house, the Oggs told Mrs. Ogg what had occurred.

Squeezing her husband's arm, Mrs. Ogg said, "I believe that's progress. At least one good thing has happened from all this craziness. From what you say, your mother seems more herself than certainly anytime since I've been here."

CHAPTER 25

On the drive back to the cottage, Fingal thanked us over and over again for speaking to his gran. "Da will be comforted much. He doesn't like to let on to Mum, but he worries about his mother."

"Well, glad we could help. I still don't understand what I'm supposed to do or why. Do you have any clue what Blanca was talking about, Greg?"

"Nae, perhaps something will come to me later."

The car pulled up in the drive. Before I could reach the handle, Greg was out the door on his side and rushing to open mine.

I paused to say, "Thanks for the lift, Fingal."

Greg dipped down and nodded. "Aye, ta."

While we waved to Fingal, I noticed the day had cleared up quite a bit and, sure enough, my phone cheerfully beeped at the change. Both Jessie and Mrs. Murphy texted, confirming the girls had arrived. Jessie promised to send photos once they were all made up.

So caught up in reading, I hadn't realized Greg stood waiting.

"I'm sorry. The girls are at friends', and I was reading their texts. I know it's silly, but I always worry when they stay with someone new and…" I petered off.

"You canna foretell what may happen outside your presence," Greg finished.

"Exactly."

"Do you still want to see my home?" Greg asked, I think, to change the topic.

Once I fired off a quick text in response and tucked my cell back in my pocket, I answered, "Yes, I would, if you don't mind."

He took my arm. Despite the two layers of clothing I wore, his fingers warmed my skin. "We can walk," he said. "It won't take but a moment."

I tugged free and stepped back. "Just a moment? Then why didn't I see your cottage when I was in the forest earlier?"

"You need to look in the right place. My home is at one with nature and hard to find."

We walked to the back of my cottage. I didn't know why I referred to it as mine. Soon enough, I'd be back in Aberdeen, but this place felt...homey. Like no other place I'd ever lived, including my house in Houston.

"May I take your hand?" Greg asked.

I gazed at him through lowered lashes and nodded. Having been married for so long, I didn't know how to act now that I was single. Things had probably changed. The good thing with Greg was that he was so isolated that he probably didn't have a clue either. His large palm swallowed up my hand. He held it, as if cradling a bird. He drew me inside the forest. I stared eagerly, determine to remember the way, but the trees seemed to shift as soon as my eyes alit upon them. I grew dizzy as he led me through the forest, step by step. The undergrowth thickened. *That shouldn't be.* In older forests, the large trees shaded the ground. Usually, there was less growth, not more. As he still grasped my hand, he used the other to hold back bushes and low tree limbs so we could continue. My head spun. The leaves changed from green to gold and red, then back again.

Greg stopped so suddenly that I staggered.

"Are you well?" he asked.

"I'm kind of dizzy."

"Sorry, I wanted to reach my home quickly so you would have time to visit and get back home before it gets dark."

It felt as though I'd taken but two dozen steps—slow ones. I opened my mouth to speak, but then he pulled back a leafy branch, and stopped. At first, I saw nothing but a tree that rivaled a sequoia with symmetrically-placed knots. I squinted hard and the knots became windows. I'd never seen anything like it. The house seemed to be built inside a hollowed-out tree, but that couldn't be right because the tree would be dead. This one had leaves and the healthy bark color of living branches. It could be that the tree grew around the house, but if so, the home's walls matched that of the tree bark perfectly. The ground seemed to smooth under our feet.

I no longer tripped over rocks or errant bushes and when I looked down, we stood on a hard, packed-dirt path which led to Greg's home. We approached it. At first glance, there didn't seem to be a door, but when Greg reached out, seams appeared delineating a person-sized rectangle and a knot protruded. Greg grasped it and pushed. The door swung open. I hesitated at the threshold. *What if I can't get back out?*

"Please, enter, Rebecca. As long as you are with me, you shall be safe." A faded, rag rug in a rainbow of shades beckoned me to step on it. So, I did.

The home had no other doors and appeared to consist of one large room like a pastoral efficiency, but perhaps all the doors only appeared when needed. A rudimentary camp bed set against the back wall and, to the right of the door, near a window, was a single table with two rustic chairs.

I saw nothing resembling a stove or grill. "How do you cook?"

"Different ways. Often, I heat stones and bury what I want to cook with them. When I come home, my dinner is ready to eat. I also eat dried meat that I cure myself. With all the trees, I don't like to make fires as often."

"Do you eat dried or raw food all the time?"

"Nae, not all the time, but probably more than most folk."

"Why do you live here?" I ran my hand over the back of a chair. The wood warmed and my palm sank into it as if it were clay. Startled, I jerked my hand away.

"Dinna fash yourself," Greg reassured me. "Please, sit."

I hesitantly perched on the edge of the chair's seat but it curved around my hips and tilted. I whooped as I slid back.

When I looked up at Greg, he shrugged. "It has a sense of humor."

The chair undulated beneath me for a moment then stopped. I wiggled and sighed. "Oh, my goodness. This may be the most comfortable chair I've ever sat in. Does it do this every time you have a visitor?"

"I never have visitors," he said shortly. For a moment a somber expression crossed his face, then he brightened. "Would you like a cuppa?"

I wasn't really in the mood. I'd drank a lot of tea that day, but I could tell Greg needed something to do, and I was curious to see how he made it with no way to heat the water. "Sure," I said, trying for an enthusiastic tone.

He waited in front of a kettle sitting on a shelf and a few seconds later, it whistled. He then put tea in it to brew.

"Okay, how—"

"You know of the fae's presence here. Staying in this forest does allow certain—"

I smiled. "Perks?"

"Aye."

A wave of dizziness hit me when the furniture in the room subtly shifted and the room expanded like a balloon filling with air. "What's going on?" As I watched, a sink popped out of a wall.

"The tree adapts to meet the needs and tastes of the individual there." He quirked his eyebrow at me. "I gather mine was lacking."

"Well, it is kinda sparse," I said. The rug morphed into a tapestry of royal blue, sage, and gold. The walls smoothed and changed to a sunny yellow. The cot disappeared.

"Oh no! Your bed's gone!"

"I think not." Greg gestured to the door that appeared. The chair propelled me upright. I guess it wanted me to see the addition. When Greg and I reached the door, he opened it, revealing a four poster, king-sized bed heaped with pillows. The walls were a restful shade of gray.

"I'm sorry. I'm messing up your home." I tried to think of Spartan rooms and utilitarian surroundings but the tree continued to alter the room adding a picture of daisies on the wall across from the bed.

"Dinna fash yourself. It will revert when you leave." He paused and slowly turned, taking in not only the new bedroom, but the changes in the living area. I said a silent prayer that the result wasn't too girly.

"What do you think of our cottage?" He placed his hands on my shoulders and guided me.

He said *our*. Did he see a future with me in his life? Could I ever live in a tree? I took my time to examine the room. An industrial style coffee table with wrought iron legs stood in front of a navy Chesterfield couch. I wandered over and sat down. Supportive, yet soft, just the way I liked my sofas. *Yes, I could live here.* Greg joined me.

When he sat, he heaved a sigh. "Perfect."

"Yes, it is." My heart swelled when his eyes met mine. "How long have you lived here?"

Greg stood abruptly and strode to a window. "I've lived here ever since I lost my family."

Way to ruin a moment, Becca! "I'm sorry."

"I thank you. 'Tis a sad tale but saddest for me. We took the wagon to the village. I left my wife and wee one at the midwife's while I visited the mercantile. There was a fire. All perished. My grief was so great that I couldna speak or even think. I hied to the forest—to solitude."

Wagon? I guess they were dead serious about not allowing cars on the island. "I lost my husband," I began tentatively. "I know it isn't the same. You lost your child too. I never thought I would stop grieving either, but at some point, I think I'll be ready and wanting to start seeing people."

"You mean men," he said flatly. Greg walked to ledge that acted as a counter, poured the tea in mugs, and brought me one.

Didn't he understand that by 'people,' I meant him? Was what I interpreted as mutual interest just wishful thinking on my part? The tea had a reddish hue. I brought it to my lips to tentatively sip to mask my confusion and, yes, hurt, and the aroma of raspberries wafted. "Believe it or not, a lot of people remarry after losing a spouse. There's nothing wrong about it, so don't you dare suggest I insult my husband by contemplating it," I said, my tone as tart as the tea.

"I didna say that." He turned to look at me, gulped from the mug, and grimaced.

"No, but I have the feeling that's what you're thinking, and it bothers me." The couch kneaded my back in an attempt to calm me, but I didn't want to be calmed and squared my shoulders.

"I canna move on."

"Well, you need to. You don't need to see other women, if you don't want to. It's more that you need to accept your loved ones' deaths and embrace the life you have. I'm sure they would want that for you."

"Yes. My wife was generous and sweet. So white, so frail."

"Frail?"

"She was sickly. I hoped to move her somewhere isolated where she wouldna be exposed to illness. I brought her to the island, thinking she would be safe. Illness didna kill her, though. A fire did."

"You can't protect everything and everybody, Greg. Stuff happens. I didn't want my husband to die, but he did. David had a long commute back and forth to work. The traffic in Houston...well, it's bad. One day, he drove to work, and didn't come home. What could I have done to prevent it? Tell him to quit his job? Tell him to stop driving? Where I come from that's not an option. Mass transit doesn't exist. I don't think you can comprehend the size of the United States if you've not been there. Texas alone is nearly the size of Europe."

"Aye, I have heard of the United States. They succeeded where Scotland didna. They fought and won their freedom."

"Well, we are quite a ways away. Made it a little bit harder for Britain to keep us under its thumb. Do you still want independence?"

"Aye." Greg's face was grim.

"On one hand, I understand that, on the other..." While sipping my tea, I paused to choose my words.

"Scotland has been a part of Great Britain for a long time. So, has Wales and Ireland. Does Wales feel this way too?"

"I dinna know nor care."

Okay. Sore spot, Becca. Time to go home before I stick my foot farther down my throat. "It's getting late. I definitely want to get back before it gets dark, and I'm utterly starving."

"I will take you back. I havena been good company, and I regret that. I value our time together and want it to be pleasant."

"Even the best of friends disagree, Greg, and I would never want to be around someone identical to me. That would be so boring."

When he reached the couch, he took my hand. "Come."

We walked to the door, and he didn't release it once outside. A sudden gale rattled branches. The leaves swirled and my hair whipped my face.

Stopping, I tried to tug my hand free. "Wait, Greg! I can't see."

He released my hand only to wrap his arm around my waist and, before I could draw another breath to speak, he lifted me. My feet dangled as he carried me along at a speed that our surroundings were a blur and the air swept my hair back as if I rode a motorcycle. My eyes teared, and I closed them tight. After a short time, only a few minutes, the wind died down.

"There you are, Rebecca." When my feet touched the ground, I opened my eyes. We stood at the edge of the forest in sight of the cottage's back door. I shook my head.

He pulled me, but I resisted. "What is this?"

"What do you mean?"

"This—place, this island."

"'Tis magic, but you already ken that, now didna you?"

He bent and his lips touched mine. I embraced him and ran my fingers through the dark locks that had tempted me. Time stood still and I willed it to stop forever. Greg drew back. Before I could say a word, he disappeared.

CHAPTER 26

I stood outside until my heart stopped racing. "Like *Alice in Wonderland* and I was never a fan of that book," I muttered as I finally felt able to walk around to the front of the house and open the door. When I checked the time, I saw it was later than I expected. My stomach growled, reminding me I hadn't had dinner. Too hungry to cook, I made a sandwich. I had just taken a bite, when Mrs. Murphy rang.

"I hope everything's going well." I assumed she called to let me know they were about to leave on the ferry.

"I think you need to come to talk to your lass."

Uh, oh. "What's wrong?"

"When we reached the pier, there was a kerfuffle. I don't ken it all, but the girls are upset and on the phone with their mums. One of the boys, Lundy, ran off. They all agree it was something young Jessica did," she finished.

"I'll be right there." My finger posed over the end call button, but I didn't touch it. "Wait. Could I speak to Jessie?"

"Aye, of course."

I heard the usual background noise and then Jessica saying, "Mom?"

"You are to stay by the ferry until I come."

"You're coming? What did—" Obviously, the mother was nearby, and Jessie didn't want to ask what Mrs. Murphy said in front of her.

"She said you did something to upset everyone and that Lundy ran off. You stay right there. I'm coming."

"Okay, Mom."

I didn't know what she did, but it couldn't have been good if she was immediately agreeing with me. Before I could say more, Jessie asked, "Oh, Mom? What about Tate?"

"If she wants to stay and she's still welcome, she can. Mrs. Murphy didn't mention her."

"She didn't do anything—well, nothing more than what we all did."

"Give the phone back to Mrs. Murphy."

When Mrs. Murphy picked up the phone, I said, "I'm terribly sorry. Jessie will wait for me at the pier. I don't want you to miss the ferry."

"I think most of the girls are going home. The movie is just not enticing enough. I'm taking my daughters there, though. If Tate wants to go, I'm happy to take her."

"May I speak to her, please?" *Ugh, maybe I should just call the girls myself instead of this ring-around-the-phonesy.*

Tate murmured, "Hello."

"Tate, you have a choice. You can go with Mrs. Murphy and her daughters to the movies, or you can wait at the ferry for me."

"I want to go home. Everyone's sad."

"Okay, I'll be there as soon as I can." I called Kay to see if she would give me a ride into town, but she didn't answer the phone, so I ran to the bus stop. As I rounded the corner, I was just in time to see the bus's tail lights receding. *Of course, I'd miss the bus.* I paced back and forth and bit my nails. While I waited, I got out my phone to report the delay, but naturally, no bars. What in the world had Jessie done? Finally, the next bus arrived. It seemed to take forever for it to reach the ferry. The girls waited alone. *Darn, I should have told them to wait at the bus stop.* I could have called them to join me and we all could have rode back home. I forlornly watched the bus pull away.

When I got to the girls, I said, "Come along. You can explain yourself while we wait for the bus." Agitated, I tugged out my phone again to see if Kay called back. When I did, the bus pass fell from my pocket. Before I could grab it, the wind took it off the pier and into the water. "Oh great. I don't suppose either of you have a bus card or exact change?"

"Sorry, Mom. I left my bus card back at Nessa's house," Jessie said, her voice barely audible.

Tate shook her head.

"Then I guess we're walking. We should have plenty of time to get back home before dark." As we traipsed toward home, I said, "Okay, Jessica—spill."

She sighed. "Well, you know I told you that Nessa has a crush on Lundy? I thought up a plan to make him notice her—or at least not want to be around the rest of us."

I waited.

"When he was at the cottage, the kitten bothered him, and I thought if he thought he was allergic to everyone except Nessa, he'd leave the rest of us alone, and she would have a chance with him," Jessie said in a rush. "Whenever I comb the cat, I've been saving the fur. I had everyone except Nessa tuck some in their pockets—all the girls at least. It worked, Mom. Lundy tried to stay as far away from us as he could, but he couldn't go far on the pier and, Mom, he growled at us, and I swear, his teeth got longer."

I thought about telling Jess that was impossible, but here, who knew?

"When he growled and showed his teeth, everyone...well, the girls, all screamed and the boys laughed at him. So he ran off. Some of the girls started crying."

"They were babies, Mom," Tate chimed in. "I didn't cry."

"Well, that was brave of you, but I'm sure there are some things that would make you cry that wouldn't bother those girls at all." I paused then added, "And you shouldn't call people names." Boy, I hoped she wasn't about to go through the teen stage early. There was no way I could handle dealing with two touchy, moody teenagers.

"Afterward, everyone told Mrs. Murphy about the hair, and she said it was mean. I didn't mean to be mean. I just wanted him to talk to Nessa since she likes him." Jessie crossed her arms and stared at the road.

"I know, hon, but allergies are serious. You don't purposely bring something to someone that you know will make them sick or uncomfortable."

"With all the rain, there were a lot of puddles and when the girls got upset, they tried to run, and some fell down. They got all wet."

"And they smell like fish," Tate said solemnly.

Jessie's lip quivered and her eyes were glassy with unshed tears. "So, I ruined it for everyone. And they all looked at me like I was some awful villain like Dr. Evil."

Not a movie I had wanted Jess to watch, but David let her. She ended up worrying about her breasts turning into missiles or, since she liked science, that she would go bald.

Jess was quiet as we walked toward the lane leading to the cottage. Tate chattered to fill the silence. I mostly nodded. I hoped Jess hadn't made it so no one would have anything to do with her for the rest of the stay. Girls could be vindictive. Hopefully, they would remember she did it for a good reason, and not to mess things up for everyone. We weren't too far from our turnoff when something growled.

"Shhh, Tate. I think I heard something." I'd been in such a hurry to get to the girls that the only thing I grabbed was my bus pass and phone. I just wasn't thinking, probably since this day had already been a magical mystery tour. The smaller wolf we saw before stalked us. The fur on its back rose so I could almost make out each hair.

"Mom?" Tate took one hand and Jess took the other.

The wolf sniffed the air. When it threw back its head and bayed, we jumped. We carried no weapons, and the wolf blocked the way to the cottage.

"Let's try backing up," Jess suggested.

As we eyed the wolf, we took two steps backward. The wolf snarled and trotted closer. I glanced around. Stone walls lined the road. The section nearest to me was boggy. I always warned the girls to avoid that side, not wanting to clean clumps of clinging clay off their shoes. I had a crazy idea.

"Girls, how much of that cat hair do you have?" *Dogs and cats don't like one another, right?*

"A lot," Tate whispered.

Jess nodded in agreement.

"Move slowly toward the wall."

We sidestepped toward the mire. I reached down, still watching the wolf, and picked up a wad of clay mud. The wolf snarled, but kept its distance.

"Give me all the hair you have." The girls fished wads of fur from their pockets and passed them to me. I rolled the hair and the clay together, so it was a sticky, furry mess, and then pinched off lumps and gave them to the girls. The hair thickened the clay enough that it held its form.

"Throw it at the wolf." The girls looked at the clay, the wolf, then me. I knew it might be the dumbest weapon ever, but it was better than nothing. Hopefully, the wolf would run. Maybe the wolf would get a kitty hate on and attack the clay balls. I didn't care as long as it left my babies alone. "On three! One, two, three!"

We pelted the wolf as hard and fast as we could. Mine and Tate's missed or barely clung to the wolf's hide, but Jessie had been on the softball team. She nailed him.

I alternated between forming furry mud balls and handing them to the girls and throwing ones at the wolf. The animal yipped at each hit. It didn't attack us, but it didn't run away either. The wolf tried to dodge the missiles. When we ran out of ammo, cat fur and clay clung to its pelt. When the balls stopped coming, the animal tried to shake and bite off the ones adhered, but they were well stuck on. Then the wolf froze, opened its mouth, and loudly sneezed. It pawed at its nose, daubing more hair there. I almost felt sorry for the poor animal. Wheezing, the wolf rolled on the path, then, with a loud snort, it hopped up and ran around in circles yipping and snuffling. We backed away and cowered behind a gnarled oak. Noticing our movement, the wolf ran toward the tree, but had a violent attack of the sneezes just as it reached it so, instead of rounding the tree, it ran headfirst into it. Conk! It staggered, then tipped over.

We looked at each other and laughed.

"That was so funny! Do all wolves act like that around cats?" Tate asked.

"No, honey. I don't think so."

Then the wolf's body seemed to suck in its fur, and, as its body convulsed, we heard cracking noises. As we watched, the animal shifted and changed until Lundy was lying on the ground. Jess turned bright red when she saw he was naked.

Tate tried to get closer, but I held her back. "Wow. He's like Kay, only he turns into a wolf," she said.

Tate must have shared her findings about Kay with Jessie since she didn't question it.

"Let's give it a few minutes and make sure he isn't going to change into something else," I said.

We waited, but the boy remained curled on his side, covered with cat hair and mud.

Tate turned to me. "We can't leave him here."

I approached and knelt beside him then poked his shoulder. "Hey," I said. When he didn't move, I said it again louder and shook his arm. Suddenly, he turned onto his back. We screamed.

He sat up and blinked at us. "Mrs. Shaw? Jessica, Tate?" He looked around. "Where am I? What happened?"

"We'd like to ask you the same question."

He sneezed again and again. When he became aware of his nudity, he tried to simultaneously cover his crotch and his mouth.

"Come home with us so you can wash off all that mud and hair."

Jess took pity on him and handed him her windbreaker. It was short, but covered the important parts. We walked home. I didn't question the lad on the way. He looked and sounded miserable. We entered the cottage, except for Lundy who stayed outside the door.

The boy tried to step through the doorway, and frowned.

"I can't get in."

"What do you mean?" I asked.

"It's like there's an invisible wall or some power keeping me from going any farther."

"The wolfsbane! It must be working." Jessie went to the door frame and removed a satchel from the top. "There, now try."

Lundy was able to enter.

"You aren't going to turn back into a wolf, are you?" Jess asked.

"I didn't plan on turning into a wolf earlier."

Jess shook the satchel at him. "Well, we have more of this and aren't afraid to use it."

"Jess! Don't threaten the guest."

"Hey, I don't want to become wolf burger," she said but tucked the potion in the cupboard.

I sent him to the shower with a pair of old baggy sweats of mine that I hoped would fit and called Conall since I didn't know the boy's number. When Conall answered on the first ring, I put him on speaker while I prepared some food to eat.

I figured the girls were bound to be hungry and teenage boys, from what I always heard, were pretty much insatiable.

"Rebecca? What can I do for you?" Conall asked.

"Actually, I need your help."

"Oh—" His voice changed into pleased, flirt mode. I rolled my eyes at the girls before I could stop myself.

Jess mouthed, "See?" at me.

"I—I found your nephew on the lane leading to the cottage. He was muddy and sneezing, so we brought him back here."

"Is he sick?" Conall asked.

"Not exactly," I hedged. "We kinda threw cat hair on him."

"Can't you just brush it off?"

I grimaced. "No, it was a lot of cat hair and it's kinda stuck on him. Could you let his dad know? Also, it would be wonderful if you could pick him up and take him home."

Jess pointed at me and her shoulders shook as she tried not to laugh. Tate had given up and run for the bedroom with her hands over her mouth. I heard her cackle and the bedroom door shut. Jess beat a path to follow her.

"Of course, I can, Rebecca. Anything I can ever do for you, you just ask."

"Thanks, Conall. There is one other thing—"

"What"

"Please, call me Becca. Calling me Rebecca makes me feel like I did when my mother was about to chew me out for something." Now if he wanted me to think of my mother whenever he spoke to me, he would keep calling me Rebecca. If anything good came from this night, hopefully it would be that he would call me Becca. I thought of Greg. He called me Rebecca and yet somehow it didn't bother me

"I'll be right over."

"Thank you." When a decent amount of time had passed after the water turned off and Lundy still had not come out, I called through the door to him. "Are you okay? Do you need anything?"

"Do you have anything else to wear?"

"I'm sorry, but nothing else would come near to fitting. What's wrong?'

He came out dressed in the sweats, but a towel was wrapped around his middle. I just assumed he was extra shy. "I made some sandwiches. Help yourself. Your uncle is coming to pick you up."

"Okay—thanks." He trudged past me and I went to get the girls.

Tate claimed the place beside Lundy and stared at him until he quit eating and looked at her. Tate saw it as an invitation to talk. "We have the kitten in our room, so it won't bother you. Is everyone in your family allergic to cats?"

"I guess, I don't know." Lundy shrugged and took another big bite of his hero.

"Have you always been able to turn into a dog? Are you like Kay?"

Lundy frowned at Tate. "I don't turn into a dog. I turn into a wolf and, no, it isn't like Kay."

"Mom said that when Kay changes, her clothes vanish and reappear. Why didn't yours? Or did you already take them off?"

Lundy spoke to his plate. "Kay's a different kind of shapeshifter. We usually remove ours before changing, but it surprised me, and I turned into a wolf before I could. They're nothing but torn shreds now.

Pitying Lundy, I said, "Tate, eat your dinner."

"I can eat and talk at the same time."

"I know, honey, but let's just focus on eating for now."

Jessie came in and sat as far away as she could from Lundy. I cleared my throat. Jessie mouthed, "Mom, do I have to?"

I nodded.

"Uh, Lundy?"

He tried to talk around a mouthful of potato chips then thought better of it, thank goodness, and motioned to her to wait while he swallowed. "Yeah?" he finally said.

"I'm sorry about the cat hair. I didn't know it would bother you that much."

"Jess—" I prompted.

"It was wrong. I shouldn't have done it. I'm sorry."

"You could have just said—you know."

"I did say. A lot. I just wanted you to give Nessa a chance. She really likes you."

"Well, I don't like-like her, and ever since we turned thirteen, everyone's been after me to go out with her. She's nice, but I don't wanna date her. I just want to be friends. I thought maybe if you and I were dating, she'd get the idea, and everyone would back off. It isn't easy when an entire village decides you should be with someone. I wish she would have just kept it to herself, but she's never been able to keep a secret and talks more than anyone I know. Heck, she talks more than anyone ever."

That was more words I've heard from the boy since I met him. "Well, it isn't easy when you like someone, and they don't reciprocate. The best thing to do is to keep on being a friend and not push them." I looked pointedly at Jessie. "And no one likes to be pushed at someone else."

"I'm sorry if I bothered you, Jessica," Lundy said.

"It's okay."

He lit up.

"But don't come onto me anymore. I'm fine being friends, but that's it."

"If you change your mind before you leave—"

"Very unlikely," she said. His face fell. Jessie heaved a sigh. "But if I do, I'll let you know."

As we finished up our sandwiches, there was a knock at the door. I opened it.

"Hello, Conall. Come on in." The wind nearly snatched the door from my hands. It looked like the weather was about to get bad again. Conall stepped through the doorway, sniffed, and frowned.

He greeted me then turned to his nephew. "What happened to you?"

Lundy blushed and hemmed and hawed. I felt sorry for him and interceded. "That's something that we'd like to talk to you about." I told him about seeing the wolf and the mud and hair and about the wolf turning into his nephew. "So, what's the deal? Are you—" I felt silly for saying it, but Tate didn't.

"Werewolves, like in the stories?"

"This isn't anything we like to talk about. It's personal."

"But—" I prompted.

"We are wulvers," he reluctantly answered. "I suppose you could call us werewolves."

"Wulvers?"

"Wulvers are…well, they can turn into wolves, but they have a second form that's manlike in that they can stand upright, but have fur and characteristics like a wolf. Their faces are slightly elongated. The ears are pointed. They have longer, sharper canines. Wulvers are pacifists. They help people and are friendly. We are told, but we don't know for sure, that wulvers are a mix of wolf, fae, and human. The fae blood made the change possible. The human blood keeps us here instead of with the fae."

"So, the wolves we've been seeing have been you and Lundy?"

"Yes."

"Why were you two growling at us in the grocery?"

"I don't know. Something's wrong, and it's affecting everyone with a trace of fae blood."

"Do you remember being in the shop with us? It was Kay, me, Jess, and Tate."

"Vaguely. It's all fuzzy. Usually, when I'm in wolf form, I'm as aware as I am when in human form, however, the wolf instincts are stronger and hard to resist. For instance—" He looked down.

"Yes," I encouraged.

"Well, if I'm in wolf form and hungry, then a rabbit hops past, I would probably go after it."

"And kill it and eat it?" Tate asked then clasped her hands over her mouth.

"Well—yes. That's what wolves do, and there isn't anything wrong with that," he answered defensively.

"Do you have to change during the full moon?"

"There's some truth in that. We do feel the urge to do so but are able to decide when and where. Now, if we refused to change for a long time, a change might be forced on us. I don't know for sure, at this point there are only rumors. We—me and Lundy—are the only werewolves here."

I thought on this for a moment. "What do you think is going to happen? What will you do if you keep changing sporadically and not remembering things?"

"I guess—" Conall paused.

"We'll have to be locked up," Lundy said bitterly.

"Wow, I'm so sorry, Lundy," Jessie said and actually reached across the table to pat his hand.

"Does anyone have any idea why this is happening?" I asked.

"You are an outsider. I really shouldn't talk to you about it." Conall pressed his lips together so tightly that they whitened.

"Okay, I get the same thing from Kay, and I am so tired of it. What can be done about this?"

Conall sighed but answered, "Greg Gillie is the Keeper of the Forest. It's his job to make sure the fae don't affect the humans in any major, detrimental way. This—" He gestured to include his nephew. "—is very detrimental."

"What's Greg supposed to do, exactly?"

"Well, he guards the fairy hill. He should know instantly when anything leaves the hill and investigate it. Lately, things are out that shouldn't be, and Greg seems to be late finding out or ignorant of it. Worse, it isn't just fae escaping. Somehow the fae's nature is affecting us and the island."

His revelation was greeted with silence as we attempted to digest it.

"Look," he continued, "it's difficult for me to talk about this. We keep to ourselves. I don't much care for Greg. There's no secret about that. There's some bad blood between my family and him. Too many of my kin have died in that forest. If he was doing what he should, tragedies like the ones my family have suffered for so many decades shouldn't be occurring. I guess it's also fair to say that the McNeils have not always heeded warnings, though, and that probably contributed to some of the deaths, but still. Memories run long here in Scotland. Feuds are common and last centuries."

"That's stupid," Jessie said. "Why don't you guys just say 'sorry,' shake on it, and if you can't be friends, at least don't be enemies."

"Because we live in a small area. And the sins of the father are indeed visited upon the son. Call it genetics or nurturing, but it's true. Greg is self-absorbed. Caught up in his own grief so that he can't see that others hurt too. No one hurts more than he does. He took all that pain and wrapped it around him. He doesn't let anyone in."

"He doesn't strike me like that," I said.

"Well, for some reason, he's different around you. Trust me when I say, he rarely spoke to anyone before you came, and if he did, it wasn't with a smile on his face."

"Well, he was pretty gruff with me the first few times we met. Maybe it's because this cottage is closest to his place. He sees more of me and the girls when he takes care of the woods."

"P'raps so."

"So, this is ultimately related to this fae hill?"

He nodded. "Aye."

"Why doesn't someone go to this hill and talk to the fairies. Explain things."

Conall and Lundy had identical expressions of horror on their faces.

"No one volunteers to go into the hill. Most never come out, and the few who do are...changed," Lundy said.

Conall rubbed his chin in thought then spoke, "I'm afraid though, that you may be right. And if someone does need to do it, it should be Greg. He's the one who's supposed to keep the peace between us and the fae."

"Maybe you should form a committee or group," Jessie suggested.

"Safety in numbers," I said thoughtfully.

"There's no safety to be had in that hill," Conall said flatly. "Greg has some power over them, but the high fae? No. Thankfully, they rarely venture forth with the exception of Puck who likes to wreak mischief. I don't think Greg has any power over him. Puck will leave when he chooses. Usually, the fae help on their side to keep what is theirs in the hill, but they don't seem to be doing it with as much diligence—or perhaps the creatures are trying harder to get out—or the barrier that usually keeps them out is weakened. I don't know, but something needs to be done and soon."

"Would the island be overrun?"

"Probably. The island was uninhabitable for centuries. A few families would move here and then vanish or be found dead. Even when my family and the other families who established this community first arrived, there were incidents so horrible, due to the fae, that there was talk of abandoning it. Then the caretaker went to the woods, and the fae's interference ceased. It could be worse than just the island suffering, even. Fae could take over the mainland too. We would be at their mercy. Truly a nightmarish situation. We've been at peace for centuries."

I shook my head. "I'm sorry, Conall." Noting that Lundy had almost finished his food, I asked, "Conall, would you like a sandwich? I could make another if you don't mind waiting a few minutes."

"No thank you. I ate before I came and I should be getting my nephew back. Thank you for taking care of him. Ready to go, boy?"

Lundy nodded and stood. When he did, the towel dropped off revealing the reason for it. I hadn't noticed it when I gave it to him, but the sweats were so frayed in the back that his furry behind was as clearly visible as though he wore gauze over it. His back was to us and when he spun to replace the towel, all three of us, even Tate, pretended that we hadn't seen a thing.

"Well, then. Thanks again. Take care of yourself. I would keep to the cottage, especially at night."

After Conall and Lundy left, I said, "I didn't want to say anything while they were here, but I think you girls should carry wolfbane with you all the time. I don't think that they would ever hurt you on purpose, but Conall did say that things weren't normal around here. Also, Jess, I'd like to look at the spell book again."

"I think it would be cool to meet a fairy," Tate said.

"Not so cool, according to quite a few fairy tales I've read. Don't get any ideas about going near that forest, young lady," I sternly warned her. "Let's clean up."

As Jess put up the food, and Tate cleared the table, I started doing the dishes. When Jess finished, she brought me the spell book and took over washing while Tate dried.

I sat at the kitchen table and flipped through the book. I wasn't sure what I was looking for. "Jessie, you need to think of a way to make up for the evening you ruined."

"Mom, what can I do other than apologize?"

"I don't know, but I'm sure you'll come up with something." I paused. "Jessie, do you remember seeing anything about protection from fae?"

"No, but I did see something about seeing through 'Glamours.'"

"Hmmm—that's something worth looking at, but I'd be happier if we could find something that affected more than our ability to see when they're tricking our eyes."

"There's a recipe for an ointment. It didn't look too hard. It had four leaf clover, marigold, mugwort, bee's wax, and a couple of other things. The hard part will be collecting them at the right times."

"Why don't you research it and see what comes up on the internet?" Tate suggested.

That would have been my first option if I'd been at home, but I was used to not having access and dealing with the library, so I'd almost forgotten.

"Good idea. Now let's see if it's up." Amazingly, I was able to get on the internet. The girls finished the dishes and came to sit at the table with me. Jessie flipped through the book and Tate read over my shoulder.

I skimmed an article. "Here's something. It says that iron is a protection from fairies. I'll bet I can find some in the shed." We read silently for a while.

"Look! This says we can leave milk and bread out and they won't bother us." Tate pointed to the paragraph.

"Again, great for when we're home, but out and about, not so helpful."

Tate's face fell.

"It's a good idea for here, though, Tate. Good eye. Why don't you get a glass and plate so we can try it tonight?"

Tate gathered a slice of bread which she insisted on toasting and a cup of milk. We left it on the front porch to one side of the door, so we wouldn't trip on it when we went out.

"Do you think it will be here when we get up?" Tate asked.

"Guess we'll find out." I figured some animals would take care of it and hoped we hadn't just invited a bunch of pests to our front door. Tate smothered a yawn.

"I think it's time we all go to bed. We can look for more tomorrow."

CHAPTER 27

The next morning, Jessie came to me. "Mom, I think I have an idea for making it up to the other kids."

"What do you have in mind?"

"Well, I wanted it to be something different from what they normally do, and I still need to figure out the specifics, but I thought I could invite them over. Have the party we were planning, but with more guests and with more to do than just watch a movie and play one game."

"It's a start. You need to plan before you ask, though. A group of teens sitting around in a cottage isn't going to be fun." *Especially not for me.*

"I'll keep thinking on it."

"You'll come up with something, I'm sure. In the meantime, I want you to write notes to everyone."

"Oh, Mom. Nobody writes notes anymore, and I don't even know everyone's address!"

"You can get on that today. Go to the grocer. As small as the island is, you could probably hand deliver them."

"Oh, no way! If I gotta write them, I at least don't want to have to see their faces when they get them and read them."

"Suit yourself."

After breakfast, the first thing I wanted to do was check for something made out of iron. Even though steel might work, iron is what I'd seen most during out research. I wondered how effective it was, but then remembered that Puck had been in the shed. If it contained something made of iron, and I would be surprised if it didn't, it hadn't bothered him. Based on that, I guess iron didn't keep them back that far. One area I could eliminate searching through, was the path that he took on his way out. Surely, if the iron touched him or he was very close, he would have reacted. I was sure I could remember. We checked the dish and cup. Both, to Tate's delight, were empty. She decided that her job would be to make sure to put some out every night. Jessie wanted to go buy some cards, so we would visit the village at some point today. I set the girls to weeding then went to the shed, opened the door, and sighed. There was a lot of stuff and it didn't seem to be orderly like the cottage.

"Might as well start, it isn't gonna sort itself." I wheeled the bicycles out and moved the gardening tools which were in the front. Made yet another mental note to have the bicycle tires fixed. I wished the shed was lit in some way. I banged the shelves with the hoe hoping to scare any critters that had taken refuge. Nothing ran out, thankfully. I found a pair of mud-encrusted wellies just beside the croquet game and shifted the items out. Then, I tugged a tarp off the nearest shelf. With a "whoomph," the dust that had collected on top went air-borne. Using the bandana, I wore to keep my hair back, I dusted myself off the best I could, and kept looking. And ancient, push lawn mower occupied one corner. Behind it, a tool chest so rusty I feared the handle would break off if I tried to lift it sat. Once I dragged it out, I used a garden spade to get past the rust and open it. It held the usual array of tools, but no nails.

On box held an extensive bottle collection. I didn't have to delve in as far back as I thought I would, but all the same, it was ten o'clock when I finally found a tin full of nails. Thankfully, it was lidded and the nails, while old, weren't rusty. I took out the tin and put everything else back inside the shed. The girls finished gardening. Jess was in the cottage trying to remember all the kids she had offended. She wanted an idea of how many cards she would need. Tate realized she hadn't fed the kitten or made the bed. She busied herself with chores I had given her. I was glad to see some initiative with the girls. By the time I finished my chores, I was a sweaty, cobwebby mess, and it was practically lunch time.

"I need to take a shower. Then we'll have lunch and go to town."

"Mom, would it be okay if we ate lunch in the village?" Jessie asked.

"I suppose we could. Any particular reason?" I toed my shoes off at the door. They would need to be wiped off before I could wear them again.

"Nessa said she'd lend me her address book if I could meet her in the village before one o'clock."

"Well then, I better hurry up."

We arrived at the shop shortly after noon and Jess was able to get the book. Kay was working, but said she'd eat with us. She had come in to help bake in the morning and was due for a short break.

"How are you doing?" she asked as she removed her apron, hung it on a nail, and came to sit.

"Yesterday wasn't a picnic. But things are looking up." I noticed that Kay took the seat farthest from all of us. I twisted in my chair to nonchalantly sniff my armpit. *Nope, I smelled fine.* We sat at a table for six, and Kay opted for the far opposite end of the table.

"What happened yesterday?"

"I'll let Jess fill you in since it mostly involves her."

Jess told Kay about the hair incident.

"Wow. I would've expected this from other weres, but Conall and Lundy?"

"There are different kinds of werewolves?"

"Of course, and different animals can be were, like werebears."

"Great. I thought when I returned to Aberdeen, I wouldn't have to worry about this kind of stuff anymore."

"It's very unlikely that you have anything to worry about. I believe they live in remote parts of the country and avoid and shun humans."

"Well, we do have a cat now, thanks to you, so I can always collect more fur to carry around."

Kay told us an amusing story about a baking disaster involving using salt instead of sugar, then asked, "Oh, what do you think about the spell book?"

"Well, it's interesting. We also did some research online since internet was up yesterday."

"What did you find out?"

"We have a few herbs in the garden that may keep fae away and apparently iron repels them." I tugged at my purse, swinging it from the back of the chair to my lap. "I resolved to bring a couple of handfuls to share with people I knew." Kay cringed.

"Why, does it bother you too?"

"Becca, a goodly portion of the village has fae blood. When someone is part fae, you never know how much, if any, the person will be affected by things like iron. For example, while it bothers me, it doesn't cause wounds on my skin if I touch it. Just makes me very, very uncomfortable."

"I'm sorry. I didn't even think about that. Will it bother Conall too?"

"I don't know, it's hard to tell how much it will affect those of us with mixed blood. Obviously, we can use it in buildings, for the most part, but that isn't the same as having a large chunk of it right beside you."

"Does steel bother you?"

"No, silly, and you already know that." She held up her spoon. "I've eaten with you and you have stainless steel flatware."

"Oh, yeah, sorry, stupid question."

We had almost finished our lunch.

"What are your plans for the afternoon?" Kay asked.

"We need to do some shopping. Jess will be writing notes and thinking of a way to make it up to her friends. Tate and I are going to the library to do more research. What about you?"

"Catch up on errands and—" Kay grimaced. "—housework. But this evening, if you aren't doing anything, would you like to come over for dinner?'

'That sounds wonderful. We're here partly because I couldn't think of anything to make for lunch."

We laughed.

Once we arrived at the library, Jessie asked, "Mom, is it okay if I stay and hang out with Nessa? She was going riding this afternoon, but changed her mind."

I paused at the entrance. "That's fine with me, but be back here by four o'clock. We'll meet up at the front desk. Tate, do you want to stay with me or go with Jess?"

"Go with Jess."

"Okay. Jess, keep an eye on your sister. Tate, behave."

Both girls stuck their tongues out at me then continued down the street while I walked up the stairs to the library's entrance. Courtney Campbell told me I could go down to the basement to look at the old newspapers. I decided to start from the beginning and scan. I might find something useful to help me deal with the fae, and I was curious about the history.

The earliest issues were predictably short since the island hosted a small population. The newsletter made a point to post new arrivals and business openings. The village experienced a spate of misfortunes—fires, disappearances, sightings of unearthly, frightful creatures. Almost half the paper in the first issues involved stories such as these. "This is interesting." There was a mention of several newcomers to the community including a Greig Ghillie, Muirne Puldreach and their daughter. "This must be the man that lost his family." I searched for the names Ghillie and Puldreach specifically and soon enough found something. An article was written about a fire in which several perished including Muirne Puldreach and her daughter, Shona. There was no mention of Greig Ghillie. In a later dated paper, I found a notice about a new family moving into Ghillie Cottage, Mr. and Mrs. Blair. *This must be Mrs. Grant's ancestor.* There was a single sentence about Mairi Puldreach, Mrs. Blair's sister, visiting to help the couple set up house. *My relative?* In later pages, it was noted that residents repeatedly claimed to have strange experiences in the forest. The constable advised everyone to stay clear of it. People who lived nearby it said they saw a man occasionally. Next, I checked the later issues. Neither the name Ghillie nor Gillie was mentioned again, not that I could tell anyway. But as the island grew, perhaps they didn't keep as good records. After the nineteenth century, very few people moved to the island. People tended to remain, and the children inherited and stayed. "Weird."

I checked my phone. It was close to four o'clock, so I put everything up and made my way upstairs. The girls were already waiting for me.

"How did it go?" I asked.

"I think I have all the addresses I need. Nessa and I had a long talk. I promised not to interfere with her and Lundy—at least not without warning her about it first."

As we waited for the bus, Tate told me what Jody, Nessa's little sister and her did while the older girls talked. When we arrived at the cottage, the first thing Jessie did was rush for a pen and paper to start on the apologies. As she worked, I cautioned her not to write the exact same thing on all of them. Kay expected us at around six.

༺༻

Since we were visiting her, we decided to leave the nails at the cottage. I grabbed a flashlight and carried a large stick from the back yard. Jess had a cane she found, and Tate toted a closed umbrella. Properly armed, we speed walked to Kay's.

"Come in, come in," she called to us from the open window. "I'm making salmon."

When she went back to her preparations, the girls both wrinkled their noses at me.

"You liked the stew. Keep an open mind and be polite," I said, under my breath.

Kay motioned for us sit on the couch and brought drinks, a glass of wine for me and glasses of water for the girls. She clinked her wine glass to mine and joined us. I told her about my research findings and asked if she knew anything.

"I don't think so, but, if somebody did mention something pertinent and I've forgotten, maybe our talk will jar it loose."

"I know that Mrs. Grant is a descendent of the sister-in-law of Mr. Ghillie. And I think we may be related. I found an identical last name on the trees, but I don't know if it was simply the same name but different person.

"Have you looked around in the cottage? Maybe there are family photos."

"I would assume that Mrs. Grant took them all with her."

"You have full reign, right?"

"As far as I know."

"Then whatever you get into is okay."

"Things have been so crazy since we have arrived, that I haven't looked further than items we needed immediately."

"Well, you may want to take some time out to search the house and possibly contact Mrs. Grant and ask her flat out."

The girls didn't care for the fish, but ate plenty of the other dishes. Kay must have suspected something because she gave them both very small portions. I thought it was delicious.

Afterward, I said, "Dinner was wonderful. Thank you."

"Let me drive you home. Things have been weird, even for the Shrouded Isle. I should have told you when I invited you that I would take you home. I wasn't thinking."

"But that means you'll be alone when you return home."

"But I'm part fae." Kay winked at me. "And I'll be in a car," she added.

"I appreciate it, Kay. Time to go, girls."

Kay loaded us in. As she turned from her lane, the weather took another turn for the worse. As she squinted at the road, the windshield wipers struggled to keep up with the downpour. "I should have had you spend the night."

"Well, when we get to our cottage you're definitely staying with us. This weather is insane."

Kay turned to me. "Thank you."

Something darted out into the street. Jess screamed and Kay wrenched the steering wheel to the left. We bumped over a broken place in the wall and hit a tree. "Is everyone okay?" Kay asked, upset.

I turned to the girls, they nodded. "We seem to be fine. What was that?"

"Becca, are all the doors locked?"

I knew I made sure the girls' were and had turned to lock mine when my door swung open and a woman leaned in. Her pale skin glowed and her wet hair hung in ringlets, scattering droplets on my shoulder. "Could you help us? My sister, she fell in the road. She's not answering me."

I didn't think. I immediately hopped out. As soon as I did, the rain blinded me. The woman grabbed my arm and tugged me into the lane. I heard Kay scream, "Becca!"

As we drew closer, what initially appeared to be a pile of clothing on the road revealed itself to be a woman.

I rushed to her side. "I'm no doctor. If we can get her in the car, I'm sure that Kay will take her to the village doctor." I didn't want to move her, but she couldn't stay on the road. I knelt and grimaced as the rain water soaked the knees of my jeans. She lay face up and still. She didn't resemble her sister at all. Though wet, I could tell her hair was blonde. Her angelic face was heart shaped, while her sister's was oval, and her nose was snubbed when her sister's was Romanesque. When I leaned closer, her eyes opened. Large blue orbs regarded me. "Oh. Are you hurt? What can I do to help you?"

"Come closer," she said.

Her voice was as beautiful as she was. Warm and kind, like my mother's voice. I realized as I knelt, I no longer noticed the rain or the chill in the air. Some part of me pointed out that that was wrong and I should be concerned, but her voice chased my doubts away. I leaned in. A hand on my neck pushed me closer.

A yowl pierced the night and the pressure on my nape vanished. I tore my eyes away from the blonde sister and turned. The large, black cat slashed at the other woman. The woman screamed as claws sank into her flesh. I sat back on my heels.

"Please help me," the blonde said.

I started to turn back to her, but Jessie grabbed me and yanked me to my feet. The woman sat up and, like a cobra, her head, mouth agape, darted toward my calf, but she missed. The creature, I didn't know what to call it, but it was certainly no woman, hissed and bared her teeth, long and fanged.

Jess shoved me toward the car and yelled, "Run!"

She swung the cane at the creature smacking it in the mouth. It screamed as blood gushed.

"Kay said don't look at its eyes, Mom!" Jessie warned me. We stumbled to the car.

"Where's Kay?" When I turned back to search for her, I saw the black cat racing toward us. I darted to the driver's side and told Jessie, "Slam the door shut and lock it when Kay gets in. I'm driving." I threw open the door and jumped inside.

"It's Kiera, Mom," Tate corrected me.

The cat leapt in the front seat between me and Jess and from there to the back. Jess slammed the door shut and locked it. I pushed the clutch and cranked the key. My driving skills were so rusty with a standard and, for a moment, I thought I would kill it, but it jerked forward and, as soon as I could, I shifted down.

"I don't see them, Mom."

"They're following us, look up." Kay had turned back to her human form. I glanced in the rearview mirror. The women flew after us as if they could swim through air.

"What in the world are they?" I asked.

"Drive faster, Mommy," Tate said.

"Mommy's driving as fast as she can, sweetie," I said.

"They're baobhan sith."

I waited and when no explanation came, asked, "What's that?"

"Creatures who need blood to survive."

"Vampires? You have vampires here?" I pressed on the accelerator.

"They usually prey on animals, which is why no one leaves a pet out. This is wrong."

My wet hands slid on the steering wheel as I took a turn. "I heartily agree with you on that. Are they still there?"

Kay, Jessie, and Tate looked back. "Yes, but they can't keep up."

"Praise the Lord for that." I didn't bother to slow down, and we fishtailed as I took the corner to our house. I ignored the lane and drove the car right up to the front door then killed the engine. "Run to the house!" I said then dove out. The others waited as I unlocked the door and once everyone was inside, I slammed it shut.

"Check all the windows. Make sure they're shut and locked," Kay said.

We rushed from room to room and looked.

I found the place where I had stored the nails and lay them at the window sills and the doors. "I hope the iron doesn't bother you too much, Kay."

"If it keeps those creatures away, I can stand it."

I heard them scratching on the door. Tate screamed and ran to me.

"It's okay, honey. They can't get in." I looked at Kay and she nodded. "Girls, go sit on the couch." It was located in the center of the room and farthest away from the windows and doors, so hopefully, the safest place in the cottage. I motioned for Kay to join me in the corner of the room and lowered my voice, so the girls wouldn't overhear. "We were lucky you were with us, Kay. I don't know what came over me."

"Given warning, you would have been prepared and able to resist them. You're strong with the magic, but caught unaware—"

"What do you mean strong with the magic?

"You were telling me of your family tree. You know that Mrs. Grant is a powerful hedge witch, yes?"

"Yes, you mentioned it before."

"And the fact that you and your daughters can see the fae, when most off-islanders can't, shows that you too have some talent. From what you have told me, you're related to Mrs. Grant somewhere far down the line."

"I haven't seen any fae before this."

"There aren't many fae at all in America, I think. Most of the powerful beings there are indigenous."

"You mean the American Indians' lore?"

"Yes. Have you ever gone to one of their holy places?"

"I don't think so."

"Houston is a new city. The States is just a new world in the clearest sense. There's the possibility that your powers were awakened when you came here since there's so much magic about, especially with the boundaries breaking down."

"I also saw that Mrs. Grant is related to the man's wife who lost his family in a fire. After he vanished, his sister-in-law, the only living heir, inherited it, so—"

"You and Mrs. Grant are related by blood and you're both related to Grieg Ghillie through marriage."

"I guess I'm lucky someone bothered to keep a record."

"I'm guessing it wasn't luck. How did you come to get your family history?"

"My mom said that someone contacted my grandmother and claimed they were related. This person asked my grandmother if she would like to see the family tree. They became pen pals."

"I bet that you'll find that person is a relative in some manner to Mrs. Grant."

"Okay, now things are getting weird. This was all planned, you think?"

"It seems probable."

"How does Greg fit into all this? He's a descendant of this Ghillie, right?"

Kay shook her head. "Not exactly." I opened my mouth, but she stopped me before I could say anymore. "Grieg Ghillie was cursed and a geas put on him regarding this island and inhabitants. Because his grief consumed him to the point that he no longer cared for others, he had to remain in the forest and keep the peace between the fae and the islanders. The geas affected the fae also. The doorway between the world of the fae and man became virtually unpassable for those in the Hill. The stronger the fae, the stronger the effect, so only the least powerful fae could pass through. They were easily handled. The Ghillie, as he came to be called, would return these intruders from whence they came. Unfortunately, the geas is failing."

"So, this Ghillie is some ancestor of Greg's?" Kay didn't answer. "Are you saying Greg inherited some family curse? That's crazy. And what's a geas?"

"A geas is a magically imposed obligation. Think on it moment, Becca."

I grew quiet and thought about all I knew and had learned about Greg and his family. About how there was no evidence anywhere that he existed. About how the last time his family name was mentioned was after the fire except for occasional forest sightings.

"Greg is Grieg Ghillie?" I asked. Kay nodded in agreement. I gasped. "But that would make him hundreds of years old!"

"That he is," Kay confirmed.

"But why is the geas failing now?"

"The curse would be in effect until the Ghillie learned to change his selfish ways and care for another."

"So—who does he care for?" I dared not to hope.

Kay nudged me, a playful glint in her eyes. "Who indeed, Becca."

"*Me?*" I felt a warmth suffice my body. Every instinct hummed, and I knew I should accept this as simple truth.

"I suspect that it started with your daughter since she resembles the child he lost. I'm guessing you look a bit like his wife too."

"He did act like I was familiar." I shook my head. "Why hasn't he fallen for someone already here?"

"I keep telling you—up until now, we rarely saw him except from afar."

I turned from Kay to pace. While I had been talking to Kay and not paying attention, Tate had moved to the window. As she stared outside, her jaw dropped and her eyes glazed over. She picked up the nail from the sill and stepped back.

"Tate! No!" I rushed to the window but before I could get the nail from Tate and replace it, the vampires broke the glass. They moaned as though in pain, but that didn't stop one from reaching for me and pulling me outside.

The sharp glass tore into my side and the vampire squealed with excitement as blood welled from the cut. Jessie shrieked in the background. I forced myself to look down and avoid staring into its eyes. Instead of feet, hooves peeped out from beneath its long dress. A tongue rasped my bleeding side. I lashed out with my fist, but it caught my arm and twisted it behind my back. Screaming, I struggled to get away. From the corner of my eye, I saw the other vampire drag Jess through the grass by her legs. Jessie twisted her body face down, her hands clawed at the ground. She freed one leg and kicked out hitting the vampire's arm. It only grunted. Tate wandered out the door in a daze. Kay kicked her shoes off as she raced outside and sank her feet into the soil. Sensing a worthy prey, the creatures released us and descended on her.

A male voice, one I'd come to know well, called out, "Back! Back to where you belong."

I looked toward him, but a bright light blinded me. The vampires shrieked. One of the creatures cackled. "The geas weakens, human. Soon you will not be tied to the land and have any power over us. Soon we will be free."

The light dimmed, and I saw the vampires at the forest's edge. In a blink of an eye, they vanished. Greg stood holding a large cross. He rushed to me, and I saw the worry and caring on his face just before I passed out.

When I regained my senses, Dr. Murphy was bandaging my side. "The girls? Kay?" I tried to rise, but the doctor admonished me to remain still.

"They're all okay. I don't think you've lost enough blood to need a transfusion, but you do need to rest. Your left side and leg needed stitches."

I apparently had cut my calf too, but hadn't noticed at the time. After tending to my other smaller cuts, he stood to leave. Kay met him at the door. He exchanged soft words with her then left.

Kay sat on the corner of the bed. "I know you don't feel well, but you need to speak to Greg."

I shook my head.

"Yes, you do," she insisted.

"I—I look a mess."

Greg peeked around the door. "How are you?"

Kay motioned him in.

"I'm alive." I tried to smile as Kay helped me sit up. "Kay told me—well, I figured out who you are, and she explained why she thought those vampire things attacked. Is it true?"

He cleared his throat. "I am careful with my feelings and a private man, but these are dire times, so I fear I must be blunt." He twisted his hands together. "When I saw your wee one and you, she reminded me of my daughter and you, of my wife."

I bristled with indignation. "Well, I'm not your wife."

"Aye, I ken. And I ken I am making a poor job of this." He walked closer. "We havena spent nearly enough time together, but I admit, I am attracted to you and I do care." He sat by the bed. "How—how do you feel about me?"

I felt my cheeks redden. "Well, I guess—I care about you too."

"There now," said Kay. "We've settled that. The next question is what are we going to do? The geas is fading more and more quickly and, by admitting your feelings, it will fall even faster."

"What do you suggest?" I asked.

Instead of answering, Kay stared at Greg. He stared back for a beat, then nodded.

"I ken what she asks," he said. I quirked my eyebrow

at him. "I must find the one who cursed me and placed the geas," he explained.

"Okay, who was that?"

"He goes by many names, but you may know him as Herne, the fae leader of the Wild Hunt."

I folded my arms around my middle and winced when my stitches pulled. "This is crazy."

Greg touched my shoulder. "Is it, Becca? You see what happens on this island. Do you think we are crazy? Do you think *you* are crazy?"

"No, but—"

"No, buts—time is short."

"Fine, but I'm going with you," I said. "It's because of me that all this is happening."

"I'll watch after the girls." Kay said.

"Thank you. Let's go, Greg."

Greg helped me up, and I limped toward the forest. Howls, growls, and unearthly sounds I couldn't identify filled the air. Because I was still weak, he lifted me in his arms, and the land blurred by, but not as quickly as it had when he had carried me before. "My powers wane. We must hurry."

We reached the large dog at the crossroads that I saw weeks ago. It growled, but when Greg held out his hand, it sniffed his knuckles and then stood aside. Just beyond, there was a hillock. I remained in Greg's arms as he sped around it and, as he did, the hillock changed and grew. As we circled, a cacophony of sound and a kaleidoscope of visions ravaged my senses. The third-time round, an opening appeared. "Ready?" he asked.

"I suppose I better be."

Though we entered the hill, we weren't underground. Instead, we were still in a forest, but such a forest! As I clung to Greg, I craned my neck, taking in my surroundings. Ash trees, their leaves turned up toward the sun, blossomed with clusters of blushed-purple flowers. Birch bark gleamed like polished silver furred with celery-colored moss. As the rich loam stirred under Greg's feet, the scent of earth, edged with mocha coffee, perfumed the air. The colors, the smells, were darker and more intense. In front of us, a magnificent oak laden with shiny acorns stood. Greg stopped and lowered me to the ground.

"I dare not go any farther. I shall call to him and hope I have enough power left for him to ken me." He shouted, "*Cernunnos, Cernunnos, Cernunnos!*"

I heard hoof beats and the howls of dogs. A party of hunters approached on horseback. Their mounts galloped toward us and, once stopped, stamped and neighed. A moment later, a pack of staghounds joined the hunting party. When I studied most of the riders, my eyes seemed to slide past, as though they were only shadows, but not so with the leader. Stag horns, larger and more magnificent than any I had seen on a deer, grew from his forehead. His umber hair fell below his shoulders and the skin of his bare arms and chest was adorned with ebony markings. These swirled, and my eyes watered if I looked at them too long. He frowned and his visage was so terrible to look upon, that I focused on his red-eyed steed instead. The horse snorted and pawed the ground as its mouth foamed.

"Why do you call me, mortal?" His voice was soft, and yet the timbre was hard as granite.

Greg shuddered but stood tall and resolute. "The curse comes undone."

"That is good news, is it not, man?"

I risked a glance. One of the shaggy dogs resembling a wolfhound on steroids growled and crept closer. At a glance from the rider, it whimpered and returned to the pack. It was large enough for Tate to ride.

"Yes, but the geas fails, and that is bad news," Greg answered. "Though becoming the Keeper of the Forest was a curse, it has become my calling. I willna have those I have long protected suffer."

The creature, who must have been Herne, leapt from his saddle and, with measured steps, approached us. "What would you have me do about it?"

"Could you—" Greg paused, studied the ground, then continued. "—remake it?"

Herne tilted his head and regarded Greg. "I could, but for the geas to maintain the barrier, there must be one to watch the borders." His glance flitted to me.

Greg looked at me, his expression full of despair. "I must stay and remain cursed then."

I shook my head. Though I had planned to return to Aberdeen, I didn't want to lose the dear friends I had made here. I was drawn to Greg. Even though I had only just discovered he had feelings for me, I very much wanted to see where this mutual attraction led. "If you stay here, you'll still be able to keep in contact with me, won't you? I know you don't have a phone, but we could write."

"The geas weakens because of my feelings for you. We must avoid all contact and sever our budding relationship completely, I fear," Greg continued.

We looked at Herne, who nodded.

I'll never see him again! He'll never find the happiness he deserves. My heart clenched and I realized I couldn't bear the thought. "No, Greg, there must be another way." I clung to him and bit my lip, trying to hold back tears.

Herne's mount neighed and reared. Without looking back, he clucked at the steed, and it calmed. "Think, man—how can you make this task a pleasure?"

Greg's furrowed forehead smoothed and his eyes filled with hope. He turned to me and, holding my hands, knelt. "We havena courted nor known each other long enough for me to ask you to be my bride, but I care about you and I believe—" He continued in a stronger voice. "—I believe in us, given time. Will you stay and give us this time?"

I thought about all I had gone through and about how I cared about the island and its people. I actually felt at home in the crazy place, and yes—strange as our unfurling courtship had been—I loved Greg Gillie. Somehow, I knew this was our destiny. "Yes, Greg. I will remain."

The horseman approached us. "They will be betrothed to each other and the land."

Greg stood, his hands still grasping mine. Herne wrapped his hand around the pommel of his sword and tugged it from the scabbard. With an eldritch cry, the blade slid into view. Greg stood between Herne and me.

"Fear not. I will unite you with the Hill—" Herne called one of the hounds forth and cut a hank of fur from its scruff. "The land—" He plucked a large blackberry from a nearby plant and mashed it with the flat of his blade. The black juice sprayed onto the fur. He turned to us. "Show me your palms."

I was afraid to do it, but even more afraid of what would happen if I didn't do as he asked. Greg and I faced each other. We held out our hands so close that our thumbs overlapped. In a flurry, Herne drew the sword across our palms and slapped the smashed fruit and fur there. He closed our hands together and murmured words that I couldn't understand. The air felt strange on my skin, as if I were wrapped in a cloth crackling with static electricity. Herne's words echoed in my head until I could hear nothing but his voice. I shuddered and swayed. Just when I thought I would pass out, it stopped.

Greg and I staggered apart. Our palms no longer bled and the fur and fruit had vanished. I rubbed my arms and shook my head then turned to Greg. His shoulders bowed as if a great weight had been set upon them. Herne nodded to us. "It is time for you to leave. The geas is reinstated."

I started to thank him, but Greg stopped me. "Never thank a fae, Rebecca. They believe, by doing so, you undervalue what they have done. They consider it an insult." He nodded at the hunter and drew me away.

As we approached the cottage, I slowed.

Greg reached for my hand. "You worry about what your daughters will say."

"I'm not even sure how to tell them."

Greg tugged me to the bench at the side of the house. "It will be all right, Rebecca. I promise." His lips met mine, and my heart sang with joyful desire. He deepened the kiss and I smothered a moan.

"We've got to go in," I gasped, my heart galloping as though I had sprinted home.

When we entered, Kay greeted us at the door. "What happened? Is everything all right, Becca?"

Jessie and Tate turned from the window, their expressions identical and solemn. I wondered if they had seen the kiss.

"A moment, Kay." Greg tugged me forward until we both stood in front of the girls. He knelt before them. "I am not your father, nor will I ever be. But I promise to protect and cherish you, Tate." He reached out and squeezed her hand. "And you, Jessica." Jessie crossed her arms, but Greg wasn't deterred. He lightly touched her shoulder. "Until life has left me and beyond."

An unwilling smile graced Jessie's face. Her eyes met mine, then she nodded, dropped her arm, and allowed him to take her hand.

Before I could even contact Mrs. Grant, the deed to the cottage came in the post with my name on it. We were home.

The End

Author's Note

Thank you for reading *Kilts and Catnip*. I hope you've enjoyed it. Please take a moment to write a short review. I'm grateful for all feedback.

Sign up for my newsletter to get the latest news and a free Shrouded Isle holiday short story at zoetasia.com. Watch for the second book in the Shrouded Isle series.

About the Author

As a child, Zoe Tasia idolized Barbara Eden, star of *I Dream of Jeannie*. However, she would have ditched the astronaut and married Captain Kirk. She can't blink and make magic, nor did she wed a Starfleet officer. Instead, life had something better in store for her. She explores her imagination as a writer, is married to an understanding Greek, has two grown sons, and a crazy cat that thinks it's a dog. Tasia grew up in Oklahoma and lived over seven years in Scotland. Now she resides in the great state of Texas, where everything's bigger and better, or so she's told by the natives. When she's not giving her make-believe friends full rein, she enjoys the opera, ballet, well-chilled champagne and books, lots and lots of books. Her first book is *Kilts and Catnip ~ The Shrouded Isle Book 1*. You can find Zoe Tasia on Facebook, Twitter, and her webpage. She also co-writes under the name Zari Reede.